Primetime Princess

LINDY DEKOVEN

Primetime Princess

amazonpublishing

Published by Amazon Publishing

PO Box 400818

Las Vegas, NV 89140

ISBN-13: 9781611099591

ISBN-10: 1611099595

Library of Congress Control Number: 2012922298

To my husband, David Israel, who gave me
the courage to run out into the traffic, and
the wisdom to avoid being hit by the cars.

Chapter One

Let the games begin.

Rosie Butler, my twenty-eight-year-old, überorganized assistant, stands at my desk dressed in a taupe Ann Taylor pantsuit, her butterscotch hair tucked neatly under her chin. Rosie's eyes are riveted to her phone sheet.

"The *Lethal Stilettos* notes meeting was moved to three. So now you have two back-to-back pitch meetings. One with Fox, the other with Warners," says Rosie. Despite the hectic pace, she remains cool and collected. "The *Of Corpse She's Alive* dailies are on your iPad. The producers think they suck and want to fire their director and hire the one you suggested. Standards has an issue on *Bunnies*; the actresses need to wear nipple covers. The female studio exec on *Alpha Male* wants to cast the guy from *Glee* in the role of Coach Bob Knight. The writers are freaking out and begging you to call that woman, whom they referred to as a first-class…well, you know."

As Rosie rambles on, I lean forward in my chair and recall the party my girlfriends threw when I landed this job three years ago. They presented me with the two stainless steel balls carefully displayed on top of my desk in a diamond-patterned black silk box. Inscribed on the front is "Now you have four." They remind me to stay strong and confident.

"Oh, and I reordered your stationery. It's under the *Variety* on your desk," Rosie continues as she watches me gather my shoulder-length dark-brown hair and clip it into a high ponytail. "I like your new Buddy Holly–style glasses. But you still look like Zooey Deschanel in *New Girl*."

"It could be worse," I say.

"The critics think she's adorable."

"Well, thanks. But I don't really want to be adorable at thirty-five years old," I say, tossing aside the *Variety* and opening the box. Neatly engraved across the top of the sheets is ALEXA ROSS, VICE PRESIDENT, COMEDY—HAWKEYE BROADCASTING SYSTEM.

Rosie continues, her eyes twinkling with mischief. "When Zooey wants to look serious and sophisticated, she puts on glasses, too."

"The difference is I need them." I smile as I tuck my white silk blouse neatly into my black pants. I take a deep breath and sit up straight in my chair. "OK, please tell Molly to join me in the pitch meetings. I'll look at the dailies in a second. Ask standards to come by after my staff meeting, and please let the writers know I'll take care of the issue on *Alpha Male*."

As Rosie exits my office, she reminds me that the staff meeting starts in ten minutes.

I pick up the *Variety* and gasp when I see the headline, "Jerry Kellner, VP at Tiger Films, Ousted for Inappropriate Behavior." Everyone's known about Jerry's so-called inappropriate behavior, but no one's reported it. Not me. Not any of his other assistants or subordinates before or after. Whoever finally did ought to be enshrined. She managed to do what others, including myself, could not.

But the great news is Jerry Kellner's no longer a part of my life. I'm no longer his secretary, slave, glorified assistant, and doormat. That was a bad time, some ten years ago. Back then, I was younger, inexperienced, and eager to please. There were times when I wasn't sure I'd make it out of that rut. But I did.

All the vivid memories of my past come flooding back this morning as I read that headline.

"Hey, Lexican, don't move! Going right for the center. OK, here it comes. Yeaaaahhh! Right between the bodacious ta-tas. Hey, where's my chai latte? Sweetheart, I don't see it. Man, you have a great ass."

Jerry Kellner's voice was like nails on a blackboard. It still reverberates in my head, even though I don't work for that shithead anymore. All the crap I put up with hoping that someday he'd promote me.

"Listen baby," he continues, *"I think I'm gonna get the drama gig at Fox. You wanna join me?"* He leaps to his feet and then turns serious. *"If you come with me, I promise, and I mean that, Lex, I promise I'll make you a star."*

A star. I peer out the third-floor window of my office in Burbank at the wraparound views of the Hollywood Hills and San Fernando Valley. I shudder when I think about those days. I was just three years out of college. I was desperate to move up and out, wondering what the heck I went to college for when all I was doing was schlepping coffee and crud. And yet whenever Jerry sensed I was about to bolt, he'd skillfully dangle that carrot, which I fell for more often than I'd like to admit.

But, hey, I had a job in Hollywood. I was the envy of all my pals. My job would put me on the executive track. I was working for the up-and-coming Jerry Kellner. I was in a highly sought-after position. At least that's what everyone told me.

As I get my notes together for the meeting, my eyes wander around the collection of framed articles, ratings, letters, and awards that adorn the walls of my handsomely appointed executive office, underscoring years of accomplishments.

The Woman of Vision Award I received last year for excellence in programming, the Face of the Future Award from Women in Media, the Creative Achievement Award from the Producer's Guild. And then there's the framed ticket to the Wimbledon Finals, which I attended last summer. What a thrill to sit in HBS's seats on center court, just a few rows behind the royal box. Who ever dreamed I'd be living this life? I take a breath and smile. I made it. The hard work has definitely paid off.

"What's with you?" asks Sylvia Radamacher, my colleague from advertising sales who just arrived from New York. She brushes past Rosie and sees me staring out the window. Colleagues always seem to wander into your space when you're picking your nose or adjusting your thong. It's never when you're speaking with confidence, making a deal, or looking important and busy.

Clad in her usual black Armani pantsuit, she throws herself on my new white Ralph Lauren Olivier sofa—something I managed to buy off craigslist and, amazingly, not get killed in the process— and plunges a hand into my bowl of M&M's, or as she calls them, "stress meds," tossing her newest Louboutins aside.

Sylvia is petite, stylish, and no-nonsense. A fast-talking, highly confident New Yorker. I often wonder if she ever second-guesses her decisions like me.

"I'm-only-here-for-the-day-got-to-get-back-to-Manhattan-I-have-a-zillion-meetings-at-McCann-over-some-problem-with-GM-not-wanting-to-sponsor-*Wild-and-Weary*-the-new-crappy-reality-show-Pete's-team-developed-with-a-bunch-of-felons-speaking-of-which-please-don't-give-me-any-stupid-comedies-to-sell-this-year-OK?" Sylvia can spew an entire run-on sentence without taking a single breath.

If she weren't one of my closest friends, I'd throw her out of my office for suggesting any of my shows are stupid. But I like her spunk and envy her strength and determination. Her stint as an attorney got her a consulting gig on *The Good Wife*, which led to a job in finance and, eventually, ad sales, where she's the lone female.

Sylvia sells our shows to advertisers, and believe me, that's no easy task. We creative types have a hard time selling our shows to our mothers. But Sylvia has real balls. Guys grab theirs when she walks by. I have fake balls—the ones on my desk, and the others I figuratively strap on every morning and pray stay in place. But mine don't put the fear of God in men the way hers do.

Maybe because I was an assistant, I empathize with their plight. I'm ridiculously careful about asking for coffee. Sylvia, on the other hand, often pushes past Rosie without even a nod and shouts, "Rosie. Coffee. Black," whips her way into my office, and slams the door. It sends shivers up my spine. I always apologize for her behavior by bringing Rosie an exquisite array of scones the next day.

I pull myself together, grab my copy of *Variety*, and quickly stuff it in the trash.

"Oh, I just read that Jerry Kellner was fired. I should be thrilled," I say, tossing my glasses into my purse. "He finally got his. But it brought back awful memories. I hate the guy. Being fired isn't enough. I want him dead."

"Oh God, get over it, Alexa, it's ancient history. Wasn't that the guy who made you schlep his stool?"

My mind drifts back to the many times I raced through traffic nearly killing myself to do some crazy errand for Jerry.

"Yup. Tearing through West Hollywood in my Volkswagen Jetta, trying to get to the lab at Cedars-Sinai at precisely eight o'clock to deliver his specimen, which was sitting in my cup holder."

"God, I can't believe that," says Sylvia.

"I remember him saying, 'I shit right into that little plastic bottle, and by the way, I don't need the container anymore, you can have it.'"

Sylvia scrunches her nose as if the bottle's within reach. It took weeks to get the stench out of my car. She leans forward, picking through the M&M's for the red ones before tossing them into her mouth.

"Jerry ended up at Fox, and I dutifully followed him there. When I asked for a staff position, he looked me in the eye and shamelessly asked what he'd get in return. I said loyalty and hard work. I'll kill for you. The next day he hired his friend Alan and shoved three scripts in my face, requesting my notes that he'd present as his. And like an abused wife, I stayed. But when Alan hired Irena Valenzuela, a popular Brazilian ex-porn star, to be his assistant, Jerry stole her and fired me."

"Put a fork in him. He's done. No one will hire him. Besides, you're way beyond him. Your shows have won Emmys. And so far your comedies have opened well. You're doing great, Alexa."

I know I've done well here and am very proud of my achievements, but I still wish I were a little more like Sylvia, whose confident demeanor is both daunting and intimidating.

Rosie flies through the door. "Alexa, here's your report. The meeting's right now in Chester's office." She looks at her watch and points to the door. I quickly gather my things as Sylvia grabs a new handful of M&M's and we wave good-bye.

Chester King is the CEO and president of Hawkeye Broadcasting System. He's a handsome dude in his fifties. He must've been some looker in his day. Everything about Chester is grand. He's got a wonderful dimple, sexy blue eyes, and a head full of salt-and-pepper hair. His office is sparse and cold. Perhaps due to his upbringing in Minneapolis, it's literally a constant fifty degrees, and if anyone has a problem there are spare jackets in his closet. The temperature doesn't adjust, you do. It's cold, but Chester isn't. The strokeman on the Yale crew, he went on to become the youngest general manager at a Boston TV station. A gregarious divorcé, he doesn't do

Hollywood parties, but he does do the girls. He produced a bunch of TV shows in the nineties and made a boatload of money. He's been very successful, as indicated by the vast collection of brass and metal trophies that adorn his office. All intended to intimidate his guests.

Ten male coworkers and I travel to Chester's office for our daily afternoon senior management meetings. As we file into Chester's outer office, waiting for his assistant to give us the all-clear signal to march on in, there's a lot of chatter about the headline in *Variety*. The guys are curious about what led to Jerry Kellner's termination. This is not a conversation I want to engage in, so once we get the signal to enter, I do. In the center of his office is a gigantic Frank Gehry desk made out of cardboard, yet strong and big enough to land a plane on. We all sink into our black leather boxy chairs, which surround a considerable marble square coffee table stacked with scripts, DVDs, and books. Some of us boast about last night's ratings, while others hide in humiliation. Our meetings are a mix of sparring, fighting, whining, and arguing, mostly about scheduling, promos, time periods, and deals.

This is the meeting of the minds. The bigwigs who plan and decide what America will watch on HBS. The heads of comedy, drama, reality, daytime, casting, promotion, business affairs, scheduling, research, and publicity are all here. We're the chosen ones. Generally, there's a lot of anxiety and tension and a fair amount of Xanax and Prozac, and a good amount of Red Bull. This is clearly the meeting of bulls and bullshit.

But I'm feeling really good today. Two of my shows opened well. I'm finally able to take a breath and enjoy my accomplishments. Sylvia's right. I'm not going to let those bad memories of my years working for Jerry diminish the success I'm enjoying today.

There's a new face in the room today. That of Frank Barnsworth, CEO and chairman of Hawkeye Industries. Hawkeye Broadcasting

System is but a pimple on an elephant's ass in Frank Barnsworth's world, which also includes movie studios, hotels, telcos, and other travel- and entertainment-related businesses. Barnsworth runs his empire out of his home state of Iowa.

We stop dead in our tracks. We've never met this guy. However, this little gimmick isn't lost on anyone. Keeping us off guard is part of Chester's management style, along with pitting us against one another. Chester believes competition and adversity lead to great results.

"Alexa, will we have any winners this year? Gonna hit anything out of the park?" Barnsworth bellows as I enter the office. This is a man who doesn't mince words. Clearly not a Hollywood guy, as no one is that direct here. Hollywood is oblique, indirect, circling, game playing, *never* a direct question or answer. Before I can even form a reply, he stands up and shakes my hand vigorously, as if we're old friends.

"I'm very happy to finally meet you, Mr. Barnsworth," I say respectfully. I'm actually scared shitless, as I hear this guy terminates and exterminates with ease. Yet all I can think about are the flats I should have worn instead of the heels, because I'm towering over this little man like the Jolly Green Giant. I start to perspire. I know that within seconds, the bronzer from yesterday's spray tan will be dripping into my eyes and on my clothes. I didn't know I'd be shaking hands with God today. I'm suddenly a wreck, thinking about unimportant things like why didn't I wear my suit? Should I secure the top button on my blouse, or will that look obvious? Didn't I remember what I learned from John Molloy's *Dress for Success*? The one day I need to look the part, I'm wearing a white blouse and black jeans. Oh God, how can I not have a blazer?

These meetings are Darwinian. The ones who yell the loudest get heard the most. It's truly survival of the fittest. This isn't great for me, because testosterone frequently wins over estrogen. Often, I scream, "Hey, it's *my* turn, I have something to say." There's a moment of silence, I jam in my point, but within seconds I'm silenced. It's clearly a guys' world at HBS.

But today is different. My male colleagues are lovely and deferential. I have to blink twice to make sure these are the same assholes I work with every day. As Sylvia says, "If it were up to them, they'd hire all guys." We refer to these meetings as "dick dances," a subliminal exercise guys engage in. Ever since I heard that phrase I can barely sit in a meeting without wondering which dick has the best choreography.

"So, Alexa, are the shows funny?" Mr. Barnsworth asks again. I guess I'm in the hot seat today.

"Well, Frank, Alexa is actually doing a great job," Chester interrupts as he pulls a piece of lint off my pants and pats my knee. "We premiered a few comedies prior to the official opening of the new season, and they're performing quite well."

Although I appreciate the compliment, I'm not thrilled that Chester came to my rescue. This creates tremendous conflict because I can speak for myself, and I also don't believe he'd pull lint off one of the guys' pants. This subtle gesture exemplifies the world I live in. I struggle with the appropriate response to these actions. Do I slap his hand away or play the role of damsel in distress? Neither. Instead, I ignore the whole thing and move on.

I came on board three years ago from Morgan Studios. While there, I developed the comedy *Everyone's Entitled to My Opinion*, based on a popular Israeli show. It became a pretty successful comedy series on ABC and stayed on for a couple of years until it was canceled for being too smart. Yes, I swear that's what the ABC executive told me when it was canceled. "We don't do smart, Alexa, we do funny." But, hey, I got a show on the air, which is no easy feat. I celebrated for days.

Morgan Studios was not in the comedy business. They were known for drama programs. During my interview at HBS, Chester was impressed that I managed to get a comedy series on the air. He said I was tenacious and had good commercial instincts and an eye for talent, so he hired me as head of comedy here. I was ecstatic. However, on my first day I overheard his assistant say that despite my great credentials, Chester also liked my boobs. What a surprise. I'm sure it wasn't the first time these double Ds have opened doors.

"Let's roll the promos, boys," Chester continues.

And with that, Steve Hansen, a surf bum who got lost on his way to the big breaks at Trestles and wound up in a suit in Burbank as the head of marketing and promotion, inserts a DVD. We're showing Barnsworth a sixty-second reel of highlights from our new shows, most of which will debut next week, the third week in September, when the official HBS television season begins. Suffice to say, it's a torturous time. We all act as if we have the greatest shows, and by the time they hit the air, we actually believe it. But every year it's the same scramble. And if the shows fail, we fail.

Sixty seconds go by in a blur. The silence has us sitting unnaturally still. Finally, Barnsworth nods his approval and we can all breathe again. There's a little more discussion about the new season, then Barnsworth announces he'd like each of us to participate in an HBS-sponsored mentoring program tutoring a student. He abruptly wishes us good luck and we're dismissed.

"What the fuck is he doing here today?" asks Steve disdainfully as we pour out into the hallway.

"It can only be one thing: he's looking to fire someone," suggests Mark Winslow, the nerdy and ever-so-serious head of business affairs, who's often blamed for making a good or bad deal. "Barnsworth doesn't appear for no good reason. This doesn't feel right." Mark is the glass-is-always-empty member of our executive team.

Network execs fear losing their jobs because the ax can fall at any time. So it's a bit disconcerting when the CEO decides to make an unscheduled appearance. It definitely has us on edge.

It reminds me of the first day I joined the network, when a producer referred to me simply as Christmas help. "Welcome to HBS, Alexa. Don't get too comfortable, you're just here temporarily." Nice.

But the truth is that producer was wrong. So far it's not been a temp job. I've survived several TV seasons and am quite proud of what I've accomplished here. We're not there yet. HBS is still behind the other broadcast networks, but we're gaining, and my contributions have helped considerably.

As I stroll down the hall back to my office, I reflect on the fact that I'm doing well and feeling pretty darn good. This is a tough job with a lot of pressure. But my track record is solid and the future is bright.

However, as I open the door to my suite, I'm stunned to see Chester standing in my office. How the heck did he beat me here? Oh my God, something's up. The mountain never comes to Mohammed. I clench my teeth and prepare for the worst as he waits for me to come inside. As I enter, the door swings shut.

"Alexa, I know what you're thinking. Relax, you're not being fired."

"I'm not?"

"You're doing a great job. And we definitely want to keep you. Your shows have done quite well, and you're a very capable executive. In fact, Barnsworth wanted me to tell you that."

I'm sweating bullets.

"He thinks we ought to consider adding four more comedies to the four already on the schedule. It would certainly increase revenue. So I expanded the budget. Let's add some more development." Chester lights a cigarette, despite the fact that it's against the law to smoke inside a building. But Chester's above the law.

"That's great, Chester. I'll get on it right away."

He turns to leave.

"Oh, forgot one thing," he says as he reaches for the door. "Barnsworth wants his sister's husband's cousin on our team. Because you've had such great success, he wants him under your supervision. His name is Jerry Kellogg or something. The guy just got canned. But he's yours now. Make it work."

And with that, Chester flicks his ashes on my fluffy white carpet, wishes me a nice weekend, and is gone in a flash.

Some days I just want to curl up and cry.

Today is one of those days.

Chapter Two

It's Monday morning, and I'm in the principal's office at Crestview Elementary School waiting to meet Gordon Harrison, a sixth-grade teacher there, and the executive director of the Kenfield Literacy Group, which matches mentors with students. I'm never any place at seven thirty, especially without my coffee. But Barnsworth wants us to participate in a mentoring program, so I'll quickly register and get to work. And then I'll have to see the dreaded Jerry Kellner.

I am sickened by the prospect of working with that sleazebag. Chester's bombshell left me speechless and ravenous. I must've gained ten pounds eating See's candy this weekend. Even the clerk knows me by name. "Hi, Alexa, nice to see you again. Do you want your usual?" The fact that the clerk at the candy store knows not only my name but what I purchase probably means I'm a candidate for Chocoholics Anonymous.

Here I am at the top of my game, finally starting to feel confident about the future and craving more responsibility. Someday maybe I can even run programming. But that great feeling came to an abrupt end on Friday when Chester announced Jerry will be joining my team. Just the thought of seeing him again has my stomach in knots.

Decked out in my black pantsuit, I lean against a dreary yellow stained wall, my black pumps planted on the nappy floor covering below. I hear the boisterous clamor of the playground outside, while the ringing bell above explodes in my ears.

My fingers tap furiously on my phone. I'm firing off text after text, trying to keep up with the endless problems and issues I deal with every day. Hopefully this won't take long, as Rosie said I just have to fill out a form. Two boys, one with a bloody nose, the other looking white as a ghost, are escorted into the principal's office by what appears to be a playground supervisor. Behind them is a well-built, athletic-looking man, probably in his late thirties, with wavy brown hair and blue eyes. My eyes travel from his old Yankees T-shirt to his faded Levi's and beat-up Reeboks.

"Alexa? Hi, I'm Gordon Harrison." He extends his hand to shake mine. "I'm sorry, I was running a bit late. C'mon in, let's talk about the Kenfield program."

I follow Gordon into a room the size of a telephone booth. We occupy seats directly across from each other at a small make-shift table that barely fits inside. The walls are plain white and somewhat dirty. One fluorescent light flickers above, threatening to give me an enormous headache. I feel like I'm on *Law & Order*, about to be interrogated for a heinous crime. It smells like old galoshes, evoking memories of my second-grade classroom. I decide to place my giant yellow H&M purse (which I purchased for a mere $16.95—I love it when I get a deal) on my lap, as there's hardly any room for it here.

"Thanks so much for coming here today. It's great that HBS has offered to participate in our mentoring program." Gordon smiles as he places his clipboard on the table.

"So, can you tell me a little about yourself?"

"Um. Now?"

"Yeah. Now would be great," says Gordon as he listens with rapt attention, his eyes steadily fixed on mine.

There's a pause.

"Oh, I thought I was just going to fill out some paperwork. Would that be OK?"

"Well, I'd prefer we talk it through," Gordon says as he slowly reveals a confident smile that feels both personal and caring. "That way I can get to know you better."

"Oh, well, sure," I say as I glance away, feeling a flush of excitement across my face.

Gordon leans back in his chair, his biceps flexing as he jiggles his pen.

"Shall we try this again?" he asks.

"Sure. OK," I say, trying to sound like this is fine, but I'm fumbling all over the place. I decide to just tell Gordon the truth. "I'm eager to start tutoring a student, I just thought I'd be filling out a form this morning. I didn't realize it was an interview. I would've scheduled more time. Unfortunately, I have to get to my office soon. Maybe we can set up another session? I'm sorry. I hope you understand."

Gordon pulls out a pair of dark-brown-rimmed eyeglasses from his pocket, places them on his face, and studies the document on his clipboard.

"Of course I understand," Gordon says as his warm sapphire eyes peer over his glasses, which rest on the lower portion of his nose. "I'll tell you what. Let's try to go through it quickly. We'll do as much as we can. How's that sound?"

"OK. I can do that." I'm preoccupied with his scent, which brings back my childhood obsession with Beeman's Black Jack licorice-flavored chewing gum.

"So can you give me a brief idea of who you are and what you do?" Gordon asks. His pen is poised to write everything down.

"Sure. I'm from Chicago. Moved here when I was fifteen. My dad died two years later," I say matter-of-factly, choosing not to reveal the pain associated with that event. I still cry when I think of him and how he succumbed to a heart attack right there in the driveway of our home. "My mom was a school administrator. She retired to Northern California. I've worked here in Los Angeles in show business for the past twelve years."

I'd be happy to talk more about myself. Who doesn't like to do that? However, my phone's vibrating in my pocket. I don't want to appear rude, but I can't withstand the temptation to pull it out. While Gordon writes, I carefully sneak it out of my pocket and notice the time. Yikes. I want to get to work early so I can prepare for my meeting with Jerry. I'm totally distracted. I feel the noose tighten around my neck. I'd really like to have a more leisurely conversation with this very nice guy who makes me feel comfortable and at ease. But I know I have to leave.

This is the first time I've seen Jerry in ten years. My stomach starts to ache at the prospect. I'm so conflicted because there's a part of me that wants to dash out of here and yet another that would like to stay and learn more about this program.

"That's your whole story?" asks Gordon.

"I don't have a complicated life." I smile. "I work. That's what I do."

Gordon pauses and then stares into my eyes.

"So, what do you do for fun?"

I'm stumped. "I don't know what I do for fun. Hmm. Clearly something I need to think about."

"Well, maybe tutoring will be fun for you," Gordon says. "Any siblings?"

"My brother's an attorney. Married with three kids. Now I'm the one everyone's worried about." I laugh nervously, as I don't really want to start a conversation about my family. I'll save that for therapy.

"Really?" Gordon asks. "Why do you think they're worried about you? You seem pretty capable."

I could really get into this. But discussing my family and my life would take a good amount of time. As I feel my phone continue to vibrate, I know I don't have much time left here. I hope he doesn't think I'm a jerk, even though I feel like one.

"Oh, you know, will I ever get married? Will I hold on to my job? You know, things people who care about you worry about." For a moment our eyes lock, and I suddenly realize this guy is kind of sexy. He doesn't appear to be a cocky asshole like the guys I'm used to being around. And he has incredibly strong eye contact, which I find both disconcerting and incredibly exciting at the same time.

I'd like to get to know Gordon and ask him questions like where'd he get that tiny scar beneath his eye? And what's his background? Why did he decide to run a tutoring program at this school? I don't know many men who choose this kind of profession. Hmm, I kind of like that about him.

He breaks the spell and asks, "So, what exactly do you do now?"

"I'm the head of comedy development at HBS. I have a great job," I say proudly, thinking this will impress him, but he doesn't say anything. He smiles nicely and writes something down.

When I reveal my position, I'm either handed a script or asked to hire a cousin, daughter, nephew, or friend as an unpaid intern. This is usually followed by a certain amount of begging. People will literally work for free just for an opportunity in show business. Gordon, however, seems unfazed. He's not the least bit impressed. This elevates him to a higher order.

I start rummaging through my purse, looking for my keys.

"And you're single?" he asks as he looks up at me, suppressing a grin.

Oh, no, I live with a fabulous guy who fawns all over me, worships the ground I walk on, and lives for my every breath. We have sex 'round the clock, and he can barely stand it when another man so much as looks at me. God, what am I supposed to say here? That

I've dated a zillion guys and can't stand any of them? And that I haven't had sex in a year and live with my dog in a one-bedroom apartment in West Hollywood? I make a good salary, but I don't have nearly enough saved for a down payment on a condo.

Sometimes I wonder whether I really want a guy, because I don't seem to work as hard at finding one as I do trying to move up the ladder. Every guy I date is turned off rather than turned on by the fact that I'm so devoted to my career. And I'm not exactly turned on when they ask if I'd give mine up for them. I'm over the days of hooking up. I want a career, and I'd like to meet a really good guy and get married someday. I don't think that's asking for much.

"Well, I'm not married, but I do live with a guy. His name is Joe." I wait a beat and watch Gordon as he checks a box on his form. "I'm kidding. The guy I live with is Joe, my four-year-old Jack Russell terrier." I crack my first big smile of the morning. Gordon looks at me again and grins. He has beautiful, clear blue eyes. They seem to twinkle.

"So, dating anyone?"

There's a pause as I contemplate his question.

"Hmm, is that on your questionnaire?" I ask, tilting my head as I glance at the paper, which he quickly covers up.

"Yup, sure is," he teases, as his warm blue eyes lock on mine.

I take my new reading glasses out of my pocket and put them on.

"Really? Invisible ink, huh?" I lean toward him peering at his paper.

"We need to know everything about our applicants. Especially Hollywood types. Really need to check you people out," he says. His eyes are filled with humor as he lowers his voice and relaxes back into his chair.

"I see. I suppose we're different from you do-gooders," I say, tuning out the distraction of a bell ringing in the distance.

"I expect that's the case. We're very committed to our work and want to make sure this isn't just fodder for a movie or reality show later," Gordon says earnestly.

"Oh, well, we Hollywood types are very picky. We don't just jump into any situation. We, too, need to check people out…carefully," I say sweetly as my face reddens. I briefly turn away to collect myself.

"So, how do I check out, Miss Ross?" Gordon asks, angling his hunky body toward me, his eyes looking squarely into mine. "Do you think you can work with me? And more importantly, do you think tutoring can fit into your very busy Hollywood schedule?" Gordon's sarcasm is tempered by his warm and very sexy smile.

There's definitely something going on here, and I'd sure like to continue this game. But my phone's vibrating in my pocket again. I have to get out of here or I'll be late. I leap out of my seat.

"Gordon, I want to tutor a student. I really do," I say, removing my glasses and shifting my attitude as I push the chair under the table. "I think it'll be great for both of us. But I have a dreadful…I mean important meeting this morning, which is why I may appear a little distracted. I'm sorry. I don't mean to be rude. But I have to get to my office. Can you please e-mail me the rest of the info? I'll get back to you right away. I promise."

Gordon stares up at me with a puzzled expression.

"Thank you so much for taking the time to meet with me. I can't wait to meet my student." I hand him my card, hike my purse onto my shoulder, and head for the door.

"I was thinking of matching you with a female student. Maybe around eleven years old. How does that sound?" Gordon asks as he jumps up from his seat.

"Great. Sounds great," I say.

"But are you really going to have time for this?" Gordon shouts as he takes off his glasses and holds the door open as I pass through.

"It's just a few hours a month. I think you'd be a great tutor for one of our students."

"Oh, yes, definitely. And yes, I can fit it into my Hollywood schedule. I'll make time," I say, smiling, mimicking his sarcasm.

Time. Something I have too little of. However I want to do this, I just have to figure out how I'm going to fit it into my day. But I'll make it happen. And boy, I'd sure like to see this guy again. I wonder what his story is.

I race across the asphalt to my silver Prius, which I got when I landed the job at HBS. I drive it like the sports car it's not meant to be and tear out of the school's lot onto the street as the radio announcer sings "Traffic on the One." I increase the volume and dart across town in pursuit of a freeway. I briskly change lanes and prepare for my drive from Culver City to the San Fernando Valley, wondering if Gordon's married. He doesn't have a ring. But that doesn't mean anything. I'm sure he has a girlfriend. But maybe not. I think he was flirting with me. It sure felt like it. But then guys just do that. Part of their DNA. I don't think it was anything. Oh, well. I liked meeting him. How wonderful it would be to find a decent guy.

I fly along the freeway to the Valley, darting in and out of traffic, thinking about my awful love life. I'm a guy during the day, or at least I try to be, and then transform into what I think a woman should be—nice, fun, and flirty—at night. But the lines blur, and I end up being some kind of hermaphrodite. I feel much more confident with my work self. And yet I wonder if that persona has totally supplanted my feminine, sexy side. It could be why I don't date much. Hmm…

As I pull into the parking lot at HBS, I feel a sense of dread. I accidentally floor the gas, then slam on the brakes and come to a screeching halt, just making it into my parking space.

I grab my bags and march through the big glass doors, past the guard, wagging my HBS badge in his face. The guard waves me through the next security door into the hallway. I head toward the commissary for some badly needed coffee.

It's nine o'clock, and I'm nearly the first person in the commissary. No one in Hollywood is even up this early. All claim to be at a breakfast meeting, and sometimes two, before waltzing in at ten. The truth is, half of them are sleeping off last night's party. The trays are stacked high. There are enough donuts to fill a stadium. I've got one hour to get settled and prepare for Jerry.

Except there's Jerry seated in the corner of the commissary, nursing his coffee. Oh my God. He's here already. I want to get a good look at him, and then I want to get out of here quickly. He's in his blue blazer, white T-shirt, and crisp, bright blue jeans with a perfect crease down the middle, along with the requisite Gucci loafers. His wavy black hair—longer now, with bits of gray—cocky demeanor, and broad smile bring back all sorts of memories. He's clearly trying to impress the young cheerleader type sitting across from him.

Instead of heading for coffee, I turn around and head for the door. I hear, "Hey, Lexican, can you believe we're gonna be working together again?" I stop dead in my tracks, close my eyes, and pray this isn't happening. But suddenly I'm engulfed in Jerry's arms. I feel a wet kiss crash against my cheek. I push him aside, straighten my clothes, and try to toss my hair, which is now plastered against my face from his sloppy kiss.

"It's nice to see you, Jerry," I lie. "I'll call you when I get upstairs."

He's stunned. He holds out his arms and says, "What the fuck?"

I can't stand how insecure I feel at this moment. I'm right back to that awful place, working for him. I felt it the second I heard his voice. But he's working for me now. I do not work for him. Maybe if I say that ten times and write it down three hundred more I'll believe it. I may be dying on the inside, but I have to appear strong and confident on the outside. I've come a long way from where I was when I worked for him years ago. This guy cannot break me. Shoulders back, chest out, and chin held high, I start to exit the commissary.

"I'll see you in my office, Jer. We have a lot to do," I say without looking in his direction as I head through the doors into the lobby.

The second I'm in the lobby my phone rings.

"Alexa, where *are* you?" asks Rosie.

"I'll be right up, but would you mind getting me some coffee?" I ask as I head toward the stairwell.

Rosie is a lovely assistant. I adore her. She isn't in my face begging for a promotion like so many other assistants. But it seems every single college grad is enamored of Hollywood. Many feel they're entitled to executive positions the second they receive their degrees. Rosie just moved here a few years ago from Florida with her cat, Mr. Pickles. She followed a boyfriend who turned out to be someone else's within weeks of her arrival. She started in a temp position on my desk, and I never let her go.

"Sure, I'm happy to get your coffee," Rosie says sweetly, and then adds, "By the way, Jerry just called and is on his way up here."

What? I just told him to wait for our call. Great. Rosie knows I hate Jerry Kellner. She saw me turn green when Chester exited my office on Friday. I wanted to kill myself. I'm beginning to wonder if it isn't better being fired. Who's ever heard of a boss reporting to his former assistant?

"OK, I'm coming." I rush past the elevator bank into the stairwell to begin my daily climb up three flights of stairs.

Elevators terrify me. I avoid them like the plague. The day before my father died I got stuck in one, as if that were a bad omen, and I've never walked into one again. I know every back stairwell in every hotel and office building. Rosie knows that I won't eat at a restaurant in the sky or go to any floor that forces me to climb more than a few flights.

Reaching the top level slightly out of breath, I walk swiftly down the endless hallway, my J. Peterman leather mailbag overflowing with dog-eared scripts written by faceless writers, many of whom I know by name but couldn't identify in a lineup. The fact that their lives are in my hands often worries me, because sometimes I wonder if I truly know what the heck I'm doing. As the famous and prolific screenwriter William Goldman once said, "No one knows anything in Hollywood."

The script bag is threatening to fall off my right shoulder. My purse is on the left one, and my phone in my right hand as I push open the door to my suite. I really need to get out of the Dark Ages, embrace modernity, and start reading scripts on my iPad. But I'm technology challenged. Just when I get up to speed on one device, a better one comes along, and I can't keep up.

"Hey, babe, you've got some cushy job, strolling in here at nine o'clock," Jerry hollers as I enter. "You're just lucky you've got me to cover your ass now, 'cause, man, I'd never let one of my staffers get away with that." I glide past the bland conference room and a couple of offices to Rosie's desk, which sits just outside my door. Jerry is relaxing on the blue tweed couch next to it, his legs lazily crossed.

"Jerry, our meeting is an hour from now. You're early. I said I'd call when I was ready." I struggle with my bag and trip over a pile of scripts blocking the doorway, which unleashes my purse and its contents. Everything flies all over the place. Rosie and I scramble to pick up the items. Lipstick, makeup, coins, hairbrush, Advil, Purell, the apple I forgot to eat in the car, and of course my Swingin-est Secret Agent metal tampon case explodes, exposing two tampons that scatter to the ground, landing right in front of Jerry's feet. He carefully leans down, skillfully picks them up, and hands all three items to me.

"Swingin-est Secret Agent, huh? Cool." Jerry smirks.

If there's ever a moment when one wants to die, this is surely it. What a great start to my new life with Jerry, who is obviously amused by my harried appearance.

"Give me a minute," I say. I quickly enter my office and slam the door. I toss my purse and script bag on the couch and crash into my black leather executive chair and rub my neck, which already feels stiff and sore. I swivel around and catch my reflection in the glass window.

It's an image of someone I'm acquainted with but don't really recognize. Is that me? I look worn-out and tired. Maybe the article I read in *Marie Claire* last night about my biological clock is true. Maybe I need to take a beat and figure out what I want more, this job or a *Leave it to Beaver* life.

God, I hate him. I can still smell his aftershave from the kiss he smacked on my cheek. Yuck.

But I want to get this over with. I pull out my mirror, check my makeup, brush my hair, open the door, and usher Jerry inside.

Rosie breezes by Jerry and hands me my much-needed coffee.

"Thank you so much, Rosie," I gush with such gratitude you'd think she just gave me her kidney.

"Nice digs, Lex," Jerry says as he quickly scans my office. He heads for the couch and eyes the M&M's, but I quickly redirect him to the chair opposite my desk. I plant myself on the other side.

This is so strange. I never dreamed I'd be on this side of the desk, with Jerry on the other. I sit for a moment and look at him, taking in this wonderful sight. I can't help but remember our last day together.

"I'm sorry I had to fire you, Lexican," he says. "But you're just not destined for greatness. It's something you either have or you don't."

I hurry out the door carrying the box containing my few personal items, as I never felt comfortable there.

"I guess time will tell that," I say, holding back tears as I rush to my car.

It still hurts to think about it. But I've moved on. I remind myself that my life is much different and better today. I pull myself together, take a deep breath, lean back, and say, "Jerry, as you know, Barnsworth wants you in my department. I'm not thrilled about this. I've never been told who to hire, especially someone I not only worked for but for whom I have rather unpleasant feelings." I hope this doesn't sound rehearsed even though I went over it a thousand times with Sylvia this weekend. I'm amazed I haven't tripped over the words. But my mouth is dry, so I reach for my coffee.

"Wait a second. What's your problem? I hired you, promoted you, geezus, I did everything for you. What're you talking about?" Jerry barks as he leans forward, his eyes bulging and that old, familiar vein running down the center of his forehead starting to engorge. He tries to continue, but I put down my coffee, pitch forward, and cut him off.

"You took advantage of me," I say matter-of-factly. "You promised me jobs and then hired your friends. You sent me on a ton of personal errands that were far beyond the purview of my job. And, let me set the record straight. No, you never promoted me, and in fact, you fired me." I fight to control my anger. I didn't realize how much pent-up rage I have toward him. My blood pressure rises, and my heart pumps wildly, but I'm not going to show any chinks in this armor.

"Ya know, Lexican, that was years ago." He's actually lounging on the chair. "Are you still carrying that around? Get over it. Geezus, *women*, I swear they just don't get it. I don't know how you girls survive in the working world."

The man has not changed.

I can barely breathe. I want to reach across the desk, grab him by the neck, and fling him out the window. Instead, I stop and take a couple of deep breaths. I have to make this work. Put the bad feelings behind me. Let it go. That was a long time ago. Life is different now. I'm in charge. He's not. I've done incredibly well. He hasn't. I'm at the top of my game. He's not. This guy can't get to me anymore.

"Jerry, we have to work together. We're gonna put the past behind us. You're working for me, and will now be a part of my team. Our goal is to create great comedy shows." I smile, trying to believe my own bullshit.

"Look, Lexican," he starts.

"My name is Alexa. That's what I want to be called. I'm your boss. Got it?" I stop and let it sink in.

Jerry stands and edges toward the door.

"Sure, boss." Just before he exits, he stops and pulls an old, crumpled tinfoil condom wrapper out of his back pocket and hands it to me. "Obviously a memento of a good time. Wouldn't want you to lose this. It dropped out of your purse along with your Secret Agent tampons." Jerry folds my fingers securely over the wrapper, grins, and is gone.

"Can you see if Chester has a second?" I call into the intercom to Rosie. I race over to my M&M's bowl and throw a handful down. What a great morning this has been. I can't believe I had that condom wrapper in my purse. It must've been there a year. Jerry should know I only used that condom as a hair tie. I'm sure it will provide plenty of material for him, along with the Secret Agent tampon case I picked up at a flea market.

Obviously a mistake. I never dreamed anyone would ever see it. After a beat, Rosie replies that Chester is in between meetings so come promptly.

Network executives are always in between meetings even when they're really at the beach. Chester isn't big on meetings. He also doesn't like bad news. He wants solutions, not problems. But I need to come clean with him.

I gulp down my coffee, straighten my suit, and head down the hallway to Chester's office. I hope this goes well.

The halls are lined with posters depicting every TV show in HBS's long history, including the famous *Blonde Logic*, *Apple's Way*, and *The American Life*. There are also photographs of famous actors from years gone by such as Patty Duke, Joseph Gordon-Levitt, Sara Chalke, Tim Allen, Jerry O'Connell, Jennie Garth, Bill Cosby, Kelsey Grammar, Brian Austin Green, Geena Davis, Ashton Kutcher, Ellen DeGeneres, Will Smith, Valerie Bertinelli, Fred Savage, and many more who appeared on an HBS show at one time or another. There's a glass case featuring several Peabody and Emmy awards. There are no windows in this interior hallway. The windows line the exterior of the building and are for the executive offices. The size and shape are among the many details discussed in every executive's long employment contract. Suffice to say, the bigger the better.

Plain brown doors guard the entrances leading to the executive suites on the third floor. There's the legal suite, the daytime suite, the publicity suite, and so on. But no one is mingling in the hallway. Generally, the hallways are for producers, agents, and writers on their way to pitch ideas to various executives who hide behind closed doors. Occasionally we'll venture outside to the restroom, where we may accidentally run into them. They'll use the opportunity to chat us up about their ideas, even following us into the bathroom, elevator, or in my case, the stairwell.

I finally make it to Chester's suite and slowly enter his sanctuary. His two female assistants are nowhere to be seen.

"What's up, Lex?" he asks without looking up as I enter his office. Hardly in between meetings, Chester is engrossed in a football game on one of his five TVs. He's supposed to watch all the competing broadcast networks at the same time. But not Chester.

Chester's happy watching sports. He has a gigantic staff to tell him what the competitors are doing.

"Chester, I officially hired Jerry Kellner today. He'll be working as a director in my department. I'll send human resources the paperwork." I hope he hears me over the sound of crashing helmets on the screen.

Chester continues to stare at the screens.

"Um, Chester, I think you should know…"

Chester lowers the volume, turns toward me, and says, "Alexa, I know you used to work for him. Make it work. This is Barnsworth's deal, not mine. Figure it out."

There's a long pause as we both just look at each other. Then, I skulk out the door and travel down the long, winding hallway back to my office.

Great. What a useful discussion.

"*The Candy Stripers* table read at Fox is in an hour, and then you have a lunch, so I think you need to get moving," Rosie yells as I brush past her into my office to begin what isn't looking like a great day. Rosie follows me and reads through the calls that came in while I was with Chester. "At three you have to meet with Richard about a standards issue on *What a Twit*, then Molly needs to talk to you about a problem on *Money Honey*. Then you have two pitch meetings, and Shawn wants to discuss your new budget, and Noah wants you to e-mail him about moving *The Candy Stripers* to nine on Wednesdays. Gordon Harrison called about tutoring. And did you approve the affiliate book? 'Cause Jane needs to know, her deadline is tomorrow. Also, Tony said *Elle* wants to interview you for a story about why there aren't more women directors in comedy, and…"

Rosie rambles on and on, spewing out more and more problems, calls, e-mails, meetings, and confrontations I have to deal with. I'll get through about half of them today. The rest will have to wait until tomorrow, and numerous people will be pissed. And I'll feel terrible. I wish I could do it all. But there's never enough time to get to everyone and everything.

"Rosie, please call Molly and Jerry into my office," I say. "Then I'll head to Fox, then lunch, and we'll place some calls in the car. I'll deal with all the other issues later."

Rosie turns on her heels. But something occurs to me about one of the calls she mentioned.

"Wait. Rosie, did you say there was a call from Gordon Harrison? Did he leave a message?"

"No, just call him back when you can." Rosie stands in the doorway.

There's a pause. Rosie waits patiently.

"Let's call him back now," I say.

Rosie walks to her desk, places the call, and within seconds Gordon is on the line.

I'm suddenly nervous. A good nervous. The butterflies-in-your-stomach kind. I'm excited and hopeful that maybe this isn't just a work call. Before I lift the receiver I glance at my reflection in the glass window. I tap my cheeks and smack my lips as if he'll see me through the telephone line. I take a deep breath, wish myself luck, and offer the most pleasant hello I can muster.

"Hi, Gordon." This sweet greeting is so not me. In order to survive at HBS I strap my balls on early in the morning, so it's hard to switch gears.

"Hey, how ya doing?" Gordon says. He has such a friendly demeanor. The second I hear his voice, my body relaxes just like it did when I tried meditation for a full five minutes.

"I'm OK. Kind of busy," I say, realizing I have about three minutes. I want to say "What's up?" My usual question when I want to move things along. But I'm really trying to slow down and call upon my nice, flirtatious self—the one that's been in mothballs for the past decade. "Do you have a student for me?"

"Not yet. Still figuring it out. I just have a few quick questions. I know you're busy, I promise this won't take long."

I look at the clock again. I want to tell him yes, I'm busy. I never have time. I'm on autopilot. I go from one meeting, phone call, and e-mail to the next. I'm not sure where my job ends and my life begins. But instead I lie because I want to talk to him.

"Sure, go ahead. I have a couple of minutes."

I can tell by Gordon's slow cadence that he doesn't work at the speed of light like my colleagues and I do. He operates on a much slower, more modulated basis. Like normal people.

"Well, first, I really enjoyed meeting you," he says. "I wish we'd been able to spend a little more time together this morning. But I'm happy you came by and that you'd like to participate in our program."

"Yes, I would've liked to have stayed longer, too. But I always seem to be racing from one thing to another." I laugh.

"Well, despite your hectic pace you seem to enjoy your job."

"On most days. Again, I apologize for leaving so abruptly."

"Oh, don't worry about it. Your smile made up for it."

"My smile?" I ask.

"Yes. You have a pretty smile."

There's a pause.

"That's really nice of you to say. Thank you."

Rosie sticks her head in the door. "They're here," she says, indicating that my next meeting has arrived.

"OK, just a second," I say back to her.

"Well, I guess I should move things along. I know you're busy," Gordon adds.

"I am. But it's nice to take a break and talk to you."

There's another pause.

"Well, if you'll bear with me, I just have a few questions. Are you by any chance fluent in Spanish?"

"No, unfortunately I'm not," I say. "But I'm pretty good at charades. Does that help?"

"That might work." Gordon laughs. "How about sports? Did you play volleyball or softball in school? Tennis? Field hockey? Anything like that? Because sometimes it's helpful if tutors and their students engage in a recreational activity. It's a great way to break the ice."

"Uh. No. I don't play sports. However, I occasionally *watch* sports. Does that count? I go to the gym. Not often, though. I only go when my friend Sylvia is here. She belongs to one of those upscale gyms. Lotsa aerobic machines and weights. I think there might even be a pool. I should go more. I just don't have the…" Oh God, what am I doing? I'm rambling. "What was the question again?"

Gordon has me tongue-tied. I'm sweating. I can't believe what I just said. He hasn't uttered a word. Is he still there? My hands are sweaty, my mouth is dry. My defenses start to kick in. I've got to take back the control. I'll become Alexa the executive now. I know that role better, and it feels far more comfortable.

"That's OK, I was just wondering," Gordon says. "No sports. No big deal. It'll be fun."

"OK, well, I better go." My tone is professional. I failed at being a potential date, so I'm going to say less because clearly in my case, it's more. "I hope this tutoring works out. You can always text me if you have more questions."

"But you like going to sporting events, right?" Gordon asks, seemingly undeterred by my detached professional tone. "Maybe we could go to a game one night."

Suddenly I'm feeling nervous again. I haven't been on a date in so long.

"Yes, I enjoy going to games and—"

"Oh, Alexa, I'm so sorry. I have to get off," Gordon interrupts. "We'll be in touch."

And just like that the call is over.

I've still got the receiver at my ear. Did this call just end? The silence screams yes, it's over. Darn. I thought he was about to ask me out. Ugh. What happened? I reluctantly hang up.

I'd like to continue my pity party, but the second I hang up the door flies open and in walk Jerry and Molly. They sit in the two chairs opposite my desk, ready for this meeting to begin. And yet I'm still mulling over the conversation I just had with Gordon. As much as I love this job, I often feel like I have whiplash going from one meeting to the next, constantly adapting to different roles and personalities.

Molly Thatcher was my assistant at Morgan. I promoted her to manager of comedy there and brought her with me to HBS. She has gorgeous shoulder-length red hair and pretty green eyes. In her late twenties, she could be the poster girl for J.Crew, as she's often dressed in a beige pantsuit, white T-shirt, and heels. She anxiously sucks on her pen and sits a little too straight in her chair. Jerry, of course, sits in his like he owns the place.

"Molly, I don't know if you've had the pleasure of meeting Jerry Kellner, but he's now the director of comedy," I say, faking a smile. "He'll need your support, and I hope you'll bring him up to speed." I try to sound genuine. But Molly knows something's up, as the plan was for her to ascend to director. I can see the disappointment in her face. Molly extends her hand to Jerry, but he ignores it and plays with the two metal balls on my desk.

"Listen, Lexican," he begins.

"Alexa," I interrupt.

"I've got to get to the bank and then drinks with some of my buddies. So, Molly, just e-mail me what I need to know, and we'll take it from there." Jerry tosses one of the balls into the air and catches it behind his back. After that stunning performance, he places the balls back in their box and swings his right leg over his left, puts his fingers through his hair, and leans back in his chair with his arms locked behind his head. I notice he's lost weight since I saw him last. But those giant brown eyes and that mass of dark, wavy hair, far more unruly than in the past, still haunt me.

I lean across the desk. "Forget the bank and cancel your drinks with your pals. We buy and develop new comedy shows. Due to recent cutbacks, we also monitor the comedies already on the network. It's a lot. So you need to get with the program." I take a breath and continue. "I want you to shadow Molly today. She's going to the *Money Honey* table read at Warners this afternoon. This is a problematic show. I want you both there," I say.

"No problem." Molly nods dutifully. "I have the revised pages in my office, Jerry. Just come by and I'll give them to you. Is that all you need, Alexa?"

"That's it," I say.

Molly exits as Jerry remains seated.

"Is there something else?" I ask.

"Listen," he snaps. "I don't do table reads anymore. Let Molly do that stuff. She can report back. I'll work the agents and get new product in here."

"Jerry, I'm not sure you get this. I'm your boss. I'm telling you what I need. This meeting is over." I swivel around to my computer, and Jerry finally starts to leave.

On his way out the door, he adds, "By the way, Molly's got great tits."

"Still married, Jerry? Olivia, right? I'll be sure to tell her how fond you are of Molly."

Jerry stops and glares at me.

"And by the way, we don't talk about tits in here. Got it?"

He swings the door open and is gone.

How could anyone be married to that slimeball? His mere presence makes my skin crawl. I can't stand to be in the same zip code with him. I'm perspiring, anxious, and exasperated. No one prepared me for these kinds of confrontations.

Rosie enters, pointing to her watch. She hands me my purse and says, "If you leave now, you can make it to Fox and then straight to Ca'Del Sole for lunch. Oh, and Gordon Harrison called back to say he had to deal with a crying student and is sorry he had to hang up abruptly. He said he'll try calling you again."

Wow. What a decent guy. He actually cared enough to call back to deliver that message.

"OK, Rosie, thanks. Please make sure to put him through when he calls."

As I ponder that thought, I grab my purse and script bag and head for the door. I'm thrilled to get outside and take in some fresh air. It's been a hell of a morning.

I pull out of my parking space, turn on some classical music, take a deep breath, and finally start to relax. I think about my conversation with Gordon. He thinks I have a beautiful smile. What a lovely thing to say. I'm going to dine out on that for a while. I play that line over again, thinking about the way he said it.

My car is my sanctuary, a refuge in which to collect myself and enjoy solitude for the ten minutes it takes to get to my next destination. I start to fantasize about Gordon and what he might be like. I roll down my window and take a deep breath of the gentle desert breeze as I exit the parking lot and coast along toward the stop sign. But suddenly I feel someone walk up alongside my car. And then I see Jerry staring at me through my open window. He bends down and leans into my face. I can smell his foul breath. I'm stunned by his appearance.

"Barnsworth is my boss," he sneers. "Not you, bitch. I'm gonna have your job in six months, so get off my back." Jerry pushes his face so far through the window I'm practically in the passenger seat, trying to get some distance from him. He lingers to make sure I get his message. Then, with a wink and a smile, he wishes me a nice day, flips me the bird, and is gone.

Chapter Three

Rosie plants herself in the seat across from my desk Thursday morning. She's reading aloud from her iPad. "Come meet Jerry Kellner, king of the Potawatomi fish boil." She laughs as she scrolls through the article she found on the Internet. "Did you know Jerry Kellner is featured on billboards that line the highway leading up to the Potawatomi Fish Boil restaurant, which his parents own, in Door County, Wisconsin? Or that he wears a jewel-encrusted crown on these billboards and is holding a gigantic kettle of fish?"

"He should go back," I say. "He's been here four days, and it feels like four years."

Rosie is obsessed. She continues reading. "His gig at the restaurant only served to fuel Jerry's great love for acting. But he desired a larger role in life. He was a cheerleader at the University of Wisconsin at Green Bay and majored in theater. After graduation, he received a gala send-off. Everyone knew Jerry was destined for Hollywood." She laughs.

"Is this from the local paper?" I ask.

"Yeah, the *Door County Times* on June nineteenth, ninety-nine. I googled him."

"I know his story," I say. "His first Hollywood job was in the mailroom at William Morris. He claims his father didn't think he'd amount to anything, like that's a new spin. His younger brother,

Craig, is a famous chef in Door County." Jerry was constantly bragging about his accomplishments when I worked for him.

"I wasn't satisfied being a big fish in a small town, Lex. I want to be a big fish, period. I have a winning personality that'll serve me well in Hollywood. I became an agent in seventeen months, which was amazing. I've enjoyed the good times with as many women as I can quite literally get my hands on." He instantly reaches over to grab both of my breasts.

I slap his hand away and race over to the copy machine as if it could save me from this lecherous asshole.

Just thinking about that moment sends shivers up my spine.

Molly appears in the doorway.

"Jerry's on his way to the *Money Honey* run-through. He knows you're coming, too." She looks at her watch. "You might want to leave soon, because it literally starts in ten minutes."

"Jerry's married to Olivia Spencer, the daughter of Avery and Millicent Spencer," Rosie reads, "who are included in New York's Social Register. Spencer is an heir to the Alliance Rubber Company, which was founded by her great-grandfather William H. Spencer, who invented the rubber band." Rosie continues to read from her iPad, oblivious to the conversation that just occurred. "They have two sons and a daughter. Did you know this?"

"Trust me, Rosie, I know everything about Jerry Kellner, more than I ever wanted to know." I get up from my desk and start to leave.

"I didn't think he was even married. Are they happy?"

"I've no idea. But I don't want to spend any more time thinking about Jerry."

As I start rummaging through my script bag, looking for the one I need to take to the run-through, I think about my own parents' marriage. Were they really happy? My dad was a traveling salesman, a job that kept him on the road, leaving my mom to raise my younger brother and me. How satisfied could she have been with that arrangement? I want to believe they were happy and that marriage is worth waiting for and that I, too, might find my kind of happiness some day.

"My guess is that Olivia's content with Jerry, and Jerry's enthralled with Olivia's connected family," I say, pouring all the scripts out of my bag. "Now, Rosie, do you have any idea where I might've put my *Money Honey* script? The one that has the last set of notes?"

"It would be so much easier if you'd download them on your iPad. You know that device has more functionality. It's more than just a flashlight." Rosie smirks as she sifts through the scripts. "Oh, it's right there, Alexa. The one on top."

"Oh, Rosie, you're the best. What would I do without you?"

"If you used your iPad—"

"Yes, I got the message, and occasionally I watch dailies on it, so I'm making progress."

"Occasionally." Rosie laughs.

"Honestly, thank you so much." I grab the script and race out of my office, down the stairs, and to my car. I hope I get to Warners in time for the run-through, but I'm already late.

Money Honey films on Stage 24, the old *Friends* soundstage at Warner Bros. The run-through's a dress rehearsal for the show that will shoot tomorrow, Friday night, before a live audience. It's the last time the studio and network executives will give their notes. Molly informed me Jerry never made it to the table read on Monday. Nice.

I drive onto the lot, get out of my car, and find my way onto the soundstage. It's large and cavernous like an airplane hangar. It's a long walk around the stage to the actual set. The floor's an obstacle course of snakelike cables and wires and is difficult to navigate in three-inch heels.

As I get closer, I can make out some of the conversation. "Oh, you must be Jerry; it's so great to meet you," gushes Wendy Grossman, a fortyish woman who Jerry clearly mistakes for a cast member's mother rather than the cocreator of the show. His dismissive hello turns into an energetic one when she introduces herself as the co–executive producer. Typical Jerry.

"We rewrote the last scene, Jerry," Wendy continues. "I know Molly had problems with it at the table read, so we tried to incorporate her notes. I hope you like what we came up with." Wendy signals to the cast and crew that it's time to start the run-through. I try to rush along but run smack into a large group of Japanese tourists who have gathered at the entrance leading to the set, which slows me down. In the meantime, I hear Jerry fawning all over the writers.

"I'm a huge fan of the show," he exclaims. "And hey, you have the *Friends* stage, how cool is that? No way you're gonna fail."

As if Jerry's ever seen the show. Let the hyperbole begin.

The audience bleachers sit across from the multiple sets on the stage. The *Money Honey* set resembles the interior architecture of celebrated New York designer Steven Gambrel, known for his finely tailored uptown homes. The set includes a living room, kitchen, bedroom, and office. It's like a big one-story dollhouse.

As I excuse myself through the group of tourists, I start to approach the stage where I see five green director's chairs lined up next to each other in front of the small kitchen set. The network and studio executives, often called the suits, will occupy these chairs to watch the run-through. They'll take notes, which they'll offer at the end of the run-through.

I finally get closer and catch a glimpse of Jerry at the far end of the row. Seated next to him are two thirtysomething Warner Bros. TV executives clad in identical black suits so similar you'd think these guys were twins. Beside them are Casey Herald and Wendy

Grossman, head writers, and Tom Swanson, a slick and very handsome director.

There's no chair for me. Ugh.

"Let's take it from the top. Places, everyone," shouts Tom Swanson as he stands.

The stage is set for the first scene. Kyle Greissman and Jenny Moran are playing a young married couple. Both are refugees from the not-so-successful show *Chix and Dix*, which aired twice on Fox. It was panned from the moment the camera started rolling. But Kyle and Jenny escaped the carnage due to their good looks and scandalous love affair. Both left their respective spouses for each other. Their affair gave *Access Hollywood* big ratings, while the show got a pink slip.

I start moving a little faster, but just as I come upon the set, I hear, "OK, everyone. *Action!*" And with that, the run-through begins. I see Kyle as he gets up from the table and moves to the refrigerator to retrieve something. I tiptoe over to the execs and whisper, "I'm really sorry I'm late. Traffic was a little rough today."

"Oh, wait," says Swanson. "Stop. Sorry, guys. We'll have to start again." The assistant director calls, "Cut!"

The room is dead quiet. I've disrupted the moment.

"Oh, Alexa, I'm sorry, we didn't know you were coming," calls Wendy from her director's chair. "We thought Jerry would be representing the network today, so we began." Jerry smiles broadly, chest puffed, waving to me. How typical that he chose not to mention that I would be here also.

"Jerry, you knew I was coming. I guess you didn't have a chance to tell them to wait?" I ask with a touch of sarcasm.

Jerry shrugs. "I guess you were just late again, boss."

I'm about to march toward him, but a skinny young intern in torn jeans and a sweatshirt magically appears with a green director's chair, placing it right next to Wendy's. I drop my purse alongside the chair and ask Tom to begin again while I glare at Jerry. He smiles back at me.

Most freshman shows have difficulty attracting and building an audience, and *Money Honey* is no different. It's aired twice. It premiered in August right after *Let's Get the Girls*, the new hit reality show featuring Miami bouncers who count how many girls they can date in one evening. Noah Stegner, the lanky but handsome, clever, and skillful head of scheduling at HBS, thought *Let's Get the Girls*, or as he calls it, *Let's Get the Ratings*, and *Money Honey*, a comedy about an upscale Manhattan investment banker and her stay-at-home husband, were geared to the same audience. They weren't. Viewers left in droves.

We watch the first scene, and when it ends, we get up from the director's chairs while the young intern and a few others sweep in to carry the chairs to the next scene about ten feet away. They're placed in perfect order while we casually saunter over to them.

Frankly, it's stunning there aren't gold limousines escorting us from one position to the next. Network executives are treated like royalty. After all, we're basically the bank. It took me a while to understand that all the praise and adoration I receive isn't about me. It's about the institution I represent. I buy the show and then decide if we'll buy more. They love me when I say yes and hate me when I say no. It's definitely fun delivering good news, but not so great when it's bad. Like in the case of this show.

The run-through concludes, and everyone applauds the actors. We praise all performances, whether good or bad. It's the polite thing to do, and we all know it comes with the territory even if the run-through was an unmitigated disaster.

The actors, writers, director, and suits now gather inside the kitchen set to begin the notes session. Generally, the highest-ranking network executive takes charge. Today, however, Jerry, who follows no rules, speaks first.

"Fannnntastic show, guys. And Jenny, you were awesome, baby!" Jerry puts his hand over his heart then throws a kiss in her direction. Jenny looks thrilled and returns the kiss.

But the show sucked. It wasn't fannnntastic at all. Jerry's interruption has created a problem for me. Now I have to deliver the bad news. Given his desire to have my job in six months, this comes as no surprise.

I have to think about how to convey notes in a highly diplomatic, sensitive way so that I don't injure these already inflated yet very delicate egos. I want to modulate Jerry's crazy outburst and soft-pedal the reality that this run-through was God-awful. So, I'm going to have to lie. A little.

"I think we have a good show. Thank you for working so hard. We want the show to succeed, and though we're doing OK, I think there's room for improvement," I say nicely. "For instance, I think we could trim the first and last scenes." I look around for agreement.

What I'm really thinking is, how am I going to get any support for this show when the ratings suck? Steve's marketing team loses interest when a show starts to tank. And this one sank faster than the *Titanic*. Because they're cheaper to produce, I'm sure there's already a new reality show waiting in the wings to take this slot.

"Well, that's an interesting idea, Alison, but I don't think we want to abbreviate that scene," Tom says dismissively. "Jerry, what else do you have?"

"Uh, Tom, have you met *Alexa Ross*?" Wendy interrupts nervously. "She's the *head* of comedy at HBS."

"Oh, I'm so sorry, Alexa, I thought Jerry was head of comedy," Tom says as he gets up from his chair.

"Not yet." Jerry laughs, as do some others, but it's an awkward moment.

"Probably not ever," I say.

"I thought he was in charge. I apologize. Hope you won't hold it against me." Tom laughs as he drapes his arm around my shoulder. I quickly pull away from his grasp. Why does Tom assume I work for Jerry? Because he's a guy? The same thing occurs when I dine with male colleagues. Invariably, the check is almost always delivered to the man. Haven't we moved beyond this?

"It's no big deal, Tom," I say. "Let's go on." Without taking a breath, I start rattling off the rest of my notes while Wendy and the others write in the margins of their worn-out scripts.

I'd like to smack Tom. I can't stand the arrogance of some of these Hollywood types. I hope I never treat anyone that way.

I finish my notes and the Warner execs offer theirs, while everyone remains huddled around the kitchen set. Out of the corner of my eye, I see Jerry slink off the stage with Casey Herald. They're engrossed in conversation. I start after him, but my phone is vibrating, and I notice twenty unopened e-mails staring back at me. I hurriedly scroll through to see if any are urgent. I stop at one that says "Gordon."

Alexa, I've selected your student. Perhaps we can discuss at the Lakers game tomorrow night? Yes, that's a request for a date. I started to ask you on the phone, but as you know I had cut it short. I know it's late. I hope that's ok. You did say you like to watch *sports. Would you like to join me?*

I smile, remembering Gordon's sweet demeanor and sexy blue eyes.

Sure, I'd like to go to a Lakers game, I respond. *I've never been.* Within seconds I receive a response.

We're set to meet at the Staples Center for the Lakers game tomorrow night, Friday. Gordon says he'll leave my ticket at the Will Call window. *Money Honey* films on Friday nights. This may be a first, as I'm putting a date ahead of work. But I'm eager to see Gordon. I know I can depend on at least Molly to cover for me.

Now I have to get out of here and figure out what to wear. I haven't had a date in ages. Maybe I can shop tomorrow morning. Darn, I can't. I'm meeting Sylvia at the gym.

Ugh, I hate the gym.

———

I hate the gym particularly on Friday mornings when I'm exhausted from a week of hell. I never go. I figure I get plenty of exercise running up and down stairwells. But Sylvia and her great body love the gym, and the gym loves her. Fortunately, she's in LA for two weeks attending the international sales meetings. I love it when she's here. But instead of meeting for meals, we meet at the gym. So fine, I get a guest pass and we go to her superdeluxe sports club, which is the Four Seasons of gyms, complete with valet parking, gourmet restaurant, LCD TVs on every single machine, and a decked-out executive locker room.

Sylvia and I work out for an hour. Well, Sylvia works out. She enjoys "Shreadmill," which challenges her body at the highest level on a treadmill while a trainer shouts instructions. Sounds awful.

The only thing I enjoy at the gym is the protein shake at the end when I'm showered, dressed, and leaving. While Sylvia sweats off whatever fat she has left on her well-toned body, I take a leisurely ride on the elliptical and watch reruns of Paula Deen preparing buttermilk fried chicken. Mmm.

We're done and off to the executive locker room, which is accessed by special code and located inside and at the very end of the regular locker room where the plebes shower and change. Our code flashes green, the door opens, and new age music and Jo Malone engulf our senses. We've reached the Land of Oz.

There are more mirrors in here than at McGowan's Infinite Mirror Maze at Fisherman's Wharf. Sylvia and I grab ice water from one of the four silver carafes situated at the end of the luxuriously appointed locker room with its bird's-eye maple-finished locker doors, fresh white towels, razors, state-of-the-art hair dryers, flat-irons, Kerastase hair products, Kiehl's lotions, and numerous other luxury amenities. I can't believe this is real. Three of my apartment could fit in here.

Sylvia, in her black Nike racerback top and matching Dri-Fit capris, her blonde-streaked hair roughly gathered in a ponytail, with sweat dripping all over her face and into her water, wipes herself off and collapses into one of the red Cardiff tweed upholstered chairs while I crash into another. I'm hardly exhausted. My white T-shirt and blue-and-gold UCLA nylon shorts are unscathed. I'm happy to take a long gulp of the lemon-infused ice water, rip off my shoes and socks, and let my toes sink into the luxuriant beige featherlike carpet below.

This is not a busy locker room, because most can't afford the astronomical price it takes to enter this haven, which includes a private locker and daily laundry service as well as the privacy and exclusivity of a room just for heavy hitters. Sylvia is one hell of a negotiator, because she managed to get HBS to pay for her bicoastal membership to this club. You'd think I'd learn something here. But I'm not sure this place is for me. Despite being a big TV executive, if I ever join a gym, I think I might be more comfortable and less intimidated at the Y.

"See those?" Sylvia points at two beautiful, curvaceous blonde women in the corner. "Porn stars. Lots of them here. They can afford this place."

Who'da thunk?

As I pretend to watch the TV screen above, my eyes can't help but notice the various landing strips and variety of breasts around me. I haven't seen this many breasts since high school. And, if memory serves me, they weren't nearly as big, nor as creatively positioned back then. Many don't match, yet occasionally, there are a set of originals. I'm also particularly intrigued by the thongs. I never knew there was so much variety. I like my Hanky Pankys, but clearly the ones to have are the sexy La Perlas.

"Ya know, Syl, as I look around this room I can't stop thinking about what a field day our colleagues would have in here."

"Yeah, it's so wasted on us." Sylvia laughs.

"Porn stars and actresses. Jerry would be in hog heaven."

"I can't believe that dick actually said he was gonna have your job in six months," Sylvia says out of the blue. She shakes her head in disbelief. "I can't stop thinking about it." She takes a long gulp of water.

"Clearly sticking the fork in him didn't kill him. You were wrong," I tell her. "I'm stuck with him, and I don't know what to do. He does whatever the heck he wants, and thinks he's bullet-proof because of his connection to Barnsworth."

Sylvia offers ways to deal with Jerry, but nothing sounds appealing. I say I'll handle him even though I haven't a clue. She tells me to discuss it with human resources, but I don't trust them, and she agrees. They'll side with Jerry, given his pipeline to Barnsworth.

"Jerry's gonna win this war, isn't he?" I say, and pray Sylvia won't say yes.

She says nothing.

Sylvia and I know that as women we need to rise above this and take these things in stride. We are the two senior female executives in this company, and as such, we must adhere to the *Never let them see you cry* rule. Roll with the punches and keep going. We can handle anything and everything. Just like the guys. Only better.

"We should get going," Sylvia says, glancing at the time and guzzling the last of her water. "Lemme know how your meeting with the dickheads goes today."

I barely have a moment to enjoy the peaceful, fragrant locker room, as I feel the constant pressure of the network and its responsibilities. I hurry to my locker, tear off my clothes, race to the shower, dry my hair, slap on makeup, and come out looking like a half-assed mess. But hey, I'm on my way and sort of on time.

I leave the tranquility of the women's locker room and about forty minutes later, arrive at the men's. Actually it's Chester's office. Or as Sylvia calls it, the Bada Bing Room, a reference to the guys-only area within the strip club where Tony and his gang met in *The Sopranos*. As I approach, I hear the sound of somebody peeing in the private bathroom just inside Chester's office. Why these guys fail to close the door never ceases to amaze me. Fortunately, I know not to look. Hearing it is bad enough.

A cacophony of male voices greets me, one trying to outdo the next, each carrying on about some important point achieved at some important game. They're poking, pushing, screaming, laughing, snorting, and shouting while taking swigs from their Diet Cokes, afternoon lattes, or Red Bulls. All that's missing is the post–Super Bowl champagne shower.

Steve Hansen exits the bathroom, yanking his zipper. I make my way around the heavy marble table in the center of the room, pretending I didn't just see this.

We take our seats while Chester leans back in his black leather chair with his feet stretched out on the coffee table, something the rest of us wouldn't dare try. He's facing the bank of TVs. Three of us sit to his right and three to his left. The four others tote chairs from across the room and sit on the periphery.

Chester signals it's time for the revelry to stop and for the work to begin. He called this meeting earlier so he could attend his son's soccer game later this afternoon. He looks to Steve Hansen, the head of marketing and promotion.

"We're preparing promos for the November sweeps. We need some stunt casting so we can promote the shows more easily," Steve says.

Preferred stunts are episodes featuring Kim Kardashian as a doctor or lawyer. A highly fantastic suggestion and one that Steve suggests over and over. I nod patronizingly. Steve's annoyed. He knows I'm not going to do this. However, Jasper Jarosz, the head of drama development, thinks it's a great idea and comes up with another super suggestion to put Snooki, from the now-defunct *Jersey Shore*, in an episode of *Frozen Appeals*, a one-hour drama about justices on the Alaska Supreme Court. Everyone applauds this wildly terrific notion, while I wonder what planet they're on. We've gotten through most of my male colleagues' reports. It's finally my turn.

"Steve, we need more promos for *Money Honey*."

Everyone moans.

"That show's over," he says. "We're not gonna waste time on it."

"Hey, if we're gonna cancel it, let's cut our losses now," offers Mark Winslow, who doesn't give a shit about anything but the bottom line, which, of course, is his job. "Warners wants the renewal on *Bunnies*, so if we cut bait on this now, it could help us with that negotiation."

"But *People* is gonna run an interview with Kyle and Jenny about their affair next week," says Tony DeMeo, the head of press and publicity. "So do you really wanna cancel it now?"

"Hey guys," I interrupt. But, Mark, Steve, and Tony aren't done. Suddenly the discussion switches to whether Jenny's breasts are real and if so, when did they go from itty-bitty titties to hooters. I sit higher in my chair and try again. Nothing. Louder. Nothing.

Chester joins the discussion, which has turned from mammary glands to the penalty kick in the Manchester United–Arsenal English Premiere League soccer game on the top screen. Suddenly it's quiet. We have to remain very still so we can carefully study and comment on the replay and then the call. The tension builds as the officials huddle to make their decision. We're on pins and needles. Midwestern guys obsessing over soccer. Anything with a ball.

Amazing. You'd think we were in the final ten seconds of the 1980 Olympic hockey game between the Americans and the Soviets, waiting for Al Michaels to scream, "Do you believe in miracles?" Finally, the call is made and the room erupts. I try again, but Tony beats me to it, talking about press tour in January.

I've had enough. I stand on my chair.

This is not fun. Getting a room full of guys to focus on the lone female in their midst is no easy task. If I shout as loud as the guys I'm a bitch. If I whine about not being heard I'm a girl. A lovely dilemma.

"Hey, I'm not sure you guys heard me. Hellooooo, I'm talking now."

Finally, I have their attention.

"We can't cancel *Money Honey*. I want to give it at least four shots. It's aired twice in horrible time slots." My feet sink into the chair's cushion. I look down at Noah, the head of scheduling, who studies a freckle on his arm. "You can't throw this away. And Mark, we don't have to cut bait on every show to accommodate a negotiation on something else. We need better and more frequently aired promos."

"I dunno, Alexa, the show sucks. It's all that *I am woman, hear me roar* crap. There's no audience for it," Steve says dismissively. Then, he looks up at me. "We don't know how to promote it. I think we oughtta just expand *Let's Get the Girls* to an hour."

There's a lot of support for that idea.

"I'm not sure, Steve," Chester says. "I think Alexa has a point. Let's see some new thirty-second spots tomorrow. And Noah, see if you can find a better time period to run it in. Maybe in Tuesday's lineup so it has a chance. Let's give it at least two more airings, and then we'll know. OK, Alexa?"

There's a pause.

"You can get down now." Chester offers his hand to guide me.

I'm dumbstruck. I won. I carefully step down while the macho chatter continues uninterrupted. Did I just win one round? Really? Suddenly I feel like Hilary Swank in *Million Dollar Baby*. I'm exhausted.

The meeting draws to a close, and Chester belches loudly, then reminds everyone to check in with Crestview Elementary to get a student assigned, that we *are* going to take this tutoring thing seriously. He asks who has their student, and I'm the only one with my hand raised. As everyone departs, Chester asks that I take a drive with him.

I like Chester. He's a good man. He's very supportive and appreciates hard work. He loves my energy. He once told a colleague that if he put a plug up my ass I'd light up all of Burbank. I won't analyze that. Just took it as a compliment.

Chester takes a lot of drives during the day. Mostly to get in a few cigarettes. Today he needs gas. I've traveled to Dodgers games, bowling alleys, diners, and even bars just for meetings with Chester. Any place where he can smoke and relieve the tension and pressure of the office. If I die of secondhand smoke, it will no doubt be due to the time spent with Chester. He drives fast and recklessly with one hand on the wheel, the other flicking ashes out the window. Kind of like Mr. Toad's Wild Ride.

I'm glued to my seat, praying my life won't end this way. The seat belt alarm pings, reminding Chester to put his on. He ignores it. This grating tone follows us all the way to the gas station. It finally stops when Chester exits the car. I stay inside. He takes another drag, parks the cigarette between his lips, and begins pumping gas on my side of the car, ignoring the signs that say do *not* smoke or use a cell phone while pumping gas. Fortunately, Chester doesn't carry a cell phone, or our chances of being blown up would be even greater.

"I want someone to head entertainment," he says from outside the car in between puffs as he squeezes the last bit of gas into his

Jaguar's tank. "I don't want to be involved in the day-to-day any-more. I think you might have what it takes to be president of enter-tainment. I'm gonna consider some folks inside and outside the network." He's talking loudly, pump in hand. My phone vibrates, but I shove it deep in my purse, as this could truly be the moment I've been waiting for. All the blood, sweat, and no sex I've endured for years just to hear these words: *I think you might have what it takes to be president of entertainment.* Finally. I can't breathe. I'm ecstatic. I've really wanted this. I've worked hard for it.

My purse is vibrating wildly. But nothing will come between me and this discussion. I want to savor it.

"Think about it." Chester says as he shoves the gas nozzle back into the pump. "Gonna get some cigarettes. Need anything?" I shake my head as he heads toward the minimarket.

Finally, I have a minute. I take a deep breath. I'm giddy. I grab the still-vibrating phone and see a bunch of e-mails. The first one is from Jerry, saying he's meeting with the president of United Talent Agency and he'll let me know how it goes. I hate him. I don't respond. Instead I eagerly e-mail Sylvia with the news that Chester just suggested I head entertainment and what a fuck-you that would be to JK. I hear Chester coming, so I cram my phone back into my bag, trying to appear calm, serious, and contemplative.

He enters the car and swings out of the gas station. "I don't want this information out there, so think about it and tell me if you want to be considered."

"Of course I'll think about it. It's a wonderful opportunity, and one that requires serious thought." I already know that *yes, yes, yes,* I want to be considered. I want to be more than considered. I want the damn job. Now. Give it to me. But I remain cool and stone-faced on the outside while my inner ten-year-old child is squealing. I have to handle this with professionalism and maturity, and at the appropriate time I'll tell Chester *yes,* I want it!

To my utter shock and surprise, this is turning into a pretty decent Friday. And I finally have a date. My first with Gordon. I'm really excited and looking forward to a great evening and am comfortable knowing both Molly and Jerry will be at the filming of *Money Honey* tonight. Now I just hope Chester gets us back to HBS in one piece. I'll worry about the cancer from secondhand smoke later.

At seven o'clock Friday evening, I drive across the Valley to downtown LA. Despite horrible rush-hour traffic, I make it relatively on time. After paying an exorbitant fee for the pleasure of parking five blocks away, I walk quickly toward the Staples Center, to the Will Call window, through security, and then up four long escalators to meet Gordon. I arrive in what can only be described as the nosebleed section. I'm slightly overdressed in my executive attire, while Gordon sits comfortably in his jeans and Lakers T-shirt. It's hard to see the players below. They look like tiny toy soldiers. Gordon smiles broadly as I approach. He takes my jacket and drapes it across the back of my seat.

"I'm so glad you could come tonight. Can I get you a drink or something to eat?"

"Oh, no, I'm fine." Actually, I'm just so happy to be here. On a real date.

The game has started and Gordon's into it. He tells me about the players and the rules and then offers his binoculars, and suddenly the game comes to life.

"Wow, this is great. I haven't been to a game in years," I say.

Unfortunately, I'm looking through the wrong end of the binoculars, which Gordon corrects.

"It helps to look through this part." Gordon laughs as he adjusts the lens so things aren't so blurry.

Gordon is relaxed and at ease. He's the opposite of the exposed nerve I can be. And his laid-back nature suggests he's not eager to impress. Gordon offers me some popcorn, which smells so darn good I have to indulge.

"This is a big game tonight. San Antonio is number one in the conference," says Gordon.

I haven't a clue what that means, but I nod anyway.

There's a pause.

"You don't know what I'm talking about, do you?" Gordon asks.

We both laugh.

"It means this is an important game for the Lakers. If they win, they move up in the standings."

"Oh, I see." I smile, leaning back in my seat.

"Not really a sports fan, huh?" he asks.

"Actually, that's not true. I'm a Packers fan."

Gordon brightens and turns toward me.

"Really? And you're from Chicago? Isn't that sacrilegious? You could get killed for less," he laughs.

"My dad worshipped Vince Lombardi. He grew up watching the Packers. Our home was a shrine to Lombardi, littered with his quotations, which my dad pasted everywhere: on the refrigerator, closet doors, and kitchen cupboards." I chuckle at the insanity.

"Yeah, well, the one I remember is *Winning isn't everything, it's the only thing.* But I'm not so sure I agree," Gordon says.

"Well, he might've revised that over time, because the ones I recall are *Winning isn't everything, but the* will *to win is everything.* And *Leaders are made, not born.* And *Winners never quit and quitters never win.* And countless others."

"Impressive. Too bad you didn't play for him. He would've loved to have you on his team."

"He died before I was born. But my dad was a dedicated fan."

"A real cheesehead, huh?"

"Yup. I still have one somewhere." I laugh. "But you like basketball, right?"

"I grew up in Kansas. No NBA team. So I was a Chiefs fan. Now I'm in LA and there's no NFL team. So it's the Lakers."

"I don't mind basketball. It's a much faster game. But I don't get the long shorts. The guys looked much sexier in the shorter ones. There's one player I remember, John Stockton. He looked great in those shorts."

"You know who John Stockton was? He played for the Utah Jazz, and you're right, he was one of the last holdouts, preferring to stick with the shorter shorts when the rest of the guys had gone to the baggier look."

"Such a shame. They clearly weren't thinking about their female fans."

"Guess not." Gordon grins at me.

There's a pause.

"I can't get over your smile," Gordon says.

"Thanks. You said that on the phone, too. That's very nice."

I feel Gordon's eyes on me.

"You're blushing."

"Yes, I know. I'm not good with compliments." My face is definitely on fire.

"Why not? You're very attractive. I'm sure this isn't the first time someone's told you that."

"Oh, yeah, I hear it every day. Are you kidding? No. Really, I'm not. Thank you, though. But I'm not."

"No, really. You are."

"I don't see myself that way."

"Well, you are."

There's a pause. I'm not used to this kind of attention. It makes me feel uncomfortable yet excited. But, fortunately, Gordon's focus has been averted as the Lakers score and our section erupts in cheers.

As Gordon chats with the excited fans around us, I peer through the viewfinder of Gordon's very snazzy binoculars, carefully surveying the arena, and then land on the floor seats.

"Wow, there are tons of celebrities here. I see George Lopez, Dyan Cannon, Penny Marshall, Jeremy Piven, and I think that's Mary-Kate Olsen."

Gordon nods. His eyes remain fixed on the game.

"Oh, and Charlize Theron and Corey Monteith, and wow, there's Leonardo DiCaprio."

Gordon cheers as the Lakers score another big one. He's clearly a huge fan, and this is serious business. He doesn't seem the least bit interested in who I'm pointing out. He doesn't care who's at the game. He's only interested in who's in the game.

I continue browsing the arena. Suddenly I catch a glimpse of someone who looks very much like Jerry. Oh, no. It can't be. No, please don't be him. No. No. No. Please, no. Not now. Ugh. I can't believe it. It's him. Sitting in the floor seats next to the Lakers bench. Beside him are Tom Dolman, the president of the United Talent Agency, and Steve Hansen. I'm nauseous. I lay the binoculars down in my lap and then, when the referee's whistle blows indicating a timeout, I pick them up again, watching Jerry as he high-fives the players returning to the bench. Tom and Steve are lapping it up. And wow, even Kobe Bryant shakes Jerry's hand. Oh my God. I can't stop looking at him. How the heck does he have floor seats? And what the heck is he doing here? He's supposed to be at the filming of *Money Honey*. Oh, great, and now two studio presidents come by. More laughter and back pats. I'm obsessed with the ease with which Jerry blends into that group and how he, my subordinate and nemesis, knows absolutely everyone. The guy who used to make me eat bananas to help him get off and leer down my blouse to guess my cup size is the belle of the ball.

"Hey, Lexican, c'mon, it's just a banana. Can't you just take one bite? Then I'll leave you alone." Jerry thrusts the banana in my face.

"Ya know, Jerry, I'm really not hungry, but thank you," I mutter, trying to maintain my dignity, hoping he'll disappear.

"C'mon, Lexi, what's the big deal?" He laughs. I grab the Chiquita and throw it wildly at the wastebasket, then race to my desk, where I pretend to be deeply immersed in tons of work, which of course I'm not. "Oh, Lexican, you have no sense of humor," he says giddily.

"I can't believe you're so into the action. That's great," Gordon says, not realizing I'm focused on some other action.

I've been here fifteen minutes and I'm miserable. I can't focus. How can I even think of becoming president of entertainment when Jerry's sitting on the floor and I'm in the rafters?

"Are you OK? 'Cause the time-out is over and the game is on this side of the court." Gordon points to the opposite end of the floor, but I'm not listening. I'm engaged in a different game, Jerry's game. My binoculars are still pointed at Jerry as he reaches down to grab his soda.

"Hey, Lexican, while you're down there, you might wanna take a look at something really special." Jerry unzips his fly and grabs my hair, yanking my head up to his crotch while I gather a pile of paper clips that he "accidentally" knocked to the floor.

"Alexa?" Gordon asks again. I feel bad. This isn't how I'm supposed to act on a date.

I finally look up, resting the binoculars on my lap.

"I'm sorry, Gordon. I'm distracted. The guy who works for me, who I used to work for, is making my life a living hell. He's sitting in the floor seats and it just makes me crazy. I'm really sorry. It's just that I wasn't expecting to see him here. In fact, he's supposed to be at a filming of a show he's assigned to monitor."

Gordon buys two bottles of water from the vendor and offers one to me. I take the time to explain the history between Jerry and myself and tell him I may have an opportunity for a promotion, but this guy is my cross to bear.

"What an asshole," Gordon says. "No one deserves to be treated that way. Why didn't you leave him?"

"I was young and inexperienced. I honestly thought that was part of paying my dues. I thought that if I was loyal and did a great job, eventually I'd get a promotion."

"He's a bully. And he really used his position to intimidate you," Gordon says. "That kind of behavior is unacceptable. You could've reported him."

"Oh, I never would've done that. I just put up with it as best I could."

Gordon reaches for my hand and holds it firmly in his. It's very comforting and feels really nice.

"I know it's upsetting to see him down there," he says softly. "But remember, he works for you now. Don't let him spoil your good time here."

I try not to, but it's beginning to sink in that Jerry is back and life is not going to be easy.

The game goes on for what seems like an eternity. I want to be personable and sweet, but I'm hopelessly distracted.

As Gordon and I exit the arena, he tells me about my female student. I tell him how happy I'll be to meet her.

"I know it's late, but would you like to grab a bite?" Gordon asks.

"I don't know. I'm kinda tired. Been a long day."

There's a pause.

"You sure? You don't want to have a drink and some real food?"

"Yeah. OK. Maybe," I say. But I can't get Jerry off my mind. "Well, no. I can't. Not tonight. I'm sorry. I'm not a great date. I'm kind of new at this."

I feel ridiculous. I'm a mass of contradictions.

Gordon looks at me and smiles.

"It's OK. I'm glad you were able to come to the game tonight. Let me walk you to your car."

"That'd be nice. Thank you."

We walk along the sidewalk toward the parking lot. Neither of us says much more. I start digging around in my purse for the keys, and soon we are right next to my car.

"Thank you for a really nice evening, Gordon. It was fun," I say, pointing my key at the door.

"You know I wanted to ask you out the second I met you," Gordon says.

I stop and look up at him.

"Really?"

"Yup. But I didn't think it would be right since we were in a professional situation. And besides, you didn't give me any time 'cause you were in such a hurry to leave."

"Yeah. That's true." I remember having to rush out to meet Jerry.

I'm starting to think maybe I shouldn't have declined Gordon's invitation to dinner. He seems like someone I'd like to know better. Why can't I enjoy the time with Gordon instead of obsessing over Jerry?

"It's cute how you tilt your head to the right when you talk," Gordon says.

"Really? I do that?"

"Yes, *really* you do," he says, mimicking my constant use of that word. "You never knew that?"

"I didn't."

"You're doing it again." Gordon imitates me by exaggerating the motion. "C'mon, I don't do that."

"You do." Gordon laughs. "Does that embarrass you?"

"Kinda...sorta...maybe. I don't know." I feel his eyes on me again. I look down to avoid his gaze.

"I think you wanted to go out with me," he says.

"Really? What makes you say that?"

"You smiled a lot during our meeting. And then when I looked at you, you'd look away. Kind of like what you're doing now."

"Oh my gosh, you notice everything."

I clear my throat and start rubbing my forearms, continuing to look away.

"Only when I like someone."

I still have my key in hand, but I'm starting to enjoy this. Gordon moves in a little closer to me. He puts his right hand gently on my arm. I feel it softly glide down to my elbow. I'd really like to go to dinner with him. He looks right into my eyes as he wraps a few strands of my hair in his index finger and strokes them with his thumb.

"Well, again, I'm glad you were able to come to the game tonight."

"Me, too. Thank you for a really nice time," I say, able to look into his eyes.

Gordon smiles at me.

I open my car door. We shake hands awkwardly. Gordon waits till my car starts and then waves good-bye.

I drive back to my apartment, feeling crappy and pissed that I allowed Jerry to ruin my night. I feel horrible. The more I think about it, the worse it is. I was more engaged in the drama going on with Jerry than my date with Gordon. He's kind, speaks slowly, and listens. His attention span is far longer than that of any of my colleagues. And, unlike so many other guys I've dated, he actually seems interested in what's going on in my life. And he thinks I'm pretty. And when he touched my arm it sent a chill down my spine. Geez. I like this guy.

But I probably blew it.

I open the door to my darkened apartment and drag myself inside. I throw my purse on the chair and crash alongside it. As miserable as I feel, I'm happy to see Joe, who is thrilled when I return home. His tail wags wildly.

"Oh, Joe. Thank God you're here. What a jerk I was tonight." I talk to him like he's a person. But fortunately, I don't have to hear his response. He'd probably agree with me.

Joe jumps up on the chair and cuddles next to me. He licks my face as if to say, *It's OK, Alexa, you screwed up but you're a good person. I love you!* I cup his face in my hands and kiss his nose as he licks me all over. He can't seem to get enough. I'm like his personal lollipop. And somehow I'm fine with that.

It's Monday. Sylvia and I sit huddled in the corner of the commissary, sipping our lattes.

"I really blew it with Gordon on Friday night," I say. "It upset me to see Jerry at the Lakers game. He was yukking it up with everyone. How does he know them all?"

"That's his job." Sylvia shrugs. "He thrives on adoration and power. He's such a freak." She shakes her head.

"How can he even afford those tickets?" I ask.

"Hey, have you forgotten about his wife? Didn't you tell me she's rich and connected?"

I nod, remembering him bragging about the perks of being married to Olivia.

"Call Jerry Bruckheimer and tell him my father-in-law got me seats on the fifty-yard line for the Super Bowl." I'm sewing a button onto his shirt, another one of the not-in-my-job-description duties. I turn and see him at his desk shirtless, mounds and mounds of black hair covering his torso. It's hard to tell where his beard ends and his chest begins. Truly revolting.

"Do you even know Jerry Bruckheimer?" I ask.

"Hey, babe, just call and tell him if he wants to go we'll take his plane. I guarantee he'll die for this."

"She said he doesn't know you from a bag of elbows and hung up on me."

I shout happily after speaking to Bruckheimer's assistant. I feel like an idiot. I'm sure she thought it was just another crank call. Which it was.

"God, Lex, you can screw up anything. Forget it." Jerry gets up and slams his office door.

"Too bad, 'cause you seemed to like Gordon," says Sylvia.

"I do like him."

"Did you get to know him at all?"

"No, not really," I say sheepishly. "The second I saw Jerry my night was ruined. I let him do that to me, which was a huge mistake."

And then, at that very moment, Jerry and Chester enter the commissary, chatting cheerfully.

"Man, let's just say her Poppins box is so dirty, you'd need a spoonful of sugar to help you go down," Jerry says loudly enough for us to hear. Chester starts to howl but stops immediately when he sees Sylvia and I sitting in the corner. The mood changes. Chester whips out photos. His children, no doubt. Jerry is effusive, offering up his as well.

Sylvia and I sit in the corner, watching this friendship develop. The fact that it's done so largely over misogynistic humor isn't lost on us.

"Jerry's been here a week, and he's already buds with Steve Hansen and now Chester," I say. "I'm gonna have to get rid of him."

"It'll never happen," Sylvia says. "He's Barnsworth's boy, remember? You think Chester and Steve don't know that? He's untouchable, Alexa. You're stuck with him. He doesn't just want your job, he wants to be your boss again."

"He's not going to get that particular job."

"What job?"

"The one I e-mailed you about on Friday. The one I told you not to discuss."

"I only got one e-mail from you yesterday," Sylvia says. "It was about product placement in *The Candy Stripers*."

"What do you mean? Didn't you get the e-mail that said Chester suggested I head entertainment and what a fuck-you that would be to Jerry?" I'm suddenly overcome with terror.

Sylvia doesn't answer. She doesn't need to. We race out of the commissary and dash up the stairs and down the long hall to my office. We're frantic. We fly past Rosie and rush to my computer. I pull up my e-mails and find the one sent from my phone to Sylvia.

"Oh my gawwwwwd!" I cry. "I sent it to Jerry instead of you. I replied to the e-mail Jerry sent about his meeting at the United Talent Agency. So he knows Chester wants a president of entertainment and that he's considering me."

There's a long pause as Sylvia and I realize what happened.

"He's going after that job, too, isn't he?" I ask.

Neither of us says a word. We know the answer.

Chapter Four

"Harper House in West Hollywood was designed by Leland Bryant, who also designed the landmark Sunset Tower on the Sunset Strip. Originally built for film industry professionals and actors in 1929, its unique blend of glamour, luxury, and community is unparalleled. The L-shaped, stark white stucco building consists of four levels of apartment units sitting atop a subterranean parking structure. Walking into the open-air elevated courtyard with its pond and fountain is like stepping back in time."

I read that ad four years before I was able to rent an apartment here. The waiting list was a mile long, and finally I was at the top. I spent those four years in a San Fernando Valley studio apartment saving up for my down payment. I've lived here almost three years, and I love this place and its tenants, many of whom are artists and writers. This apartment building has been home to stars including Bette Davis and Carole Lombard, who were among the first to rent space here. I often think about who might've lived in my apartment. I want to believe it was Bette Davis because I admire her forthright nature. A woman before her time. I learned she was the first president of the Academy of Motion Pictures Arts & Sciences. I had no idea.

The other tenants and I often get together on Sunday nights and barbeque by the fountain. We've had block parties and book parties. I really enjoy the tranquility of this wonderful complex. The place offers a much-needed respite from HBS.

A whole week has passed since that awful Monday morning when I realized Jerry got the e-mail intended for Sylvia. But I love Sunday. It's the day I most treasure. I'm in my sweats, hanging out with Joe, my beloved dog, the one (furry) person in my life who's happy to see me no matter what.

He and I are stretched out on my comfortable down-cushioned window seat overlooking the fountain in the courtyard. Across from us is my shabby chic yellow-and-blue floral couch, a gift from my mom, along with a tall white tweed chair and small glass coffee table, a great find from Cost Plus. The blue-and-white-striped roman shades are pinned high, exposing a wonderful large dormer window, which is slightly ajar. The Santa Ana winds blow softly, offering just a hint of smoke from the Malibu fires, which have engulfed the city the past week, leaving traces of ash on the windowsill.

We have a wonderful view of the San Bernardino Mountains, which boast gorgeous white peaks, although they're clouded in smoke today. As Joe rests his head peacefully on my calf, I watch my best friend, Emily. Her looks and demeanor closely resemble the actress Catherine Keener as she sits on the floor, pitched against the wooden leg of my white tweed chair, knitting a small pink cap for her sister's baby girl. Chopin's "Prelude No. 2 in A Minor" plays softly in the background.

"I never heard from Gordon," I say wistfully, staring out the window.

There's a short pause, something Emily uses for effect now that she's a full-time shrink, often practicing on pals like me. Her days writing freelance articles for *Seventeen* are a thing of the past.

"If you want to see him again, call him," Emily says without looking up from her knitting. "I don't think he thought you were interested."

I turn away from the window and look toward her. "I'm supposed to tutor an eleven-year-old student next week. I'll see him then."

"If you want a personal relationship with him, you need to let him know. He thinks you're too into your job."

I'm not sure what to do. There were many times over the past week I thought of calling Gordon, but something stopped me. Maybe I'm afraid of getting close to someone. Gordon seems authentic, sensitive, and caring. I think that frightens me. If he's the real deal, I could see myself falling for him.

I've had just one real boyfriend. I loved him and thought he loved me but discovered he was screwing someone else. I'd heard this happens but never dreamed I'd be a victim. I still can't believe I didn't know about it. Danny Rowland. What a jerk. I thought he was the one. He came into my life just after Jerry fired me and before I became an executive. Emily calls him a Band-Aid, said he helped smooth that transition. But in the end, he might've made things worse. It seems they always leave me for one reason or another. And after losing my dad and then Danny, the only guy I really loved, well, I'm not sure I want to try this again. I think I'll just love me for a while.

"I'm afraid to go there, Em. I like Gordon, but frankly, I'm worried about putting myself out there, ya know?"

"Alexa, he likes you. He'll be flattered. You didn't give him a chance. Don't be so afraid. From what you said so far, he doesn't sound like he's a player. Try to have a little fun. It's just a date. You don't have to marry the guy." Emily continues knitting with laser-like focus.

Emily's my rock. I couldn't be happier she's no longer writing, and instead, shrinking heads. She's the polar opposite of Sylvia. She speaks slowly and deliberately. She practices Tai Chi and yoga every day. But unlike the Hollywood girls, she doesn't do it to look skinny and toned. It's about insight, balance, and a sense of inner calm. We're so different. I'm impetuous. Emily's introspective. I want more. Emily wants less. I trust her the most, as she's my very best pal.

We met in our twenties and have maintained our friendship for over a decade. Emily's married to Chuck, an architect, and they have twin boys. Because they live in Santa Monica, I don't get to see her very much. Emily keeps me grounded. She believes showbiz folks think they're above everyone else, entitled and immune to punishment. She also thinks the horrible behaviors and excesses of show business are too easily accepted. She may be right. I don't ever want to fall victim to that.

Emily's scent fills the air. It's a mixture of pine and mint. She tells me it's from an organic detergent she uses. Whatever it is, I can't get enough. It reminds me of the red-and-white mints my dad offered when we took walks together at night. We never had a destination in mind. It was just our time alone. We talked about everything, but mostly school and my increasing conflicts with my mom. I was a raging hormone-filled teenage girl who resisted and rebelled against virtually everything.

Emily says there's more to life than work, and that as wonderful as it is to have a great job and make good money, it helps to have a little balance. I ignore her, but I know she's right.

"I think it's great that you're going to tutor this student. It'll be wonderful for her and good for you. And then maybe you can tutor Sean. God knows he could use some help with math," Emily says.

"I was never good at math. I can barely balance my checkbook. I'm the last person you want helping your son with numbers," I say. "I just hope I have time for this."

"Make time. It's important. You can't disappoint this girl. She's going to depend on you."

"I know. I'm looking forward to meeting her."

I pull Joe on my lap and massage his ears as he closes his eyes. He's clearly in heaven. Emily readjusts her position without losing sight of her knitting. She has amazing powers of concentration.

"I want that job. The head of entertainment," I say.

"OK, but only if you promise not to develop shows like *Hoarders*. I'm shamelessly addicted to that dreck."

"Not a chance. Except I caught a glimpse of a woman who had forty-seven dogs and cats. It was sick. And yet I couldn't stop watching. I was sucked in, too." I laugh.

"It's a train wreck. I guess that's the appeal." Emily puts down her knitting and shifts her eyes toward me. "Look, if you really want that job, go for it. But think it through before you make the decision. Because you're going to have to give up a lot for it."

"Yeah, I know," I say hesitantly.

"Jerry's a guy," Emily says as she comes over to the couch, pushing Joe aside. He offers a gentle growl, letting her know he's not happy his space is being invaded. But Emily doesn't care. "He already has a leg up 'cause he's got balls. Real ones. Not those fake metal ones on your desk. He's going to Lakers games and sitting in the floor seats. Can you handle that? You're working in a very traditional boys' club. There's never been a female president there. You might be able to get this job, but you'll never get a key to the men's room. And what they say in there can make or break you."

"You mean I need a key? I can't just barge in there?" I try to lighten the mood.

Emily is getting to me. I'm starting to worry. I know she's right. I have so much to think about. Do I really want this?

"Jerry's well connected, Alexa. He's going after that job, too. And he doesn't care who he runs over to get there. He may not have your creative skills, but he wants it very badly. Have you thought about why you really want it?"

"Yes, I know exactly why I want it," I say. "I want it because I'm good at developing shows for HBS's audience. I love collaborating with creative people and challenging myself and others to reach beyond the usual fare. I want to set trends and inspire our viewers. It's great when shows can actually impact our culture. But mostly I want to offer programs that provide laughter and relaxation after a hard day."

There's a long pause. Emily looks squarely into my eyes and then puts her hand over mine.

"Then go for it. You're very passionate about what you do. And you work so hard there. They'd be lucky to have you in that job."

Thinking about what's ahead for me at work is exciting and nerve-racking at the same time. I know what it's going to take to get to the top. I reach into the candy dish and help myself to a few mini Milky Ways in anticipation of Halloween. Kids rarely trick-or-treat here, but I stock up. A month in advance. Just in case. So glad I did.

I walk to the kitchen and get a Diet Coke, thinking maybe it will offset the chocolate I'm eating and the weight I'll be gaining.

"By the way," Emily shouts, "not to change the subject, but how's your mom? Have you talked to her lately?"

Uh-oh. I don't seem to have any more Diet Cokes. And I need one now. Panic sets in. I hope I'm not addicted to the destructive ills of this beverage. Meanwhile, Emily retrieves her knitting and shoves it in her bag, letting me know she's planning to leave.

"Yeah, last week. She's fine." I frantically move everything around to make sure there isn't just one Diet Coke hiding in my overstuffed refrigerator. Aha. Found one. Panic attack averted. "She only wants to know who I'm dating. She thinks it's great I have a job but is far more concerned with the fact that I'm not married, especially since I'm over thirty; a fate worse than death."

"Hey, my mom still wonders why I didn't end up with Scott the banker. Remember him?" Emily asks.

"God. That douche bag?"

"Yeah, she loved him." Emily rolls her eyes.

"I guess you couldn't tell her the whole thing was about great sex, huh?" I laugh.

"Uh, no. Didn't want to go there."

We both laugh conspiratorially.

"C'mon, walk me out. I have to stop at the market to pick up some food to make for dinner tonight," says Emily as we link arms and walk to the door. "Oh my God, I can't believe I just said that. I've turned into my mother."

"Eh, you're not quite there yet," I say as we enjoy one last laugh and hug good-bye. Just before I close the door, Emily turns around.

"Go for the job, Lex. You deserve it."

When Emily is out of sight I slowly close the door and mull over our conversation. I decide to take Joe for a walk and gather his leash and adjust his collar. He's out of his mind excited and can't wait to get out the door. We make our way down the stairs and into the courtyard.

It's a beautiful day. I wish I could just sit out here all afternoon and enjoy it. But I have ten scripts to read and notes to do before the week begins tomorrow. Joe and I move swiftly toward the grassy area in front of my apartment building. As Joe takes care of his business I think about mine and whether I have what it takes to go the distance.

––––––––

As I lie in bed thinking about my discussion with Emily, my eyes catch a ray of light that happens to illuminate a photo of my parents on my dresser. I found it in my mom's album. It was taken about two weeks before my dad passed. My mom never framed it, but I did. It's one of the last photographs of my father. I stare at it and wonder what my dad would say. Would he say, *Go for it*? Would he want me to take on this battle? What kind of advice would he offer? As I ask myself these questions, my eyes start to close, and soon I'm fast asleep.

It's eight thirty in the morning and I'm in the office. A little over a week has passed since the Sunday Emily gave me "the talk." I've had a whole week to think about whether I truly want to be president of entertainment. I'm sipping coffee, waiting to see Chester so I can tell him what I've decided. I left a message on his voice mail saying I wanted to see him.

I want the job. And I want Chester to know I'm the best person for it. I know I may not get it. But I really believe I've had enough experience to take this on. I want to break the glass ceiling at HBS. It's not lost on me that I'd be pioneering new ground. Being a woman is an asset, given that our audience is primarily women. I know what they like. I understand the characters and stories they relate to. Chester told me I'm a good executive, which is why Barnsworth put Jerry in my department, so why shouldn't I get the job? I believe I can work with everyone, bring a unique perspective, and build HBS into the powerhouse network it once was.

Hmm, should I end with that line? Or another? As I mull over my speech to Chester, I hear Rosie marching briskly to her desk as the phone rings. I feel awkward staring at the blinking light, as I'm perfectly capable of picking up the receiver, but instead I wait for Rosie to answer. I don't want to be distracted or blindsided by an unexpected call when I'm focused on what I want to say to Chester. Rosie yells through my open door, "Alexa, Chester said to come up now."

I'm wearing my lucky suit. It's never failed me. I got my job in this suit. I spoke briefly at a press tour in this suit and did better than I expected, even though I was scared shitless. It's a simple but expensive black blazer, white tank top, and black pants.

As I make my way down the hallway to Chester's office I think about the article I read in the *New York Times* that said women have trouble asking for what they want. In fact they apologize for it. Whatever they get is more than enough. Whereas men demand raises and promotions. And they won't stop there, they'll ask for more. Whatever they get isn't enough. They feel entitled. Women don't. I've decided I'm going to be like a guy and say what I want.

Even though I'm nervous and trembling inside.

I move swiftly down the hall, telling myself over and over to be strong, to stand up straight, and to appear confident. I pray Chester won't notice that I'm anxious and hyperventilating.

"Hey, Alexa," says Jan, one of Chester's two assistants. "Go on in." The door magically opens. Chester stands next to the desk in his maroon jogging suit and Bruno Magli loafers, a cigarette dangling from his mouth. The second I enter he shoves an article in my hand. It has *Deadline Hollywood* across the top. This is a blog written by Nikki Finke, who's the ultimate resource for any and everything Hollywood. She not only reports it, she comments on it. She makes careers and destroys them. The goal is not to ever be the subject of her blog. However, it appears I am today.

This is not my lucky day, nor my lucky suit. It will now join the other unlucky clothing dumped in the far corner of my closet, never to be seen again. It will be hauled away to Goodwill when I get around to it.

"You might want to take a look at the headline that says, *Alexa Ross to Head Entertainment for HBS.* Then you'll see an e-mail below it, which you apparently wrote to Jerry Kellner a few weeks ago, saying you'd be getting this position and what a great fuck-you it is to him." Chester continues pointing to the article, which is now shaking in my hand.

The blood drains from my body. I'm suddenly dizzy and feel faint. How am I going to defend this? Is this e-mail debacle ever going to die? Is it going to haunt me the rest of my life?

The second I open my mouth, Chester interrupts.

"I believe I mentioned that if you were interested, I'd consider you along with several other folks. I think it's rather presumptuous of you to e-mail Jerry within seconds of our conversation, boasting about this appointment."

"I'm sorry, Chester. It's not what I intended. If I could just explain—"

"I don't think there's much to explain," he interrupts again, sounding more annoyed.

I don't know what to say. My body won't stop shaking. My lips are twitching. I can't think of any way to get myself out of this mess. I'm embarrassed and humiliated. How can I say, "Oh, that e-mail? Oh, that was supposed to go to Sylvia, not Jerry." As if that would make it better. I just want to get out of here.

"I'm sorry, Chester. I'll talk to Jerry." I start to leave.

As I approach the door, I hear Chester toss the article in the trash. "Did you want something else? Jan said you wanted to see me this morning."

"Oh, nothing. It's nothing," I say.

It's quiet but tense. Chester glares at me as he moves toward his coffee table, signaling that the meeting is over. Thank God. I can't get out fast enough.

I race to the nearest restroom, hoping not to run into anyone. I just want to get into a stall quickly, as I'm not sure I can hold back the sea of tears much longer. There are three stalls, two occupied and one for me. Whew. There's a lot of flushing and talking, so I'm safe, as no one saw me enter. I'll just wait for them to leave so I can be alone.

Two women are washing their hands, and from the conversation I realize it's Chester's assistant Jan and Steve Hansen's assistant, Dawn. They're chatting quietly, but loudly enough for me to hear.

"Do you think she's still in there?" asks Dawn.

"Oh, I'm sure she is. Chester was furious when I showed him the article. He said, 'Get Alexa in here now.' I thought, Oh boy, this ought to be interesting." Jan laughs. "And it turns out she *wanted* to see him. She's gonna regret that!"

"You know, Jerry seems like a good guy. He offered me tickets to the Breeders Cup when he saw a photo of my daughter's horse on my desk. Isn't that nice?"

"He's terrific," Jan says. "Frankly, he ought to head entertainment. Alexa's crazy to think she'd ever get it. No woman has risen to that level here. What makes her think she can?"

"She's sure not in the boys' club."

"Yeah, Alexa doesn't get it," Jan says. "Chester will promote either Jasper or Jerry. In fact, he and Jerry are going to the Dodgers game in an hour. Oh man, I have to give Chester the tickets." She and Dawn mercifully exit the restroom.

I'm in a state of shock. It's one thing to wonder what people think of you and another to hear it. I can't move. I'm numb. I just want to sit here forever and never get back to my life.

I think about what Emily said: "Can you handle this? Do you want it that badly?" Those words reverberate in my head. This morning I thought I knew what I wanted. But can I handle the politics? Can I endure the fight getting there? Chester will undoubtedly pit me against the other candidates. He'll want to see who emerges unscathed and who is left bloody. Do I want this job badly enough to endure that?

After a few more minutes I finally drag myself out of the stall, wash my hands, and look in the mirror. I look dreadful. I rinse my face and tap my cheeks, trying to instill life and color back

into them. Without any makeup or hairbrush, I'll have to impro-
vise. I run my fingers through my hair, straighten my clothes,
and tuck my white top deep inside my black gabardine pants. I
pull on my matching black jacket and button the single button
in front.

I stare at myself in the mirror a moment longer. I think about
my dad. He'd probably say, "This is a minor setback, Lex. Pick
yourself up and keep going. You've worked hard for this. You
deserve this. You can do it." And then he'd repeat the words made
famous by Coach Vince Lombardi, *It's not whether you get knocked
down, it's whether you get up.* Those words continue to resonate with
me years after I first heard them when I was all but sixteen and
failed to get the job I really wanted at Bloomingdale's. But my dad
said this was the first of many rejections I'd face in my life and that
I needed to be resilient in order to be successful.

I finally get myself together and leave the restroom. I walk
steadily down the hall repeating the phrase *It's not whether you get
knocked down, it's whether you get up* over and over to myself. Soon
I'm back at Chester's office.

"Hi, Jan," I say nicely as I approach her from behind. She whips
around, startled to see me.

"Is Chester still here, or has he left for the game already?"

"Yes, he's still here." She seems worried.

"Great. I'll just let myself in." I barge into his office. Chester
has Dodgers tickets in his hand. Before he has a chance to speak,
I say, "Chester, I want the job. I've thought about it, and I want it.
I'm the best person for it. I deserve it, and I'm going to show you
why you should hire me over anyone else."

"OK," Chester says, startled by my outburst. Just as he's about
to speak, Jerry appears in a T-shirt and jeans, a Dodgers cap tucked
in his waistband.

"Hey, secret agent, how's it going?" he asks, smiling broadly.

"It's going well, Jer. I just told Chester I want to be president of entertainment and that I'm the best candidate for it. Wouldn't you agree?"

Jerry's broad grin disappears. His face drops. He looks at Chester for a response. Chester looks down. Neither looks at me. They both seem very uncomfortable. Good.

"Hey, have a good time at the game, boys," I say sweetly. "I'll hold down the fort while you're away. Oh, and Jerry, I want to see you in my office when you return. I want to know how that e-mail I accidentally sent you made its way into *Deadline Hollywood*."

Jerry glares at me. He's not a happy camper.

Chester exits the office. Jerry turns toward me. But before he has a chance to say a word, I wink, smile, give him a thumbs-up, and walk out.

Chapter Five

I spent too much time on the toilet in the ladies' restroom yesterday. It wasn't very comfortable in there. But it felt a lot better than sitting across from Jerry, which is what I'm doing now in my office. My legs are planted firmly on the floor, hands in my lap. I'm trying to look like a leader even though I'm shaking inside. I look directly at Jerry, happy that there's a coffee table between us, a great obstacle should one of us engage in physical warfare. A tiny wooden toothpick dangles from his mouth. He sits at the far end of the couch, his right hand on the armrest, the left playing with a piece of wool from the seat cushion.

"What were you thinking?" I ask. "You sent an e-mail that was obviously not meant for you to *Deadline Hollywood*? Why, Jerry?"

His eyes are focused on the fur thread. He plays with it until it comes loose, then kneads it into a tiny ball. Meanwhile, his legs are bouncing wildly, a habit I find annoying and obnoxious.

My eyes drift to the coffee table, which is vibrating to the rhythm of Jerry's legs. My coffee cup creeps toward the edge. It's moved about six inches in the last several minutes. I grab it and take a swig. Meanwhile, the silence is excruciating. Jerry continues to avert his eyes. I'm reminded of the time he was worried sick that a photo of him and starlet Natalie Jones, his mistress-of-the-moment, would appear on Perez Hilton's blog.

"Aleeexxxxaaaa!" Jerry screams as if he's on fire.

"What?" I say breathlessly, my heart racing, expecting to see Jerry engulfed in flames. (Not that this would've been bad…) Instead, he's waving a pink message slip and looking absolutely horrified.

"Perez Hilton wants the name of my girlfriend for the photo he's running on his blog tomorrow. Get him on the phone. I would die to be on his blog, just not like this," Jerry barks.

Just as Perez comes on the line, Jerry rips the phone from my hand.

"Mr. Hilton, you can't run that photo. I dunno who that girl was. She just appeared next to me. My wife would die. Then I'd have to kill myself. Do you want blood on your hands?"

I roll my eyes at his dramatic plea.

"Oh, thank you. Thank you." Jerry hangs up and breathes a deep sigh of relief. But within a second his demeanor changes. "Wait two minutes, then call back and ask if he'll cut her out of the photo."

"What? Why?"

"I want the photo of me. Not her. I wanna be on his blog. It would be so great for my career. I'll pay you extra for the notes you're doing on the next script. Please?"

The silence is broken when Jerry says, "It really wasn't that big a deal. Get over it."

"Really? Well, it was certainly a big deal to Chester."

"He never mentioned it at the game."

"That's because you report to me. Not him. And it's my responsibility to make sure you know that it's not something we do here. We may be competitive, but we aren't out to destroy each other."

"Yeah, OK, what else?" Jerry's legs start to relax.

"I know you better than anyone here," I say. "Lest you forget, I was not only your professional secretary, but your personal slave. I was privy to a lot of private things in your life. You want to play dirty? I can play that game, too. I'm happy to send an e-mail to Nikki Finke and tell her to research the time you were arrested for smuggling dope from Mexico, which was skillfully dismissed by your rich and connected father-in-law." Jerry's legs start bouncing again. "I have plenty more and you know it."

"We're done." Jerry gets up.

"You may be done, but I'm not."

Jerry walks to the door. I know he isn't concerned.

"I know you wanna head entertainment," I say, following him. "And so do I. So you're gonna have to beat me bloody. I know you'll enjoy the prospect. But you don't know what I'm capable of now. And at this moment you still work for me."

We stand eye to eye as Jerry places his hand on the doorknob, ready to fling it open. "Alexa, you talk a good game. But you're out of your league." He smirks as he swings the door open and leaves.

I collapse on the couch. My heart's pounding, my palms are hot and sweaty. He utterly exhausts me. What a way to start the day. Jerry's more than a handful. He brings out the worst in me. And then, as I lie there totally wiped out without even a moment to take a breath, Rosie pops her head in the door.

"Alexa, you have an appointment at noon to tutor at Crestview. You wanted to schedule one this week. Do you want to cancel it?"

"Oh gosh." I pick myself up, look at the clock, and sure enough, it's still Tuesday morning, now eleven fifteen. I feel like I've gone eight rounds with Manny Pacquiao. "When's my next meeting?" Rosie says three o'clock. I have some time, so I'll go.

I never do this—leave the office in the middle of a workday for anything but a meeting. If I ever have time to breathe, it's to return calls or e-mails, or catch up on scripts. But today I have tutoring, which I'm excited about. I'm glad I could fit it in. Frankly, it'll be good to get out of this place and clear my head.

I get in my car, turn on my iPod, and start listening to classical music, hoping it will offer some relaxation. But I can't help but think about Jerry. I think of all the different ways I'd like to kill him. Death by paper cuts is number one on my list.

My thoughts are interrupted by a call from Rosie telling me we need to use the next twenty minutes to place phone calls. I reluctantly turn off the iPod and give up my much-needed relaxing drive. In between calls I think about what I'm going to say to Gordon because I sure didn't end our date well, and I'd like to see him again.

After fielding several calls I finally approach Crestview. As I swing into the visitors' lot I notice how this neighborhood has suffered. It used to be a nice suburban area, but clearly things have changed. There's graffiti everywhere. Next door is an old gas station with broken pumps and windows. It doesn't look as if it's been operational in years. Old tires, couches, and mattresses lean against an unoccupied industrial building across the street. I watch as mothers of the kindergartners hover around the gate outside the school grounds, waiting for their children.

I leap out of the car, grab my phone, and toss my purse in the trunk. As I approach the main office I see Gordon helping a young boy with his heavily weighted backpack. I can't help but wonder what the heck these kids bring to school. In my day, it was simply a few notebooks and some books. Now kids look as if they're embarking on a trip to the Himalayas.

Gordon looks great in his Levi's, navy-blue polo shirt, and what appears to be a thick American Eagle belt and REI hiking boots. His shirt accentuates his broad, sculptured shoulders. I didn't realize he had such a nice body, yet he doesn't seem like someone who spends one moment thinking about it. I stroll up alongside him.

"Hey, I'm so glad you could make it. C'mon in," he says cheerfully. We file into the office. There's a Hispanic girl with long dark hair that looks like it hasn't seen a brush in a lifetime sitting in a chair across from Gordon. There are only two seats, so I lean against the wall, hoping Gordon won't shut the door, as this room is smaller than an elevator and my claustrophobia could easily bring on a panic attack.

"This is Marisol Guittierez. She's your student."

I extend my hand to shake hers. Marisol very reluctantly offers hers back. Her eyes stay fixed on Gordon.

"Hi, Marisol. So glad to meet you. I think we'll have a good time together," I say, trying to break the ice. And then my phone vibrates. While Gordon talks to Marisol, I lift it from my pocket and tap out a few replies, hoping no one notices.

Gordon puts his hand over Marisol's, leans toward her, and says, "Alexa is going to help you learn to read so you don't fall too far behind." But Marisol is nervous. She seems like she doesn't want to be here. When Gordon says she can return to her class she's gone in a flash. I take her seat. My phone continues to vibrate. I retrieve it and scroll through the new e-mails. Gordon shoots me a slightly disapproving look.

"Do you think you might be able to put that away for just one second?" His tone is lightly scolding.

I'm looking at an e-mail from Steve Hansen about a new promo he wants me to see. I reply as I feel Gordon's eyes on me. I shove the phone back in my pocket as he leans back in his chair, hands behind his head.

"Are you ready for this today?"

"Yes, yes, I'm ready. But I'm not sure Marisol is into it. She escaped pretty fast," I say, wondering if she might've been put off by me or something I said, even though the amount of time we had together was less than a minute. I don't think it was me, but this is not exactly my comfort zone. "I've never done anything like this before. I don't know if I'll be any good."

"How do you know if you've never tried?" Gordon asks, putting his hands on the table and leaning in toward me. "It's going to be fine. You're both nervous. But you have to take the lead. Marisol is scared. She doesn't know the language well. She's one of ten kids. Her father's a laborer. They're on welfare. Her parents are Spanish-speaking."

"OK. But I don't speak Spanish, remember? You asked me that on the phone. Maybe I'm not the right one for her and—"

"Alexa, relax," he interrupts. "You'll be fine."

Gordon smiles and gets up.

"I'm going to take you and Marisol to the school library. Just read with her. Go over the words slowly. Get to know her. Let's get rolling, OK?"

Before I have a chance to reply, we're out the door and on the playground, where Gordon is treated like a rock star. His adoring munchkin fans maul him along the way, all vying for his attention. I'm about six steps behind, having a really difficult time navigating my way over the rough asphalt in my three-inch heels.

I realize this may be the only time I can talk to Gordon. So, despite the playground distraction, I decide to give it a shot.

"I'm sorry about our date," I yell as we traverse the playground, dodging flying balls and kids. This is clearly Crestview's version of Iraq. Instead of artillery, I'm being attacked by soccer balls.

"I'm sorry, too. I guess it just wasn't meant to be," Gordon shouts, his back to me, plowing ahead in pursuit of Marisol's classroom. A young girl grabs his hand and skips the rest of the way, tugging him along.

An elbow jabs into my back, and a young boy shouts, "I'm sorry," as he grabs a ball and rushes away. "Gordon," I shout, trying to hold his attention. "I know I was too distracted at the game. But I really want to get to know you. Can we try it again?"

I hope his reaction won't be too terrible. I rarely allow myself to become this vulnerable. I wish he knew what a big deal this was for me. But he doesn't respond. "I don't want to believe it wasn't meant to be," I yell, not the least bit concerned who might be hearing this now. Gordon moves faster. I'm desperate to keep up with him but I'm not cut out for kid wars, as I just barely escape being swatted by a jump rope.

"Let me think about it," Gordon says as I finally catch up. We enter a classroom and are greeted by pandemonium. The teacher, Jorie Simon, seems glad to see Gordon. I don't know which is worse, the insanity in here or out there. It's utter chaos. I wonder how Miss Simon will take control of this class. But apparently, we won't be around to see. Gordon points to Marisol and escorts her out of the room. The three of us head to the library.

Gordon and Marisol lead the way while I try to keep up, wondering if I should take off my heels and walk barefoot the rest of the way, which might get me there faster. I'm lagging way behind as we finally approach the school library. I follow Gordon and Marisol inside. He tells us to look through the books until we find one that sounds interesting. I peruse the tiny shelves and see some familiar titles from my past, *The Phantom Tollbooth*, *Charlotte's Web*, *The Island of the Blue Dolphins*, *Little House on the Prairie*, *Mr. Popper's Penguins*, and a few others that evoke pleasant memories. Gordon takes one out. It's *Beezus and Ramona* by Beverly Cleary.

"Oh my gosh, I love this book," I say. "My mom read this to me."

"Good. I think this might be a relatively easy read for Marisol. It's third-grade level, but if you can get her to fourth, we'll be doing well."

"But she's in the fifth grade."

"She'll get there. That's why she has you." Gordon winks at me. "I have to go. Check in before you leave, OK?" He smiles and then sails off, leaving me with Marisol, who looks uncomfortable and anxious. It doesn't help that I'm sitting at a table intended for two very tiny people. I feel as if I'm living among the Lilliputians.

I'm not even going to try to get my legs under this thing. Instead I take out my glasses, sit alongside Marisol, and read the first page of *Beezus and Ramona*. Marisol hasn't said a word. She's transfixed by the drawings opposite the text. I point to Ramona's hair, and then to the word "hair," and then to Marisol's hair. I say the word *hair* a few times. Marisol just stares at the page. I don't know if she's getting this or not. I place my index finger under every word. Marisol smiles when we get to the word pretty. Ah, maybe I'm making progress. I read the last sentence, which says, "Beezus was happy." Marisol laughs. I notice for the first time that she has an awfully pretty dimple. We tackle a few more sentences. After a few fits and turns we make it to the end of the first chapter. The bell rings, and Marisol leaps out of her seat and heads for the door. Apparently, the end of our session couldn't come fast enough.

"It was great to meet you, Marisol. I'll see you next time, OK?" Marisol nods and sprints out of the room.

I hike back across the playground to my car. However, this time I'm carrying my heels. Note to self: bring flip-flops, because this is not the best terrain for bare feet.

"Hey, so how'd it go?" Gordon shouts from the school's entrance as he sees me approaching my car. "Will you be back?"

"Yes, I'll definitely be back," I say. "She's really shy. But once we get to know each other I think it will be better. Today was a bit challenging."

"Well, I can't think of anyone more suited for the challenge," Gordon shouts back. I smile as I reach the car and then hear Gordon yell, "What about this weekend?"

"What about it?" I ask as I finally reach my car.

"Do you wanna catch a movie or dinner or something?" Gordon shouts.

"I thought you needed to think about it."

"I did."

I'm sitting in the driver's seat with the door open, wiping the grit off my bare feet and dumping the gravel that collected in my shoes on the ground. Gordon darts over to my car. He squats down alongside me so his face is about even with mine.

"So, it was really OK?" Gordon asks softly.

"It was. I like her," I say, smiling.

"And?"

"And what?" I slip on my shoes as Gordon moves in closer, wiping his brow and catching his breath.

"Did you have a little fun?" Gordon smiles.

"I did. I think it's really great that you run this program," I say as I study his warm eyes and clean-shaven chin.

"Well, thanks. That's nice."

"No, really. Maybe you can get more schools involved?"

"That's the plan. I'd actually like to extend the reach of this program. But it'll take time and a good amount of fundraising."

Gordon moves in closer. He has almost no wrinkles and a few faint freckles around his nose. We both hold each other's gaze.

"Is that a tiny scar beneath your eye?" I ask.

"Hmm. I guess my concealer wore off." Gordon laughs. "It's from a bicycle accident on Turkey's Turquoise Coast a few years ago. Fell smack into a rock."

"Ouch."

"Yeah, it wasn't fun."

"Though it sure sounds exotic."

"I wouldn't call being stitched up at the Ahu Hetman Hospital in Marmaris particularly exotic." Gordon scrunches his nose. "Maybe we'll go together sometime."

There's a pause as I think about what he just said. Then Gordon leans in closer. He takes a lock of hair that's swept onto my face and slips it behind my ear. He looks deep into my eyes.

"Is this uncomfortable for you?" he asks softly.

"Why would it be uncomfortable?" I say, flirting for the first time in months.

"I don't know. You seem uneasy," he whispers.

His face is about an inch from mine. It's unsettling but exciting.

"It doesn't bother me. I kinda like it," I say, thinking about how turned on I am by this guy.

"We might've had a difficult first date. But I'm willing to try it again. I definitely want to get to know you better. What do you think?"

"I think yes," I say softly. I can hardly believe he's for real. I feel tingly and nervous at the same time.

But I can't hold his gaze any longer. I have to avert my eyes, as it's feeling really intense. My mouth is so dry I'm worried I might have bad breath, and yet I can almost taste his, which has a fresh minty scent.

"I'll pick you up at seven on Saturday. Be downstairs," he whispers back.

"I might have plans. I'll check and—"

"Change them," Gordon interrupts.

There's a long pause.

"But you don't know where I live."

"I know a lot about you. And I want to know even more," Gordon says. He places his hand on my left knee. "Be ready. We're gonna have a great time." His eyes twinkle with excitement, and then he rushes back to his office.

Whew. I sure wasn't expecting that. I pray my deodorant is working because I'm hot and sweaty and even a little shaky. I've got to pull myself together and get back to work even though I'm anything but focused on that right now. As I roll down the window and start my trek back to HBS, I'm totally engrossed in Gordon. I think about the way he knelt down beside me and placed his hand on my knee. I can't get over his penetrating blue eyes and how they were transfixed on mine. There's something really sexy about him. I can't put my finger on it, but I'm really feeling it. Oh my gosh, I haven't felt this way in years.

I'm so mired in my thoughts that I almost don't hear the phone ring.

"Chester canceled *Money Honey*," Rosie blurts out as I secure the Bluetooth on my ear, forcing me to drive erratically off these mostly desolate streets onto the insanity of the freeway.

"What? Just like that? What do you mean he canceled it, Rosie? How do you know?" I ask, jolting myself back to reality.

"Well, you're not gonna love this, but apparently Chester told Jerry to cancel it."

"Chester told Jerry to cancel *my* show? Seriously?" I want to kill Chester, but since that's not going to happen, I bear down on the accelerator and head back to the office.

How could Chester do that? It's *my* job to talk to the producers, not Jerry's. The more I think about it, the angrier I get. But strangely, as much as I want to focus on that anger, I can't stop thinking about Gordon. I want to press Rewind and play that scene in the parking lot over and over again. I'm completely absorbed in the details of our conversation. I mull over every word and gesture. I'm definitely attracted to him. How can that be? I hardly know this guy. For a moment I actually thought he was going to kiss me. His mouth was so close to mine I could almost feel him on my lips. And I think I would've liked it. Wow, what's happening to me? I can still smell him. I reflect on every detail, like the bits of gray in his sideburns, the ring of sweat under his right arm, the hint of a black sock between his pant and boot, the tiny beads of perspiration on his forehead, the shape of his nose, the intensity of his eyes, the way he said my name, his wink and his smile and the tender way he touched my knee.

My phone rings again, and I hear Rosie say, "Chester's on the line." Again I'm jerked back to reality. My respite is over. I'm almost back at HBS yet wondering how I managed to change lanes and dodge traffic without even noticing I was doing it.

"Hi, Chester, I heard you canceled *Money Honey*."

He says he had no other choice, that last night's numbers were too low. The network is hemorrhaging and this is a show that was never going to make it.

"I just wondered why you asked Jerry to cancel it when you know *Money Honey* is my show," I say, since I bought the idea, developed the script, and fought to get it on the air. But Chester claims ignorance. He changes the subject and asks that I hurry back, as he wants to start the meeting early.

Sure. I'll exceed the speed limit just so I can star in the next LA car chase in order to get to Chester's meeting on time. Whatever.

My time with Gordon and Marisol is now ancient history. I fly into the HBS parking lot, praying I'm not too late for the start of the afternoon staff meeting. I open the trunk, grab my purse, and dash upstairs.

I sweep by Jan and breathlessly enter Chester's office. I'm stunned that I'm the first to arrive. Chester's on the balcony, chatting on his cell phone and flicking ashes onto the cars in the HBS parking lot below. He starts to wrap up his call as I claim my usual chair, and he enters the office, closing the screen door behind him. He tosses his phone on the desk, saunters over to his big leather chair, and lights a brand-new cigarette.

"So, you want to head entertainment?" he asks without any kind of preamble. I'm startled, but say yes, I do.

He picks up the remote and aims it toward the entry. Magically, the door to his office closes. Neither of us says a word until it shuts completely.

"Why?" Chester asks.

"Why do I want to head entertainment? Because I think I can inspire others to develop commercially successful shows and start winning again," I say, completely forgetting what I had memorized.

Chester takes a long puff on his cigarette and stretches both feet onto the coffee table. I notice a tan line just above his ankles and that his black Nike sweat suit seems a little frayed at the edges. All five TV monitors are on, but none carry any sound. He takes another puff and stares at the screens. I sit expectantly, not knowing if I should fill the silence with more words or leave it alone. Just as I think of something to say, Chester says, "Leadership is about challenging the troops, taking reasonable risks, embracing change, and getting others to follow you. It's a team effort. It's about common goals, collaboration, getting everyone to pull their weight." He takes another hit off his cigarette and asks, "You up to that?"

I sit up straight in my chair and say, "Of course I'm up for it, and—"

"You'll need to earn the respect of the team," Chester interrupts. "You need to show your colleagues you're not only a good developer and have good relationships with the community, but that you can manage crises and lead the team to a Super Bowl win."

Sports metaphors are something I've grown accustomed to at HBS. I understand what most mean. The ones I don't know I look up on Wikipedia. Obviously, I know what leading this group to the Super Bowl means. In TV terms, it means winning the sweeps and the season, which would make us the most-watched television network.

"I can do that. I'm very confident in my managerial skills and my ability to develop good shows."

Suddenly Chester rises and walks toward his private bathroom several feet away from where I'm sitting. I hear him turn on the water faucet. And then, with the water running in the background, I hear the sound of the toilet seat as it thumps against the commode and then the sound of him urinating. I scrunch my nose and roll my eyes.

You'd think he'd close the door.

"You'd be the one everyone looks up to. It's a difficult role. Whether it's managing success or failure, it's not easy," he shouts from inside the bathroom.

Within moments I hear the toilet flush, and the faucet is turned off. But a little too quickly. It doesn't sound like he took the time to wash his hands.

"The most important part is working with your team, showing them the way, leading them, and ultimately guiding them to victory." Chester exits the bathroom, adjusting his pants. He walks back to his chair, plops himself down, and then suddenly the door flies open and Jan appears.

"The guys are here. Are you ready?"

Chester takes a puff on his cigarette and motions to Jan to let them in. So ends our impromptu meeting. One of the biggest meetings of my life, one I was totally unprepared for, has come and gone in an instant. I'll no doubt beat myself up for not saying something great. I'll examine every single thing Chester said and what he didn't say a gazillion times. It's also unclear if this little meeting was planned or unplanned. I never know with Chester. All I know is that was my moment.

There's a lot of chatter as the guys enter the room. It appears they were watching a porn film Steve downloaded on his cell phone, which creates a lot of excitement.

"No means yes, and yes means anal!" Steve joyfully announces as the guys howl and shriek their way into Chester's office. They tumble into their seats and begin to settle down as Chester parks his cigarette in the ashtray.

"I wanna get through the November promos," Chester says, reminding us that although this is the first week in October we have to plan for the November, February, and May sweeps, as they determine advertising rates. The bigger the rating, the better chance we have of keeping our jobs. "Steve has a few to show." Chester retrieves his cigarette, dropping some ashes on my foot, which makes me flinch. However, no one notices because Adrienne, Chester's gorgeous temp secretary, has just waltzed in with his requisite coffee. Adrienne is tall and slender with a beautiful olive complexion, light-green eyes, and long, straight auburn hair. Her Hawaiian good looks and melodic way of speaking soothe the animalistic tone of this group.

"Hi, gentlemen, hope you have a good meeting." Adrienne hands Chester his coffee and glides out of the room. Suddenly it's very quiet.

"We're gonna show a sixty-second spot for *Let's Get the Girls*, which we think should run during football on Sunday," says Steve as he loads a DVD in the player. A gorgeous, scantily clad Penelope Cruz look-alike fills the screen. She's lying on a lounge chair in a very revealing red string bikini with her eyes closed and a giant cherry dangling from her surgically enhanced lips. Around her is a Caribbean landscape, a beautiful, rich, blue sky against a sea of green, glittering water. We are at some fabulous resort. The girl is an absolute knockout. There's no dialogue, just Maurice Chevalier's "Thank Heaven for Little Girls" playing softly in the background.

The actress sucks on the cherry, popping it inside and outside her mouth. Finally, she holds the stem between her teeth as the cherry rests on her chin. Her body rocks back and forth in slow motion to the rhythm of the song as if she's in some trance. The music is lowered and across the screen appear the words, *Come Pop My Cherry. Let's Get the Girls. Sundays on HBS.* And it fades to black.

The guys are ecstatic. They come out of their stupor, cheering and whooping for this great promo. I wouldn't be surprised if they were trying to hide their woodies.

"Pretty good stuff, Steve," says Chester, trying to contain his excitement. "I like it." All the sycophants do. Steve takes out the DVD and puts in another.

"If you're trying to get men, then fine, but women aren't gonna respond to this," I say.

"We only care about getting men." Steve rolls his eyes disdainfully. "*Let's Get the Girls* is for guys."

"But why don't you want to try and attract women, too? Why not create an additional promo that appeals to men *and* women?" I ask.

No one says anything. Steve inserts another DVD.

"Because this is a guys' show," Steve says. "It's great if women watch. But if not, who cares? The show is doing unbelievably well with men."

"I know men like it," I say, refusing to acquiesce. "I just don't see why we can't encourage women to watch this show, too."

"Because it's a guys' show," says Noah, who feels the need to rescue Steve from my villainous questioning. But I'm not done. If Chester wants to see my ability to lead, then fine, here we go.

"I think you guys ought to develop another promo that appeals to women. The show is about dating. Girls like those shows. You know, like *The Bachelor*? I don't see a downside trying to get more female viewers for this show. We're a broadcast network, guys. This isn't Spike TV. We want to bring everyone into the tent. Why not just try?"

I've offered a pretty good argument, but it's clear no one wants to acknowledge it. Then, finally, Chester speaks up.

"Well, it's a good idea. Why don't you create one for women, too? No downside." Chester is patronizing, but I'll take it. Steve rolls his eyes and writes something down.

Steve would like nothing more than for me to disappear. I complicate his life with what he considers insane requests. I can't get over these guys. It's like they're programming for an audience of men stuck in the 1950s. I'm their worst nightmare, reminding them that no, we are now in the new millennium. And surprisingly, women vote and work outside the home. Something I'm sure they secretly wish wasn't the case. And then, just when I think we might be making some progress, they unveil a new promo that's better suited for the Playboy Channel.

"Let's see the next group," says Chester, changing the subject. We roll through about ten more, each one worse than the last. At least, that's my opinion.

Everything is about sex. The lack of it, the need for it, how great it is, how great it can be. I know sex sells, but I often wonder, is the audience really this vapid? Are we catering to the lowest common denominator, or are we offering shows that *are* the lowest common denominator?

We're finally done and start to leave.

"We can't leave yet. I've got a scheduling issue," Noah says. "We need something to replace *Money Honey*." Noah moves shows around like pieces in a puzzle. He makes sure HBS has something on twenty-four seven. His greatest achievement is that we've never gone to black. Everyone stops to listen.

"Uh, didn't anyone think about that before it was canceled?" I ask.

"We thought we had two new episodes of *I'm Da Man*," Pete Jenkins, the head of reality programming, interrupts. "It would've been great, but the star, Ashton Silverlake, has hepatitis, so they had to shut down."

"We need to cover two time periods in the sweeps," Noah says. "We could run *Bunnies* back-to-back and probably get a number or see if we can find something else."

"Well, I might have a solution," I say. "I spoke to Vince Vaughn's agent, and it's possible he could host a comedy special."

The guys like this. Lots of excitement.

"Well, that's great for next season, but I need something for November. Something fast," adds Noah.

"His agent told me he's in between movies and would consider doing something for TV," I say. "I can always ask."

"Not a bad idea," says Chester. "Go get it."

"But we've gone after him before," whines Jasper. "He keeps turning us down. He doesn't want to do television. We've heard that over and over."

"I spoke to his agent the other day," I say. "Unless I'm in the early stages of Alzheimer's, I can say with confidence that he told me this."

Jasper rolls his eyes and I wonder if I'm getting snookered.

"Can you get into it right away?" asks Noah. "Because we need something fast."

I pull out my phone and text the agent.

As if on cue, the door opens and Jan waves Jerry Kellner inside. Everyone turns to see why he is being admitted to our precious man cave.

"Sorry to barge in on you guys, but I have great news. I want to share it right away." Jerry is eager and excited. This is worrisome.

Jerry stands in front of the five screens, fist bumping Steve and Noah. All eyes are on him.

"What've you got?" asks Chester, who seems neither thrilled nor dismayed by Jerry's interruption.

"If we could have one single interview in primetime right now, what would it be?" asks Jerry.

No one has a clue. We're stumped.

"C'mon, guys! Think! What would be *the* thirty-share interview right now? Who does America want to hear from?" asks Jerry, whose eyes are as wide as saucers.

Jan stands in the doorway, waiting for the answer as well. We're all on the edges of our seats, exactly where Jerry wants us. His face is red. His eyes are popping out of his skull. He's beginning to perspire. But he's beaming. Jerry loves an audience. The whole thing makes me anxious. What in the world did he come up with?

"Who would you pay a million dollars a minute if you could get it back in triplicate?" Jerry shrieks.

No one answers. We're all just staring at Jerry.

"C'mon, guys, I'm practically spoon-feeding this to you. How can you not think of who this might be?" His voice is at a fever pitch.

And then it occurs to us. All at once. Of course. It's Ivor James. The famous baseball player who fell from grace. We've all been fascinated by his Shakespearean fall. His life completely unraveled when a tabloid revealed details of his multiple affairs and use of steroids. The national press ran with it while Ivor hid out in his zillion-dollar mansion in Atlanta. No one has seen or talked to him in weeks. Ivor James's sterling image was shattered. Everyone wanted the first tell-all interview. Could Jerry have gotten Ivor to talk to HBS? No one could get that interview. Ivor turned down *Sixty Minutes*, Oprah, Brian Williams, and Diane Sawyer. How in the world did Jerry get it?

"Unbelievable. You got Ivor James!" shout Steve and Noah in unison.

"Very big play, my man," Chester says. "Great score."

They are over-the-moon thrilled. Jerry is literally jumping up and down so hard and so fast I think the floor will give way.

I can't believe it. Ivor James, who led a seemingly perfect life with his perfect wife and perfect children and threw it all away in favor of prostitutes and drugs, losing all his sponsors, has been in rehab for months. No one's heard from him. There's just speculation and a paparazzi photo here and there. And Jerry Kellner has somehow scored his first, and what could be only, interview.

Jerry is besieged with questions. He triumphantly shouts that he landed the big one. He'll deliver Ivor to HBS for a two-part live interview to air over two nights during the November sweeps. Noah is overjoyed. Jerry has single-handedly provided the solution to Noah's problem. He's not only saved the day but might be responsible for HBS's first sweeps win in ages. I have to admit this is huge. My phone vibrates, and I see a text back from Vaughn's agent that says, "Sweetie pie, Vince is not interested in TV. He will never do TV. Stop bothering me about it. He's a feature star." Nice.

"Jerry, I want to hold a press conference," Chester instructs. "Get the deal worked out with Mark." He squashes the butt of his cigarette into the HBS ashtray, gets up, drapes his arm around Jerry, and walks him to the door. The guys slap Jerry on the back as they file out of the room, offering congratulations. The room empties out except for me. I remain on the couch trying to think of some great reply to the agent's condescending text. Chester sees me sitting there.

"Lex, don't go after Vaughn, we don't need him." I get up, smile sheepishly, and exit.

As I walk down the long hallway back to my office, I can't help but think that despite my attempt to show Chester I can lead and inspire the team, there's nothing that can compete with a ratings extravaganza like the first Ivor James interview. Jerry has stolen the show. It certainly appears that if anyone's keeping score—and at this place *everyone* is—Jerry is beating me one to nothing.

Sylvia and I are in the locker room, having just worked out for an hour on the treadmill. She ran ten miles while I ran three. I'm exhausted. She's exhilarated. It's been two days since Jerry's grand announcement. I needed to work out. The stress is building. And now even the new clerk at See's Candies knows my name. She has eight milk Bordeaux in a bag waiting for me. Ugh. This is bad.

I guess it's better than buying the five-hundred-dollar Cole Haan boots that caught my eye on Bluefly the other day. Chocolate and shopping seem to ease the pain at least temporarily. Although an emerging belly and a big MasterCard bill create a vicious cycle.

Sylvia reports that Ivor James's interview will air on the first and second Thursdays of the November sweeps. It's set to begin four weeks from today. Sylvia says ad sales have gone through the roof. We're gonna make a ton of money.

I tell her about my meeting with Chester on Tuesday.

"He probably thinks the role of president is a stretch for you," Sylvia says. "You know he thinks a guy can easily assume the role, but he's not sure a woman can."

"Well, it's not lost on me that every time a woman is made president, a man becomes chairman. But, if a man is elevated to president, his is the final word. When is there going to be a woman in charge of everything?" I ask.

"Hey, you think it's bad in our business? Take a look at Wall Street. There's not one female CEO of a major Wall Street firm," Sylvia says.

"That's pathetic. No wonder Wall Street is so screwed up."

"How about Congress? I read an article yesterday that said there are three hundred fifty-seven men and seventy-eight women in the House. Can you believe that?" Sylvia asks.

I can't. Where the heck are the women?

We're both buck naked, standing beside our lockers in the fancy executive locker room, trying not to stare at any other naked bodies, including each other's. But I do notice Sylvia has a teeny butterfly tattoo just below her belly button. I never would've guessed that about her.

"So, did you hear how Jerry got the Ivor James interview?" Sylvia whispers as she plucks her clothes out of the locker and places them on the bench.

"I can only imagine," I say, grabbing my thong and twisting it every which way, trying to find the front so I can get it on correctly.

"This girl Georgia was bonking both Jerry and Ivor. She told Jerry about a sex tape she made with Ivor. So Jerry sent Ivor an e-mail saying Georgia gave him a tape of Ivor doing Georgia, which he's eager to discuss with the press."

"What?" I ask, wiggling into my bra. "Tell me this again. Are you saying Jerry blackmailed Ivor into giving him the interview?" I'm shocked he'd actually go that far.

"Yup," says Sylvia, who's already dressed. She tosses her gym clothes in the laundry bin and heads for the makeup table with a giant mirror surrounded by lightbulbs. I jam a foot in my pants and hop my way over, trying not to fall in the process.

"I can't believe it."

"Believe it."

"Who told you this?"

"Georgia," Sylvia says matter-of-factly as she applies mascara. "She's my colorist in LA."

"What? Your colorist? Are you kidding me? And she's a hooker on the side?" I race back to my locker, grab the rest of my clothes, and finish dressing as Sylvia puts on the rest of her makeup.

"Well, she's not a hooker. She's VP of guest relations at Drai's in the W Hotel. Her job is to make sure the VIP clients are, shall we say, well taken care of."

"So she told Jerry she screwed Ivor James?"

"God, Alexa, didn't you hear me? She *filmed* them screwing, and she was happy to get paid any amount of money for it." Sylvia finishes applying her makeup.

"I don't understand sex tapes. Does everyone set up a camera and film themselves having sex now? Is this the new thing? I mean, it's been so long that I'm probably not up to speed on this." I tuck my shirt into my pants and cram my feet into my heels. "So what did she get out of this, Syl?"

"Jerry gave her ten grand."

"He paid her for the tape?"

"In cash. Out of his own pocket, so it's not traceable."

"Does he actually *have* the tape?"

"I assume so. Georgia said he bought it from her." Sylvia starts blow-drying her hair.

"But why would she do that to James? Why would she sell a tape of them screwing? And why to Jerry, of all people?" I shout so Sylvia can hear above the noise of the hair dryer.

Sylvia turns off the hair dryer and looks me straight in the eye.

"I don't know the answer, but I think she was in love with Ivor. I guess it was the usual stuff. He wouldn't leave his wife for her. You know, a woman scorned kind of thing. Why she sold it to Jerry? Because Jerry happened to be the client she cried to. He offered her money. It was a very lucky moment for Jerry and a very unlucky one for Ivor James." Sylvia switches the hair dryer back on as I yank a sweater over my head. I'm finally dressed.

I suddenly remember what Jerry said in my office last week. That I don't have the connections he has. I also don't have the chutzpah. It would never occur to me to blackmail someone to get what I want.

Maybe Emily was right. I may not have what it takes to get that programming job. I'm not a killer like Jerry. I won't stop at anything to get what I want. I could probably tell Jerry's wife, Olivia, about this. But who would I really be hurting: Jerry or Olivia? And in the end, would Jerry honestly care? He's gotten what he needs from Olivia's family. And I wouldn't be surprised if Olivia hasn't turned a blind eye to his indiscretions.

"What Jerry did was disgusting, Syl. Aren't you the least bit shocked by this? It's blackmail." I'm truly stunned. I can't believe Sylvia isn't as outraged as I am.

Sylvia stops.

"I've observed his behavior. I'm not surprised anymore. Jerry is a cold-blooded monster. He's soulless. He's not someone we'd ever choose to know. He's a fucking shark."

Sylvia has completed her transformation from gym rat to executive. She grabs her purse and reaches for the door to exit.

"Lex, you're gonna have to come up with something if you want to get that job. 'Cause, guess what? He's winning."

Sylvia flies out the door and is gone.

Chapter Six

Gordon and I are having a lovely dinner at Craig's, a showbiz hangout in West Hollywood. It's an unusually chilly Saturday night, but we're huddled inside a curved blue leather booth framed by dark wood and soft lighting. We chose this place because it's fairly close to my apartment, and I love their comfort-food menu, something I crave after a stressful day at work. We share the fourteen-ounce prime New York steak and opt for french fries instead of mashed potatoes. I'm determined not to screw up this date, but I can't seem to stop ranting about my job.

"Jerry sounds like a jerk," says Gordon as he munches on some fries. "Can't you just get rid of him since he reports to you?"

"Not really. He was placed in my department by the chairman of HBS."

"Ah. Not an easy fix. Your business is so cutthroat. I'd hate it."

"I'm not sure I'm going to make it."

"Oh, c'mon, you seem like a tough woman," he says. "You don't strike me as someone who shrinks away."

"I have to be strong all the time," I say, as I take a bite of my steak. "And I don't know if it's me, or who I want to be, or who I have to be. I'm not sure who I really am anymore."

Gordon wipes his hands on the napkin and asks the waiter for a large glass of water.

"Alexa, can I get you anything?" asks the waiter. "Would you like some more wine?"

"Sure, Julian. Thank you."

"Guess this is your place, huh?" asks Gordon.

"Julian is an aspiring actor. I've gotten him a few meetings with casting directors. So he takes good care of me here."

"I'll bet he does. That's a really nice thing to do."

"It's no big deal," I say, taking a sip of wine. "I'm happy to help him."

Gordon angles in toward me, placing his arm around my shoulder.

"But it is a big deal," he says. "There are lots of actors who'd give their eyeteeth for a meeting. I'm not in your business, but it's hard to avoid hearing about it if you live in LA. It's very generous to offer him an opportunity like that."

There's a pause as Julian pours more wine.

"Yeah, it seems like everyone in LA is in show business, doesn't it? You can't enter a Starbucks without seeing at least three people writing scripts on their laptops."

"Despite the stress, I think you really enjoy your job," Gordon says.

"I do. I like it very much. But I don't want to sacrifice everything for it, nor do I want to become my job. I'm determined not to make it my life. I don't want to drink the Kool-Aid and become Jerry."

Gordon offers me more french fries, which I'm only too happy to accept.

"So what about you?" I ask as we both take a sip of wine. "Do you love what you're doing?"

"Very much. I wouldn't trade it for the world." Gordon shifts his arm off my shoulder and onto the top of the banquette while using the other to pierce his steak.

"That's nice. I'm not sure I get the same kind of reward. At least I'm not getting it right now," I add dejectedly.

"Hey, you can turn this around. You just have to get tougher. You're dealing with a macho group of guys. You may have to be a little more aggressive about what you want." Gordon moves even closer to me. "Look, from everything you've told me, I hate this guy, Jerry. He's a beast. But you can't let him get away with stuff. You've got to go after him. You've got to find his weak spots and nail him." Gordon takes a sip of water. "You're working with a rough group in a very competitive race. But you also need a little balance to give you some perspective."

"Ha-ha. What's that? I don't have time for balance."

"Yes, you do. You need to carve out time. It's important; it will give you a better perspective on life. Maybe tutoring will help. It'll take you out of that environment for a while."

Gordon reaches for his wineglass.

"So, lemme ask you something," I say, grabbing the few remaining french fries, which I've tried to avoid, and cram them into my mouth before I change my mind. "Didn't any of my colleagues register for tutoring?"

"No," Gordon says as he stabs his fork into his last chunk of steak without looking up. "No. Never heard from anyone else." There's a pause. "Which shows what kind of person you are. That you actually want to enrich other people's lives as well as your own. I think that's an admirable trait." He smiles.

Gordon takes my hand, and within seconds, his soft lips are on mine. Every muscle in my body relaxes. I'm no longer trying to be the unbreakable broad but instead, the sexy girl in the red bikini sucking on the cherry. I let go, and it feels wonderful. I love his gentle touch and seductive manner. Gordon slowly pulls away, leaving me breathless and, for a change, speechless.

"Wow," I say.

"Liked it, huh?" Gordon says.

My face is on fire. God, can he tell I'm turned on? I can't believe I'm falling for him.

"Ya know, I really don't go out on dates that much," I say, leaning back into the banquette, sipping more chardonnay and trying to sound cool and collected, even though I just want to do it again and again, each time longer and deeper than the next.

"Gee, really? I'd never have guessed that." Gordon takes out his reading glasses and cleans his lenses with the edge of his napkin.

"I mean, I really haven't had much time to date. You know, with work and all."

Gordon puts his glasses on and reviews the check. I try to take it from him.

"No, this is on me tonight. I invited you to dinner," Gordon says.

"OK, but next time it's on me. I don't believe the guy always has to take the girl out. That's kind of old-fashioned."

"Hey, I've no problem with that," Gordon laughs. "Sure, next time it's all yours."

"Hmm, he didn't charge us for the wine," Gordon says as he reviews the check and signals for the waiter.

"No, he won't," I interrupt. "Julian takes it off."

"Why?"

"Oh, it's his way of thanking me for the meetings."

"Wow. You clearly are a very powerful woman. I'm sure glad to know you." Gordon grins.

"Do you think being powerful is sexy?" I smile coyly, sipping the last drops of wine, feeling Gordon's eyes on me.

"I think you're sexy," Gordon says softly.

"No, seriously, what do you think?"

Gordon moves in close and whispers, "Seriously, I love looking at you. And seriously, I think you're sexy whether you're powerful or not."

Before I can get another word out, Gordon pulls me toward him and once again I'm entwined in his arms, enjoying a wonderful, long, and passionate kiss. Just what I was hoping for. I'm totally blown away by this guy. Gordon suggests we head back to my apartment. I thank him for dinner, and we exit the restaurant.

We stroll over to the valet stand, where it's suddenly gone from toasty to bone-chilling cold. For some reason LA is in the low forties, which is considered freezing here. I wrap my long wool sweater around me as I'm starting to tremble. Not sure if it's because I'm so excited to be with this guy or just seriously cold.

The valet brings Gordon's red '76 Alfa Romeo convertible to the curb. He opens the passenger door to let me inside. Suddenly this very chilly night turns into the Arctic as we pull away from the restaurant into traffic. My hair is flying, my teeth chattering. Why in the world is the top down?

"Um, ya know, it's really cold," I shout. "Don't you want to put the top up?" Windswept hair flies all over my face and inside my mouth.

Gordon looks at me and smiles as he speeds away from the curb. "Oh, c'mon, it's invigorating. Doesn't it feel good? Makes you feel alive, doesn't it?"

"No, it makes me feel cold," I scream. "I'm freezing."

"Well, try to hang in, 'cause the top won't go up. Haven't had the time to fix it. I've been restoring this car for years. Was hoping we'd catch a warmer night. I'm sorry. It's just a few blocks to your place, right?"

I nod and shiver at the same time.

Gordon takes my hand, squeezing it tightly while steering with the other.

"Look up at the sky. It's a beautiful night, isn't it? You can actually see the stars."

I look up, and sure enough it's crystal clear and I actually can see some stars right above me.

"Did you ever wish upon a star when you were a kid?" he asks.

"Yes, I guess I did." I'm still shaking.

"Did your wish come true?"

There's a pause as I turn toward Gordon. I pull the windswept strands of hair off my face and try to park them behind my ear. He seems so happy and almost oblivious to the cold.

"I don't know. I don't remember," I say, trying not to sound as miserable as I feel right now. My teeth are chattering so loudly I can barely hear myself think.

"Every time I look up at the sky and see a bright, shining star I think about making a wish. I guess it's been ingrained in me," Gordon says as he pulls me close and rubs my shoulders to warm me up.

"I remember dreaming about having more than I had at the time. Clothes, a toy or something," I say, enjoying the feeling of having Gordon's arm around me.

And then I hear Gordon humming softly.

"What're you humming?"

"'Dream a Little Dream of Me.'" Gordon smiles, and I can't help but smile back. "I know that one."

"Then sing it with me. It'll keep your mind off of the cold."

"No, I don't sing."

Gordon pauses, and we both smile at each other as the wind rips through the car.

"I'll help you. Let's do it together," Gordon says.

Gordon sings and then looks at me expectantly.

"Don't be so self-conscious." He's smiling, but I can't seem to conjure up the nerve to join him.

"I don't have a good voice," I say sweetly.

"Like anyone's gonna hear you?" Gordon laughs as he takes my hand firmly in his. "C'mon, give it a shot."

After a moment, I finally give in. I don't know what's come over me, but I start to feel comfortable and let myself go...a little.

Gordon tightens his grip on my hand as he sings back to me.

I'm actually enjoying this now and decide to chime in. We sing our hearts out about leaving our worries behind and craving a kiss, laughing along the way. And just as Gordon promised, I've forgotten that five minutes ago I was freezing my ass off.

Gordon coasts along Sunset Boulevard, past the House of Blues and The Standard hotel, and just before we hit Harper Avenue, we come to a stop signal. Finally, I'm able to grab my hair and put it into a makeshift ponytail so it isn't blowing all over the place.

"You seem to know that song pretty well," Gordon says.

"My friend Emily and I took her niece to the set of *The Voice*. They were rehearsing a dance number to 'Dream a Little Dream of Me.' It stayed in my head for days. I love the melody. It's very romantic. I can't believe you know the lyrics. I figured you for Coldplay, Springsteen, U2, and maybe even LMFAO. Hardly Mama Cass."

"You're right, not my usual fare. My mom used to sing it to me and my sister. She was a big fan of The Mamas & The Papas, so I'm well acquainted with their music," he says.

"Gosh, that's so nice," I say, trying to think of a time when my mom might've sung to us.

"Yeah, she was also very big on dreams," he says wistfully. "Always encouraged us to follow our passion, to do what makes us happy. You know, that kind of thing."

No, I don't know that kind of thing. But I think it's too early to divulge that my mom's dream was to simply keep a roof over our heads and food in our mouths. A young widow, her passion was survival.

He reaches into his pocket and pulls out his wallet. He hands me a ten-dollar bill.

"I'm going to pull over by that curb," Gordon says as he points to the street corner. "See that homeless vet on the corner with the sign? Can you please do me a favor and give this to him?"

I look in the direction Gordon's pointing and see a man lying on the ground inside an entryway to a big building on the corner. A shopping cart is next to him. He's huddled inside a blanket next to two glass doors leading into the building.

The Cadillac SUV behind us starts honking. But Gordon doesn't move. I hop out of the car and walk briskly up the sidewalk toward the entryway. The man is nestled deep inside a grungy blanket. I cautiously approach and look back to make sure Gordon is within sight. Gordon nods. I offer the money to the vet. The man nods a few times, takes it, and smiles appreciatively. I notice the rough, dry texture of his hand, his toothless grin and sad eyes. He tries to say something, but all I hear are grunts. Horns are blasting and cars shrieking. I tell the man to sleep well and hurry back, wondering how in the world people are able to sleep out here. I feel terrible for them. It must be especially hard for vets. As I approach Gordon's car, the honking escalates. I see a few middle fingers pointed at me. I dive into the passenger seat. When my seat belt is safely secured, Gordon reaches over and hugs me.

"Thanks. I really appreciate you doing that. It's cold out. I just felt badly for that guy."

"Hey, it's likely you just made one of his dreams come true," I say, smiling at Gordon, who squeezes my hand, revs up the engine, and flies around the corner to my street. He finds a parking space right across the road from my apartment building, parallel parks, and turns off the ignition. The wind is fierce. Now even Gordon is shivering. I have frostbite.

"So, what do you think? Are you going to invite me in, or should we sit in my car and freeze to death?" he asks. He's buried in his jacket, his Lakers hat pulled so far over his eyes I can barely see them.

We both crack up as we leap out of the car and race up the concrete stairway to my apartment complex. We're laughing and gasping for air, going as quickly as we can, trying to stay warm. When we reach the entryway, I put my key in the door and lead us inside the small foyer, which has an elevator on the right and stairs on the left. I opt for the stairs. Gordon follows behind.

"Hey, don't you want to take the elevator?" Gordon asks.

"No, I'm elevator phobic." I always dread this conversation. "And I'm just up one flight. So it's no big deal."

"You don't take elevators? Ever?"

"Nope."

Gordon and I finally reach the top of the stairs, where there are just two apartments. Gordon blows on his hands to warm them up as he watches me put the key in my door.

"Well, what if you're in New York or something? How do you manage to get to a high floor?"

"It's not fun. I usually ask a guard to take me up. It's a problem," I say, tossing my purse on the entryway table just inside my apartment

"Well, have you tried hypnosis? I'm sure there are other—"

"I don't like to talk about it," I interrupt. "It's not something I'm proud of. It makes me feel weak."

Gordon finally gets it, and the conversation is over.

"That was a really nice gesture," I say, trying to change the subject. "You know, to give that homeless guy some money. I'm sure that will help him."

"Well, I feel badly for the vets," he says, as I unbutton my sweater and he takes off his hat and jacket. "It doesn't seem right that some vets return from service only to live on the streets. I figure ten dollars can at least buy him a meal."

Fortunately I left the heat on, so we start to warm up. Gordon takes his first look around my apartment and sees Joe. But Joe isn't thrilled to see another male on his turf. He makes that very apparent as he ambles over, raises his leg, and pees on Gordon's. It's a lovely habit he seems to have acquired of late.

"Oh my gosh, I'm really sorry," I say, so embarrassed I could die. I tear off my sweater, toss it on the couch, and rush to the kitchen to get some paper towels. "This is Joe's way of welcoming you into our home."

"Am I the only one who gets this wonderful reception, or do others enjoy this fine tradition?" Gordon helps me wipe off his pants.

"I'm so sorry. I really have to break him of this habit. I'll pay for the dry cleaning. I feel terrible." I can't believe I finally have a decent date and Joe does something like this. I shoot him a scornful look. But he responds with a slow burn as if to say, *Hey, this is my territory, what the heck is he doing here?*

"Don't worry about it," says Gordon. "I have a black Lab. These things happen. Not quite like this, but they happen." He hands me the towels and I throw them in the wastebasket in my bathroom.

When I return, I see Joe perched in the center of the couch, making it virtually impossible for both Gordon and me to sit there. Do I detect some envy going on? I walk over to the couch and point to the floor. Joe knows I mean business. He sheepishly jumps down, then climbs aboard the window seat, keeping a watchful eye on Gordon as he replaces Joe on the couch.

"Can I get you something? A drink?" I ask as Gordon settles into the little warm imprint Joe left behind on the couch.

"I don't need anything but a chance to look at you," he says.

He takes my hand and pulls me down so that I'm sitting beside him on the couch. He gently brushes my cheek with his hand, and before I know it, we're entangled in each other's arms. It feels so good. I can't remember the last time I felt this way. He kisses me again and again. It's deep and passionate.

We both come up for air and gaze into each other's eyes.

"Hey, I saw *Lethal Stilettos* the other night," Gordon says. "That's your show, right?"

"Yes, I developed that one and struggled to get it on the air. But it's holding up pretty well. Did you like it?"

"It was very funny. I have to admit I laughed out loud."

"You just made my day," I say as Gordon takes the opportunity to kiss me once again.

"Three macho guys working in the world of fashion just to meet girls is funny. Your idea?" Gordon asks.

"It was, actually. I read an article about guys who did that and suggested the area to the writers. They figured out how to make it into a show."

"Well, they pulled it off. It held my interest, and it was definitely funny. And guess what? I got a season pass. I'm hooked," Gordon laughs.

"That's great. I'm so relieved you like one of my shows. Thank goodness."

"It's a very unusual and conflicted work environment, that's for sure."

"Well, did it make you think of me?" I ask.

"It did. But I don't need a show to help me think of you. I think of you often," Gordon says softly and then kisses me again.

Soon he's nuzzling my neck. And within seconds, the antique studs on my gray silk blouse pop open, exposing my new black lace bra, which couldn't be more perfect for this occasion. It's part of the La Perla bra and panty set I got on sale at Saks after I witnessed how beautiful they looked on the porn stars in the executive locker room. I feel his lips approaching my breasts. And then I wonder, what am I doing? How far am I going? Does it matter? Do I have any condoms? I don't think so; just an old condom wrapper, thanks to Jerry's skillful retrieval. Note to self: I really need to throw that wrapper out before it results in another humiliating scene. It's been so long. I hope it's OK to sleep with him. I really don't want to just hook up. What if that's all it is for him? What if he never calls me?

I try to live in the moment, but it's not something I do well. I decide to push all those thoughts out of my head and just enjoy the fact that I'm about to have sex for the first time in God knows how long. I pray I remember what to do.

Gordon reaches behind my back and skillfully unfastens my bra with one hand, which indicates he's had lots of practice. And then the phone rings. I whisper that the machine will pick up because I don't want anything to interrupt this delightful moment. But everything comes to a screeching halt as we both hear the message as it plays loudly on my ancient answering machine.

"Oh my gawd, Lex," Sylvia shouts into my machine. "Are you watching the news on HBS? Did you see Jerry and Vince Vaughn talking about their new comedy special? Do you know about this? Are you watching? Oh my God. He's so obnoxious. He's literally coming all over Vince." It doesn't end there. "Lex, are you there? You're always there. Where are you? You should be home with Joe. What's going on? Maybe you're in the shitter. I'll call you back in ten."

Talk about killing the moment. Gordon has moved off of me. He sits beside me, tucking in his shirt. I button my blouse. Neither of us says a word. Gordon asks where the bathroom is, and I point. I disconnect the answering machine, something I should've done earlier. I look at Joe, who stares at me as if I just committed a crime.

He's clearly not happy that he's on the window seat and I'm on his couch. I hear the toilet flush, and Gordon comes out, adjusting his shirt. He appears sexier than he did before. His hair is mussed. He looks sleepy. His cheeks are flushed. His black V-neck sweater is rumpled, and his white T-shirt hangs below it. And he forgot to fasten one button on the fly of his jeans.

"I'm sorry," I say, as Gordon pulls on his bomber jacket and heads for the door. "You don't have to go." I jump off the couch and join him as he moves into the entryway. I want to beg him to stay, but I know that won't go down well.

"It's late," he says, sounding tired. "It's not your fault. I have to get home. I've got a long drive back to Venice. But I really enjoyed being with you tonight. Can we do it again?" He doesn't wait for an answer as he locks me in an embrace and kisses me for a long time. I rest my hand on his belt, wishing we could pick up where we left off. I let it drift below the buckle, taking a risk, but Gordon reaches for it, indicating no, we're not going there tonight. Darn. He holds me tight and comes in for what will be the final kiss of the evening.

"I had a good time. I hope you did, too," he says, as he brushes a piece of hair from my cheek.

"I had a great time," I say, smiling. "I wish you didn't have to go."

"Me, too. But I've got an early morning softball game and a long ride back home."

Gordon reaches for my hand and draws it to his lips, kissing it softly. He stares into my eyes, and I stare back, waiting. But after a beat, he reluctantly lets go, pulls on his Lakers cap, and opens the door.

I watch as he escapes down the steps, shouting that he'll call me. I sure hope he doesn't freeze to death on the way home, because I'd sure like to see him again. I stand in the hallway, looking out the tiny chrome window that overlooks the street. I watch as he pulls away from the curb and fades from view.

I go back inside and crash on the couch. I'm so upset. Jerry Kellner, the bane of my existence, strikes again. I turn on the TV but the news is over. We're now into *Saturday Night Live*. Then it suddenly occurs to me that Jerry is doing a show with Vince Vaughn. Oh my God. Who did he have to pay to get that? His agent gives Jerry the show but not me? Why? What's that about?

I can't deal with this now. I'm too tired. The wine is getting to me. I'm pissed and sexually frustrated. How could Gordon leave just like that? I lie down on the couch, close my eyes, and start to replay this lovely evening from beginning to end. I mull over every detail in my mind, thinking about this new man in my life and how I want to see him again and again.

And never go back to the office.

———

"You have *The Candy Stripers* table read at Fox in an hour. Then a meeting with Noah about the schedule. Then you have pitch meetings. Two from Paramount and one from Sony. Then there's a casting session with Wayne in his office. Then Molly needs three directors approved for *Married Women, Single Men*. Then you have lunch with Kathy Kloves at Pinot Bistro. Then a rough cut of *Of Corpse She's Alive*." Rosie takes a breath. "And there are a slew of calls. I told most to just e-mail you, but some still insist on talking. Also, Sylvia wants to know if your landline is working because she left you a message Saturday night. She called repeatedly, but your machine never picked up again. Are you there? I don't hear you."

It's Monday morning. Bring it on.

"Yes, I'm here. My Bluetooth fell out. Probably due to the over-load." I'm trying to find some humor in this, but Rosie will have none of that. She continues.

"The *Elle* interview is tomorrow at two thirty. Tony DeMeo will be in it with you. He wants to go over it today, so you know what to say."

As if I wouldn't know what to say. Do I need a ventriloquist?

"After that you have tutoring. So I'm going to move the casting session for *Mean Girls Grown Up* to Thursday," Rosie says. "You have three pitch meetings in the afternoon also."

I haven't even entered Burbank and already my day sounds difficult. I sip my latte as I drive over Laurel Canyon on this chilly Monday morning. The weekend is but a memory. No word from Gordon since he left my apartment on Saturday night. I hope he got home. But as I start my week, I can't worry about such things. I have to stay focused. Can't let romance get in the way of a good career. At least that's what I'm trying to tell myself.

"Let's go back to *The Candy Stripers* table read this morning. Why isn't Jerry attending?"

"Oh, he can't. He called in sick this morning."

"Gee, why don't I believe he's sick?" He's certainly sick in the head. But sick? Jerry? I'm sure there's something else going on. "Please get him on the phone, Rosie. I'll hold."

I take another sip of my latte and navigate my way onto Ventura Boulevard.

"Hey, Lex, what's up, babe?" Jerry says sleepily.

"Not too much, *doll*. Why aren't you at *The Candy Stripers* table read?"

"Whoa. Is that *this* morning? Oh, gee whiz. I thought it was next week." He chuckles.

"Yeah, probably because you and Vince were so busy developing your new show."

"Ah, gotcha, Lexican. Yes, I was able to pull off yet another huge deal. Another touchdown. What can I say? I'm simply the best."

"Hey, whatever it takes, Jer. And who knows that better than you? I'm sure you did whatever you could to land that deal."

"Are you suggesting nefarious dealings? 'Cause if you are, you're dead wrong. I'm just a far better salesman than you. The agent wanted Vince working with me, not you. That's just the simple truth."

"Why don't you just tell Barnsworth you want to be the head honcho? Why bother earning it?"

"Lex, baby, relax. You need to get laid. How long's it been? You still using the vibrator? Seriously, drop that and get the real thing."

"Jerry, get your ass to that table read now, or you're fired." I can't believe I just said that. I've reached my breaking point. We both know I can't come through on that threat, but it slipped out of my mouth. I wish I could take it back.

"Ha, well, of course you know that can't happen. But you can dream, sweetie pie. Tell you what, I've gotta get my act together, and once I do, I'll head over there. What time did you say that run-through is today?"

"Table read, Jerry. *The Candy Stripers* table reads are on Mondays. It's Monday. I know life's complicated for you, but we're shooting sitcoms, not heroin. It starts in an hour. Have a nice day, Jer." I hang up and swing into my parking space. What a great way to begin my day.

I sail up the stairwell to my office, lugging my bag, holding my phone as it vibrates wildly. I'm hoping it's Gordon. As I enter my office suite, I see Molly, my associate, sitting by Rosie's desk. She jumps up and follows me inside.

"I just need three directors approved for *Married Women, Single Men*. Evan Greenstreet, Mike Thompson, and Antonio Garcia. The CW's going after them, too. The producers want to get at least one of them to do the last two shows in the sweeps."

I fling my bag on the chair, take a quick glance at my e-mails, but again, none say Gordon. Damn.

"Sure. I like all of them. Go ahead," I say, "but, Molly, see if you can encourage the producers to consider a woman to direct an episode. We haven't had one on this show." Molly nods and flies out of the room.

"Your lunch canceled. Do you want me to get you something from the commissary?" Rosie shouts through the intercom.

"No, thanks, Rosie. I'll run down and pick something up later."

"Noah's here for your scheduling meeting," Rosie says. I tell her to have him come inside.

The morning whips by in a blur. There's one meeting after the next, a ton of e-mails, phone calls, script notes, dailies, rough cuts, pitch meetings, casting suggestions, approvals, standards notes, legal issues, scheduling problems, promos, ads, press coverage, and the usual pleas for more money to make shows bigger and better. I've made it through the first four hours of my exhausting day.

Before I head downstairs to get a salad for lunch I take one last look at my e-mails, but again, none from Gordon.

It's so hard when I like someone because I really want them to like me back. I'm not great with rejection.

Despite the hellacious nature of my day, it's gone by in a flash, and tomorrow I'll be seeing Marisol, and hopefully, maybe even Gordon will be there. Rosie and I returned most of my calls. I got through the meetings and did a long prep with Tony for the *Elle* interview. He's worried; I'm not. I'm finally able to take off my shoes, lie down on the couch, and relax for a bit as I watch dailies from *Lethal Stilettos*. I still can't believe Gordon liked it. That makes me so happy. Rosie and I stay till eight o'clock, order pizza, and by ten call it a day. We walk to the parking lot and bid each other good-bye, knowing we'll see each other in just under twelve hours.

Unfortunately, things don't always go as planned. My car won't start the next morning, so Rosie sends a car and driver because I have a full workday and need to get moving. Jeremy Cahill, our TV intern, arrives along with Armand, the driver. Jeremy will wait for the tow truck and accompany my car to the shop. I'm sure it's not something this Ivy Leaguer ever thought he'd be doing. But in today's world, Jeremy is thrilled to be getting paid experience in his field of study. He's very agreeable and eager to please, so I expect he'll go far in this business.

A car and driver are but one of the many perks that come with my extraordinary job. Having these benefits available certainly makes my life much easier. However, I feel a bit apprehensive accepting them. Sylvia, on the other hand, doesn't think I utilize them enough. She has a permanent driver, dines at expensive restaurants, and even charges HBS for her daily floral deliveries. Sylvia figures we won't have these jobs forever, or we'll surely suffer cutbacks if the shows don't do well, so we might as well enjoy the perks while we can. I suppose she's right. I rarely take advantage of the fringe benefits because I'm so focused on the work at hand.

Armand escorts me to his black stretch limo, which is double parked outside. I give Jeremy the keys, and he heads to my garage. There's nothing like a stretch limousine to attract the neighbors' attention. I feel like I'm going to the prom. Hardly an understated vehicle. I quickly hop into the backseat, hoping to fade into oblivion, as this lap of luxury feels a bit ostentatious for the times.

Armand announces that we have two stops this morning. One is my breakfast meeting at the Four Seasons hotel, followed by a set visit and then straight into HBS. He says we're on a tight schedule, as Rosie made sure to remind him that I have an interview this afternoon and she wants me there on time.

As I stare out the tinted window at the scenery I can't help but think about Gordon. Maybe everything is fine. Maybe he'll call

Friday and ask me out for Saturday. He doesn't seem big on planning dates in advance. I just miss him already, which concerns me because I haven't been this attracted to a guy in an awfully long time.

We pull into the driveway at the Four Seasons hotel, and I make my way into the dining room, where I'm set to meet Shane Snyder, who is the head of comedy development at Sony Television. When Catherine Davis, the hostess, sees me approach the line waiting to get in, she greets me warmly then pulls me aside and leads me to Shane's table, where he's seated with his three lieutenants. Before the hostess leaves she asks if the table is all right, if I would rather the one by the window. When she feels confident I'm comfortable, she instructs the waiter to take care of us. There isn't anything we can't have. The waitstaff assures us that the chef will prepare whatever suits my fancy. So I decide to go for it and order the oatmeal brûlée with stewed fruits and toasted banana nut loaf. I'm already salivating.

Given my tight schedule, Shane and his team make sure to discuss all items that pertain to Sony's shows. We spend less than an hour together. The conversation is all business. Satisfied they've come away with information that might help them sell even more shows to HBS, Shane presents his credit card to the waiter and we all air kiss good-bye. Wow, that was fast. My guess is Shane has another breakfast at a nearby restaurant.

As I start to exit, I run into several colleagues who want to know if I've had a chance to read their scripts. They follow me to the door. But the hostess appears out of nowhere and whisks me off to the entrance where Armand and his black limo await. She asks if everything was all right and thanks me and HBS for dining there.

I feel like Cinderella. I'm convinced that at a certain hour this great adventure will be over and I'll turn back into a pumpkin. TV network executives are treated like rock stars. It's intoxicating.

Who wouldn't want to live this life all the time? Jumping in and out of limousines, being offered the best table at the most exclusive restaurants, never having to wait in line, ordering any meal you desire, and having others perform your menial tasks. I can't believe this is happening to me sometimes.

It's a fairy-tale existence. I better enjoy it while I can.

My great ride continues as Armand races across town to a home in Hancock Park that's being used as a set for one of our comedies. I rarely do this, but Jensen Winnick, a beautiful young actress who just completed a movie for Spielberg, agreed to guest star in this show. I want to make sure she knows how thrilled we are to have her on HBS. It's good talent relations and a great excuse for me to get out of the office.

Armand pulls onto a lovely residential street. Production vehicles line the road while dollies, cables, tracks, and crew members encroach on this normally quiet community. As we park alongside the curb, Elizabeth Crane, a young and very attractive production assistant, opens my door, shakes my hand, and escorts me around the tracks and into the home.

"Alexa, the director is waiting for you to arrive," Elizabeth says. "He wants to do the next setup while you're here. Please follow me, and be careful of all the equipment." Elizabeth reminds me of myself when I was her age. She's very efficient, focused, and probably a little nervous, as she's in charge of the network executive.

As I enter the living room I meet Jensen, who's getting ready to film her scene. Then I'm greeted warmly by the cast and crew, who make a huge fuss offering me a chair, food, drink, and my own headphones so I can hear the audio. With all this attention, it's difficult to determine who's the bigger star: me or Ms. Winnick.

I could definitely get used to this.

I've enjoyed a full thirty minutes on set and would love to stay here all day, but Armand signals that it's time to move on. The director, producer, and a few cast members walk me out. Another production assistant offers me a bottle of water. And Elizabeth hands me a basket of T-shirts, caps, and various other items from the show, which Armand puts in the limo. My parting gift.

The thrill and wonder of this job never cease to amaze me. What other profession offers this much fun? Having the chance to watch a scene come to life as it's being filmed and offering ideas to enhance and improve the show is an extraordinary opportunity. Who wouldn't want to see the fruits of her labor on TV a few weeks later? It's why we endure the harder times: because the good times are rich and rewarding.

As we head over the hill to HBS in Armand's fancy car, I feel relaxed and happy. Two feelings I don't express often. Maybe Sylvia's right. I ought to take advantage of the perks. I watch the traffic move around me, but I don't have to navigate it; I'll leave that to Armand. I can indulge in the snacks and the *New York Times* that share the enormous backseat with me. The world of Jerry Kellner and the anxiety I feel about not hearing from Gordon have been cast aside. At least temporarily. I've had a wonderful morning and feel confident that I made the right decision to try and move up the ladder at HBS. Today reminds me of the great work we do, the terrific people involved, and how much more I could contribute if I were to take on a bigger role with more responsibilities.

Armand drives into the HBS parking lot and drops me off right next to the big glass doors leading to the lobby. I grab my bag and basket and thank him for a wonderful morning.

"Hey," I say, sprinting through my suite, energized by my visit to the set. "What's going on?"

"Tony called," Rosie says. "He's on his way up. The writer from *Elle* is early, so he's bringing her shortly. I told him you'd be here soon."

"OK, sounds good," I say as I head into my office, tossing my bag on the couch. "Rosie, c'mon in and take a look at this lovely basket. Let's see what there is."

Just as Rosie and I are about to tear into the basket Tony knocks on the door and pokes his head in. "Hey, babe, Patricia Wielding, the writer from *Elle*, is here. You ready?" There's simply no downtime. No transition. No time to catch my breath. Just on to the next. Without waiting for a reply, he opens the door and lets them both inside as Rosie carefully moves the basket off the couch and onto the ground and then quietly slips out.

Tony is a handsome, single thirtysomething from New Jersey. He moves fast and talks fast. He has the attention span of a gnat. He wants to get in and out quickly. If we dare delve into anything that requires a lot of thinking or strategy, he's out to lunch. He's constantly checking for messages on his BlackBerry. His slick black hair, ever-present five o'clock shadow, and fancy suits suggest a highly successful man on the make. He knows everyone and dates everything.

As I introduce myself to Ms. Wielding, Tony retreats to the corner of my office, tapping away on his phone. While he's engaged in something he believes is far more important, I escort Patricia to the couch. She notices the metal balls on my desk, and I tell her about the party my girlfriends threw for me. She takes one out of the box and smiles as it rings softly when shaken lightly. Just as she returns it to the box, Tony appears. He plops down next to me and begins talking even though Patricia and I are in midconversation.

"This is a story on female directors," Tony interrupts.

"Yes, I know," I say, startled by his awkward interruption. I guess he wants to start this meeting so he can get to his next one. Plus, he's anxious, and I know why. The truth is, we have a woeful number of female directors on our comedy shows. So we need to deliver our spin. For that reason, Tony insisted on being at this meeting. God forbid I go off script.

"Wow, look at this gigantic bowl of M&M's. I don't think I could have this in my office," Patricia says cheerfully. "It's far too tempting. I'd gain a pound just looking at them."

"Well, you'd be amazed how they alleviate the stress," I laugh.

"I'll bet," she adds. "I'd go through a bowl a day."

Patricia, a Peggy Noonan look-alike, is a real pro. Her job is to make me feel comfortable so I'll slip and say more than I should. She needs to make this interview feel like we're just two girlfriends sitting around, dishing. Her light-pink sweater set and gray skirt belie the shark underneath. But I know not to judge a book by its cover. Patricia's a freelance journalist known for hard-hitting stories, many of which appear as exposés in *The New Yorker* or *Vanity Fair*. So I'm on guard.

She places a small tape recorder on my glass coffee table to capture every word, pause, and emotional hiccup. Tony sits beside me so he can pinch my arm if I go off course.

"Like I said," says Tony, "Patricia is doing an article about the lack of female directors, particularly in television. I've already told her we don't necessarily agree with that premise, that at HBS we've hired several female directors on our pilots and series and expect to do that more and more, wouldn't you agree, Lex?"

"Well, Tony, I appreciate your input, but I want to be more specific, so if you don't mind, I'll ask the questions," Patricia says, and we're off to a roaring start.

Clearly, Patricia doesn't care for Tony and would prefer he was anywhere but here.

"Alexa, I've gone over the comedies you have on the air and notice that, although you certainly have a few female directors employed, they're still a tiny minority. And the numbers don't change from year to year." She reaches for a document. "For example, it appears that white males have directed more than eighty percent of the top forty series. And apparently, out of those shows, ten didn't even hire any women directors. Why is that?" she asks as she glances at her tape recorder to make sure the red light is on.

Tony interrupts, "Well, Patricia, I'm not sure where you got those numbers. I can surely get you a more accurate representation, particularly of the comedy shows we have on HBS."

Patricia doesn't flinch. Her eyes stay fixed on me. Her pen is poised to write whatever comes out of my mouth, which is dry and desperate for some water. But I wouldn't dare ask for some now.

"We at the network encourage producers to hire experienced directors on their shows," I say, carefully calibrating my words but wishing I could say more. "The problem isn't that we don't want women directors. The problem is that not enough of them are getting the opportunities to break in, so they aren't getting the experience necessary to get them directing positions on network shows. It's important they get entry-level opportunities so they can grow."

Tony looks at Patricia, praying I've said enough and that there won't be a follow-up question, but of course there is. Patricia consults her notes and starts reading from them.

"Well, look, Alexa, frankly, I don't want to hear the company line. I've heard it over and over. I've heard gains across series for female directors have been dramatic, that you've come a long way, but there's still more to go. I've heard that you're extremely proud of your initiatives and expect to increase the number of female directors. I've heard you've made progress, blah, blah, blah." Patricia stops reading her notes and looks up at me. "I was hoping as a woman in charge of a division at HBS, and frankly, the highest-ranking woman at HBS, that perhaps you might have a different perspective. I mean, surely it wasn't easy for you to rise through the ranks. You must know how hard it is to succeed in this business. Particularly if you're a female director."

I have a feeling Patricia and I are going to be dancing around this. Just because I'm a woman doesn't mean I represent women. I represent the network. I always have the network's best interest at heart. It's been drilled into my brain. But it doesn't mean I don't try to provide opportunities for women. If it's between a man and a woman and they're equally qualified, I try to give the woman a break she might not get elsewhere.

I start to formulate my answer, but Patricia looks down at her notes and starts reciting more information.

"You currently serve on the Board of Women in Film, and you were a panelist at the Hollywood Radio & TV Society luncheon about the lack of diversity in television. You were also the keynote speaker at the USC Women's Cinema Program. And, oh, here's one more. Just recently you spoke to the Women's Division of the Writers' Guild of America about the lack of female show runners."

Patricia stops reading and looks up at me. A real "gotcha" moment.

"Clearly you know how difficult it is for women to break through. What advice would you give them?"

Tony interrupts, saying, "I'm not sure Alexa can really answer that because, as she said before, when HBS producers hire directors they want experienced pros behind the camera. The way to rise through the ranks is to start on cable shows and get experience there." Tony's words are sophomoric at best. Once again, Patricia ignores him and looks to me for the answer. I find Tony's interruptions insulting, and though I'd really like to say more, I'm the good soldier and will continue to echo the company line, at least for now.

"Patricia, it's simply about hiring the right person for the job. We don't make decisions based on gender. That would be crazy. Women are a big part of the workplace now. We occupy positions of power, and we've made great strides. There may not be enough women directing TV shows, but in time, there will be. We encourage our producers to hire the best directors they can find. And each year we seem to bring more and more new ones into the fold."

Tony is beaming from ear to ear. He offers a thumbs-up when Patricia looks down at her notes. I know the lingo. I've been trained well. Stay on track. Don't rock the boat. Defend the company. Be a team player. Whatever you do, don't say what you really think. This isn't about you. It's about the company. Before Patricia has a chance for a follow-up, Rosie peeks in the door.

"I'm so sorry to interrupt, but Chester's on the phone, and you're going to have to leave soon to get to Crestview by four o'clock," she says.

Tony jumps up gleefully and escorts Patricia to the door. We say our good-byes, and Tony winks to make sure I know I did a good job. However, Patricia isn't done. She takes a business card from her purse and hands it to me.

"I sure wish we had a little more time. We were just getting into this. I'd really like to discuss this further when you have some time. Do you think we could do that? I'm writing my cell number on here in case you want to talk later." I look carefully at the card and put it in my pocket. Tony tells Patricia she doesn't have to bother me. He tells her to call him anytime. He whips out his BlackBerry and escorts her out of my office.

I return to my desk and grab the phone. Chester wants to know if I think Jerry should announce the Ivor James deal at press tour.

"Sure, Chester. That'd be fine," I say. It's really not fine at all, but what other choice do I have? "Yes, it sounds like a wonderful fix for *Money Honey*. Thank God he was able to pull this off. Yes, I agree." I hang up the phone. Once again I'm the team player, cheering on my colleague, playing the role of the company robot.

Rosie tells me that Jeremy said my car just needed a new battery and parked it in the lot. She reminds me that it's past three and that if I want to get to Crestview, I'd better hurry. I gather my things and head out.

I begin my trek over the hill into Culver City, listening to Rosie as she apprises me of the calls and meetings I missed as well as the latest gossip. But I'm distracted. I'm deep in thought, wondering why Gordon hasn't called. Was there something I said or did that turned him off? As Rosie drones on and on, I keep thinking about Saturday night and what might've been had Sylvia not left that message. I never should have kept the answering machine on. I keep coming back to the same place: I thought we had a good time. He seemed very conflicted about leaving and then said he would call. So why hasn't he? I'm beginning to wonder if he's like all the other guys I've dated.

I'm in the school's parking lot and wishing I'd remembered my flip-flops so I could change out of my heels. But I was moving too fast this morning. I take one last look in the mirror, paint on some lip gloss, brush my hair, and add some blush. I get out of the car and look toward the main office. The door's closed. Could he be gone already? It's much later than I usually arrive. I look around the parking lot for Gordon's red Alfa and don't see it anywhere. I walk across the playground, which is empty and quiet, till I come to Miss Simon's classroom.

As I enter the class, I'm surprised to see how orderly it is. There are five students quietly working at their desks. Miss Simon looks tired but happy in her blue jeans and gingham shirt. She's correcting papers at her desk, and when I approach, she nods and points to Marisol, who's reading a book at the back of the room. I tiptoe over and watch as she mouths each word, tracing it with her index finger. She lights up when she sees me.

"Marisol, it's great to see you," I say softly. "How've you been?"
"Good."

"Hey, since it's a nice day, why don't we work outside instead of going to the library?" I ask.

Marisol likes this idea, so we exit the classroom and sit down at a picnic table. Marisol places her book on top and opens it to the middle.

"Whoa," I say. "It looks like you're all the way into the fifth chapter. That's great. Did you understand what you read?"

Marisol nods.

"So tell me about the story. What's going on with Beezus and Ramona?" I ask.

"Well, Ramona has a pet lizard. His name is Ralph. But he's not real."

"So he's an imaginary friend?" I ask.

"Yup. He's like Luiza."

"Luiza? Who's that?" I ask.

"She's my girlfriend. We talk a lot when I'm cleaning the house and making dinner. And she sleeps with me, too."

"Hmm. Well, I had an imaginary friend also," I say.

"You did?" Marisol asks, looking right into my eyes.

"When I was about your age I had trouble understanding what I read sometimes, too."

I place my hand on her back and move a little closer to her.

"And do you know that I called my imaginary friend Lois?"

"That's funny. Lois and Luiza." Marisol laughs.

Just as Marisol starts to tell me how much she's starting to enjoy reading, Miss Simon appears with her purse on her shoulder and keys in hand.

"It's almost five thirty. I'm glad you got some time together, but we ought to pack up and get on home. The others have left. Marisol, I'll give you a lift. Why don't you get your backpack, and I'll meet you out here."

"OK, bye, Alexa," Marisol says as she jumps out of her seat and returns to the classroom.

"Thank you so much for taking the time to work with Marisol," Miss Simon says. "She was looking forward to seeing you today.

It's really terrific that you volunteer for this. I'm never able to give one-on-one instruction anymore. There are just too many kids." She drops her purse and reaches behind her head, tying her long, blonde, curly hair into a ponytail.

"Well, I'm happy to do it," I say. "I wish I could spend more time with her. I'm thrilled she's enjoying the book."

"Well, she even seems more confident, and it's only been a week. Imagine what it will be like in a few more. Thank you again for doing this. It means a lot."

There's a pause. Then I decide to pop the question. I figure, what the heck.

"Um, do you know if Gordon is still here? I want to let him know Marisol and I had a chance to work together today."

Marisol has returned, carrying her backpack.

"Oh, he's with Barbara. I think they went to Newport Beach for the day. Nice for them to get away, huh?" Miss Simon grabs Marisol's hand. "It was nice to see you. Have a good night." And with that she and Marisol head toward the faculty parking lot, waving good-bye.

I'm stunned. I want to say, *Who is Barbara?* But I don't want to reveal that I don't know. Instead, I call out that I'll schedule another time soon and walk to my car in the visitors' lot.

I don't know what to think or feel. But something tells me Barbara isn't Gordon's mother, sister, or dog. So that wonderful feeling isn't so wonderful anymore.

I get in the car, turn on the ignition, and just sit for a while. I feel the corners of my mouth sag as disappointment sets in.

Chapter Seven

A week has passed since I heard about Barbara, whoever she is. And nothing from Gordon. I was ready to sleep with him. And now I learn he has a girlfriend or maybe even a wife. Ack. You just never know with guys. What was I thinking? I'm still upset, but I remind myself that there will be another man. Someday. I hope.

I was hoping to tutor Marisol today. This would've been our third session. However, I can't get to Crestview this afternoon. I tell Rosie to cancel. I want to honor this commitment but I'm being pulled in every direction. I have so much on my plate. Especially now. Yet I really enjoy the time I spend with Marisol. It's meaningful and gives me a better perspective on life. Gordon was right. It reminds me the world isn't just about winning time slots and killing the competition. Although today that message will once again be heard loud and clear. The press conference Chester arranged for Jerry to announce Ivor James's first interview takes place in one hour on Stage 19 on the HBS lot. Stage 19 is where *The Virgin Wife* is filmed. One soap opera replacing another.

I pull into the parking lot, grab my stuff, flash my badge, and head to the entrance. As I enter the lobby, I see a flurry of activity. There are several reporters and camera crews. They're whisked through security and on their way to the stage. No one seems to know what this is all about. It's been a well-kept secret.

I cross the lobby toward the elevator bank, where I see Chester and Barnsworth waiting. As I approach them, Chester calls out to me.

"Hey, Alexa, you remember Mr. Barnsworth," he says.

"Well, of course, Mr. Barnsworth, how are you?" I stop and extend my hand. "It's so nice to see you." Once again, I'm in pants and a sweater. I forgot my blazer in the car. Damn. Although I don't want to be clad in strong-shouldered 1980s pantsuits, I still believe it's important to appear professional.

"I hear you're developing some good shows," says Barnsworth.

"Oh, yes, things are going really well." I offer my loveliest saccharine smile.

This is such bullshit. But it's a typical Hollywood conversation. How are the shows? They're sensational. Everything looks good? You bet. Here's the more truthful conversation: We bought shows from good writers. We hope they'll deliver a great pilot. But who knows. What they think is great, we often think sucks. And vice versa. Will they come through? Maybe. It's a crapshoot.

But no one wants to put a negative spin on anything. We have no problems. No worries. I've often wondered how productive this is. Why not take some time and discuss the issues? Work together to solve the problems. Push the boundaries and find alternate ways of achieving different and sometimes better results. Instead the focus is always on the spin. HBS's motto should be *Truth is our enemy. Spin is our friend.*

I've never been terribly comfortable with this approach. I believe in transparency. Even if it's bad news. Let's deal with the issues, not shove them under the rug, where they'll resurface later and be much worse.

Suddenly, the elevator door opens and Chester and Mr. Barnsworth usher me in ahead of them. But I don't move.

"Um, I don't take elevators," I say, fidgeting with my purse and feeling tightness in my chest. "Actually, I take the stairs. For exercise. You know, to get a little aerobic activity."

And then, just as I open the door to the stairwell, who should appear but Jerry. He flies through the entryway to the elevator bank, screaming to hold it open so he doesn't have to wait for another one. And to his surprise, there's his hero, Mr. Barnsworth.

"Hey, Mr. B, great to see you," he exclaims. "Are you here for the big announcement today?" Jerry leaps inside the elevator and presses a button. As the door closes, I hear, "I think I might've single-handedly saved the sweeps for HBS." They disappear, and I wish I could, too.

I drag myself up the stairs, berating myself with each step. When I reach the third floor, I open the door and see the backs of Barnsworth, Chester, and Jerry as they make their way down the hall toward Chester's office. I should be part of that group. This is how my phobia inhibits my ability to succeed. If I'd been able to handle a three-story elevator ride, it would've been me, Chester, and Barnsworth. Jerry wouldn't be in the picture. I just gave him an opportunity to best me again. I skulk down the hallway and enter my office suite.

"Are you going down to the press conference?" Rosie asks as I shuffle through the suite into my office.

"No. I don't really want to be there. I'll watch it on the monitor."

Rosie is silent. She watches as I toss my bags on the couch and flop down next to them.

"Is something wrong?" she asks.

"No. I don't want to get into it. I just want to sit here and die for a while."

"Why would you agree to let Jerry get up there? What do you think that suggests?"

"I know what you're thinking, Rosie. But honestly, it's a show that he brought in. Chester wants him to announce it."

"You need to be there. You should go to the stage and watch. You need to be seen by your colleagues and the press," says Rosie.

She's not wrong. I wish I could always do the right thing. I wish I could please everyone and meet all their expectations. I wish I could be the perfect executive all the time. But I can't. I'm not perfect. And frankly, I feel like crap, hating myself for not being able to get in that stupid elevator.

Rosie gives up and leaves my office. I turn on the TV and select the in-house feed so I can see what's happening on the stage. Stage 19 has been altered to look like a theater. There's a platform with four brown upholstered chairs sitting side by side on a beige rug. Below it are about five rows of seats from one end of the platform to the other. About twenty seats per row. Suddenly I hear ambient sound. It appears to be the settling of the audience, which is not visible on the monitor. There's a one-camera perspective. We, the viewers, watch the chairs on stage through the eyes of someone in the audience.

After a while, Rosie pokes her head through my door holding a bowl of freshly made microwave popcorn. The aroma is intoxicating.

"C'mon in," I say.

"I thought this might come in handy." Rosie laughs as she sets the bowl on my coffee table in front of the TV.

"Ah, the perfect complement to M&M's," I say. "Chocolate and salt. OK, now I'm ready to watch the show."

Rosie turns up the volume and then sits next to me on the couch. We both cast our eyes on the screen as we gobble down the treats. The stage manager counts down, three, two, one, and then suddenly the lights go on, the stage is lit, and Barnsworth, Chester, and Jerry walk up to the platform and take their seats. Tony stands in front of them on stage at a small podium. It's interesting that his BlackBerry is nowhere to be seen. I think it must take a vacation when he's around Chester and Barnsworth.

"OK, we're going to begin," Tony says, trying to quell the commotion. "As you know, we have an announcement to make today. I think you'll find it very interesting."

Tony's trying to titillate the audience. However, this is an audience of cynical reporters who cover entertainment for TV and print. They never think anything is as big as we make it out to be. That's because we live in the world of spin, and the press wants to know the truth. They'll decide what to write and how to spin it for their own purposes. Tony wants to gain control of this unruly group, who want to know why the heck they're there. From what I can tell, none have a clue this is about Ivor James.

"Chester, there are rumors that you're gonna step down and have someone else run entertainment. Is that true?" asks a reporter from the *Los Angeles Times* who's in the audience. It's suddenly quiet. No one ever thought he would actually step down. So we're all anxious to hear his answer. Chester's none too pleased that he's suddenly on the hot seat. Reporters don't care. They ask what they want, often making TV executives who only function in well-controlled circumstances uneasy.

"I'm not stepping down, John. But yes, I want to hand that position to someone else. Mr. Barnsworth and I think it's time I take on more global responsibilities and have someone else oversee and manage day-to-day programming." I'm sure Chester's desperate for a cigarette. Tony, who moved aside while Chester was speaking, takes center stage.

"Well, who will take on that role?" asks the reporter again, not letting this go so easily.

"Not sure yet. That's something we're handling internally. As soon as we know, you'll know."

"We've heard rumors it might go to one of your lieutenants, Alexa Ross or Jasper Jarosz," interrupts a journalist from the *Los Angeles Business Journal*.

Chester is taken aback. Before he attempts an answer, Tony finally does his job and takes control. "Hey, I don't think anyone is interested in the personnel issues at HBS. I think it's our programs the world wants to know about. So, without further ado, I'd like to introduce Jerry Kellner, who is the director of comedy at HBS. He's going to tell you about an important addition to our lineup, which will debut in the November sweeps."

"Did you cancel *Money Honey* because of the scandal between the two leads, or was it just bad ratings?" interrupts someone from *LA Weekly*.

As silly as it sounds, this is a common question. I wish someone would say no, it wasn't due to the abysmal ratings. We here at HBS thrive on bad ratings. We love waking up to bad ratings. Who cares that we killed ourselves for that show and it tanked last night. We love the looks we get from our colleagues who want to kill us. We particularly enjoy a bad day all around. Why would we cancel a show with bad ratings?

"Look, we gave that show a good shot," Chester says. "We wanted it to succeed. We poured a lot of time and money into it, but unfortunately, the audience didn't respond. We had to cut our losses and move on."

Another question starts, but Tony interrupts, saying, "We're here to discuss a change in the lineup for the November sweeps, so Jerry?" Irritated, Tony looks at Jerry, who is still sitting next to Chester on the platform. "Why don't you come up and make the announcement they all want to hear?" Jerry leaps to his feet, fist bumps Tony, and takes his spot at the center of the platform.

"Hi, I'm Jerry, and I'm thrilled to be here today," he says, grinning from ear to ear. He loves this. "No, I'm not the new head of entertainment *yet*"—he laughs heartily—"but remember my name, because today I've got great news." Jerry starts walking back and forth across the stage. Like Tony Robbins, he's gesticulating and using high-pitched tones to excite and motivate his audience. He's very relaxed and excited. I can feel his adrenaline pumping.

Jerry launches into the same presentation he gave in Chester's office. "Who does everyone want to see on TV?" But this is a different audience. They're skeptical, and not nearly as desperate as we were that day.

"Michael Jackson," says one, and everyone laughs.

"Better than that," says Jerry, who won't take the bait.

"Elvis," shouts another.

"Oh, c'mon, guys. OK, I'll put you out of your misery. Ready? Drumroll, please." And sure enough there is one. After all, this *is* Hollywood. Rosie and I roll our eyes. I notice that Barnsworth is enjoying the show, happily engaged in Jerry's act.

"This better be good," shouts Jon Nuger from the *Hollywood Reporter*. "I can't think of anyone other than Ivor James, frankly, and he's in Europe right now."

And with that, Jerry points to the center aisle. The lights dim, and a dramatic single spotlight illuminates someone who enters from the back of the room and begins walking slowly down the center aisle to the platform. It is Ivor James.

Ivor is about six two, thin, with blond, disheveled hair. His beautiful blue eyes are only a memory; they're focused on the ground as he walks nervously through the crowd of reporters and cameramen, who snap photos rapidly as he goes by. Invited guests and employees take photos with their smart phones as recorders are thrust in his face. News crews turn on their lights and blind him. It's utter pandemonium. Tony and his team of publicists miraculously appear and help Ivor onto the platform. The atmosphere has turned electric. Ivor stands unsmiling beside Jerry.

He straightens his brown-and-oatmeal wool argyle vest, which he wears over a brown oxford shirt. The shirttails have come out of his khaki pants. He retucks them as Jerry drapes his arm around Ivor's shoulder like they've known each other for years. Ivor seems extremely nervous. He hasn't said a word. His eyes remain downcast. He looks like a schoolboy who's just been scolded for stealing candy. He stands still and quiet. Jerry's beaming.

"You got it, guys. Ivor James is gonna give his first big interview to HBS on Thursday, November first at nine o'clock eastern standard time, so set your DVRs. That's the first night of the November sweeps, and HBS has the interview *live*." Jerry emphasizes the word *live* so loudly his voice cracks. He squeezes Ivor's shoulder and rocks him back and forth like he's a rag doll. Ivor looks limp and anxious.

"Now it's my pleasure to introduce the greatest reporter of all time. A Peabody and multiple Emmy winner. He'll have the honor of interviewing Mr. Ivor James on Thursday the first and the following Thursday, the eighth. *Live*. Ladies and gentlemen, the incomparable Mr. Carl Sandler." Jerry shrieks his name like he's running for office. I can't believe I'm the only one who finds this nauseating. It's so over-the-top. Like a circus.

Carl Sandler, a Brian Williams look-alike, leaps onto the platform. He shakes hands with Jerry, then Barnsworth, then Chester, and finally, Ivor James. Sandler drapes his arm around Jerry and tells the audience about James's accomplishments on the baseball field. Then he talks about how his life took a terrible turn when his wife found him in bed with her best friend, which opened up a whole can of worms, and we, the viewing public, were exposed to story after story about Ivor James's descent. Carl lists all of James's indiscretions, one after the other, while Ivor stands with his hands in his pockets, looking at the ground.

He's humiliated.

I feel badly for him. He's miserable. I can't watch it anymore. I grab the remote and turn off the TV. Rosie looks at me. We both shake our heads in disbelief. Without saying a word, Rosie returns to her desk.

I walk to mine and check e-mails. I hear Rosie listening to the voice mail. I can't help but think about poor Ivor James and how he was blackmailed into this by Jerry. Another victim. It's amazing how far his tentacles reach.

To me this is the dark side. Sometimes I wonder how far we'll actually go for a rating point. If we put on a live execution we'd get huge ratings. But is it worth it? How low can we go? Where's the line? Is there one anymore?

"No one really called for you," Rosie says. "There are just a few messages for me, and, oh, Gordon Harrison from the tutoring program."

"Huh?" I'm wondering if I heard her correctly. "Gordon?" I can't believe I'm excited. I shouldn't be. I have to remember he's just another asshole.

"Yeah, he said to call when you have a chance," Rosie continues. "Oh, maybe it's because I called earlier today and canceled your tutoring session. Do you want me to call him back?"

"Well, did he call for you or me?" Now I'm confused.

"I think it was for you, but I'm happy to return the call. Are you going to the *Even Nerds Have Standards* casting session tonight? It's at Gower Studios. They think it will start around six." Rosie is standing in the doorway with her call sheet in hand.

"Well, can you find out if Gordon wants to talk to you or me?" I ask.

Rosie just stares at me.

"I don't want to call him back if he wants to discuss the tutoring session."

"Why don't I just call and see what he wants?" asks Rosie, who waits for me to answer. "Is there something else going on that I'm not aware of? Because I get the sense this is a bigger deal." Rosie's on to me. We hardly have any secrets. But I don't say anything, which reveals that yes, something *is* going on here. "OK, let me know what you want to do," Rosie says. "In the meantime, you have a pitch meeting with Molly in one hour. It's with the Ferrazzi brothers."

Do I want to talk to Gordon? Or would I rather hear whatever he has to say from Rosie? Why can't I shake this guy? God, I need to get out of here. I'm going to get some air.

"Rosie, I want to take a break. Just going downstairs to get a Diet Coke. That press conference was horrible." I want to focus on something else for a while, so I grab my purse and head out the door. "I'll go to the casting session tonight at Gower. Please have them send over the list of who'll be reading, OK?"

"OK. Also, you wanted me to remind you to grab your blazer out of the car for your meeting this afternoon."

"Oh, yes, thank you," I say as I walk out of my office and down the stairs. I approach my car and unlock the door. Someone appears from behind and places his arms around my waist. Oh God. Not now. Without turning around, I say, "Jerry, get your fucking hands off of me."

"I'm not Jerry." The second I hear that voice I know it's Gordon. I rip myself out of his grip and turn around to see his face. He's looking right into my eyes, smiling. I don't know what to think.

"My God, what're you doing here?" I ask, completely bewildered by his presence.

"I wanted to see you," Gordon says as he leans casually against my car.

"Why are you here? You never called me back after our date," I say nervously, wanting to know what the heck happened.

"I know." Gordon looks at the ground.

I feel awkward standing here, as I know my colleagues can see me from their windows above. I don't want to be watercooler gossip, so I suggest we take a ride. I tell Gordon to get in as I drive out of the lot onto a side street, where I park and turn off the engine. Gordon breaks the silence.

"I had a great time at dinner," Gordon says. "But I felt like things were moving a bit fast and thought maybe we should slow them down."

"Really? And you didn't want to share that information with me? Especially when you said you'd call?" I'm pissed. "We only had two dates. I hardly think it was moving fast."

"Oh, c'mon," Gordon says, staring at me. "You know where we were headed that night."

"I don't know what to think," I say, pausing slightly. "I don't really know you. I mean, what're you doing here? Are you stalking me? How'd you know I'd even be getting something out of my car? It's kind of freaky, you know?"

Gordon moves toward me. He takes my hand in his. His eyes look sad.

"I'm sorry if I hurt you," he says softly. "I understand that you're confused and may not trust me. But I really like you. I had a long relationship that didn't work out. And, well, I know I've handled this poorly. I don't expect you to really understand."

"Who's Barbara?" I ask, unable to hold it in any longer.

"My boss, Barbara Kenfield." Gordon's confused. "She runs the Kenfield tutoring program. Why do you ask?"

"Do you have a thing for her?"

"For Barbara?" Gordon laughs. "Are you kidding? She's married with grown kids. Why would you ever ask that?" Gordon's perplexed, and I'm relieved. I shrug. Boy, did I miss that one. "There's one other thing," Gordon says.

Oh God, there's more?

"Once I realized this could get serious, I felt uncomfortable dating you because you're a volunteer with the Kenfield program.

I had to check to see if it's OK to go out with a coworker. It took some time to get an answer."

I'm starting to get the picture. There's a long pause as Gordon looks at me, waiting for a reaction. I take some time and then turn toward him.

"I like you," I say, looking squarely into his clear blue eyes. "I missed seeing you and was really disappointed you didn't call me."

We hold each other's gaze, aware of the strong chemistry between us. I look down at Gordon's hand, which is now on top of mine, resting on the center console between us. It bears traces of the world he lives in. There are paper cuts, pen marks, and a blue Band-Aid with white stars on it. He has long fingers, short nails, the perfect amount of light-brown hair on his knuckles, and a few light freckles. While I contemplate Gordon's hand, I think about the tutoring program and how much I enjoy spending time with Marisol.

"I want to stick with tutoring," I say. "But sometimes things get crazy here, like today. Will you make sure Marisol understands? I don't ever want her to think she's unimportant. I really like her, and I know we can work well together."

"I think you're a great match," Gordon says as he brings his hand to my face and softly brushes my cheek. "I'll definitely tell her how much you value your time with her. So will you give me another chance?" Gordon's fingertips linger at my cheek.

I nod and smile as he gently takes my hand in his and brings it up to his lips.

He kisses the back of my hand before releasing it. "Can I take you to dinner tonight?"

"That would be nice. I'd like that," I say. "Oh, but I have a casting session at six, so I can't get there till about eight. I'd really like to see you, though. Could that work?"

We agree to meet at Jar, a restaurant on Melrose I haven't been to in ages. I start my car and head back to HBS. I have just five minutes to spare before my pitch meeting.

I drop Gordon off outside the HBS parking lot; his car is on the street.

"Hey, how'd you know I'd be getting something out of my car at that precise moment?"

Gordon ducks down to talk to me through the passenger window.

"Just a lucky guess." Gordon smiles then taps twice on the top of my car and races across the street to his Alfa.

When I return to my office I see Rosie sitting quietly at her desk. She looks like the cat that ate the canary. Then it occurs to me. Rosie. She must've told Gordon to come by. Soon, she's in my office with her call sheet. She starts going over the ones I missed and preps me for my pitch meeting. Suddenly she stops. I look up, and she bursts out laughing. I do, too. Rosie and I can communicate without saying one word. She does know me well. Really well. Here I thought she hadn't a clue about my feelings for Gordon and it turns out she's known all along. After a moment of levity, we pull ourselves together and then, without missing a beat, we put on our work faces and it's business as usual.

My day rips by. I fly from one meeting to the next, trying to stay on time and in the moment. At five thirty, I head off to the casting session, which I hope goes by fast because I'm looking forward to dinner with Gordon.

We have a great session, which actually starts on time and allows me to get out of there and arrive at Jar at exactly eight o'clock. Gordon pulls up behind me. After some discussion, we decide it might be better to grab some food at Bristol Farms and make dinner in my apartment.

Joe isn't thrilled to see Gordon again. But Gordon came prepared. He purchased some dog treats to bribe his way into Joe's heart. It seems to work, as Joe's willing to share his woman this evening. No peeing on Gordon, and no hogging the couch.

But Gordon and I never move from my kitchen table. We talk about anything and everything for a very long time. Our conversation drifts from our families and friends to the unrest in the Middle East. We discover we have the same aversion to spinach and love chocolate. Although me more than him.

"You're a little monster," I laugh. "I can't believe it."

"I love Lady Gaga. I've even traveled abroad to catch a concert. OK, so tell me something I'd never guess about you."

I look up at the ceiling trying to come up with something equally as shocking. "You'll never believe this, but I know who won the World Series last year," I say.

"OK. Bring it on."

"St. Louis Cardinals," I say proudly.

"Whoa!"

"They beat the Texas Rangers."

"That's huge. How could you possibly know this?" Gordon is dripping with sarcasm.

I ease back into my chair and notice the crescent moon in the upper edge of my kitchen window. I quietly exhale and bite my lips to keep from smiling.

"My Aunt Nellie lives in St. Louis. She sent me a World Series hat, which comes in handy on bad hair days."

"I have an Aunt Nellie also. What're the odds?"

We discover that we love reading anything by Dave Eggers and are shamelessly addicted to *Angry Birds*. We'll never part with our Kindles, although Gordon often misplaces his. He prefers the aisle, while I like the window. But neither of us can get over the fact that I live with Joe and he lives with Josephine. However, Josephine, his black Lab, could eat my little Joe for dinner. So we decide to postpone the introduction. But it reminds me that we once had a black

Lab also. I go to the living room and return with a photo album and start looking for a photograph of that dog.

"This is a really nice picture," Gordon says, pointing to one where I'm standing in front of my parents outside our home in Chicago.

"Yeah, I must've been around eight years old," I say, recalling good memories of those times.

"Your dad looks so young there. How old did you say you were when he died?"

"I was just seventeen."

"I'm sorry."

"It's OK," I say, trying to lighten the mood. "It was many years ago."

"Yeah, but not something you ever get over," Gordon says as he brushes the back of his hand against my cheek.

"He died of a heart attack," I say, thinking it might be safe to share what happened. It's not something I feel comfortable talking about, and certainly not with just anyone. But Gordon's exquisite, soft blue eyes are fixed on mine and seem to suggest that he's waiting for more.

"My dad had just pulled his car into the driveway after a routine errand on a bright and beautiful Saturday morning," I say, taking a deep breath. "My mom was in the backyard, planting pansies, and I was in my room talking on the phone to my best friend, Elyse Field. Suddenly there was loud banging on our front door and two men yelling for my mom. I heard her come barreling through the house. I quickly hung up the phone. We ran to the door, and one of the men grabbed my mom's hand and pulled her to the driveway, where my dad lay motionless on the ground. Another man was pumping his chest while another yelled to the neighbor to call nine one one."

I stop for a moment as Gordon reaches for my hand, clutching it tightly in his.

"My mom knelt beside my dad, and I noticed a small brown paper sack next to his hand. I guess it was from his errand that morning. I moved closer to my mom, who was sobbing on my dad's chest, but Mrs. Raskin, an elderly neighbor from across the street, came running over and pulled me away."

I release my hand from Gordon's and get up from the table to get some water.

"Do you want something?" I ask, grabbing a bottle of Evian from the fridge, but Gordon shakes his head. I take a big gulp, lean against the refrigerator door, and notice that Gordon's eyes have not left me for one second.

"My parents were surrounded by firemen and police," I continue, recalling that image so vividly. "Mrs. Raskin draped her arms around me and walked me across the street to her house. I can still hear the sound of my mom crying in the distance. They got into the ambulance. I thought my dad would be OK. But he wasn't. Later that day, my mom returned. And in the small bedroom in the back of Mrs. Raskin's little yellow house, my mom told me my dad had passed."

"I'm so sorry, Lex," Gordon says softly as he reaches for me to sit back down at the table beside him. He moves his chair close to mine and pulls me close. My head rests on his shoulder, and I can feel his chest rise and recede with every breath. "It must be extremely painful to lose your dad at such a young age," Gordon says as he strokes my hair soothingly. "I can't imagine what that would be like."

He holds me as we sit silently, taking in the enormity of that memory. I forgot how wonderful it is to have a guy hold me. Just being engulfed in his arms. Just being held. I cherish this moment. I wish we could sit like this forever. I wish we didn't have to be someplace tomorrow. But it's now eleven thirty and we're both fighting to stay awake. We're dead tired.

Gordon says he has to get up early. He's yawning. I'm barely able to keep my eyes open. I walk him to the door. We stand for a moment, staring into each other's eyes. Gordon cups my face in his hands.

"You're very special, Lex. A beautiful girl both inside and out. But mostly I'm intrigued with your tenacity and ability to power through tough times. I don't think you realize just how strong you really are. You definitely inspire me." Gordon smiles. "In more ways than one."

Then he slowly puts his mouth on mine. He wraps his arms around me. I can feel his heart beating against my chest.

"I was so excited to see you today," I whisper. "I'm so glad you came over."

"And I'm pretty excited to be with you now," he teases. "As you can probably tell."

"I can tell, and frankly, it's kinda sexy."

Gordon places his right hand behind my ear and runs his fingers through my hair. His eyes are firmly fixed on mine. With his left hand, he gently unbuttons the top three buttons of my silk blouse. I feel the softness of his lips as they lightly graze down my neck. My eyes close as I start to give in to him.

"I love the way you make me feel." His voice is steady and soft, his lips now very close to my ear.

And then I'm literally swept off my feet as he carries me into the bedroom.

After an extraordinary night of lovemaking, we finally catch our breath and stare deeply into each other's eyes. It's really late. But I've totally lost track of time. I'm lying in bed beside Gordon hoping this night will never end. Gordon reaches behind my neck with his right hand, bringing my face close to his. He offers a long and deeply passionate kiss, arousing my whole body all over again. I'm absolutely blown away by his unselfish and sensuous manner.

When his eyes close and I hear the sounds of him drifting off to sleep, I stare at the ceiling above and smile.

Gordon has to be at Crestview at the ungodly hour of seven thirty in the morning to greet his sixth-grade social studies class. Gordon and I stand in the hallway, wiped out and tired, but promise to see each other as soon as our schedules permit. We embrace and kiss good-bye. I watch as he skips down the steps to his car and hope this isn't the last time I'll see him.

I shower, get dressed, and jump in my car to start the morning drive to HBS. As usual and right on time, the phone rings. I adjust my Bluetooth and say my usual good morning to Rosie, only to hear Gordon's voice.

"I had a great night. I hope you did, too."

"I did. It was fantastic," I say happily. "I'm so glad you called."

"Do you know that lyric, *I want to be your favorite hello and your hardest good-bye*?" Gordon asks.

"No, I don't. But I like it."

"It's from a song," he says. "I can't recall the name of it. But I remember hearing it and thinking, *I wonder if I'll ever feel that way about someone*. It's how I feel about you. I miss you already, sweetheart. Have a good day. Let's check in later."

I can't wait to check in later. In fact, I wish later was right now. Why do I have to wait till later? And then just as I take a breath, relax, and think about my awesome time with Gordon, the phone rings again. Oh, please be Gordon. But it's not. The caller ID indicates it's Rosie. Oh God, can't I get a break? I just want to reflect on last night and go over every detail. I want to lose myself dreaming about every single thing that happened and replay it in slow motion. I don't want to think about work. Or HBS. Or Jerry. I just want to bathe in the pleasure of my night with Gordon. I'm truly falling for him. Something I promised myself I'd never do.

"Alexa, you need to get to *The Candy Stripers* set," Rosie says. "There are standards issues, and the writers won't back off. Richard said he needs you in the writers' room ASAP."

It's highly unusual for a network executive to be in the writers' room of a comedy show. It's the place where the great creative minds exchange hysterical jokes, each trying desperately to top the previous one. The bigger the laugh, the better the rating. If I'm called over there, something's really wrong.

The Candy Stripers is a half-hour comedy set in 1965, featuring four young female hospital workers who share an apartment in New York City. On the heels of the successful TV series *Mad Men*, we thought a comedic approach to this era in a medical setting might be unique and worth trying on HBS. It's holding its own, which is a lot more than I can say for some of the other shows.

Jack Fickinger and Brian Sanderson are the head writers. They had a long and illustrious career writing jokes for *The Daily Show* and *The Simpsons*. They created this show and pitched it to Molly and me. I bought it in the room, and we worked together to get it on the air. But this was no easy task, as Jack and Brian are two macho guys who have little understanding of female sensibilities. It's been a real struggle trying to get them to appreciate that women and men don't always enjoy the same humor. And there's only one female writer on this staff, someone I practically had to force down their throats. I thought it was important to have a female perspective, as the show is about and for women.

I'm driving onto the Fox lot, entering the guard gate just off Pico Boulevard in West Los Angeles. I'm a zillion miles away from HBS, which is on the other side of town, in the Valley. I give my name and driver's license to the guard, who makes sure I'm not a terrorist. He checks my trunk for explosives, then lets me pass through to the parking garage.

I park my car on the rooftop, as there isn't a space anywhere. I walk down six flights of stairs, dreading the climb back up.

I worked on this lot when Jerry was promoted to director of drama at Fox Studios. This is also where he fired me. Suffice to say, I don't have an affinity for this place. But I know my way around because I did many an errand for Jerry, especially commissary runs.

"Make sure you get the Chinese chicken salad with dressing on the side," Jerry shouts as I begin my journey to the commissary across the lot. "I want the chicken chopped coarsely, not finely. Last time you screwed that up. And make sure to get a French roll, not sourdough."

"I've got the order, Jer. It's the same thing every day." I roll my eyes.

"Well, then why is it always fucked up?"

I'm almost at Bungalow 34, *The Candy Stripers* writers' offices. As I approach the front door I hear a lot of laughter, commotion, and rowdy behavior. When I enter, a basketball flies in my face. I instinctively swat it away and come inside.

"Hey, Alexa, how ya doing?" says Jack Fickinger as he runs after the ball, which lands under the empty reception desk just off the entryway. To my left is a big conference room with a brown Formica conference table that seats about fifteen. A TV set hangs from the wall on one side of the room, and a huge white grease board is on the other. There are multicolored index cards taped beside the board, along with quotations, clippings, cartoons, and letters, both formal and informal. There's a small typing table in the corner with a desktop computer and tons of yellow Post-it notes stuck to the wall above it.

On the other side of the room is a square card table. Every kind of junk food imaginable sits on top. It's stacked high with Ding-Dongs, Wheat Thins, Oreos, Cheetos, and Red Vines. On the shelf above is a microwave oven that's seen better days, a coffeepot that should've been thrown out years ago, napkins stolen from Starbucks, used coffee cups, straws, and some already chewed gum. It looks like something out of *The Hangover*.

Gathered around the table are eight people dressed in shorts, jeans, T-shirts, and hoodies. Everyone looks the same. They're all white. They're all men. They're all in their twenties or thirties. If you didn't know they were big-time comedy writers making a shitload of money, you'd think they were a bunch of nerdy college boys. They could easily be the guys in a Judd Apatow movie who sit home and jerk off to Megan Fox. Not handsome. Not sexy. Not fuckable.

Sophie Lavie, an attractive young woman in her twenties, is the writers' assistant. She sits at the typing table, taking down every single solitary word that's uttered in the room so there's a record of all the jokes that were tossed around. There's only one other female, sitting at the opposite end of the table. Merisa Newman, the lone female writer on this staff. And so far she's written the best first draft this season. She sits at the far end of the table in *The Hangover* corner.

Because it's Wednesday and *The Candy Stripers* shoots on Friday, the first run-through of this week's episode will be this afternoon. The writers are finalizing the script, making changes and revising the story.

I turn off my phone and enter the writers' room. Everyone is glaring at me. Comedy writers don't pull any punches. They don't like suits, and they sure don't like our notes. Frankly, I don't really want to be here either.

"So tell me what's going on," I say, taking off my jacket and draping it across the back of the chair.

"Your idiot standards guy wants us to take out a urine joke," Jack barks. "He thinks it's too crude for network TV."

At that moment, Richard Stevenson, who is the vice president of broadcast standards for HBS, enters the room. He's tall, soft-spoken, and impeccably dressed in a black-and-white tweed blazer, white oxford shirt, finely pressed dark jeans, and what look like Cole Haan loafers. Richard is a clotheshorse. He enjoys shopping and fashion. He and his partner live in West Hollywood and know all the best restaurants. He's polite, professional, and picky. He takes a seat across from me and next to Jack and Brian, the head writers. The four of us sit at one end of the table while the rest of the writing staff is at the other.

"Sorry you had to come here today, but we can't seem to come to an agreement," Richard says, biting his lip and pulling his cuffs forward. Richard decides what's acceptable and what isn't. He has to be sure nothing in our programs will upset the advertisers, who don't want to offend their customers. He may have the worst job at HBS, always being the bad guy. "The joke at the end of the first scene features the main character's boyfriend urinating on the floor. We could risk advertiser defection if we go ahead with this."

"You have a character urinating on the stage?" I ask incredulously. "I don't recall reading that in the script."

"We added it last night," Jack admits. "We think it's integral to the story and feel strongly about keeping it in. It's a setup for a joke later on. I don't see what the big deal is." The other writers all nod their heads in unison.

"Are you suggesting that your main character take out his penis and urinate right there on the stage?" I ask. "Are you kidding?"

"Well, our lead actress could piss on his head, which could be pretty funny, too," adds Hank. "Give him a golden shower!" Everyone finds this hilarious except Richard and me.

The guys are laughing themselves silly while more ridiculous ideas are tossed around. Richard's phone rings. He steps out of the room to take the call. Probably dealing with another crazy request on a different show. As Richard exits, he reminds me of the issue we had on last week's show when one of the actresses wore a really low-cut shirt so the men could play a game of boobsketball.

"Hey, I remember when I was at camp in the Catskills and this girl went off into the bushes," Brian says. "We were screaming, 'Show us your tits,' but then suddenly we see her squatting down and a string's dangling from her ass. Was pretty gross. Hey, we could add something like that in the second act, ya know? I'd love to see the string dangling. That'd be great."

"Uh, let's go back to the first scene and an actor urinating on stage," I say, trying to stay on topic. "I'm not sure we want to do this. Richard's right. We're going to get plenty of flack from advertisers. Isn't there some other way you could get to the joke you need at the end?"

"How about if she has sex with her dog?" asks another writer I've known for years who's particularly nasty and hostile toward executives. "Would you suits prefer that?"

"I'm not sure why we'd ever prefer that," I say, gritting my teeth and wondering why in the world he would even say such a thing.

"Look, the guy's a poontang magnet," Jack says. "We pay it off later. It's not like last week's episode, where they have sex and he pulls out, leaving her coated in population piss. This is no big deal. You guys are freaked out over nothing."

Brian throws the basketball that almost knocked me in the face at one of the guys, who isn't expecting it, and it bops him right in the nose. The guys think this is exceptionally funny. They're howling with laughter. One guy grabs the ball and slams it into Brian, who catches it expertly, then sticks his tongue out at him.

"She oughtta play the skin flute," another one laughs.

"Hey, baby, does that get you wet?" asks Brian, who directs his question at Sophie. She ignores him and keeps typing while Richard returns to the room, taking his seat at the table.

"Hey, how's my cootchie catcher?" shouts one of the guys, who grabs the ball and slams it across the room, almost striking Jack in the head, but Jack isn't the least bit fazed and instead offers him a thumbs-up.

"That's two more fuck points!" someone shouts from the other side of the room.

I'm stunned at the offensive nature of this conversation. As I listen to these so-called hilarious suggestions I wonder if this is an opportunity for emotionally stunted men to get a rise out of the few women in the room—or to mentally masturbate with like-minded men.

My eyes wander to the lone female writer at the end of the table, who feigns a laugh. She's trying to stay connected to this fraternity party. I glance at Sophie, the writers' assistant, who is rigidly focused on her computer. She's used to this. She types furiously, trying to keep up with the latest joke in case she's asked to recall what was discussed a second or two ago.

"You suits just kill jokes," says Jack as he gets up from the table to retrieve the ball, which lands near the door. "This is fun-neee. Do advertisers want ratings? If they want ratings, you go with funny. I'm sick of these stupid arguments."

I get up to leave. But before I go, I say, "Guys, you're not gonna have an actor urinating onstage. It's not happening. It's not funny. It'll be cut out of the show. Figure something else out." I start to exit and hear, "What a fucking cunt," as I walk out the door.

"Thanks for coming over, Alexa," Richard says, standing on the steps outside the bungalow.

I stop and look back at him.

"It wasn't even funny, Richard. It was gross. It was adolescent boy humor. We're doing shows for a broad adult audience."

I turn and start walking toward the parking structure.

"Alexa," Richard shouts. "I got a call while you were with the guys. The actor is going to urinate on the stage as planned. Jerry Kellner told Brian he would make it happen. He said it's drop-dead funny and not to listen to you."

"Oh, really?" I turn around again and look directly at Richard. I'm furious. "And when did Jerry become the head of comedy?"

"About two hours ago," says Jerry as he skips alongside me. I'm stunned to see him suddenly appear next to me.

"What're you doing here?" I ask.

"I told you I'd have your job in six months. Except I was wrong. I got it in just under six weeks."

He's grinning.

"Eat me!" he shouts.

Jerry races past me up the steps into the bungalow, where he's received like a conquering hero with loud applause and hugs from all the writers inside.

Chapter Eight

"Jerry just got to you first," says Chester as I struggle to attach the Bluetooth to my ear, almost colliding into a Dodge van as I make a right turn out of the Fox lot into traffic. "I called earlier, but your phone was turned off."

I'm exploding with anger, flooring the accelerator, but my Prius can barely get up the modest incline. I take a deep breath and give Chester the opportunity to explain.

"Since you both want the top post, I think it's time for Jerry to take on a more responsible position. He's going to run comedy and you're going to run drama. You would both need experience in these areas to effectively oversee all of programming."

I'm livid, but I have to calm down. "Chester, I chose the comedy scripts that are being developed now, which I intend to read over Christmas break. Then I'll decide which ones to recommend to you. I'm very familiar with the writers and their concepts. Do you really think this is the best time to make a move like this?"

"Maybe not." Chester seems to be genuinely contemplating the idea.

"Jerry doesn't even know the comedy writers, and I haven't worked in drama in years. There's going to be a steep learning curve for both of us." I'm exasperated trying to get Chester to understand the ramifications of this decision. "It's going to be a game of catch-up, Chester, and we're right smack in the middle of development season. And wait a second, what about Jasper, who is currently the head of drama?"

"Oh, I had to let Jasper go. I'd like Molly to work with Jerry in comedy, and you can decide whether you want to keep the gal who worked with Jasper."

"I just think it's a mistake, Chester," I say.

"Honestly, Lex, Jerry had a competing offer. He brought in two terrific shows, the Ivor James interview and the Vince Vaughn comedy special. I had to promote him. You have to admit he's doing an outstanding job."

Yeah, sure, I have to admit it. I hear Chester take a hit on his cigarette.

"Jerry had the leverage. He wanted to head comedy," Chester adds.

"I haven't been in dramatic programming in years. I don't even know who the key players are anymore."

There's a long pause. I feel sick and worried. I sure wasn't expecting this.

"Jerry is out there," Chester says. "He knows a lot of folks. He's the consummate salesman, and we need him at the network. I didn't want to lose him. He's a good piece of manpower."

Yup, manpower.

"OK," I sigh. "I'm sorry it didn't work out with Jasper."

"Oh, he'll be fine. He's gonna be president of Straus Enterprises, which does reality programming." Suddenly I hear Chester's assistant come on the line. She tells Chester he has another call. The discussion is over.

This is how Hollywood works. Jerry hustles an offer so he can better his position. Chester needs to keep Jerry. The loser, Jasper, gets ousted. But Chester's friend hires him. So, Jasper enjoys a soft landing and fails upward. The Peter Principle at work.

So Jerry gets my job, and with it, all my good comedy development. He also gets Molly, who will make sure it all stays on track. I inherit Jasper's drama development, which is less than stellar. Jerry will skate through with a few rough spots, and I'll work my ass off to make sure the drama development is competitive with my old comedy development. I'll be competing against myself. But hey, everybody's happy. Everyone wins.

This couldn't come at a worse time. We're about to go into the holiday season, when everyone leaves town. I'll need to get new drama scripts into development and rush them along. Jasper's never had a winning drama season. That puts more pressure on me to find good ideas and great writers. So much for downtime.

Despite the fact that Gordon lives and works on the other side of town, we've enjoyed most evenings together. It's been a whirlwind two months, and now Christmas is right around the corner. We may get out of town for a few days, but right now I'm happy to be home and not have any calls, meetings, or drama for a while because January is the beginning of the most dreaded time in TV land: pilot season.

Thanks to Jerry, HBS did, in fact, win the November sweeps. The first time in five years. Ivor James's interview went through the roof and was followed up by a great live comedy special featuring Vince Vaughn. Two tremendous shows that resonated with the viewers and the guys in charge. Jerry is more than a mere executive these days. He's a superhero.

Everything shuts down tomorrow, the last Friday before the holidays. No one will be back until January sixth, and even then, it will take a week before the engines are at full speed. Jerry and his family are vacationing in Costa Rica, far away from here. Rosie is off to Florida. Chester's skiing in Aspen.

I'm taking the day off. The first time in a year. Instead of rushing across town to Crestview Elementary, I enjoy a leisurely drive. I stop at Starbucks and pick up a latte. No calls. No Rosie. No Jerry. And later today, my best pal, Emily, and I will have lunch.

I want to see Marisol one last time before the holiday. She seems far more comfortable with me, although she's not fond of the fact that tutoring sometimes takes place during recess, which she really misses. I get that. But she's making good progress. Today I'm bringing my favorite Beverly Cleary book, *Ramona the Brave*, which I managed to find used at an online bookstore.

I'm wearing jeans and a sweater along with my Jack Purcell sneakers so I can sprint across the playground to where I see Marisol waiting in her usual spot on the beige wooden bench outside the library. It's so great to feel relaxed and comfortable. Marisol is with Olga Hernandez, her best friend. When they see me approach, Olga leaves but waves a friendly hello as I come toward them.

"Hey, Marisol. How ya doing?" I ask as I sit down beside her on the bench.

"OK."

"You know, it's almost Christmas. Do you have a tree?" I ask. Marisol shrugs.

"Well, I brought you something for Christmas," I say as I take out a gift that's wrapped in a pretty pink ribbon with Marisol's name on the front. Marisol rips it open.

"Ramona." Marisol smiles.

"That's right. This is called *Ramona the Brave*. She reminds me of you, Marisol. Because she's got spunk. Do you know what that means?"

Marisol shakes her head.

"It means she has courage, she has nerve, she's determined." I clench my fists, emphasizing my point.

Marisol laughs.

"I think you have that, Marisol. I think you're trying really hard to learn English. And that takes a lot of work. I know it's difficult for you," I add.

I drape my arm around Marisol's shoulder and pull her close. It's chilly out. But she seems comfortable in her short-sleeved top. I wonder about her family. Where do they live? What is life like with nine brothers and sisters? What will she make for dinner tonight? Does she ever get new clothes or just hand-me-downs? I wish I could take her shopping and out for a nice meal, just one time. But it's against the program's rules. Gordon nearly bolted out of his chair when I begged him to let me do it.

Marisol and I talk about her other classes, and she asks for help with a math assignment, which I'm only too happy to do until I discover it's identifying x-y coordinates on a graph, which takes me a while to figure out. When in the world will she ever need to know this?

"Will you be here next week?" Marisol asks.

"No, not next week. Next week is Christmas. You'll be on Christmas vacation. At home with your family. Won't that be fun?"

Marisol says nothing, just shrugs. I can't seem to get her to talk much about her family.

"I'll be back in January. That's not far away," I say reassuringly. "How about reading this new book I got you?"

Marisol nods and we open the book to page one. Just as we begin, Gordon appears.

"Hey, my two favorite girls. How're you doing, Marisol? I heard you weren't in school this week but came back today. Was that to see Alexa?"

Marisol shakes her head, smiling broadly.

"Why weren't you in school? Were you sick?" I ask.

"No. Had to take care of babies," Marisol says.

"Oh, you had to help your mom with the younger kids?" asks Gordon.

Marisol nods.

"That's good, but I'm glad you're here today spending time with Alexa so you can get some reading done."

Marisol smiles, and I notice she's moved closer to me.

"Lex, come on over to my office before you leave," he says as he starts to walk away. I'd really like to kiss him, but we're careful not to reveal our relationship. Instead, he winks and I smile as he heads back to his office.

"Is he your boyfriend?" Marisol asks.

"Ummm…why would you ask that?"

"He likes you." She grins.

"I like him, too," I say sweetly.

Marisol cracks up, and we both laugh.

I reach into my pocket, grab my glasses, and start to read *Ramona the Brave* out loud while Marisol puts her finger under each word. She's learned to sound them out slowly. She's making progress, and I feel great. She's far more relaxed and interested in reading. We both get excited when she solves a problem. I'm so proud of what she's accomplished.

The bell rings, signaling that recess is over. Marisol jumps up.

"Hey, how about giving me a hug?" I ask.

Marisol wraps her arms around my waist and hugs me tight.

"I hope you have a really good holiday," I say as I stroke the top of her head.

"OK," Marisol says, and then releases her grip and rushes off to join Olga and her other classmates, who are heading to Miss Simon's classroom.

I approach the main office and see Gordon correcting papers in the tiny room where we first met. I walk inside, and he gently closes the door. He grabs my hand, pulls me close, and whispers in my ear.

"You're so beautiful and sexy with your glasses on. I think I need to see you every single day."

"I wouldn't mind that," I say softly as he puts his mouth on mine and starts kissing me.

"I think I'm actually wearing you down."

"It's Christmas. I'm more relaxed," I say, smiling. "Not sure it has anything to do with you, though."

"Oh, c'mon, I'm doing a good job, don'tcha think? I think I'm growing on you."

"Maybe." I won't give an inch.

"What do you mean by that?" Gordon asks.

"Oh, I'm just teasing. But I do hope you can handle me," I say, placing my arms around his neck and looking into his eyes.

"I'm not sure you give me enough credit," Gordon says as he kisses my forehead. "I don't think you're that difficult to handle. I've gotten to know you. And I know that beneath that rough and tough exterior, you're actually a very sensitive, sweet, and caring person. I know you don't love hearing that. I know you want to be like the guys, but trust me, you're not a guy."

"This is going to be a nice, relaxing two weeks," I say, releasing myself from his grip. "But then hell begins. Pilot season is treacherous. We won't be able to see each other as often."

"That's OK." Gordon makes light of it. "We'll survive."

"I'm serious," I say as I lean against the wall a few feet away, looking directly into Gordon's eyes. "I don't think you understand what's ahead for me at work. I've got to do a great job because I want to be promoted. I don't want to work for Jerry ever again. If this doesn't work out, I won't have anything to fall back on. I don't know what I'll do. I've only worked in the TV business. It's all I know. I don't do anything else, and that scares me."

Gordon sits down at the table, puts his feet on the opposite chair, and wraps his arms behind his head. But his eyes never leave mine. He just watches me intently.

"You know your life is different," I say. "You've had a lot of stability. Your parents were doctors, you have two masters degrees, and you enjoy a variety of interests."

I clear my throat and cross my arms. "I didn't have that kind of upbringing. I worry about the future. I know how things can change in a split second."

Gordon sits quietly. He's an extremely good listener, something I'm so unfamiliar with. No one really listens in my world. They all talk *at* each other. Gordon smiles as I continue to lean against the wall. He looks squarely into my eyes and waits expectantly.

"You've traveled the globe," I say wistfully. "Biking in the French countryside and volunteering to help others in places I've never even heard of. And then you donate the money you win betting on basketball games to homeless shelters. I mean, Gordon, I've never known anyone like you. You're an incredible guy. I'm just not sure I could ever do what you do."

Gordon leans forward in his chair and reaches across the table for my hand. He stays seated as I move away from the wall, uncross my arms, take his hand in mine, and sit down across from him.

"You done?" Gordon asks, squeezing my hand.

I nod.

"Our paths were different," Gordon says softly as he leans forward, still holding on to my hand. "You suffered a terrible loss when your dad died. I had a more stable upbringing. I was afforded more opportunities. I didn't have financial hardship. We haven't had the same life experiences. But that's OK. And we may have varied interests, but we share the same values, and what we don't know we can learn from each other. I don't want you to be like me. I like you for who you are, separate and apart from me. That's what's exciting about you."

Gordon kisses the top of my hand. "We'll figure it out. I'm a patient guy who thinks the world of you. I don't want to be with anyone else. I know you're going to be busy. I can handle it."

Gordon loosens his grip and is suddenly obsessed with a fly that's infiltrated his space. He sits back in his chair but is watching the fly's every move. I get up, pace back and forth, and then lean against the wall. I run my fingers through my hair and finally exhale the breath I have been holding. "OK, then, just so you know, the second January arrives, it's a nonstop roller coaster till May, when the season ends and the networks all announce their new shows for next season," I say, watching Gordon, who is fixated on the fly.

"Are you listening?" I ask, wondering why this stupid fly has his full attention. "This is really important. I want you to know how it works. I have to go to New York and present our shows to a few hundred advertisers at Carnegie Hall. I've never spoken there before. Chester's done it on his own in the past. This is my big moment. I need him to see that I can easily handle the responsibilities of the job and speak convincingly to a roomful of very skeptical executives."

"I'm listening," Gordon says as his eyes follow the fly. He grabs his clipboard, trying to figure out when to take a whack at this thing.

"I've got to read a ton of scripts over the next few weeks. Then in January I'll pick the drama pilots and recommend them to Chester. Then casting, table reads, rehearsals, shoots, dailies, rough cuts, the whole bit. And then two weeks of watching the pilots and discussing which ones will get on the air. And it culminates at the upfronts in New York. Pilot season is a killer. Are you listening?" I'm hyperventilating, my heart is racing, and I'm starting to perspire just thinking about this.

"Take a breath." Gordon smiles as he gets up from his chair and cups my face in his hands. "You love this, Lex. It's who you are. It's not like you can't handle it. This is what you live for. It's what I love about you. You're passionate about what you do. I think it's great, and I'm absolutely confident you'll pull this off successfully."

Gordon reaches for the door, and just as he opens it, the fly escapes. It'll live to see another day.

"I want you to do well," Gordon says, kissing my forehead. "If we can't be together for a while, that's OK. Let's not freak out until there's something to freak out over, OK?"

I can't get over Gordon's supportive nature and calm disposition. There's nothing I can't do, nothing I can't conquer. He's the most positive, optimistic guy I've ever met.

Just as we're about to part, my phone rings. It's Emily saying she'll be late for lunch, but to get a table. I tell her I'm on my way. The second I hang up, the phone rings again. I turn away from Gordon, as I know how much he hates the phone. He rarely uses his and almost never listens to his voice mail, which I find terribly frustrating. At least I've gotten him to text once in a while. But social media sites like Facebook, Twitter, Pinterest, and others have no place in his world. He has as much interest in them as I do in extreme cave diving in the Bahamian Islands, something Gordon has on his bucket list.

"Hey, Sylvia, what's going on?"

As I listen to her, Gordon looks at his watch and says he'd better get going. I put my hand over the receiver and tell him I'll see him later tonight. He kisses my neck and whispers, "Mmm, you smell good, baby." He throws me a kiss and leaves the room.

"Sure, I'll meet you for breakfast on the tenth," I say as I head out of Gordon's office to my car. "We have that sexual harassment seminar the next day. That oughtta be fun."

I drive quickly from Culver City to Brentwood and manage to find a parking space in front of The Daily Grill. I insert my credit card in the meter, and then make my way up the escalator through the revolving door into the restaurant. Just as I'm seated, Emily appears.

We sit across from each other at a small table for two in the corner. We quickly order so not one minute is wasted. This is a highly anticipated lunch at which we'll finally have some time to share our lives.

"I have a boyfriend, Em." I take a long sip of Diet Coke. "I really like him. He's amazing."

"I know you like him. I can tell from your e-mails. And he's now made it to boyfriend status. Hmm. Serious business." Emily smirks.

"Yes, I think we've graduated to that point."

"You're glowing. I haven't seen you this way in years. You must be having great sex," Emily says as she dumps three stevia packets into her iced tea.

"Why do you think it's just about sex?" I ask.

"Your purple thong is a dead giveaway. Saw it peeking out of your pants. You're very Monica Lewinsky, wearing dating underwear now," Emily says.

I yank on the back of my jeans and pull down my sweater, trying to hide the offensive attire.

"Actually, I wear them all the time."

"That's 'cause you're finally having sex," Emily says, smiling.

"No, I left the bikinis behind when I saw the girls wearing thongs in the locker room. I was a relic from the past," I say.

"But thongs go right up your crack," Emily whispers. "How can you stand that?"

"Hey, no VPL. You need to get out of the past. More thongs, more sex," I laugh. "And the answer is he's a great guy. Very down-to-earth, a good man."

"Why hasn't he been married?"

"He lived with a girl for eight years. They broke up two years ago."

"Do you think it's really over?" asks Emily in her typical shrinky way. Our salads arrive. Emily's has bacon, despite her asking that it not be included. But rather than making a fuss, she simply picks out the pieces and puts them on the bread plate.

"Yeah, I'm pretty sure. Gordon said he always felt like something was missing. That something just wasn't right. Later, he discovered she'd been seeing someone else for a year. Kinda shitty, huh?"

"Yeah, well, I hope he's not one of those guys who's commitment phobic now," says Emily. "It seems to be a contagious disease in LA. I can't tell you how many women enter therapy asking how to get their boyfriends to marry them."

"We'll see. He's very relaxed about everything, the complete opposite of me. But I'm intrigued with his adventurous personality. He offers a whole different perspective, which I find exciting."

"He sounds really nice, Lex. I'm glad you're happy. It would be so great if you could have a nice relationship to balance that crazy work world of yours," Emily says. "By the way, how's it going with your old boss?"

"Jerry's doing well. He sold his soul to the devil, and it keeps paying dividends. Chester made a point of telling me how valuable he is to the company. I about puked." I stab my salad with my fork.

"Oh, he'll burn out. He can't keep up the pace."

"You think? I don't know," I say. "The man wants to rule the world."

"Jerry really has a self-esteem issue. Too bad he never got any therapy."

We both laugh at the mere thought of Jerry in therapy, which would be like me in an elevator. The two don't mix.

"Just do your job. That's all you can do."

"I wish that's all it took," I say, trying to underscore the gravity of my situation. "But it's not. I have to do more than just my job. I want that promotion, Em." I sip my drink. "At least I think I do. Although sometimes I wonder if I'm cut out for this. It's really tough. And Jerry's no walk in the park."

"What does Gordon think about all this?"

"He's been great. He wants me to go after what I want. He's not the least bit threatened by me or what I do and believes I can handle all that's thrown my way. I hope I don't blow this, 'cause I'm lucky to have him in my corner."

"He's lucky," Emily interrupts. "He's dating a great girl. I only care that you're happy and that he's kind and respectful."

"I hope he hangs in with me," I say as I put down my fork and lean in toward Emily. "I'm not as comfortable in drama, so I'm gonna be stressed to the max from January to May, trying to pick the right shows and prove I deserve the promotion. It's going to be torture."

"You'll be great, Lex." Emily puts her hand over mine. "I'm proud of you. You know there will be plenty of obstacles, but you may actually become the first female president of HBS."

I take a long sip of my Diet Coke as my eyes scan the restaurant. I notice a number of men sitting together in their white shirts and black ties. Their navy-blue blazers drape across the backs of their chairs. I see only a smattering of women at those tables. I can't help but wonder, if there are so many more women in the workforce, why are so few of them at the top?

"I wanna meet Gordon," Emily says, finishing her salad and ordering a refill of iced tea. "He sounds pretty darn good. I bet your mom's happy."

"She is. Gordon and I thought we'd drive to Carmel for a few days next week so they could meet. But she just booked a flight to see my brother."

"Oh, so where are you guys planning to go instead?"

"Well, my mom offered to cancel her trip so that she could meet my soon-to-be-husband," I say, rolling my eyes. "But I managed to dissuade her of that idea. Instead she suggested we stay at her home while she's away. She'll leave the key and plenty of food for Joe, her grand-dog."

"Wow, that actually sounds great."

"It does. She's just thrilled I have a boyfriend. Finally."

"Well, in her world that's what matters." Emily smiles sweetly.

"Yes, that's important to her. But you know what's important to me?" I whisper as I lean in close to Emily and look around to make sure no one is listening.

"What's that?" Emily whispers back, angling toward, me thinking I'm about to reveal a tightly held secret.

"Sex!" I say loud enough so the men at the next table can hear. "And guess what? I'm finally having some."

Emily and I high-five as the men at the next table offer their congratulations and toast my success.

We're on our way to Carmel. Fortunately, Joe, my nine-pound tan-and-white frisky terrier, is a great traveling companion. He sleeps soundly in the backseat of my Prius as Gordon drives it along Highway One, the scenic ocean route from LA to Carmel.

The city of Carmel-by-the-Sea is situated on the Monterey Peninsula. It's famous for its artistic history, white sand beaches, upscale shopping, art galleries, great restaurants, hiking trails, and cycling. It's a quaint community with storybook architecture and hidden alleys that lead to charming shops. My mom lives a stone's throw from the center of town. It couldn't be a better location.

After a five-hour trip, with just two stops for Joe and one to satisfy my craving for a See's butterscotch square (I'm finally over the Bordeaux), Gordon drives into the city of Carmel. We travel along Ocean Avenue, which is decorated with sparkling white tea lights and holiday-themed ornaments this time of year. We slow down to admire the stone-paved alleyways, curlicue-roofed shops, art galleries, and restaurants. Some of the storefronts feature Santas, snowmen, gingerbread houses, and fireplaces. A spinning Christmas cake shaped like a carousel captures the smell of the fresh-baked goods. Soon we reach my mom's home on the corner of Junipero and Tenth Street.

Like all the homes in this area, my mom lives in what can only be described as a cottage. At just fifteen hundred square feet, it has three bedrooms and sits on a beautiful oversize corner lot. Unlike me, my mom has a natural flair for interior design. She finds items for five bucks at a flea market that look like five hundred when displayed in her home. Somehow that gene didn't make it into my pool. She meticulously remodeled this single-level home with blond hardwood floors, white walls, upscale fixtures, a chef's kitchen, stone fireplace, and four sets of French doors that lead out to a sun-filled, glorious garden, patio, and spa. My mom moved here after I left home. But I sure would've liked living here.

I take the key from the mailbox and let us inside. The second we enter we see a new white-and-gray plush dog bed. Placed at its center is a white nylon bone larger than Joe. Within seconds Joe is deeply engaged with his new toy.

"This is a really great place. I've been to Carmel a few times, but never to someone's home here. It's quite beautiful," Gordon says as he places our bags to the side and glances around the room. I head to the kitchen.

"Can I get you something to eat? My mom usually has plenty of food, especially if she knows I'm coming."

"Sure, whatever you're having is fine." Gordon steps down into the sunken living room and looks outside at the garden. I start rummaging through the kitchen cabinets.

"I'm gonna call Bay Bicycles and see about renting a couple of mountain bikes for us tomorrow morning," Gordon says.

Great. I can hardly wait. I promised Gordon we'd go on a bike ride. I sure hope it's true that one never forgets how to ride a bike, because I haven't ridden one in years. I finally find some potato chips, which seem like a good lunch. I put some in a bowl for Gordon and bring them into the living room, while I eat mine right out of the bag.

Gordon's on the phone writing down the location of the bike rental store and discussing all the gear we're going to need.

I look over at Joe, who's slobbering all over his new bone. He's euphoric.

As I munch on the chips, I peer out the window at the beautiful greenery in my mom's garden. I love seeing the rich foliage in Northern California. We have so little of it in LA. While Gordon continues his conversation with the clerk, I stroll across the room to my mom's antique pine credenza and peer at the photographs placed on top. Many are familiar pictures of my brother, his family, my dad, my mom, and myself. I notice an old framed anniversary card. It's from my grandmother to my mom. It says, *Always be kind and thoughtful to one another. Love, Mom.* I pick up the frame and examine it closely. I notice the ink is all but faded and the paper is chipped and yellowed.

"Hey, how about if we quickly unpack and then take a walk on the beach?" Gordon asks as he hangs up the phone.

"Sounds great," I say. I'm already feeling relaxed just being out of town, something I remind myself I should do more often. "But I really need to give you something. I was going to wait till Christmas. But I think I should give it to you now."

Gordon looks puzzled as I go over to my suitcase and pull out a shiny red plastic bag with a green bow that was crammed deep inside and hand it to him.

"Well, you did a pretty good job of hiding this," Gordon says as he releases the bow. He pulls a Giro Ionas bicycle helmet out of the bag. "Man. This is fantastic. It's got the wind tunnel ventilation and everything."

"I know you wanted a new one, and I heard you asking the clerk about it, so I thought I should give it to you now. And I love that it's blue and black. Very cool, don't you think?"

Gordon puts the helmet back in the bag and embraces me.

"It's very cool. Thank you. I love it. And I needed it badly. I'll think of you every time I wear it." Gordon smiles.

"I'm glad you like it," I say as I kiss him on the lips. "Now let's get unpacked and take a walk."

I make sure Joe has enough water and food, though he seems delighted to be on his bed with his new toy. He's very intense and singularly focused. He's been here several times and knows his way around, so I don't worry about leaving him alone. In fact, he probably prefers it to my apartment, as he has his own private doggie door leading to a fenced-in garden. I think he, too, will enjoy this nice vacation.

Gordon takes my hand as we leave the cottage and stroll down the hill toward Carmel River State Beach, just a few blocks away. We hear the roar of the heavy surf as we get closer.

"That is a super-fine helmet you got me. I'm very impressed," Gordon says as we wind our way past the parking lot and eventually down the stairs leading to the beach.

"Well, as dorky as it looks, I can't wait to see it on you. A regular Lance Armstrong sans the drugs."

Gordon smirks.

Carmel State Beach is a mile long with a lagoon formed by the Carmel River. It's rarely crowded here. Tourists really don't know about it, which is great for the locals. This area is an oasis of incredible beauty. Gordon and I walk hand in hand, struggling at times to navigate the rocks that line the water's edge. Finally, Gordon sees a secluded area on some rocks above the lagoon. We take off our shoes and climb on top. We're perched on a hill just above the ocean. It's positively gorgeous up here. The weather is pitch-perfect. There's a cool, comfortable breeze. We breathe in the salted scent of the crisp ocean air. Hearing the rhythmic sound of the waves crashing is soothing. We can hear the tiny bubbles of foam come up the shore and then sink back into the ocean. Barely a cloud in the sky. Christmas in Carmel.

"This is pretty darn nice. I could see myself living here," Gordon says, his hair blowing softly in the wind as he peers out at the ocean.

"It's lovely. Whenever I visit my mom I come down to this beach. I love the sound of the waves. It has such a calming effect on me."

"Well, then we may have to buy you an ocean," Gordon laughs.

"Hey, I'm relaxed, aren't I? Have you seen me look at my phone once since we arrived?"

"You haven't. You're right. I'm proud of you. We may have to come here more often," he says.

"Well, that would be great," I say as I turn toward him. "There's nowhere I'd rather be than right here with you. I don't want to think about anything else. I just want to enjoy this time away from everything." Gordon reaches for my hand as we both sit for a minute, taking in the peaceful setting and rich environment. After a moment, Gordon breaks the silence.

"I have something for you."

"You do? What?"

"Just a little gift."

"A gift?"

"Yeah. Do you think you're the only one who thought to bring a Christmas gift?"

Gordon retrieves a small box that's lodged in his jeans pocket and tries to restore the original shape of the box—the top got crushed, having been there for a while—and then hands it to me.

As I lift the top I see a beautiful, sparkling charm bracelet. I slowly bring it out of the box and let it rest in my left hand. I'm overwhelmed by the crystals, which sparkle in the sunlight.

"It's a Green Bay Packers charm bracelet," Gordon says.

"It's beautiful," I say, stunned. "Wow. I don't know what to say. Well, thank you, that's what I should say: thank you. Thank you so much. This is so generous…so kind."

"There's room for thirteen charms. I got you started with these," Gordon says as he points to each one. "A Green Bay Packers jersey, a helmet with their logo, a gold football, and a cheese-head."

I finger the bracelet's four emerald-green beads. "Are they jade?" I ask, unable to take my eyes off it for one second.

"They are," Gordon says. "I saw this bracelet in a catalog, but I wanted to create my own. So I went to a jeweler and selected the charms. I also wanted jade, because when I was in Egypt I learned jade is the stone of love, inner peace, harmony, and balance. Can I put it on you?"

"Are you kidding? Of course!"

Gordon carefully fastens one end of the bracelet to the other. It fits perfectly. I wiggle my wrist, watching as the charms dance up and down. I'm enchanted by the tinkling sound of the bracelet.

"I love this, Gordon. It's beautiful, and it's so thoughtful. I can't thank you enough. And you had it made for me. Wow."

"Can you see what's inscribed here?" Gordon asks as he points to the gold football charm. Without my glasses, I have to squint closely at the football but see the words, *It's whether you get up.* "I couldn't get the whole quote on there, so I settled for the last part."

I can't imagine how much thought and time went into this. I'm unbelievably grateful. I reach up and cup Gordon's face in my hands, and then I lean in and kiss him gently on his lips.

"I don't know what to say. I've never received anything so lovely. I'll treasure it forever," I whisper and kiss him again.

Gordon places his arm around my shoulder and pulls me close. I lean into his chest, all the while gazing at my new bracelet, which is twinkling in the sun. I admire it up close and then extend my arm and do the same from afar. Wherever it is, it looks positively stunning. The charms sparkle even brighter in the afternoon sun. I'm mesmerized.

"This is absolutely beautiful," I say, smiling broadly. "I'm never taking it off. Never. Not even in the shower or swimming or anything. You're just going to have to see it on my wrist all the time."

"I'm glad you like it," Gordon whispers. "I was hoping you would."

After a moment Gordon turns toward me and places two fingers on my cheek and runs them down the side of my neck. It sends a tingle through my whole body. He leans in close and kisses me again and again. His lips move down the side of my neck and follow the same path his fingers traced, finally ending at the first button on my blouse. I stroke the back of his head as he nuzzles at my breast. And then I bring his head back up and kiss his lips.

We both sit quietly looking out at the ocean, listening as wave after wave crashes against the rocks around us. I feel like I'm in a movie. Everything is perfect. The weather, the setting, the boyfriend, the bracelet. Life doesn't get much better than this.

"I love that you're still a Packers fan," Gordon says after a while. "It says a lot about you. It's part of why I love being with you." Gordon cradles my body in his arms.

"You're so good to me," I say, looking into his eyes. "The guys I know, the ones I'm around every day, they're just, well, you know… different."

"Yeah, well, competing with the Neanderthals you work with isn't exactly difficult," Gordon says, smiling. "And I'm sure there's at least one who'd be happy to get in your pants."

"Well, I guess I'm just plain irresistible. Hard not to love. Ya know?"

"Yup, so many things to love about you, Lex," Gordon says as he looks toward the sky, grinning and pulling me close. "Let's see. Maybe it's the Hershey wrappers all over your car. That's a really attractive habit. Or the half-empty Diet Cokes around your apartment. Or maybe it's the way you speed out of the parking lot with your purse on top of the car."

"I only did that once," I say. "And I was in a hurry. Very funny."

"You're always in a hurry." Gordon grins. "Although there's one thing I really do love, and that's the way your breasts bounce around in your black turtleneck."

"Seriously?" I say, pulling away from him. "I can't believe you said that. God. Ohhhh my God. That is so gross! My breasts do not bounce around like that. Oh man. Do they?"

"They do." Gordon laughs, but then his eyes soften when I wrap my arms around his neck, press my body against his, and kiss him tenderly. His hand runs up my thigh and bright lights prick my eyes. I feel breathless. How have I given him this power over me? After a moment he stops kissing me and gazes into my eyes.

"Maybe it's your competitive spirit," Gordon says as he takes a breath, loosens his grip, and grows more serious. "I love that you're confident, independent, and passionate about what you do. I think that's very sexy. And I like that you can be sensitive and forceful and occasionally, and I mean just occasionally, can even laugh at yourself. But I said 'occasionally,' got that?" Gordon teases as he tilts my chin up and kisses me again.

We hold each other awhile longer, watching as the sun sets over the ocean. We don't move for a long time. After a beautiful sunset we realize it's time to leave and head back to my mom's.

———

Later, we take a stroll down to the Mission Ranch Restaurant for dinner. The view from the outdoor dining room is spectacular. There are sheep grazing in the meadow, and even though the sun has set we can still see the Santa Lucia Mountains in the near distance and hear the waves crashing against the shores of Point Lobos.

"I can't stop admiring my bracelet," I say softly, reaching across the table for Gordon's hand. "You remembered what I told you about my dad...well, it just...it just blew me away."

"Of course I remembered," Gordon says as he takes a sip of wine. "And it means a lot to me that you like it."

"I love it." My eyes linger on Gordon's white oxford shirt with rolled-up sleeves, which exposes his beautiful tanned arms and just a hint of his chest. "I can't remember when I've had such a great time. I'm really enjoying this trip."

Gordon reaches for my hand, brings it to his lips, and kisses it.

"You know, earlier you said some really nice things, and I kind of wanted to return the favor," I say, feeling a little nervous and vulnerable.

"OK. And what would that be?" Gordon smiles.

"Well, I want to tell you what I enjoy about being with you. Like I love that you know the lyrics to so many songs and aren't afraid to sing them out loud."

"Well, you're getting there. I noticed you sang a few on the way up," Gordon adds.

"I love that you wanted to ask me out the second you met me," I say, taking Gordon's hand in mine. "And I'm so relieved you're not a game player. You're incredibly honest and direct. And I love that you think I'm capable of doing more than I think I can."

My voice grows more serious and soft, almost at a whisper as I lean forward across the table.

"I love watching you watch me when I enter a room. And I love that your mom taught you to believe in dreams. My world changes when I see you, Gordon."

Gordon stares at me longingly, and his eyes look warm, accepting, loving in a way I've never seen in a man's eyes before. I stare back at him, still clutching his hand in mine.

"Oh, and one more thing."

"There's more?" Gordon asks.

"Yup. I always save the best for last."

"OK. I'm waiting…"

"Being with you…you know…in bed."

"Yes…"

"It's…well, it's amazing…"

"Well, then why are we wasting time here?" Gordon laughs and reaches for his wallet to pay the bill.

As we leave the restaurant and walk back to my mom's home, I think about this romantic, picturesque town with its leaning cypress trees, oak-lined cottage-filled streets, world-renowned art galleries, and serene atmosphere. I never dreamed this place would be so romantic. In the past I'd come for the weekend, see my mom, and drive back. I was never able to fully enjoy what this city had to offer, nor was I able to share it with someone as wonderful as Gordon.

I can't remember when I've been this crazy about a guy. For the first time I'm actually thinking, is he the one? I've been resisting loving someone for so long, so afraid to get involved with anyone, so worried about getting hurt. And now I find myself caring deeply about Gordon. It's scary and yet rousing at the same time.

We barely get inside the house, and Gordon pulls me into his arms and begins kissing me passionately. He scoops me up and carries me to the bedroom. Nuzzling my neck, whispering in my ear, he makes me feel hot. Then cold. I feel my nipples rise. I feel my breath go shallow. I want him…I've never wanted anyone more.

"I couldn't wait to get you out of that restaurant," Gordon whispers. "I couldn't hang on any longer."

"I know," I say softly. "Me, too."

Gordon undresses himself. I watch. How incredibly masculine he looks. Fit. But not in a vain way. Real. Delicious. And then he lifts me gently onto the bed as I wrap my legs around his hips and we slowly begin to make love.

———

Later, unable to sleep, we turn on the TV. Strangely, we find ourselves watching *Elf*, a movie neither of us has ever seen. We laugh and sing to Leon Redbone and Zooey Deschanel's rendition of "Baby, It's Cold Outside."

"By the way, has anyone ever said you resemble Zooey Deschanel?" Gordon cracks himself up because he knows I get this all the time. But for some reason tonight I'm eager to accept the compliment.

Then Lena Horne belts out "Let it Snow," and Eartha Kitt croons "Santa Baby." It's sixty degrees, but we're snuggled up under the covers, singing our hearts out like it's thirty below.

———

The next morning we wake up bright and early. Gordon's unbelievably excited about our bike ride. I'm not. But I come around when Gordon agrees to some shopping in town after our ride. That perks me up.

The clerk at Bay Bicycles has me outfitted like a competitor in le Tour de France. I'm wearing royal-blue spandex shorts, a yellow shirt, giant helmet, and special sneakers. A bottle of water is attached to the handlebars, a protein bar Velcroed to my waist, and a light backpack sits on my shoulders. I look and feel ridiculous. I can't imagine I'll be able to do ten miles of the seventeen-mile course Gordon's planned.

And I don't.

However, I do make it as far as the lone cypress tree, a big tourist attraction along the world-famous seventeen-mile drive from Carmel to Monterey. We decide this is where I'm going to relax and enjoy my protein bar while Gordon rides a few more miles and then collects me on his way back. He's proud I did six miles in addition to the trek over here from the rental shop, which had to be a few more. That was more difficult than the nice bike path. Dodging cars on a bike when I haven't been on one in over twenty years isn't exactly my idea of fun.

Afterward, we take a leisurely ride around town, stopping at PortaBella restaurant for lunch. I'm starving. The pathetic protein bar didn't do the trick. I also can't wait to dump this crazy outfit and get into the jeans I brought along in my backpack. I change the second we get to the restaurant. As soon as we're seated we hear Dean Martin singing "La Vie en Rose" playing quietly in the background. It reminds me that I miss the scratchy recording of Edith Piaf singing it in French.

But now the fun part of my day begins. Shopping. The trade-off for getting up at the crack of dawn and wearing those unflattering bike shorts. We leave our bikes at the restaurant and spend the afternoon strolling by the many shops and galleries, gazing at things we can't afford now but hope to in the future. This is Gordon's least favorite thing in the world. He'd much rather be zip lining in the Philippines or paragliding in the Dolomites. I'm happiest eating and shopping. But hey, relationships are about compromise, right?

We've had a wonderful trip, but it's now the morning of the last day. We have a long drive back to LA. We reluctantly pack our bags and load up the car. I lock the door and take the key. Joe hops in the backseat, and suddenly our brief, beautiful, romantic, and relaxing vacation is over. But we'll be left with sweet memories.

I don't ever want to forget this incredible time with Gordon. Our first few days away together. Joe pokes his head out the backseat window, enjoying the seventy-mile-per-hour wind whipping at his face. Gordon attaches my iPhone to the dock, presses the

U2 playlist, and floors the gas. We're singing wildly along with Bono as we speed along the freeway back to real life in LA. As the ocean begins to disappear behind us, signaling the true end to this memorable trip, I listen to the faint tinkling of my bracelet as it rests comfortably on my wrist and am giddy at the thought of my new life with Gordon.

Joe and I are enjoying our Sunday sitting on the window seat. It's been a cold couple of weeks with some rain, which is typical of winter in LA. I open the hatch just a bit and smell the humidity outside. Joe dashes over to the light, plops down, and sticks his tongue out to catch the raindrops as they fall. I lie back on the pillow alongside him. What a perfect day. I'm in my comfy Gap sweats and thick cotton socks. My hair is gathered in a ponytail, and my Diet Coke sits on the coffee table beside me, along with a pile of scripts. Beethoven's "Moonlight Sonata" plays softly in the background. Before I contemplate the scripts, I think about the wonderful respite I've had away from HBS.

The weeks between Christmas and New Year's have gone by swiftly. It's the calm before the storm. Gordon and I saw each other almost every day. I'll never forget how I simply melted when he gave me the bracelet, which clings to my wrist. I am hopelessly in love with him.

I dread going back to the office tomorrow. January sixth is less than twenty-four hours away. I'm up to speed on all the drama scripts. I've had the time to read and make copious notes. I bought some more interesting concepts and put them on the fast track. I've even had a few phone calls with the writers, so we are moving along on time.

As I swing into my parking space, I see Sylvia smoking a cigarette in front of the glass doors leading into the HBS lobby. I grab my bag and greet her.

"Hey, what's wrong? What're you doing out here?" I try to balance my purse and the bag full of scripts on one shoulder.

Sylvia takes a puff but doesn't say anything.

"Why don't we go to my office and talk?"

"No. I'm not done with my cigarette. I need every inch of it right now."

"OK, fine. You sound stressed. How about if we take a walk?"

We enter the building, flash our badges to the guard, and walk through a short corridor. We exit onto the back lot and stroll alongside the stages.

"I can't sell their damn reality shows," says Sylvia as she takes one last puff on her cigarette, then throws it to the ground. She grinds her black Jimmy Choo four-inch heel into it with more force than necessary. We lock arms and begin walking up the road between the soundstages. There are a few cars and trucks loading and unloading equipment.

"You can sell anything. What're you talking about?" I ask.

"I can't sell this shit. *Texas Cheerleaders* is full of sex and violence. This show belongs on MTV, not HBS. I dunno how to get our advertisers to sponsor shows like this."

"Did you talk to Pete?" I ask.

"Fuck Pete," she says. "Pete doesn't care. He's getting numbers. The problem is we need more scripted shows. That's where the ad dollars are. If we become a reality network, we may gain viewers, but we'll lose dollars. Suffice to say, I'm feeling the pressure."

"Well, it's not your fault," I say. "Your job is selling shows to advertisers. You can't give them something that doesn't exist."

"I have to bring in revenue, period. It doesn't matter how I do it," she adds.

We stop. I look at her, wondering what that last remark meant. Sylvia looks back at me. She lights another cigarette as we begin our walk back toward my office.

"Why don't you come upstairs so we can talk this through? I've got a meeting at ten. Maybe we can just bury our heads in the M&M's bowl and stay there the rest of the day." I try to lighten things up, but Sylvia won't budge.

"Nothing more to say. Got my work cut out for me. These guys are gonna kill me."

"No, the cigarettes will," I say. Sylvia rolls her eyes, takes another puff, and then squashes it as we enter the building.

"I've gotta meet Larry and some others now. They're in town from New York. We're meeting at the Beverly Wilshire. They wanna talk to me about actors urinating in our shows. They want to discuss the advertiser defection we had on *The Candy Stripers*." Sylvia's not happy.

"Well, tell them to talk to our pal Jerry, the comedy genius. He overruled Richard," I say.

"Yeah, sure, Jerry, the hero who brought us a sweeps win. Sure, tell that to them. Jerry's not gonna take the heat. I am."

We walk back inside the lobby.

"I'll see you at the sexual harassment seminar," Sylvia says.

"Yeah, that oughtta be interesting." I laugh.

"The guys call it the sexual her-ass-meant–everything seminar."

"Why doesn't that surprise me?"

"Total waste of time," Sylvia says. She rushes out of the building as I begin my journey upstairs.

The second I enter my office suite I see Rosie waiting at my door. We barely say hello or discuss our vacations. It's as if no time has passed. Rosie has her call sheet and appointment book in hand. She starts reciting the calls that came in over the past couple of weeks at lightning speed. I barely have my wits about me.

I get into my office, throw my bags on the couch, and within a second I hear Rosie's phone ring, then mine, then the pinging of multiple e-mails. Then Noah Stegner and Mark Winslow, who have scheduling and business issues, arrive at my door. Then Rosie rushes in and throws a few sets of dailies on my couch. Then Stacey Toobin, Jasper Jarosz's former director of drama development and my new subordinate, appears in the doorway with a box full of scripts that just arrived this morning. Shit. More work.

Kill me now.

This week has been hell. Everything came crashing down on Monday. Did I just have a vacation? I can't remember. It's suddenly Thursday, and I don't know where the week went. I've been underwater for days and haven't seen Marisol since before the holidays. I sure hope to get there next week.

However, today will be different. Chester's scheduled a sexual harassment seminar from one to five for senior and middle management. This seminar will be offered up and down the ranks of HBS so everyone is aware of exactly what constitutes sexual harassment. No one wants to go. It will interrupt our day. Mostly, however, it will be unsettling. There are plenty of perpetrators and victims among us.

At a little after one, we file into conference room C, which has a U-shaped table with ten chairs on each of the three sides. There's a lectern set up in the open space, and standing behind it is a guy who resembles President Obama. His name tag says Mr. Michael Weaver. He's looking down at his notes as we enter.

Sylvia, Molly, Stacey, Chester, Steve, Jerry, and the heads of business affairs, press, and scheduling, along with others, spread out around the table, quietly and almost guiltily taking their seats. The whole scene is strange and devoid of the usual boisterousness that accompanies HBS meetings. This one resembles a memorial. My colleagues are sitting uncomfortably with their hands folded in front of them as if in detention. It's amazing to see the rowdy and unrestrained personalities I'm so accustomed to silenced by the mere fact that they're at a sexual harassment seminar.

Chester sits alongside Clyde Bennington, the vice president of human resources. They're seated on one side of the table, directly across from Jerry and Steve. Sylvia and I sit along the center facing the open end of the U. There are about twenty-five men and, including myself, five women. Clyde gets up to introduce the seminar.

"HBS is required to offer a four-hour sexual harassment seminar for all their employees. And all employees of HBS are required to attend. This particular session is for senior and middle management. There are adhesive name tags in front of you. Please write your first name on the tag and stick it on so it's in full view. Also, please turn off all cell phones, iPads, et cetera." Clyde says.

We all do as he instructs, though there are audible moans.

Maybe it's me, but the men in this room seem to be particularly uncomfortable. They really don't want to be here. It's like everyone remembered their Prozac today.

"I'd like to introduce Mr. Michael Weaver," Clyde says, "who is a representative from the Ranger-Wilde Consulting Group, which offers sexual harassment training to employees of large corporations. He's going to lead the discussion."

Clyde returns to his seat as Weaver, who wears a wireless microphone on his lapel, stands behind the lectern and begins addressing the group.

"Good afternoon." Weaver not only looks like Obama, but has the same soft-spoken, even demeanor. "Thank you for coming. I know many of you have probably taken sexual harassment training before and may find this repetitive. But we believe it's important to repeat the workplace guidelines so that everyone is fully aware of what sexual harassment is and how to prevent it."

Weaver walks out from behind the lectern into the interior of the U-shaped table, pausing now and then to make eye contact with each employee.

"Managers need to develop the necessary skills to prevent sexual harassment by maintaining a harassment-free workplace. They need to communicate expectations about workplace conduct, recognize and respond to inappropriate behavior, and maintain an environment where employees are comfortable bringing forward concerns. This seminar should provide an understanding of the business risks of sexual harassment."

I look at Jerry and Steve, who completely ignore Clyde's instructions; they're texting each other under the table, even though they're sitting side by side. I'm sure they're watching downloaded porn or tweeting to their followers. So far Weaver has missed this, unless he has eyes at the back of his head.

"Let's explore the definition of sexual harassment. Does anyone know what it is?" Weaver asks. No one moves. I wonder if anyone is breathing. It's eerily silent.

"Sexual harassment is a form of sex discrimination," Weaver continues. "The legal definition is unwelcome verbal, visual, or physical conduct of a sexual nature that is severe or pervasive and affects working conditions or creates a hostile work environment. Now, does anyone know what a hostile work environment is? Because that's usually the most misunderstood area."

I don't expect anyone to answer this question, but to my shock and surprise, Mark Winslow, the head of business affairs, raises his hand. We're all stunned that someone is actually participating.

"I can't be certain of the exact legal language," says Mark, "but I know that if you, as a manager, are innocent of any kind of sexual harassment yourself, it may not matter because if the workplace you manage is considered sexually hostile by just one of your employees, you and your company can be held liable in a court of law."

"Absolutely correct," says Mr. Weaver. "And because many of you are managers in a high-profile company, you must be cognizant of these facts. So let's start by doing a little role-playing, shall we?"

Weaver asks Jerry and Steve, who are sitting in the first two seats to Weaver's left, to come up and stand beside him at the open end of the U-shaped table. They both turn red. They look like schoolboys caught masturbating under the sheets. Weaver may, in fact, have eyes in the back of his head, because he didn't even look in their direction when he called their names.

"OK, now we need a woman. How about you?" Weaver points to Molly. "Can you come up here?"

Of all people, he had to pick Molly. She's trembling as she cautiously approaches the front of the room. She faces both Jerry and Steve. Her eyes remain on the floor.

"Jerry and Steve, let's say you're over there at the copy machine." Weaver points way across the room. "You're telling an off-color joke and aren't aware that Molly is standing right here. Molly hears your joke and is offended. Is that considered sexual harassment?"

Neither Jerry nor Steve responds. They just look down.

"Molly, do you want to take a guess?"

"Yes, it is," Molly says, her voice barely audible. "It's considered a hostile environment."

"That's correct. It's interesting that this young woman knows that and you guys don't. That's something you need to know. OK, thank you. You can all sit down."

Jerry and Steve mosey back to their seats. I see Molly wiping her eye. For a moment, I wonder if she's crying.

We sit upright in our chairs, watching and listening, although every now and then I see the guys stealing looks at their phones under the table. I notice that Noah even has his iPad there. Chester strolls in and out of the room to smoke. I guess he's above this.

We're cooped up in this room for four hours without access (supposedly) to phone calls, e-mails, or meetings. We review handouts. We're quizzed. We're lectured. We're asked questions. Some of us engage. Most do not. Weaver reiterates the message over and over and over: sexual harassment will not be tolerated in the workplace. It is a federal law. There will be consequences if that law is broken.

I wonder if it applies to HBS. I wonder when he's going to discuss the consequences for the whistle-blower. That doesn't come up.

Weaver goes on to discuss the new sexual harassment laws related to e-mail, text messaging, sexting, and social media. He discusses how things can be misconstrued in written form.

I look at Molly, who just stares at the handouts in front of her. She seems tense and anxious, as does Stacey. Jerry leans back in his chair, looks at his watch, and makes eye contact with Pete and Tony across the room. They roll their eyes. Everyone knows all of this. What a complete waste of time. Everyone's been through these boring seminars.

The fact that Jerry was fired due to inappropriate behavior is not lost on me. How quickly they forget that just a few months ago it was blasted all over the trades. We all know what inappropriate behavior means. He was fired because he no doubt sexually harassed someone at Tiger Films. But it's not discussed. It's a verboten topic. The giant elephant in the room no one will ever address. Like it never happened. And even if it did, it happened someplace else, under someone else's watch. Not our problem. You'd think there'd be a rehab center for sexual harassment offenders. But when there's no physical evidence, all that happens is a talking-to, a firing, a rehiring, and a soft landing.

My heart's racing. I feel as though I've ingested twenty Cokes. But I haven't. I've been sipping water. My hands are clammy. I'm sweating. I think four hours of this is a bit much. Maybe this is hitting too close to home. I'm feeling awfully anxious.

Anita Hill was the first one who brought the term "sexual harassment" to the attention of Hollywood in general. And I learned there was a name for something I thought was just an aspect of the workplace I'd always have to put up with. Yet even with the new laws, so few come forward. Myself included. Part of me wants to jump up and say, "Jerry Kellner, you did this to me. You should be prosecuted." But then I'd be persecuted.

I'm starting to perspire. I need a break. I feel as if I'm having a panic attack. Maybe I'll slip outside and get some air. I get up, push in my chair, and just as I'm about to exit the room, Mr. Weaver fires a question at me.

"Alexa, tell me about subtle sexism. Do you know what it is?"

I freeze. I glance around the room. All eyes are on me. I look at Jerry. He leans back in his chair. His feet are on the desk. He's not looking at me. He's looking at the clock above the entryway. I see Steve tapping on his BlackBerry under the table while Noah scrolls through his.

Chester glances at his watch. I scan the room and see that everyone seems worn out and tired. I look at Molly and Sylvia, who are yawning. I glance at the clock. It's four fifty-five. We're five minutes away from the end of the seminar. Five more minutes. Just five minutes and this torture will be over.

"I think subtle sexism is harder to identify because it's usually unconscious," I say slowly. "It may be that men are just culturally more comfortable dealing with other men."

The room is quiet. No one says a word. I hear Jerry's chair creaking in the distance.

"What do you think of her statement, Chester?" asks Weaver.

"I think she may have a point," Chester says. "What do you think, Jerry?" asks Weaver.

"About what?" Jerry asks, as he rocks back and forth in his chair with a smug expression on his face.

"Did you not hear what Alexa just said?" Weaver asks.

"Yeah, I heard her. I always hear her." Jerry smirks, and there are a few other soft chuckles heard around the room.

"Well, why don't you repeat what she said, then?"

"Something about sexism. That it's unconscious. And I think that's probably true. I don't think any kind of 'ism' is necessarily a conscious act," says Jerry.

"Sylvia, we've not heard a lot from you today. What do you think subtle sexism is?" asks Weaver.

"Mr. Weaver, with all due respect, I think this is a waste of time. Sexism and sexual harassment exist. Women are used to it. We live with it. It's part of our environment. If we choose to challenge it, we get fired. Yes, it's against the law, but women are afraid of losing their jobs. It is what it is."

"Sylvia, I hope you don't feel that way," Chester interrupts. He bolts out of his seat and stands alongside Mr. Weaver. "We don't want women at HBS to feel they can't report sexual harassment. We really are committed to a sexual harassment–free environment."

Clyde jumps up as well and joins Chester and Mr. Weaver in the middle of the open space.

"Yeah, right." Sylvia laughs.

Chester is surprised. The idea that a female executive would speak out like that is terrifying and possibly contagious. I return to my seat.

"Sylvia, please let us know if there are any infractions. You must report them to human resources," says Clyde.

She just smirks.

You can cut the tension with a knife. And then suddenly, the big hand reaches the twelve and everyone leaps out of their seats and charges out of that room like elephants escaping a herd of predators.

Why is this reminiscent of Marisol jumping out of her chair the second the bell rings? Are these guys fourth graders? Weaver shakes his head in frustration and starts to gather his papers. Clyde offers his hand and thanks him for a job well done. No one else goes over to him. The room empties in a nanosecond. Everyone is gone except Mr. Weaver and me.

"Thank you, Mr. Weaver," I say. "That was an interesting seminar."

"Glad you enjoyed it," Weaver says.

I linger as I make my way out the door, and then Weaver hands me his card.

"Call me if you want to talk," he says.

I hold his card in my hand and stare at it. I look at him. He looks at me expectantly. Do I just say, *You can't begin to imagine all the infractions that go on here. All the laws that are broken on an hourly basis. But do you honestly expect me to report my coworkers? What about the women who did? Where are they now? And what about the young women who ask me what they should do? Do you really want me to encourage them to compromise their careers and report their colleagues? I feel that if I report anything, I'm the problem. That's the message we hear. Why would my employer want to support me with the threat of a lawsuit hanging over his head?*

I take Weaver's card and put it in my pocket. I thank him again and walk back to my office. On the way out, I stop in the restroom. There's only one stall occupied, and I can tell the shoes belong to Molly.

She's crying.

"Molly? Are you all right? It's Alexa. I know that was brutal. Are you OK?"

She doesn't respond, but stops crying and opens the door.

"I'm pregnant," she says. She tosses a tissue in the trash, opens the door, and is gone.

Chapter Nine

It's three o'clock on Friday, the day after the sexual harassment seminar. Molly and I made plans to meet at a coffee shop a few minutes from the office. It's a no-frills, old-fashioned hangout for showbiz types at breakfast and lunch.

There's hardly anyone in here at this time. I see Molly sitting in the back against the wall in an old green leather booth and walk briskly toward her.

"How're you doing?" I ask as I slide into the booth.

Molly shrugs. "OK."

There's a long pause. I watch as Molly plays with the corner of her napkin. I'm not exactly sure how to begin this conversation.

"Do you wanna talk about it?"

"I'm pregnant."

"I know. I'm sorry, Molly. I'm sure this is weighing heavily on you. Do you want to tell me whose it is?"

"Steve Hansen," Molly says.

"Huh?"

"You heard me."

"Oh my God."

"Yup, oh my God."

"Has this been going on for a while?"

"Yup," Molly says as she twists a lock of her hair into a Shirley Temple curl. "We kind of got to know each other over the holidays. Then we started having sex, and then, well, I got pregnant. I'm not that far along. Just six weeks. But Steve wants me to quit. He doesn't think we should be working at the same place."

There's a pause. This is quite a shock. I need to digest this information.

"Um, you know Steve's married?"

"Yes, of course, but he's going to leave his wife," Molly says dismissively. "She's really a shrew. He hates going home. He's spent almost every evening with me since Thanksgiving."

I can't believe what I'm hearing. And yet I can. How many times have I heard it? A zillion. A married male manager takes advantage of a female subordinate. A coworker. The young woman's flattered by the attention from an older, powerful, successful, and handsome male. The married man will never leave his wife for her. But he wants the young woman to leave her job for him.

Gee, why does this sound familiar? It takes me back to a place I was a long time ago when I was attracted to men who weren't available. Some were married, some were not. Fortunately, I didn't get drawn in the way Molly did, but I remember feeling I couldn't really be rejected if the guy was already unavailable. But it became complicated very fast because inevitably I wanted more, and that wasn't going to happen. Fortunately, Emily talked some sense into me, and I was able to extricate myself from the last of those situations.

Molly's playing with her earring now. She has no idea of the heartache that awaits her.

"Molly, you don't need to quit your job." I touch her arm. "It's not your fault you're pregnant. As you know, it takes two. Have you and Steve decided to keep the baby? Is he going to support you?"

Molly just stares at me.

"You've spoken about this, haven't you?" I know what the answer is by her expression.

"Well, no," Molly says, flicking the corner of the paper placemat with her thumb. "But I'm pretty sure Steve's going to tell his wife. And then I think he's going to leave."

There's a long pause as I reach over and take her hand in mine.

"He's not going to leave his wife, Molly," I say softly, looking squarely into her eyes, but she drops her lids. "Steve's a player. Everyone knows that. He's had other affairs. I don't want to hurt you, but I do want you to know the truth."

"Oh, yes, I know," Molly says, pulling her hand from mine. "We talked about that. I know you don't think that I'm the one, but he's told me I am. He's just got to find the right time to tell her it's over."

Molly seems convinced. Yet I can see right through her. She's a bag of nerves. The waitress finally arrives. I order a Diet Coke, and Molly has an iced tea.

"Having a baby is a big deal," I say, leaning back into the banquette. "You've got to make arrangements. And if Steve wants you to quit, then he'd better help you find a new job, because in this economy, with all the cutbacks, it's not exactly easy."

All I want to do is strangle Steve Hansen. How am I ever going to look at him without wanting to slam his head into the wall?

"And I don't want you to quit," I say.

"But I think I need to," Molly says as she blinks to hide the tears about to well up. "I know I should tell Jerry, because he's my boss now, but I don't want him to know what happened."

"Yes, he's your boss," I say, pulling a few napkins out of the holder and handing them to her. "If you quit, you need to tell him. But you're not quitting. So you won't have to tell him anything. At least not yet."

The mere thought of Molly discussing this with Jerry makes my skin crawl.

Jerry bullies the weakest around him. There's no way I'm gonna let him near Molly.

Molly dabs her pretty green eyes with the napkin. Her glorious red silky hair looks dead and limp. She's unable to look at me, and instead remains focused on the soggy paper placemat under her iced tea. I lean across the table and again put my hand on hers.

"Women get pregnant and work till they deliver the baby," I say. "You're young and healthy. You've worked extremely hard to get to where you are. Steve's marital issues are his problem. Not yours. If you really want to marry this guy, then fine, that's your business. But I'm not going to let you quit your job today."

As if on cue, my phone rings. I dig inside my purse. It's Rosie reminding me that I have a four thirty appointment. She wants to know when I'll be back. Leaving the office in the middle of the day when I don't have an outside meeting isn't exactly my pattern. She probably thinks I'm having a quickie with Gordon. It doesn't matter. I'm not about to betray Molly's trust.

"I have to get going, Molly. I have a meeting. I wish we had more time." I leave cash on the table, gulp down the last of my Diet Coke, hike my purse onto my shoulder, and slide out of the booth. Molly remains at the table, sipping her iced tea and continuing to stare at the mat.

"You're a very smart young woman," I say as I bend down to look into her eyes. "I want and need you on this team. I'm here if you need me." As I approach the glass door to exit the coffee shop, I turn around and shout, "You're not quitting."

I guess there will always be sexual energy in the workplace. The temptation exists. But why does it seem to be about the powerful and the powerless? Can women really compete and succeed in such a sexualized environment? Is it really a fair playing field?

As I saunter back to my car, I actually contemplate not answering the phone that's vibrating deep inside my bag. What other fires do I have to put out today?

"Hey, sweetie," says Tony. "I think you killed at the *Elle* interview. It's gonna run in next month's issue. So it's cool, babe."

"That's great. I'm glad you're happy with it," I say, sliding into my car.

Less than twenty-four hours after the sexual harassment seminar and he calls me *sweetie* and *babe*. I swear I'm working with a bunch of blockheads.

"Tony, were you so focused on your BlackBerry that you didn't realize you were in a sexual harassment seminar yesterday?"

"Yeah, babe, I was there."

"Did you not get that words like *sweetie* and *babe* aren't acceptable in the workplace?"

"Oh, yeah, sorry, hon, but listen, you're gonna be on the stage with Chester and Jerry taking questions from the press at the TCA on the twenty-second. That's in two weeks. I wanna know if you've picked any pilots and if there's casting. We need big stars. Please don't get us actors we can't sell. I need names, babe. I mean hon."

And then comes the clincher.

"Jerry just delivered Will Smith's kid. Got some good traction with that one. So see if you can come up with something, OK? Ciao." Tony hangs up.

I'm incredulous. Sylvia was right. What a waste of time. How does one change a paternalistic and sometimes misogynistic culture that has been embedded in corporate America for centuries? Tony doesn't get it. And I don't think he wants to get it. And frankly, I'm not sure he has to get it.

I drive onto the HBS lot and travel up the stairs to my office, where I see Rosie coming down.

"Steve and Jerry are in your office. They need you for a second. Then your four thirty is waiting. Where've you been?" asks Rosie. Together we walk up the stairs to my suite. As we enter, I see both Steve and Jerry standing in the doorway to my office. Uh-oh, what's up? This doesn't look good.

"Have you heard?" asks Steve. I walk past him into my office. What I really want to say is, *Yes, Steve, I did just hear. I heard you screwed Molly and now she's pregnant and you want her to quit. You're a lecherous, lowlife asshole.* But of course I bite my professional tongue and close the door.

"Ivor James killed himself this morning. Hung himself with a dog leash," Steve says with little emotion. I look toward Jerry, who plops down on my couch and reaches into the M&M's bowl.

"That's horrible," I say, trying to take in this very troubling information. "I'm so sorry to hear that."

"Yup, it's pretty bad," Steve says. "I'm just glad we were able to air both interviews during the sweeps. And that he managed to hang in till now. Ha, hang in till now, get it?" Steve laughs at his own sick joke, takes a seat next to Jerry on the couch, and they both grab handfuls of M&M's.

I can't believe what I just heard and pause in stunned silence. Finally I walk over and stand by Steve and Jerry.

"Are you serious?" I ask. "The man just killed himself. Probably due to the fact that you, Jerry, outed him. Don't you feel kind of guilty?"

Steve grabs a *People* sitting on top of a pile of scripts on the coffee table. He starts thumbing through it, munching loudly on the chocolates while Jerry sinks further into the couch, tossing handfuls of M&M's in his mouth.

"No, I don't have any guilt," he says after a while. "The man's dead. He wanted to die. Not my problem. I feel bad for his family. Although, man, he'll leave a fortune." Jerry moves forward and grabs another handful, popping several in the air, trying to catch them with his tongue. Something my eight-year-old nephew enjoys doing.

"Hey, did you see this?" Steve points to a photo of Kate Hudson in *People*. "She looks pretty hot here, don'tcha think?"

Jerry leans over to take a closer look. "Yeah, but she's got fake tits."

"Who cares!" Steve says.

I'm dumbstruck. I rip the *People* out of Steve's hand and put it on the table.

"This is disgusting. Do you realize we crossed the line? We wanted ratings so badly that we caused this guy so much suffering he felt his only way out was to kill himself."

"Oh, Alexa, that's pretty dramatic," says Steve as he grabs another handful and then gets up to leave. "No one causes anyone to do anything. He chose to do the interview. He didn't have to. We were the lucky recipients of great ratings. It is what it is."

"Jerry," I say, looking right at him. "You lost your brother. You know how devastating that is—"

"Don't go there." Jerry glares at me.

"OK, listen," says Steve. "I need you both to start getting footage so we can show clips of the pilots at press tour. I'm sure Tony told you, we need lotsa star power."

Steve grabs his last handful of M&M's as he and Jerry head toward the door.

"You lost your brother? Man, what happened?" Steve asks.

"Nothing. Car accident. Long time ago."

As they head out of the suite into the hallway, Steve answers his ringing phone, and I sit on the couch wondering what the heck I just witnessed.

Two hellacious weeks have passed. I feel horribly guilty because I haven't been able to schedule a time to see Marisol. Fortunately, Gordon put Marisol on the phone with me so I could reassure her that I'd be there again soon. But pilot season has begun with a vengeance. It's taking every ounce of my energy. I decide to keep Stacey, who's pretty darn good. She's very focused, a great manager, and a tremendous help for me.

Today is HBS's press tour, which is held at The Langham hotel in Pasadena. It's an opportunity for us to tell the TV reporters what might get on the schedule next September. The day concludes with a big party that also includes all the actors on HBS's shows. It's great fashion, big hairdos, lots of cleavage, *Entertainment Tonight*, bloggers, and paparazzi.

At the executive session, which occurs early in the morning, the journalists fire questions at the president of entertainment about anything and everything. Nothing is off-limits. Chester wants Jerry and me to sit on the stage with him this year. An indication that we're the two vying for his job. He wants to see us perform.

At seven thirty this morning I had my makeup done and my hair blown while Tony shot sample questions at me to make sure I knew how to respond. Interestingly, Jerry didn't have to endure this inquisition.

"Isn't *The Investigators* just a rip-off of *CSI*?" asks Tony.

"No, not at all. We're focusing on private investigators in Jackson, Mississippi. I don't see any resemblance," I say.

"Great. Good answer, keep it short. Less is more. OK, next one: Don't you think some of your shows dumb down the network? Like what about *Mother, May I Sleep with Danger?* Why would you want to develop a show like that?"

"Our job is knowing what our audience wants. We're mindful of our demographic and what's worked in the past. Based on that information and plenty of research, we feel confident we can deliver shows that will appeal to our audience."

"Fucking great, Alexa. Again, keep it short. Details can only get you in trouble, darlin'." Tony high-fives me. I guess I passed his test or he wants to get back to his BlackBerry, which was vibrating madly as he interrogated me.

Turns out Tony's questions were the softballs.

The executive session is about to begin. We're seated on a riser at the front of a very large meeting room. The space has been transformed to look like a stage, with a large screen behind us depicting a few of HBS's noteworthy shows. Spotlights are on us. Cameras flash and digital recorders take in our every breath.

I'm nervous looking out into this rather unfriendly-looking audience. Chester isn't nearly as bothered by them. He's in his finely pressed dark-blue jeans, white button-down shirt, and blue blazer. He and Jerry must have coordinated, because they're wearing virtually the same uniform. I'm wearing a Rachel Roy beige sheath dress, a string of pearls, and nude pumps.

"Some of us were at the press conference you held in November announcing the Ivor James interview," says a reporter from the *Orlando Sun*. "As you know, the man killed himself a few weeks ago. Do you think HBS might have gone too far by subjecting this very troubled man to two live TV interviews?"

"Well, of course we're deeply saddened by Mr. James's untimely death," says Chester. "We've set up a memorial fund in his name and don't plan to air the interview again any time soon. Of course, no one can predict this kind of outcome. Our thoughts and prayers are with his family."

"Jerry, we heard there was some sex tape. Do you know anything about that?" asks the reporter.

"No, sir, I don't." Jerry shifts uncomfortably in his chair.

"Is there another question?" Tony quickly asks from just off-stage. "Yes, Bonnie Hoffman from the *Baltimore Sun*, in the back, go ahead."

"Why isn't there more diversity in your shows?" Ms. Hoffman asks in a strong, firm voice. "You're the only broadcast network that has fewer than five African-Americans and zero Latinos in any of your primetime series. How can you get away with that?"

Chester sits higher in his chair and is about to respond, but Jerry beats him to it.

"Actually, we just picked up a pilot called *Hey, Good Lookin'*. It's a hilarious sitcom about a homophobic guy who realizes the girl he's been living with was formerly a man. It stars Keshawn Mitchell. We think it's a breakthrough show. The entire cast is African American."

Before Ms. Hoffman can follow up, Tony interrupts and asks for the next question, clearly not wanting to spend too much time on that one.

"Miss Ross, didn't you once work for Jerry Kellner?" asks a reporter from the *Denver Post*. "And if so, what was it like having him work for you in comedy development? And now it seems you're both candidates for the top job at HBS. How are you handling this?"

Suffice to say, I'm a little surprised. Where the heck are the questions about our shows? How am I gonna dance around this one? I wish I had all the answers at my fingertips the way Jerry does. I look offstage and see Tony shaking his head. He's worried I can't handle this. Jerry leans back in his seat, smiling. Chester is happy to be off the hot seat and fiddles with his lighter. He's anxious to get offstage and back to his cigarettes.

"I was Jerry's assistant a long time ago," I say. "It was interesting having him work for me. But he's done a great job at HBS. We're all on the same team and only wish each other the very best, because at the end of the day it's about the shows. We compete against the other networks, not each other." A bead of perspiration trickles down the side of my face. I hope my deodorant is working, because I'm dying, what with the lights and the tension.

"Hey, we may be on the same team, but I intend to win this one." Jerry laughs. He gets some cackles from the audience as well.

"Jerry, it appears you're going to be on the cover of *GQ* next month," says Hy Oringer from the *Los Angeles Daily News*. "Sounds like you're becoming a real player in this town. How do you account for that, particularly in light of the allegations of inappropriate behavior when you were at Tiger Films last summer?"

"As you may have noticed, there was no legal action. It was an unfortunate experience. I don't hold it against Tiger Films. In fact, I ordered one of their comedy scripts to pilot, so no harm, no foul." Jerry laughs again. "But in terms of my sudden celebrity, I attribute it to good salesmanship. I know a good idea when I see it, and I go after it. I'm here to win. TV lacks showmanship today. I intend to change that."

I don't hold it against Tiger Films? Brilliant. Jerry is a genius at the blame game. I would never think to say that. The press is infatuated with him. Let the love fest begin. Chester slaps Jerry on the back.

I'm fielding no questions at all. How am I going to turn this around?

The rest of the questions are for Jerry. Either no one is interested in my area, or I'm just not as much fun. I certainly don't have the colorful background or wonderful sound bites that come so naturally. Every time I try to say something, he or Chester outmaneuvers me. This is painful.

After an hour, the session ends. The reporters rush onstage and shove recorders in our faces. Tony tells them to meet us outside, as the next session is about to begin, and then leads Chester, Jerry, and me to the main lobby, where we're greeted with more questions. However, most want to know more about Ivor James and crowd Jerry, who skillfully dodges them by offering stories about the Potawatomi Fish Boil and his brother the chef, who Jerry is proud to say may be the star of a new reality show.

I've had enough. As I leave the lobby I run smack into Sylvia.

"You were great," she says.

"I sucked," I say, because I know I did.

"Oh, c'mon. You did a good job. Let's go sit by the pool. I need a smoke."

She puts her arm around me, and we walk together down a long hall to the pool behind the building, far away from the meeting rooms. Sylvia pulls out a cigarette, and for the first time since I was twenty and smoked for a bit, I'm tempted to join her. We rest on a couple of lounge chairs. There's nobody here, probably because it's overcast and cold. But it's great for us. Some time away from the assholes.

"OK, how bad was I?" I ask. "Tell the truth. I sucked, didn't I? Wait. Don't answer that. I don't know if I can handle it."

"Relax. You were fine." Sylvia's lying, and I know it. She takes a long puff on her cigarette and looks out over the pool instead of at me. "Jerry made the *Entertainment Weekly* Power One Hundred List. He's number forty-nine. That's pretty impressive for someone who's never been on it, and he's the keynote speaker at the Creative Artists Agency retreat next week."

Sylvia flicks her ash on the ground next to her chair.

"He knocked it out of the park. I think you know that," Sylvia adds, kicking off her shoes.

Of course I know it. I feel sick. I stretch my legs out on the lounge chair and bum a cigarette off Sylvia. We both just lie here saying nothing, as the silence speaks volumes.

"So, what're you saying, Syl? Are you saying give it up? He's got the job, you don't have a chance?"

"Pretty much. Why kill yourself? He wants this more than anything. Why beat your head against the wall?"

I hear muffled conversations in the distance indicating that the press tour is in full swing. I wonder who's on the hot seat now.

"Oh, and in case you didn't know," Sylvia says, "Jerry's wife filed for divorce. He's a free man. Got what he could from her. Including invitations to join Barnsworth on the golf course and lunch at the country club. Nice, huh?" Where and how Sylvia gets all her information—which is always accurate—is a mystery to me. She reaches across the small table between us and puts her hand in mine.

"Give it up," she says. "You're not gonna get it, and frankly, I don't know why you'd even want it. HBS is all about creating a false and misleading impression that we're going to be the top-rated network. But it's all smoke and mirrors. And Jerry's the perfect foil. The fact is, none of his shows stick. They're all one-offs. He couldn't develop a good series if his life depended on it. But I'm not sure it matters."

Sylvia lets go of my hand and takes another long puff.

"This is a shitty place to work," Sylvia says as she pulls her legs up to her chest. "It's a horrible place for women. Why don't you run Lifetime or some women's network where your hard work and creativity would be appreciated instead of frolicking in this junkyard? I just don't want to see you get shit kicked in your face all the time. I just hate it."

I take another drag off my cigarette and notice it's already down to the butt. But I don't care. I need it. We both just sit for a while without speaking. Then Tony appears out of the blue.

"Hey, I've been looking all over for you, babe. What're you girls doing out here?"

Tony doesn't wait for a response. He's really not interested in one. "I just got a call from *Elle*. They're gonna dump the story.

Sorry, Lex. I thought we could get you out there, but they didn't feel they had enough. Thank God. I don't think there was an upside to that article, anyhow."

Tony brings a chair over and places it between Sylvia and me.

"That's too bad," I say.

"By the way, not to add salt to the wound," Tony says as he lights a joint. "I couldn't get you into the Fifty Most Powerful Women edition of the *Hollywood Reporter* this year. CBS and ABC cashed in a lot of favors to get their gals in there. You got edged out. Kills me that Ali Tamarisk, the lit agent from Paradigm, got in and you didn't. That one made no sense. Maybe next year. Anyway, we'll keep trying. Buck up, babe."

Tony's phone rings. He looks at the caller ID but doesn't take it. Instead he takes a long hit and slowly exhales.

"Man...that's the magic puff right there," Tony says, closing his eyes and relaxing. His phone rings again. "Geesh, a guy can't puff a skinny." Tony shoves the phone in his pocket, leaps out of his seat, and with the heel of his brand-new loafers, smashes the joint into the ground. "Call my office tomorrow, Lex. Let me give you the name of a publicist who might be able to help you. I just don't have the time to start someone's career. May cost you a few bucks. But it might be worth it." Tony winks, smiles, and is gone in a flash.

I just don't have time to start someone's career, he'd said. My career hasn't started yet?

Sylvia is smart enough to keep quiet. We both just lie here. After a minute I decide it's time to turn on my phone and see what other great things have been going on. Within an instant the phone rings. It's Gordon.

For the first time I'm ambivalent about taking his call. I feel terrible, like I just hit rock bottom. I want to be upbeat and personable, but I'm not sure I can fake it.

"Hey, Gord," I say, trying to sound nice and friendly, even though I feel like someone just kicked me in the gut.

"Hey, darlin', how's your day going?"

"Shitty. How's yours?"

"Oh boy," he sighs. "This doesn't sound like a great time to talk, so lemme ask you this, do you think you could possibly make time to see Marisol later today?"

"No."

"Are you too busy? 'Cause you haven't seen her since before Christmas. So I was wondering if you might be able to find some time this week and—"

"I can't," I interrupt. "I told you January to May is horrible. I'm just overwhelmed with work. I like her. I want to see her. But I can't do it right now."

"You made a commitment. It's not just about you, Lex. You have a girl who depends on you now. You can't just walk away."

"I'm not walking away," I say, trying to keep my voice down as I watch Sylvia, who's pretending not to hear this conversation. "I'm walking away right now. I know this isn't what you want to hear. I'm sorry. Please don't press me on this."

I wish he hadn't called. The timing couldn't be worse. I think we're about to have a fight. I'm having an awful day and feel a headache coming on.

"Maybe this isn't a great time to talk," Gordon says softly. "You sound really upset. I'm not sure we want to argue. What's going on? What happened?"

"Nothing. OK? Nothing," I say, feeling badly, but not wanting to get into it right now. Certainly not in front of Sylvia. "I have to go. I'll talk to you at the party later."

"OK," Gordon says. "By the way, what do we wear to this thing?"

"It's a Hawaiian-themed dinner, so it's casual."

"Hawaiian theme? Why?"

"Oh, it's to promote *Hawaiian Leis*, a reality show about six housewives from Palm Beach who are forced to live with Koa warriors in the remote mountains of Molakai."

"You're kidding, right?" Gordon laughs.

"No, it's a real show," I say, not finding the humor in it right now. "It's set to premiere in a few weeks. The guys think it's a slam dunk."

"Of course they do."

"I should really go," I say, suddenly remembering that I also invited Gordon's boss, Barbara, who I'll be meeting for the first time. "OK, well, I'll see you guys later."

"Poor guy," Sylvia says as she swings her legs off the chair facing me. "He hasn't a clue how brutal this business is. He should only know the hell you go through in this job."

"I can handle more than you think, Sylvia. I'll be fine." I get up, and without another word, I walk back to the lobby and to the valet outside. I don't feel like seeing anyone right now. I just want to disappear. I hand my ticket to the attendant and tell myself that I'll take a ride back to the office, where I'll freshen up, and then return here later for the dinner party. I just need some time alone. I can't let this get me down. I've got to pick myself up and keep moving forward.

I feel badly about snapping at Gordon. He's the last person I want to hurt. I'm just stressed and upset. When my car arrives I quickly call Rosie to find out what's been going on.

"Oh, the usual insanity. You have about thirty messages, mostly about casting, a few standards issues, and—"

"Fine, let's start rolling calls," I interrupt. Rosie is stunned. I'm rarely, if ever, short with her.

"OK, well, first Molly wants to talk to you and—"

"Great. Put her through." After a moment, I hear Molly's voice and ask her what's up.

"Well, I just wanted to say that though I appreciate your taking the time to talk to me, I've decided to quit. I appreciate your concern, but Steve thinks—"

"I don't care what Steve thinks!" I scream into the phone. "Steve's a selfish asshole. He's not thinking about you. He's thinking of himself. 'Cause guess what? He's a married guy who had an affair with a coworker that resulted in a pregnancy. Weren't you paying attention in the sexual harassment seminar?"

"I don't work for him, Alexa. It shouldn't—"

"It does matter. It does. He's in a position of authority. And he's scared. 'Cause I can go right to HR and tell them what's going on and he could be fired," I say, but quickly wish I hadn't.

There's a long pause. I don't hear anything. Did she just hang up on me?

"Molly? Are you there?"

"Please don't do that," Molly says softly. "I told you this in confidence."

Molly's right. The stress is building to the point where I just want to go home, get in bed, and curl up under the covers. It's just not a good day. And I'm taking it out on everyone else.

"He wants you to quit," I say, turning to my professional self, "because he thinks if you're not around he won't get in trouble for what happened. But at some point, people are going to want to know who the father is. And you guys need to decide how you're going to tell everyone."

"Well, all the more reason why I shouldn't really be there anymore," Molly says as I tear off the freeway and head toward the HBS parking lot.

"You're making a huge mistake," I say, distracted and upset, feeling like I'm at the end of my rope. "I'm sorry, I don't think I can help you."

Molly hangs up abruptly, and I feel horrible. I pull into my parking spot and turn off the ignition. I close my eyes and bury my face in my hands. After a while, I take a few deep breaths to calm myself. I really don't want to wreak any more havoc on the poor unsuspecting people in my life. I need to relax. Molly's right. She doesn't report to Steve. People have affairs all the time. I have to calm down. This is just so emotionally charged for me. What a morning this has been. I'm wiped.

After a couple of minutes, I look at my watch and realize I only have a short time here before I have to drive back to the hotel and join the rest of my coworkers at the after party.

I drag myself out of the car and head upstairs, where I spend the next couple of hours catching up on calls, e-mails, and dailies and use the time in between to replenish my makeup and brush my hair while Rosie removes a coffee stain from my dress, something I didn't know till she pointed it out. I even take a moment to rest on my couch. It's a brief break, but I need the time to recharge before I go back into the lion's den.

"I know you're having a rough day," Rosie says. "Things will improve. They always do." Rosie checks the stain to make sure it's all out and hands me my purse. I thank her for being so attentive and haul myself back to the car, hoping she's right, that things will get better.

Soon I'm back at the hotel. I leave my car with the valet and enter the lobby, and the first person I see is Chester.

"Alexa, why don't you join us?" Chester says. "*Fortune* is doing a piece on the dearth of good comedies. You should talk about your shows and where they might fit on the schedule. C'mon by our table."

Before I have a chance to respond, I'm greeted by Gordon and Barbara, who just entered the lobby. Barbara is the spitting image of Melissa McCarthy, who appeared in the film *Bridesmaids*. Suffice to say, she stands out among the anorexic young actresses who parade along the red carpet, stopping as they greet the hosts from

Access Hollywood and *Entertainment Tonight*. Most are actors cast in pilots that may or may not make the schedule. They're young, just out of college. If they even went to college.

"Hey, you look great," says Gordon as he kisses me on the cheek and then immediately introduces me to his boss, Barbara Kenfield, who greets me warmly. I'd like to engage in conversation, but I'm distracted by Chester's invitation to join him. I don't know how I can leave Gordon and Barbara alone. It wouldn't be right. As I ponder this dilemma, it becomes increasingly clear that I made a huge mistake inviting them to this event when it's clearly a business function. What was I thinking?

I lead Gordon and Barbara to the tent where we're seated at a small table in the back. I survey the area and notice there are no spouses, no guests, just journalists, actors, and colleagues. I beat myself up for moving too fast and not thinking things through. I was eager to meet Barbara and figured why not just include them tonight.

"This is really nice," Barbara says. "Thank you for inviting me. I've heard so much about you and am thrilled you're involved in the tutoring program."

"It's been a fun experience," I say, smiling briefly while my eyes dart around the room, looking to see what my colleagues are doing and who they're with. "Why don't we get some food at the buffet?"

Gordon lets Barbara go ahead of him and then moves up alongside me as we get in line.

"Hey, sweetie," Gordon whispers. "I know you had a difficult day. You're being kind of cool. Are you OK?"

"No. I'm not OK," I whisper back, but since we're behind Tony and Noah I don't want to share what I have to say with them. Instead I pretend all is hunky dory and introduce them to Gordon and Barbara. But Tony and Noah have little to no interest in talking to them. It's obvious that Gordon and Barbara are not actors, reporters, or showbiz folks. So why bother? What's in it for them? They offer perfunctory handshakes and quickly turn around, continuing where they left off. Then I watch as they take their plates and join the columnist from the *New York Times* who's preparing a story about scheduling. Another opportunity for publicity and spin. More ways to alter reality.

"Hey, you were great today," Jerry says as he cuts in front of me.

"Brace yourself," I whisper to Gordon. "You're about to meet the infamous Jerry Kellner."

"Can't wait," Gordon whispers back.

"Jerry, this is my boyfriend, Gordon Harrison."

"Nice to meet you," Gordon says, though I know he's lying. I see it in his eyes.

"And this is his boss, Barbara Kenfield."

"So, what brings you here tonight?" asks Jerry while winking at the Hawaiian dancer serving him spare ribs from behind the buffet table. "And hey, Barbara, weren't you the gal that got kicked off *The Biggest Loser* the other night?"

Gordon and I are horrified. Barbara extends her hand graciously and says no, she wasn't on *The Biggest Loser* but hears it's a good show.

"Oh man, I swear you look just like that heavyset gal who passed out and threw up after the hike in the dessert. Not you, huh? Oh, well, then what're you guys doing here?"

"Alexa invited us," Gordon says with a scowl. He suddenly wants to whip through this line. Gordon grabs a plate and shoots me a look. I am mortified.

"So, what do you do, Gordo?" asks Jerry.

"I head a literacy program and teach sixth-grade social studies," Gordon says as he hands his plate to the next Hawaiian server, who offers teriyaki chicken skewers.

"Cool. A teacher. I figured you for a fancy bank guy, maybe a jock, lawyer, even a brain surgeon. But a teacher? Well, hey, to each his own. OK, see ya. Have a good time, kiddies." Jerry takes his plate and waltzes away from the buffet to his table.

Gordon and I stagger back to ours and see Barbara, who's already seated.

"Barbara, I'm so sorry. My coworker, Jerry, isn't especially diplomatic."

"Oh, don't worry," she says. "I'm used to working with children."

"He's a jerk," Gordon says as he puts his plate on the table, eager to trash Jerry and his indelicate remarks.

But I don't want to talk about Jerry. I'm miserable enough. I'm seated in the corner of the tent while Noah and Chester discuss my shows with the reporters from *Fortune* and the *New York Times*. Jerry's with a writer for the *Los Angeles Times*. Another opportunity for a feature story on him. Sylvia and her boss are with Steve and two guys from the *Wall Street Journal*.

Every one of my colleagues is doing business except me. I watch photographers snap pictures of everyone but me as the action is on center court, and once again, I'm in the bleachers. Those photos will be all over the Hollywood trade papers and blogs tomorrow. Yet part of me would rather sit with Gordon and get to know Barbara. At this point I'd do anything for a relaxing dinner, one that doesn't require being *on* every second. Just an easy, calm, hang-loose meal. But this is hardly the time for that. I have to prove I have what it takes to earn that promotion. I can't let my guard down for one second, especially among my colleagues. Somehow I've to get out of here and over there without appearing to be an asshole.

"So, what do you do at HBS?" asks Barbara.

"I develop drama shows," I say. "I was in comedy. Now I'm in drama." Snappy, short answers. Less is more. Now I'm talking like Tony. My eyes scan the room. They go from Chester to Jerry to Steve to Noah and back again. I'm looking everywhere but at my boyfriend and his boss, who are enjoying their meals while I haven't touched mine. Hoping to move things along, I tell Gordon I'm going to the dessert table. Before I know it, he's behind me.

"What's wrong with you?" he asks, grabbing my arm, which I shake off. "What the heck happened today?"

"Look, I made a mistake," I hiss as my eyes search wildly around the room, making sure no one is watching or listening; this is hardly the place for our first argument. "This is a business party. I never should've invited you here. Much less Barbara."

"Then why did you?"

"I don't know what I was thinking. I just wanted to be with you instead of them. But this is the wrong place and time. I'm sorry, Gordon," I say as I start rubbing the back of my neck. "I got the shit kicked out of me today. This was the one chance I had to redeem myself, and I blew it. I should be schmoozing those guys. I'm supposed to be hyping my shows to the press."

I take a breath and try to calm down.

"It's not your fault. I'm just having a really crappy day."

I'm practically in tears, which Gordon notices and tries to comfort me by placing his arm around my waist, but I jerk it away.

"I'll be fine. Don't do that here."

Gordon's shocked by my behavior. I'm not particularly proud of it either, but I'm upset and angry at myself. Not him. But he's not loving this.

"Ya know, I think we should leave," he snaps and starts going back to the table. "I don't want to be here when you're like this."

I sure didn't handle that well. Instead of making things better I made them a lot worse. I follow him back to the table, smiling and pretending nothing's wrong. After a few minutes Gordon announces that he has to get up early and though he'd like to stay longer, he really has to leave. He apologizes to Barbara, who seems perfectly happy to go with him, as she senses the tension between Gordon and me.

"Thank you again for dinner," Barbara says. "It was so nice to finally meet you, Alexa." She shakes my hand and starts to leave with Gordon.

Gordon's pissed. He gives me a peck on the cheek and follows Barbara to the valet. He doesn't even say good-bye.

I'm a total shithead. Sylvia sees me sitting alone and waves frantically for me to come join her at Chester's table. The conversation is about advertising and the deep cuts the network has endured due to diminishing ratings. I listen carefully, feeling really awful about what happened with Gordon and realizing that I have virtually nothing to add to this discussion. I'm just an interloper. After a while the party starts to thin out. Jerry, Steve, and Noah, who've all had one too many, sit down with us. Jerry occupies the empty seat next to me.

"So, you're dating a teacher?" Jerry says, slurring his words. "Can't you do better than that?"

"I like him. He's a good guy."

"You can do better," Jerry says, slapping me on the back. "You need more confidence. I always told you that. You don't aim high enough." Jerry angles his chair close to mine, draping his arm over the back. I shove it away and steer my seat toward Sylvia, who shoots Jerry a dirty look.

Chester orders a round of drinks even though everyone has had quite a few already. It's getting late. We have to be back at work the next morning. But Chester's not ready to leave. And because he's the boss and we're his children, we do as we're told.

Most of the reporters have gone to their rooms to file stories. It's just us HBS colleagues now. We're left drinking, laughing, and partying, the stress of the day behind us. Thanks to the alcohol, life doesn't seem as bad as it was a few hours ago, and Chester announces a management retreat in Hawaii over Presidents' Day weekend in February, which is just a month away. We're all thrilled and raise our glasses. A chance to go to Hawaii, all expenses paid? Just to do a little work? Fantastic!

Jerry moves to another table. His hand is practically down the dress of the actress sitting next to him. Steve is pawing one of the Hawaiian servers. And Noah, who I thought only had eyes for his wife, seems quite enthralled with Gina Gleysteen, Pete's new assistant in reality. They both disappear. I can't get over these guys.

Sylvia says she's had enough and is done for the night. She retreats to her hotel room and I head to the valet. I don't expect a call from Gordon but take out my phone and scroll through the messages anyway. Nothing. I sure don't blame him for being angry with me. I'm sure he's furious. As I think about whether I should call Gordon now or wait till the morning, I feel Chester stroll up alongside me. He hands the valet his parking ticket.

"Think we had a good day, don't you?" Chester asks.

"Yeah, I think it went quite well."

Chester lights a cigarette and flicks the ashes into the wind. "Beautiful night." He takes a puff. "Went from cold to summerlike. Only in Southern California. We've got it all here." Chester pauses as he takes another drag. "Glad it's the weekend. By the way, I think you did OK this morning, Lex."

"Whew, thank you. I needed to hear that," I say. Chester's not one to offer compliments. So I'll take it.

Chester taps his ashes onto the pavement.

"But you need to get out there more," Chester says, looking away from me. "You gotta mingle, you know, start bringing in some big deals. Like Jerry. I think you can really learn from him."

I hate this conversation. I don't say anything; instead I just stare at the ashes as they fall to the ground and disappear.

"Ya know what I've been thinking?" asks Chester.

I can only imagine. Again, I just wait.

"I may split the entertainment job. Maybe have you head programming." Chester flicks his cigarette again.

"What do you mean by that?" I ask as I turn toward him. "Because the president of entertainment encompasses loads of other areas, including programming, promotion, reality, daytime, business affairs, and some others, right? So, I'm a bit confused."

"Yeah, well, Jerry might do well overseeing those areas."

This is not going well.

"So I would oversee programming and he'd oversee everything else?"

"Yeah. Maybe."

"So co-presidents?"

"No. No. Not co-presidents."

"Well, what exactly do you mean, Chester?"

At that precise moment both of our cars appear. Chester leaps to the driver's side of his and tips the valet so he can make a quick getaway. He clearly doesn't want to elaborate.

The other valet holds my door open, waiting for me to come over. But I haven't moved. I'm staring at Chester, waiting for an answer. But he's in his car, about to pull away.

"Hey, I think you guys would make a great team," Chester shouts as he puts the car in gear and drives onto the street.

Chapter Ten

"Hi, this is Alexa Ross. Tony DeMeo suggested I speak with Nancy Calloway. Is she available? Yes, I'll hold." The phone is lodged against my ear as I coast up the escalator to the second floor of Neiman Marcus. Why in the world is it so crowded here on a Monday morning? Don't these people work? I always wonder what lucky person gets to shop during the week when the rest of us schleppers are at the office. I rarely get to department stores. Never have time. Thank God for the Internet, my own personal shopping mall that sends me a present every day.

"Yes, hi, Nancy? Thank you for taking my call. I'll just get to the point. I'm interested in some publicity. Would you have time to meet?" I ask.

"Later this afternoon for coffee? The Polo Lounge at five? Great. I'll see you there."

Nancy's not one for long conversations. Boy, that was fast. At least I don't have to worry about making small talk. I can hardly wait for this meeting.

I can't pussyfoot around anymore. The score is Jerry one hundred, me three. I'm trailing badly. It's time I take control. I never thought I'd need a publicist. But if Sylvia's right and perception trumps reality, then I better get myself some. If I want to win this battle, I have to pull out all the stops. I don't like that Chester sees

Jerry in the role of president and not me. He couldn't even say it. It makes me crazy. I need to change things. Fast.

I'm turning a corner. Not wasting time. A new Alexa is emerging. Gordon's still angry, and frankly I don't blame him. The pressure's unrelenting. I've got pilots to cast, scripts to read, notes to do, dailies to watch, calls to make, rough cuts to see, and Jerry to bury. I refuse to live in his shadow.

This is a really busy day. Starting at Neiman's. Then on to the Beverly Hilton hotel for the *InStyle* Golden Globe Nominees Luncheon. Three of the actors on my shows are up for awards in television comedy. Later, I'll meet Nancy at the Polo Lounge in the Beverly Hills Hotel.

I rush off the escalator and pass Jessica Chastain. Wow, she looks fabulous. I'm dying to tell her how much I enjoy her work, but that would be so lame. I'd be banned from the business. Instead I pretend to look past her, presenting an indifferent and disinterested attitude.

I quickly find the office for Gabriella Mannucci, who will be my new personal shopper. Apparently, there's a whole new world I never knew about behind the designer collection on the second floor of Neiman's, where Gabriella resides. I think I may have found nirvana.

As I enter the suite I'm greeted by a tall woman with long, blonde, wavy hair and big, square, bright-red-rimmed eyeglasses that shield her penetrating blue eyes. Her name tag says Gabriella. Her facial structure is similar to Cher's. She must've been a model at one time. She's an awesome presence. Probably in her forties but could easily pass for thirty. Her gorgeous hair spills onto what appears to be a vibrant-purple Prabal Gurung ruffled silk chiffon blouse with georgette sleeves and button-fastening cuffs, a Tom Ford black pencil skirt, lightly textured smoke nylons, and very sexy black sling-back Manolos. Wow, Manolos. So *Sex in the City*.

How I long for just one pair. She's really put together. I hold her business card and extend my hand.

"Hi, I'm Alexa Ross. Sylvia Radamacher's friend?" I feel small and insecure. I thought I looked great when I walked in wearing my J.Crew white cashmere sweater and black Theory skirt, which I got for a mere eighty bucks on Gilt. But now I feel as though I couldn't dress myself if my life depended on it. Gabriella shakes my hand and ushers me into her office.

Gabriella's office is about the size of Gordon's, but that's where the comparisons end. Her walls feature celebrity fashion photos ripped from magazines from all over the world. A very large bulletin board sports stickers, business cards, scraps of notes, Post-its, and wisps of hair. A nail polish chart is on the opposite wall.

Her desk is a mess. There are the usual office items, pencils, notepads, desk accessories. But they're buried beneath bras with oversize tags, unopened boxes of Jimmy Choos, a beautiful white St. John blazer, two black Spanx tank tops, a Victoria Beckham tiny kelly-green dress, a magnificent creamy Givenchy blouse, a pair of black Armani trousers, and six pairs of red Cosabella lace and satin thongs. I'm mesmerized. I don't know where to look first. There's just too much to take in.

"So, you want a makeover," Gabriella says in her heavy Italian accent. She looks me over from head to toe. When she meets my eyes, she offers a shrug. "What can I do for you?"

"I want to look professional and attractive. Know what I mean? I want to change my image. I don't need a whole new wardrobe, just an upgrade. Can you help?"

Gabriella just looks at me.

"OK. Fine. Sexier…I want to be noticed."

Gabriella wastes no time. We spend the next three hours rushing around the second and third floors of the store. Gabriella grabs pants, tops, suits, dresses, skirts, sweaters, and lingerie, and makes a quick stop to the shoe department on the ground level. We make several trips back and forth to the dressing room, where I try on more clothes than I have in my entire life. I pray I can afford this without going bankrupt. I'm perspiring as I pour myself into clothing I would never select off the rack.

"You've got a great body," Gabriella says, as if she's accusing me of some crime. "What's wrong with you not to show off such a beautiful figure? *Tsk tsk.* We have to change that. Look at you. Look how a lovely you look." I'm standing on a small base in front of three mirrors that don't hide a thing. I feel like a bride, but instead I'm wearing a very flattering Azzedine Alaia red jersey dress with a plunging neckline and insanely expensive but gorgeous pale patent leather Christian Louboutin pumps.

I spend the entire morning in this store. Rosie forwards calls as if I'm in the car, but they're impossible to take here. While I struggle to get into a bra that apparently lifts and separates better than the Victoria's Secret ones—which are "caca," according to Gabriella—Rosie finally screams into the phone that I have to leave *now.* I guess three hours is more than enough time.

I race out of the store with enough bags to open my own boutique. A light drizzle is falling, but my mood has lifted. I find my car around the block. I'm delighted I didn't get a ticket in the one-hour zone. I load up my trunk and head over to the Beverly Hilton hotel for the Golden Globes Nominees Luncheon.

I need to go shopping more. It's amazing how buying new clothes brightens my mood. And having my own personal shopper is pretty cool. Man, Sylvia really knows how to live. I could get used to this.

It must be my lucky day, because I find a great parking space on a residential street a block away from the hotel. Gabriella suggested I toss the outfit I arrived in and opt for another, particularly since I'm going to this big-deal luncheon today. She put me in The Row's black stretch jersey miniskirt, white T-shirt, Haider Ackermann merlot wool-blend tuxedo blazer, and my new three-inch Louboutin "come fuck me" heels, which I'll be sure to wear with Gordon. They look terrific, although I can't walk in them. But hey, I look fabulicious, which was Gabriella's departing word as she sent me on my way and then reminded me to get a spray tan before stepping into the red dress. I sure hope I get a bonus this year, because if not, I'm going to need a bank loan to pay for this shopping spree.

The Beverly Hilton hotel on Wilshire Boulevard opened in 1955. It was built by Conrad Hilton. For years it was owned by Merv Griffin, the former talk show host. It has been the venue for the annual Golden Globe Awards. Today's luncheon attracts not only the nominees for television shows and theatrical films, but also stars who just want to be seen. Some publicists had to sell their souls to get them on the red carpet. It's always a thrill to see movie stars. I don't care what anyone says, when Johnny Depp walks in the room, we're all starstruck. I mean, c'mon, who wouldn't be?

As I carefully walk across Wilshire Boulevard toward the hotel, I begin to see the pandemonium associated with anything star-driven. Unlike the Golden Globe Awards show, this is a smaller production; there aren't the usual bleachers and hoards of fans dying to catch a glimpse of their favorite stars. However, even this minievent draws a crowd. It's glitz, glamour, and fancy luncheon attire. As I walk around the corner onto the hotel grounds, I see the huge, sprawling, U-shaped driveway with the red carpet rolled out in front. About sixty camera crews and still photographers are lined up waiting for the stars to arrive. Syndicated and cable talk show hosts wait eagerly for their prey. It's very cool, and frankly, I'm thrilled to be here.

I walk alongside the red carpet, trying not to fall off the narrow strand of sidewalk reserved for everyone else. I glance to my left. There is a slew of gorgeous celebrities being nudged along by their very focused publicists, who want them interviewed, photographed, and discussed by every fashion expert and celebrity stylist. The cameras and the crowd never tire of these events. Flashbulbs pop every second. Fans are held behind barriers, shouting the name of each celebrity who is escorted onto the red carpet. Occasionally an actor will stop and wave to the crowd. The fans are delighted to be acknowledged and quickly snap photos.

I notice Amy Poehler, who's instantly drawn into an interview. She's dressed in a simple black skirt and short jacket. And, wow, Anne Hathaway, next to Tom Hanks. And I almost don't recognize Cameron Diaz. She's so thin. In fact, they're all really thin. Don't these people eat? As I move farther toward the front of the hotel I see Natalie Portman in a beautiful pink satin pantsuit. I try to stay focused on what's in front of me but can't help but slow down to admire Brad Pitt. Now that's cool. My all-time favorite movie star. Just inches away. What I'd give to have him in a show for us. Dream on, Alexa. What a star-studded event. A simple luncheon turns into a global extravaganza when the movie stars show up.

Just as I'm about to step inside the double doors leading into the Hilton's grand lobby on my way to the International Ballroom, which will be the venue for the luncheon, I receive an elbow to my chest. The person attached to it quickly turns around and apologizes. I almost lose my balance when I discover George Clooney's hand on my arm, frantically apologizing for this minor collision. It takes about a minute for it to register that this very famous and unbelievably handsome dude has his hand on my forearm and is within inches of my face. But before I can even say it's no big deal, Billy Bush grabs Clooney's arm and moves him toward the *Access Hollywood* camera.

I can't get over that George Clooney's hand was on my arm just seconds ago. Oh my God, I can't wait to tell Emily. If she were here, she would've quickly taken a photo, tweeted it, and posted it on Facebook.

Interestingly, once we're inside the ballroom there are few celebrities. They're in the green room, where more cameras and interviews await. Instead this room is a sea of white men in black suits, white shirts, and colorful ties. All of them look as if they could be actors themselves. They're well groomed, good-looking, and sexy. They reek of success, power, and money. The few women in the crowd are dressed like men, in dark-colored suits, completely desexualized. These are my colleagues, many of whom are film and TV executives, agents, and a smattering of writers and producers. Drinks and hors d'oeuvres are passed while we wait for the luncheon to begin. I remind myself that I have to transform into Alexa the executive and shake off the ecstatic girl who is still giddy over George Clooney's hand on mine.

"Hey, Alexa, we rarely see you outside the network," says Andy James, an agent at ICM whom I've spoken with many times but couldn't pick out in a crowd. Thank goodness he recognized me, because although I talk to these people on the phone, I rarely see them.

"I don't get out as much as I should." I smile. "Too many network meetings. I'm glad to see you."

I'm doing what everyone else is doing—talking to the person in front of me but peering above and beyond to see who else is here. Everything is about selling. What kind of deal can I make? Who can I push to buy my product? Who do I want to know better so I can further my career? It's a room full of selfish ambition.

As the lights begin to flicker, signaling the start of the luncheon, I pull out my ticket and search for my table. On my way I'm accosted by Rob Persinger and Gary Rothchild, who are TV packaging agents at the Creative Artists Agency. They're dapper, smooth, intimidating, and purposeful. They offer the obligatory air kisses. We greet like good friends. However, I know when and if I ever leave the network, they will not know me. My power is in the chair. They'll be as gracious and wonderful to the person who succeeds me as they're being with me now and forget I ever existed.

"You look beautiful," Rob says in a sexy voice. He looks me up and down. It gives me goose bumps, which I'm sure is what he intended. Rob is gorgeous. It's amazing he isn't an actor.

"Thank you, Rob. It's nice to see you again."

"We'd like you to consider Steven Jacoby to direct Toby Anderson's pilot," says Gary, getting right to the point. "It's our package. If Steven directs it, I'm sure we can help cast it as well." Gary and Rob double-team me. Rob plays the schmoozer and Gary gets the job done. I get their point. If you hire our midlevel director, we'll help you get the feature stars you want for your pilot. It's an offer I'll definitely consider.

"That's interesting," I say. "I'd like to get Zac Efron for the lead. What do you think?"

Gary looks at Rob, and through some sort of mental telepathy, they arrive at an agreement. Gary says, "I think we can work that out. Let's talk later today."

Their job is done. They quickly move on to their next victim, who is the president of Warner Bros. Television. I move across the room and grab a glass of chardonnay off a silver tray and run smack into Drew Barrymore and Justin Long. Weren't they a couple at one time?

What other businesses offer this much fun? This luncheon is just one part of my very busy day. It's something I take for granted. I stop for a moment and absorb the setting. It's really amazing to be here amid some of the greatest entertainers in the world. I'm lucky to be in this field and not afraid to admit that it's pretty darn exciting.

But all comes to a screeching halt when I see Jerry Kellner in the corner with the president of FX. I decide to stay put so as not to ruin my day. I take a sip of wine as my eyes dart around the room. I see a few more familiar faces. This is nerve-racking because it's basically an all-male cocktail party. There are definitely women here, but they're clearly the minority. However, I guess if you're a woman on the make this might be a good place to meet guys. With the exception of Jerry, most aren't interested in pussy. They're interested in making deals. Their friendly manner is just a facade. They're all sharks out for the kill.

"Hey, sexy, how ya doing?" asks Peter Galenson, a guy I dated years ago. Actually, I'm pretty sure I slept with him. Hmm, yup. I did. Unimpressive, as I recall. He's an agent at Paradigm representing TV writers. "Nice to see you're doing drama now. Have you read Peggy Brenner's spec pilot? It's really good. I hope you might consider her to run *Handsome Dude* if you guys pick it up."

"Sure, Peter," I say with a smile. "I'd be happy to read it. I remember when she wrote for *CSI Miami*. Please send it." Peter's work is done. Peggy was the flavor of the month, but then never quite got it back. This is Hollywood. Hot one day. Cold the next. Not a business for the faint of heart.

"Alexa! How ya doing?" asks Chris Joseph, one of my favorite agents at William Morris Endeavor. "So great that you're in drama now. Do you love it?" We hug as though we haven't seen each other in years, even though it's been a few weeks. Whenever he's at HBS, he always stops to say hello. An affable agent with terrific writers, Chris was promoted from a literary agent to a packager. The bigger shark tank. I think he might possess a *genuine* gene, as he may even acknowledge me after my stint at the network is done.

"Please help me get some great actors for my pilots," I say. "I need big names. Tons of pressure. Can you help?" I feel very comfortable with Chris. He and I started our careers around the same time. He was in the mail room when I worked for Jerry, and now he's married with a kid on the way.

"Whatever you need. I'm here for you. Let's grab breakfast and I'll help ya out," Chris says. "By the way, hang in there, kid. I remember when you worked for Jerry. Man, he's a crazy cat. Watch out for him. He's bad news." As if I don't know that. Nice to know the town is engaged in our battle.

The talent has entered the ballroom, and lunch is being served. Chris and I air kiss good-bye. I'm seated between a talent agent at ICM and Todd Fields, the writer of the very successful drama series *Corporate Jungle* on TNT. Both spit over my salad as they greet each other.

Todd and I hit it off right away. He tells me about *Corporate Jungle*, a show I've seen twice, and goes on to describe another idea, which I want to buy. He's stunned. But not more than me. I don't even have next year's budget, but I want this very successful guy writing shows for HBS. I'll figure the rest out later.

The president of the Hollywood Foreign Press, which gives out the Golden Globes, takes the stage and introduces the nominees. Everyone applauds. I notice Jerry sitting across the room. The second the show begins, Jerry leaves. His work is done. He's about the schmooze, nothing else.

It's just after three o'clock, and the luncheon is over. However, I have to stay in Beverly Hills to meet Nancy Calloway later at the Polo Lounge. I've been there several times, always as someone's guest. I look forward to the day I can get my own reservation without spelling my name a hundred times. R-o-s-s isn't exactly difficult to spell. But the hostess insists it's R-o-t-h. Welcome to Beverly Hills, where R-o-t-h is more common than S-m-i-t-h.

My feet are dying in these new shoes with the beautiful red soles. I dread the long walk back to my car. Interestingly, most of the celebrities have slipped out either during the luncheon or shortly thereafter. It's all about the red carpet. Their work is done.

Boy, there's nothing like breaking in a brand-new pair of heels. Why didn't I just leave my car at the valet? I didn't want to deal with the long wait afterward. Instead I'll be dealing with blisters for days. After what seems like five miles, I limp up to my car. I cannot wait to take off these pumps. As I approach, I see a ticket on the windshield. Fifty-eight dollars? Are you kidding me? I might have to return something to Neiman's. Well, this sure was a bad decision. I crash into my seat and tear off my shoes. I call Rosie, who runs through a slew of messages including one from Molly saying she's at work. Apparently my persistence paid off. Steve is not going to win that one. Yay!

For the next two hours I remain in my car and run HBS's drama development from a residential street until it's time to leave for my appointment with Nancy. While Rosie places calls I take care of the most important piece of business, which is to send Emily a text about George Clooney. What girlfriend wouldn't appreciate that story?

As I happily think about that split second next to George, Rosie interrupts saying Gordon's on the line. We spoke briefly after he and Barbara left dinner the other evening, but as easygoing as Gordon is, he wasn't nearly as forgiving as I had hoped. Things are still a bit frosty.

"I got your message, what's up? Have a class starting in a few minutes." Gordon's irritated tone isn't lost on me.

"I'm really sorry. Are you going to be angry with me forever? I screwed up and—"

"Look, I don't know what to think. I thought you were really rude and insensitive the other night at your press function, and I didn't like it."

"I know," I say, trying to sound as apologetic as possible. "As I said, I'm having a difficult time. I tried to explain the kind of pressure I'm under and—"

"Alexa," Gordon says my name, and it feels awful because I know what's coming means he's not happy. He never calls me that. It's always Lex or Lexi, but never Alexa. Uh-oh. "We're all under pressure, OK? We all have our stuff. Some of us just handle it better. And I think that's something you need to think about. Look, I've got to go. Let's try to move on. We're both busy. We'll have to table this."

"OK, but can we be friends?" I ask, sounding ridiculous, but I'm starting to wonder if we even are anymore. "I made a mistake, but I think we're allowed to make them occasionally."

"I'm coming, I'm coming," I hear Gordon say to someone in the background. "We'll figure it out. Talk later." And then all I hear is dead air and then there's a text from Rosie reminding me to meet Nancy in ten minutes.

I turn on the ignition and head toward the Beverly Hills Hotel, which is less than a mile away. I replay the conversation with Gordon, hoping this is now behind us. I drive up the long tree-lined driveway to the entrance.

Sometimes I literally have to pinch myself because I can't believe I've made it as far as I have in my life. As a kid I remember dreaming about what it would be like to just walk inside the lobby of the Beverly Hills Hotel. And today it's no big deal. I've been here numerous times. I'm living a life so different from the one I left behind.

Suddenly I hear a door slam and a woman yelling for someone to get her car. I snap out of my stupor. A brand-new silver Mercedes sedan is parked alongside. Nancy Calloway slams the door, grabs the ticket, and marches into the hotel. I've seen Nancy's photo many times. Much has been written about her, though she tries to remain behind the scenes. She frequents all the parties, award shows, and trendy Hollywood restaurants. She's a Hollywood trailblazer and workaholic. She's also aggressive and relentless.

I wait for Nancy to pass. I fiddle around in the car, pretending to look for something. When the coast is clear, I jump out, grab the parking ticket, and hike under the famous green-and-white canopy and head over to the Polo Lounge. I hope this goes well. I'm already intimidated.

Nancy has barely entered the restaurant and is already holding court. The hostess waits patiently as Nancy glides by each table, offering hellos, kisses, and in special instances, hugs along the way. I wait at the entrance for the hostess to seat Nancy. I look across the Polo Lounge and see Bruce Willis and Jeff Bridges at one table, and directly across from them are Naomi Watts and Maggie Gyllenhaal. They seem far more relaxed than when I saw them earlier on the red carpet at the Hilton. When the hostess returns, I follow her to the table. What a scene. My eyes dart from one table to the next, getting quick glimpses of some very famous people everywhere. Our table is at the back of the outside terrace in its own alcove. A lovely private banquette that could seat four.

I slide in, order a Diet Coke, and peer around the garden, where I notice Samuel Jackson dining with Quentin Tarantino. God, this is some place at five o'clock on a weekday. I definitely need to come here more often. Nancy is chatting with the chairman of Disney. She's extremely personable. I'm beginning to wonder what the heck Tony was thinking. How am I going to be able to afford her?

"Hi, Alexa, nice to meet you," Nancy says breathlessly as she slides into the booth across from me. She wears a yellow sweater slung over her shoulders, crisp white blouse, and feminine black pants, and Chanel sunglasses rest on top of her platinum-blonde hair. Her Carolina Herrera appearance is both striking and daunting. Probably in her sixties, but admitting to fifty, she orders the

McCarthy salad sans bacon, eggs, and cheddar cheese with just a touch of balsamic vinegar on the side. We were meeting for coffee, but I guess she missed lunch, although a bowl of chopped lettuce doesn't sound especially appealing.

"So, what can I do for you, hon?"

I'm sure she never meets with anyone on my level. If Tony weren't the head of publicity at a major broadcast network, there's no way Nancy would give me the time of day. She's doing him a favor, and she'll expect one in return.

"I'm trying to get promoted at HBS," I say. "It appears I may need a little outside help to raise my visibility and flaunt my accomplishments. Frankly I need to get my name out there."

Nancy glares at me. She knows I'm a neophyte.

"I googled you," she says flatly. "There's not much there. You were head of comedy and just switched to drama, correct?" I nod. "You're not even on the *Hollywood Reporter*'s Fifty Most Powerful Women list. And you're a senior executive at a major broadcast network? That's not good."

Great. More wonderful things to hear. "Well, that's why I'm here. Tony said he doesn't have time to help me start a career. I actually thought I had one, but according to Tony—"

"Tony doesn't know shit," Nancy interrupts. "First of all, it's his job to get you out there. But Tony's a misogynist pig. We all know that. He's not going to help you unless it helps him. That's just who Tony DeMeo is." I'm startled by her assertion but don't disagree. "OK, look, I know what you need. I'd have to charge you five grand a month. You're gonna have to meet journalists, get some on-air training, and do plenty of interviews. It won't happen overnight, but we can get you started."

"OK, it's a deal," I say, wondering where the heck I'm going to find the dough, but I'll worry about it later. Nancy's meal arrives. Or rather a dollop of lettuce and an ounce of chicken at the bottom of what looks like a serving bowl. I figure three forkfuls and she's done.

"What's your background?" Nancy says, plunging into her salad without glancing at me.

"I have a degree from San Diego State in communications, but it really serves as a wall hanging. It was my typing skills that opened doors for me," I say as my thumb and index finger tug at my earlobe, a habit I resort to when I'm feeling anxious. "I got a temp job as a junior secretary working for a lowlife producer in the Valley, and then, uh…well, I was an assistant to Jerry Kellner, who I followed to Fox, and—"

"Actually," Nancy interrupts, enjoying the last bite of her happy meal, "I just want to know what you've done as an executive, but forget it, we'll talk about that some other time. We have a lot to do. We'll need to get moving."

And then, just like that, the meeting's over. Nancy's done. No small talk. No personal conversation. No laughs. No fun. Just business. Straight and to the point. She signs the check and starts to leave.

"Alexa, you're not an assistant anymore," she says, glaring at me. "You want to be in the boys' club? Then change your attitude. You need to embrace the power of your position."

She shakes my hand and whisks off to another table, greeting more colleagues as she makes her way out. I'm left sitting in the booth like debris from a hurricane.

———

It's only been a week, but my world is about to change. Nancy didn't waste one second. I have a ton of interviews and meetings. I've had to push many of my general duties on Stacey. Rosie is picking up the slack. It's all about getting me out there and building my brand. I've already spoken to a few reporters and done some radio interviews. Nancy suggested I get highlights and new makeup. I spent the weekend doing that.

I visited her hair salon. Next to me was Jennifer Love Hewitt, who was buried in a script the whole time. She hardly looked up. Sitting under the dryer reading from her iPad was Halle Berry. Where in the world do you see famous celebrities carrying out mundane tasks like this? And yet no one in the salon was gazing at them. That's LA. Celebrities are like wallpaper. No big deal. Except for the paparazzi waiting outside.

Gordon's been out of town at a seminar with Barbara while I've been running around like a maniac. The whole Hollywood scene means nothing to him. He enjoys hearing about it but has no patience for the narcissistic attitudes. I'm not sure I can share all that I'm doing with him. I don't think he'll love my transformation, as he's all about authenticity. I hope he understands I have to make some adjustments to beat Jerry.

As I head into HBS, Rosie tells me that Chester moved the staff meeting to ten. So I need to hurry up.

"OK, well, I'm on my way so that should be fine."

"You have a ton of other stuff to do. Nancy has about six interviews scheduled. God, she's amazing."

We'll see how amazing, as today will be the first test of my new makeover, which I spent the better part of the weekend on. I'll be curious to see the reaction in the staff meeting. I blew Sylvia off this morning. If I have any time, I'll *try* to get to Crestview this afternoon to see Marisol; if not I'll make it up to her somehow. Fortunately, I made it out there last week, even though it was a short session. I promised Gordon I'd stick with her till I leave for New York in May, although I may need to discuss this with him at dinner tonight, our first chance to see each other in about a week.

I rip into my parking spot and go directly to Chester's office. It's a little after ten. I'll be late, but I'm over that now. The guys are never on time. Why should I be? All the things I thought mattered in life don't anymore. New attitude. New me. I enter Chester's office suite and fly past Jan, who actually gasps as I breeze by.

The gang's all here. The meeting must have just begun. I'm a mere five minutes late.

I walk across the room toward my chair. I'm wearing my new Louboutins and sexy, low-cut red silk dress. My push-up bra emphasizes my ample bust, something I hid in the past. I am in full makeup, highlights, and the obligatory spray tan, which Gabriella said must accompany the red dress.

No one says a word; however, I feel every single pair of eyes on me. There isn't one person who isn't gazing at me. I get to the chair, cross my legs, which shows off my new bronze tan, and smile cheerfully.

"Holy shit, is that you, Alexa?" Tony asks, nearly falling out of his chair.

"Wow, what did you do to yourself?" asks Noah.

Chester hasn't stopped looking at me. I'm actually feeling a little uncomfortable. I'm not used to this kind of attention. Particularly from *this* group.

"Uh, well, I guess we," Chester is discernably tongue-tied, "well, we were talking about, uh, a show. Right guys? The Babbit show...I think."

Like dogs in heat, they can barely keep their tongues in their mouths and bob their heads in unison. There's one person who's not turned on. Jerry Kellner. Having acquired the role of vice president of comedy, he's now a member of the dick dance club and would sure like to get the focus off of me and onto him.

"We're discussing Donald Babbitt's pilot," Jerry says. "I'm pretty sure we can cast it."

"Is the script good?" I ask. "Because the concept was kind of lame. I bought it because Mila Kunis was attached to star. Is she still on board?"

Jerry has trouble holding his own when it comes to developing scripts, which would require reading them—something Jerry dreads. It's where I'm strong and he's weak. I wonder if he's even read this script or had someone either read it to him or provide a synopsis, which is the way he often *reads* scripts.

"Jerry, is Kunis still in it?" asks Chester.

"Uh, no. She passed," he mutters.

"That's too bad," says Chester.

"Has it gone to other actresses?" asks Steve.

"Yeah. We've been to about six so far," says Jerry softly.

"Well, the only way we'll go forward is if we get a famous actress in the lead role," says Chester. "You can cast around it, but without a star, it's dead."

Without missing a beat, I continue to destroy Jerry.

"I had a great talk with Todd Fields," I say. "Chester, if we can find money in next year's development, I can get him in here. He gave me an idea I think could work for us."

"Great," says Chester. "Mark, get into that today. What else you got?"

"It looks like *Dad's New Wife Bernard* on NBC might be canceled," I say. "If so, Dex Holland will be available. I spoke to his agent, Rob Persinger, who said he has a lot of offers."

"Well, how do we get him?" asks Chester.

"Already taken care of," I say. "Rob wants his client, Steven Jacoby, to direct Toby Anderson's pilot. We can make that happen. In return, we'd get first crack at Dex. I also let him know we're very interested in Zac Efron if he ever decides to do TV."

Chester lights a cigarette and smiles. When no one is looking, he taps my knee with his free hand, suggesting his approval.

"Jerry, I want to see some names for those comedy pilots," he says. "If we don't get a star, we'll push it to next season. Let's get to work on that, OK?"

Jerry shrugs. He can't even look at me. I'm lovin' this. My transformation, both internal and external, is beginning to work. I'm determined to turn things around. I'm not reporting to Jerry Kellner. Ever again. I don't care what it takes, it ain't happening. And he's not getting promoted over me.

"Oh my gawd," Rosie says, looking me up and down as I enter my office suite. "You look gorgeous."

"Thank you," I say as I teeter down the hallway in my fancy Louboutins.

"Are you going with Gordon to some great place tonight?" she asks.

"No. Why?" I'm confused.

"Well, you look beautiful. I've never seen you this dressed up."

"Get used to it, Rosie. Things are about to change." I move on. "What's happening?"

Rosie grabs her phone book, reciting the calls I missed, and follows me into the office as I sit at my desk and begin sorting through e-mails.

"You had a free morning, but Chester wants you to attend a casting session with Jerry on Donald Babbitt's comedy pilot. That session starts in fifteen minutes. But you have a notes call with the producers of *Forced to be Family* at that time."

"Have Stacey do that call." I stop what I'm doing. "That's odd. Chester wants me to weigh in on one of Jerry's shows? Did Jan say why?"

"Nope."

"Chester said that pilot might not even go forward if they don't get a star," I say.

"Well, this casting session is for a minor role in that show," adds Rosie.

"OK. Then later I need to stop by two locations in the Valley, right? And then Marisol this afternoon. And then I'm meeting Gordon for dinner. Did he tell you where?"

I listen to Rosie while scrolling through e-mails. A new one just arrives from Gordon.

Thinking about you. Hope all is well. Luv u sweety. CU l8tr. Rosie has info.

The muscles in my neck soften, and my heart rate slows down as soon as I read this. Gordon's always had that effect on me.

Luv U2. Can't wait to CUL. xo

I take off my shoes and hike up my dress, sitting cross-legged while massaging my toes, which are freezing. My boobs are falling out of my dress, but no one can see this except my computer screen.

"Oh, Sylvia wants to see you tomorrow," Rosie yells from outside my office. "And Emily called. I forgot to mention that earlier. Sorry. Oh, and Nancy wants you to do an interview with the *New York Times*, which sounds fantastic."

"I can't see Sylvia," I shout. "Tell Emily I'll get back to her when I can. And tell Nancy whenever she wants me, I'm there."

I'm sure Rosie's starting to wonder what's happening to me. I'm wondering, too. But right now I'm doing what I have to.

I take care of a few more e-mails, put myself back together, and start off to the casting session down the hall. I can't wait to see the look on Jerry's face.

Wayne Cedar, the diminutive and balding vice president of casting for HBS, has a beautifully appointed office. The walls are light gray, providing a lovely backdrop for the black-and-white photographs by Toni Frissell, Aneta Kowalczyk, and others of that ilk. Along the opposite wall are photographs of actors Wayne hired early in their careers: Hillary Swank, Jerry O'Connell, Julia Stiles, Paul Rudd, and Ryan Reynolds. All the actors auditioning for roles in this room today long to be on that wall tomorrow.

If Jerry isn't able to secure a famous actress for this pilot, it will die or roll to next year. The fact that Jerry chose to keep this meeting and cast around the lead is interesting. I'm sure he doesn't want the writer, Donald Babbitt, to know the pilot may be going south. Jerry's not good with bad news.

I greet Donald, who gives me a friendly handshake and obligatory air kiss. He embraces me warmly and asks if I had a boob job. Charming. Jerry and Molly arrive and see me sitting between Donald and Wayne on the couch. Jerry stops when he sees me.

"What're you doing here?"

"Chester asked me to sit on this session," I say, smiling.

Jerry smirks, trying to hide his anger, and takes a seat alongside Donald. Molly plants herself behind me. While the three men are chatting, Molly taps me on the shoulder.

"I had a miscarriage over the weekend," she whispers.

I turn toward her and ask if she's all right.

"I'll be OK. And Steve and I are through, and that's probably best. You were right. Thank you," Molly says sweetly.

"I'm sorry you had to go through all this," I whisper as I squeeze her hand.

I want to talk more, but the first actress has entered for her audition. She's a very beautiful woman in her early twenties with long, golden hair and gorgeous green eyes. "Hi, y'all, I'm Raven," she squeals as if she's in the seventh grade, then takes a seat on a straight-backed chair facing us. I can't help but notice how thin she is, like she hasn't eaten for days. Raven begins her audition. When she's done we all applaud while the casting director escorts her out the door and brings in the next actress.

Vanessa Armstrong, also in her twenties, has long, wavy chestnut hair and a chest that's bursting out of her green tank top. She greets each of us with a big white toothy smile, and when she stumbles by Tom we can't help but notice the top of her bright-pink thong peeking out of her tight capris. It's clear Vanessa's audition isn't nearly as good as Raven's, but as she exits we all tell her how great she was.

"Va-va-voom, that's the one!" shouts Jerry as the door closes. "We found our Sofia Vergara."

I roll my eyes, knowing it was Vanessa's appearance that appealed to him more than her performance.

"Well, she sure doesn't have the chops, but I understand the allure." Wayne laughs.

"I like her look, too," Donald says. "She's got great tits and terrific cleavage, but I'm not sure she can go the distance."

"I have to get to my next meeting," I say, getting up to leave. "Look, Raven is clearly the better actress. Vanessa has the looks you guys want, but you have to remember this show is targeted toward young women. Better make sure the actress you pick is someone they can relate to. Vanessa is no Sofia Vergara, who's funny and warm as well as sexy. Women love her. You guys better think with your heads and not something else."

"Oh, Alexa, go fuck yourself. You're such a buzz-kill. It's always about your woman bullshit," Jerry says.

"Jerry, go fuck your own self," I shout back. I'm not going to let him get away with this insulting behavior. "This show isn't even ordered. Did you tell them that Chester said it's not going till you hire the lead actress? This is a total waste of time." I start to exit, and when I shut the door, I hear Donald screaming at Jerry. I'm happy. My job is done. Finally, a small victory. I'll take it.

I sweep into my office, grab my bag, and head off to Crestview to see Marisol. Rosie follows me into the stairwell reading off the latest issues of the day.

"Nancy said you're going to be featured in *Variety*'s Most Powerful Women issue next month," Rosie says. "And *The Wrap* wants to do an interview with you tomorrow. She wants you in full makeup for a segment on *Access Hollywood*, discussing the pilots you've ordered. This is amazing. She's really doing a great job."

Finally some good news, which makes me feel a lot better. I can put Jerry and the casting session behind me and resume my day. As we head out of the stairwell, I ask Rosie to get me an iced tea from the commissary. I think this might be the first time I've ever asked her to do something like that. She seems surprised, but I don't really care. While she's gone, I call Nancy and go over exactly what she needs. I'm starting to like this. I'm winning for a change and liking my new attitude.

Rosie hands me my drink as I get into the car. It's going to be torture walking on that playground in these insane heels, so I tell Rosie to make sure Marisol meets me in Gordon's office because I don't want to navigate the playground. As I start to pull away, Rosie says Molly needs to talk to me, but I've given Molly more than enough time, and pass on calling her back.

When I approach Crestview, I see Gordon standing in the entryway of the main office.

"Wow. Where did this come from?" Gordon asks as I reach his office. We step inside, he tosses his glasses on the table, takes a beat, and smiles broadly as he surveys me from head to toe.

"Ah, I take it you like this?" I say flirtatiously.

Gordon's enthralled with my new look. I think it's the first time he's seen me in a sexy dress.

"Uh, yeah. You look fantastic."

"I do?"

Gordon takes me in his arms and pulls me close.

"Very hot," he whispers. "You are one sexy broad."

Gordon starts kissing my neck.

"Hey, slow down," I laugh. "I'm going to see you in a couple of hours."

"I know. But do we really want to have dinner?"

I move gently from his embrace.

"Yes, we're having dinner at Craig's, where we had our first romantic dinner, and then you can come over," I say, kissing him gently on the lips. "I'm here to see Marisol, remember?"

"Oh, yes. And Rosie said you want to see her in here?" he asks. "Why? Can't you meet her on the playground? I was going to work in here."

I point to my new heels.

"OK, I get it. But just this time, 'cause this room is for brief meetings. I can't always use it. I'll be on the playground, grading papers. Not my idea of fun."

"Well, just think about tonight," I say, tilting my head and flashing just a hint of my new printed bra. "We'll have plenty of fun later."

Gordon pulls me closer, but at that very instant the door opens and in walks Marisol. Gordon releases me, says he'll see us later, and darts out the door.

Marisol and I sit across from each other at the table as she shows me her new book, *A Wrinkle in Time* by Madeleine L'Engle. This seems a cut above where we're at, but it's clear she wants to tackle it.

"You look really pretty, Alexa," says Marisol.

"Why, thank you so much," I laugh. I stand up and do a quick pirouette so Marisol can get the full picture. "This is the new me. Do you like it better than my other, boring outfits?"

Marisol nods, and I pull my chair around the table so I'm sitting right next to her.

"So what's been going on?" I ask as I put on my glasses. "I know I missed some weeks. I'm so sorry. Remember I told you this is a really busy time for me? I may not be here on a regular basis for a while. I hope you understand."

"I do." Marisol looks down at the book and opens it to the first page. "Olga is reading this book. Can we try it?"

"Sure, I know this story well. I think it's great. It may be a little hard at first, but let's give it a shot."

Marisol stares at the first page. But I notice something different. She doesn't have that cute smile today. She doesn't seem comfortable. I can't explain it. But something's off.

"Um, before we start, is everything OK?" I ask. "Maybe because I haven't seen you in a while. You just seem different."

Marisol shakes her head and just stares at the page. I wait to see if she'll say anything more, but she's not forthcoming.

"OK, well, then let's begin."

But Marisol doesn't say anything. Her finger is under the first word, but there's just silence. I wait.

"I missed you." Marisol speaks so softly I can barely hear her.

"Oh, I missed you, too."

There's a long pause. I put my arm around her and bring her toward me.

"It's going to be difficult for me to get here for a while," I say. "I have a lot of work. You have to promise that you'll keep reading. OK?"

Marisol nods but won't look at me.

"Let's try to start this book. Then, when I return, I want you to tell me all about it. I read it a long time ago and I'm eager to hear what you think of it."

Marisol begins to read, stumbling over a few words, but she's actually doing better than I expected. I'm really impressed, and I tell her so. I even see a glimpse of that cute little dimple. Whew, she's not completely lost. I help with more words. She's frustrated, but once I say the word, she says it over and over. She's really concentrating, and when I move my finger under the next word she sounds it out slowly and smiles.

"You're doing great, Marisol. I'm so proud of you."

Marisol grins broadly but doesn't lose her concentration. She keeps moving her finger along the page.

My phone's vibrating. As Marisol continues reading I scroll through the list of messages many that say *urgent*. More problems. I let Marisol finish the chapter, but even though our time isn't up, I know I have to attend to these issues. And I just got here. Ugh. I hate this.

"Marisol, you did a great job. Bravo. I'm so proud of you," I say, raising my arms above my head, underscoring my enthusiasm for her accomplishment.

Marisol smiles sweetly. And then I put my hand over hers, and she offers a disconcerted look. She knows something's up.

"I have to end early today," I say softly. "I'm sorry. I'm just overwhelmed right now."

"But you still like me?"

"Of course I like you. Are you kidding?"

There's a pause as I put my arm over the back of her chair and look squarely into her eyes.

"I like you so much. I really do," I say. "Believe me, I would much rather spend time with you than deal with work right now. It's just a really crazy time, and as much as I don't want to leave, I know I have to."

I stand up and toss my glasses and phone into my purse.

"Am I going to see you again?"

I bend down and gently touch the top of Marisol's head.

"Of course you are. It may not be next week. But it'll be soon. I promise."

There's a long pause. Then for the first time, Marisol looks up at me. She looks straight into my eyes.

"I really like you, Alexa. I learn a lot from you. I'm so happy when you come."

I can't move. I've never heard her say anything like that before. I can't just leave, nor do I want to. I'm so darn conflicted. I'm really attached to her. I set my things down on the table and decide I'm not leaving so fast.

She stares up at me and I stare down at her.

"Come here, Marisol. Let me give you a hug."

Marisol leaps out of her chair, and we both stand in the middle of this little room embracing each other. I never knew the depth of her feelings for me. I realize for the first time how very important this time is for her and how she's come to depend on me.

We continue to hold each other.

"Do you think I'm going to leave and never return?" I ask, tilting her chin up. She nods. After a moment I kneel down on the ground so we're at eye level. "I made a commitment to you and to this program. I'm your tutor, and I want to help you read. I know it's hard because I'm not here as often as I had hoped. But I want to see you succeed. You're doing so well. I don't want you to stop trying. You have to keep reading." I tip Marisol's chin upward again and look right into her eyes. "I'll be back, Marisol. I promise. You have to believe me." Marisol offers a weak but appreciative smile. "When I return I want to hear all about *A Wrinkle in Time*. OK?"

Marisol nods as I take her hand and we both step outside.

The second the door closes, Marisol rushes to the playground. I watch as she greets her friend Olga and places her book in her backpack. Just as I'm about to turn the corner I see Marisol. She turns toward me, smiling as she waves good-bye.

When I get in the car, Rosie informs me of problems on the sets and some deals that haven't closed. I handle most of these issues on the phone on my way back to the office. But given the traffic and the time, I decide it's too late to go to the Valley. Instead I stop at home, feed Joe, take in the mail, and freshen up.

I get to Craig's a little early and sink into the booth along with my phone, iPad, and call sheet. Julian greets me right away and pours some wine. I set everything on the table so I can finish work before Gordon arrives.

But I'm distracted thinking about my time with Marisol today. I had no idea how much tutoring meant to her. I thought it was a hassle for her. I recall the conversation I had with Emily, who said I can't disappoint her, as she'll come to depend on me. Boy, did she call that one. But I've also come to depend on her, which I didn't expect. As much as I give her, I'm getting plenty in return. It's a wonderful feeling, and I'm thrilled with the progress she's made in such a short period of time and love that she wants to keep up with her classmates. I really treasure our sessions and think about how good I feel being with her and how being a part of her life has also enriched mine.

The time goes by quickly, and soon Gordon arrives, whips off his jacket, and then kisses me as he sits down beside me. He orders a bottle of Merlot, though I've already had two glasses thanks to Julian.

"I don't know why we're here," Gordon says. "We should've just picked up something and brought it back to your apartment."

"Oh, I think it's nice to go out to dinner, particularly here," I say, brushing my hand against his cheek. "I remember our first kiss was right over there in that booth. It was such a turn-on. I knew you were a keeper."

"And I knew I was in big trouble because you looked so beautiful and sexy. I couldn't wait to get out of here."

"Oh, so that's why you tore down Sunset Boulevard? We were freezing, remember?"

"I do." Gordon smiles. "But it took you forever to invite me up to your apartment."

"Oh, there's no way you weren't coming up that night," I say coyly. Julian pours the wine while Gordon orders filet mignon, asking that it be well done on the outside, while I opt for the honey truffle chicken.

As Julian scoops up the menus, Gordon turns toward me and brushes his hand on my cheek.

"You look hot like this. I need to get you home," he whispers as he kisses me again, and then I rest my head against his chest. "When I Fall in Love" plays softly in the background, and I listen carefully to the lyrics. It seems to be about true love. When both lovers give of themselves and commit deeply to their relationship it can last a lifetime.

I can't help but wonder if this is about us. And how I've come to rely on this guy. How our worlds are intertwined now. And then I wonder, will it be forever? I can't imagine not being with Gordon. He's an integral part of my life.

"How was it with Marisol today?" he asks.

"I had a wonderful time," I say. "I discovered how much she values our tutoring sessions. She's doing remarkably well. I'm so proud of her."

Gordon smiles and kisses the top of my head.

"I knew you'd be good at this," he says. "I can't tell you how great this makes me feel. It's so important for these kids. And especially Marisol, who gets so little individualized attention in the classroom or at home. I'm glad she's making progress."

"Her reading is getting better, and she's selecting books that are more challenging. I'm really happy for her."

Gordon drapes his arm over my shoulder as I tear off a piece of bread and feed it to him. We both take a sip of wine, and then Gordon pulls me close and whispers in my ear, "I'm so lucky to have you in my life."

We take another sip of wine, enjoying every second of our time together. My body is so relaxed. I'm not grinding my teeth or picking my nails. I feel light-headed and a little sleepy. However, I catch of glimpse of someone coming through the door. It appears to be Jerry. I open my eyes wide to make sure it's him. And it is. He shakes Craig's hand like they're old friends, but I know they're not. I've come here plenty of times and never seen Jerry. Craig leads him to a large table in the back, where he sits alone, glued to his BlackBerry. Gordon knows something's up. He follows my gaze, then turns back toward me and rolls his eyes.

"Oh, no, you have to get over this guy. You can't let him dominate your life."

"I hate him," I say, feeling agitated. "And I can't get over him. He's trying to get the job I want. And if he gets it, I'd have to work for him again. And that's never going to happen. Never."

"Well, you could quit," Gordon says as he removes his arm from my shoulder. "What about working someplace else?"

"Gordon, I can't quit," I say as my eye starts to twitch. "I've worked hard for this opportunity. I'm very invested in my job. And I want to be promoted. You know that. I'm trying to balance everything, but it's not always easy."

"Well, maybe you better figure out when enough is enough," Gordon says as he moves his arm, creating a little more distance between us. "Because I can't stand when you're like this. It's like you become this other person. Like the night of your press tour. I never want to see that side of you again."

"All the sides you see are a part of me," I say, feeling testy and biting the inside of my lip. "I'm sorry if you don't like them all. They're all me. I can't be what I'm not."

Neither of us says anything more. Jerry's presence alters my world. I continue to stare at him. And then I see the Creative Artists agents Rob Persinger and Gary Rothchild, along with the writer Todd Fields, who I offered a script commitment to at the luncheon last week. Oh my God. This is *my* deal. What in the world is Jerry doing having dinner with them? What's going on? I take a big gulp of wine.

"I can't take it," I say. "I'm going over there." Gordon grabs my hand, trying to hold me back, but I yank it away. "I'll be just a second. I promise. I just need to do this." Gordon rolls his eyes as I stroll across the restaurant toward Jerry, who is astonished to see me.

"Hey, Jer, what're you guys doing here?" I ask in the sweetest way I know how. I tug on my dress a teeny bit to make sure that push-up bra's still working. I can't believe I've resorted to a sexualized self. This was never my mode of operation.

"Alexa, how are you? Please, sit down," says Rob Persinger. "We asked Jerry if you could join us tonight, too, but he said you were busy."

Jerry glares at me, and I return the favor.

Rob pulls a chair from the adjoining table over so I can sit next to him. No one bothers to ask why I'm here or who I'm with. They must assume I just wander through restaurants until I get an invitation to join a table. But I don't make a fuss, as I want to know what this meeting's about. Jerry's not happy. Of course not. He didn't want me here.

Rob orders drinks for everyone, and suddenly I'm mired in conversation. It's going so hard and fast that even though I know Gordon is across the room waiting for me, I don't bother to get up. I feel terrible on one hand, and glad Jerry wasn't able to pull one over on me.

It turns out Todd Fields's idea is a dramedy, which frankly could fall under either Jerry's area or mine. Apparently, the agents thought it best to discuss the issue with at least one of us.

Fortunately, I have something Jerry doesn't. I know how to create a good story. I have suggestions and ideas. I love working with writers. Jerry hates it. He hated it back when I worked for him.

"This is a fabulous concept," I say. "One of the things we could do is offer a satirical approach. Remember the movie *Fargo*? There might be a way to develop your show in a similar way. It would be a departure from our usual fare. Something we don't see often."

Todd eats this up, and we go back and forth exchanging comments, getting more excited about the show and what it could be.

I love the creative process. Building and shaping ideas from a line or two and turning them into hit shows. When the creative juices get flowing, there's just no stopping me. Todd and I go at it while the agents and Jerry just listen. We spend what must be a half hour tossing out more and better ways to develop this idea. The deeper we get, the more I realize this could be a hit for us. I'm so excited about it I can't wait to tell Chester.

"Alexa, I'm bowled over by your passion and excitement," says Todd. "I want to work with execs who are collaborative and who also encourage writers to take chances. I've been looking for someone who will grant me the opportunity to reach beyond what we normally see on television. And you seem like someone who will do that. Where do I sign?"

We agree that Todd will do the pilot for me and shake on it.

"I have to get going," I say. "But I'll confirm with you in the morning and follow up with Chester."

Jerry's had enough and decides to leave. Like a twelve-year-old, he pouts his way out of the restaurant. I offer my gracious thanks to the agents and tell the writers we'll speak soon. When they're all gone, I'm left alone and dread the fact Gordon's been at the table for such a long time waiting for me. I sheepishly return.

However, Gordon's not here. Instead I see my cold, congealed chicken sitting alone on the table. On top of it is a napkin with the words, "You've drunk the Kool-Aid."

Chapter Eleven

Ten days have passed since that night.

No matter what I try, Gordon won't speak to me. I'm beside myself. He won't respond to my phone calls, e-mails, or texts. I send his favorite cookies, only to have them returned. So I eat them, each bite more miserable than the next. It appears to be over. Hardly the way I expected it to end. But then it never is. I decide to give it one more try, as I have to leave for our retreat in Hawaii tomorrow morning.

"It's eleven o'clock at night," Gordon answers without saying my name, but he knows it's me from his caller ID. "Aren't you in some meeting? I thought you Hollywood types work twenty-four seven."

"Wow. Nice to talk to you, too. Look, I'm sorry, Gordon. I know you're angry. You deserve to be—"

"I deserve to be?" he interrupts. "How nice of you to say that. Apparently you believe that apologies grow on trees. You sure use them often. Or is that just another Hollywood tradition, tossing out apologies along with cookies and expecting things to be copasetic again?"

Welcome to the other side of sweet Gordon. Occasionally it rears its ugly head, and I end up drowning in his sarcasm. But I'm not giving up.

"What I did was terrible," I say. "I know that. I'm not perfect. I've not been in a relationship in years. Remember? Apparently, you're better at it than me. I'm still finding my way. I was hoping you'd cut me some slack."

"Why?" he asks. "Why should I cut you some slack? Your behavior was stunning. This just isn't working for me. I don't want to play this game anymore."

"One night? I screw up one night and it's over?" I ask, trying desperately to hang on and not crumble. "We're going to break up over this? What about all the other good stuff in our relationship? Yes, I should've come back to the table sooner. I'm sorry. I didn't mean to hurt you. Really. I really didn't. I wish you'd forgive me."

"I don't know, Lex," Gordon says as he takes a deep breath and I hold mine, wondering what will follow. "I don't know if this is going to work. You're right, you did prepare me for this battle you're waging at work, but I didn't realize the toll it was going to take on our relationship. I'm unclear about your priorities. I don't know if you're really in this with me or, frankly, if I really even want to be in it anymore."

Why was I so anxious to talk to him? Maybe I should've taken the hint when he didn't respond so I didn't have to hear that last sentence. The lump in my throat is so large I can barely swallow. Fortunately neither of us says anything for a while, which gives me some time to think and recover.

"You're right," I say, trying to get the words out. "My drama at work is taking over my life, and that's not fair to you." I take a breath and continue, though my heart is racing 'cause I don't want to lose him. "Whether we break up tonight or not, I want you to know that I care deeply about you. You're the best thing that's ever happened to me. I take full responsibility for my actions that night. It was a nasty thing to do. It was wrong, and I know I hurt you. And that's the last thing I want."

I hear Gordon breathing on the other end, but that's about it. Not a word. The silence seems to go on forever.

"You better get some sleep," Gordon says. "Aren't you leaving for Hawaii in the morning?"

I take it as a good sign that he remembers I'm leaving town. Changing the subject may mean I got a reprieve. But I'm not sure.

"Yes. But, um, well, are we going to be OK?"

"I don't know if we'll be OK, Lex," Gordon says, sounding pretty darn serious. "But tell you what. Apology accepted. When you're back maybe we'll get together and see if our relationship is worth salvaging."

"Please don't say that," I say. "It is worth it. And I don't want to wait to see you."

"You're only gone for a couple of days, right?"

"Please. Can I see you before I leave?"

"It's late. You're leaving in the morning," Gordon says, softening. There's a long pause. "I know what you're thinking."

"You do?" I ask sweetly.

"It's too late for make-up sex." He laughs. "And I have to get up early also. How about if we take a rain check for when you return?"

"What do you mean it's too late?"

———

My bags and I schlepped across town to Venice last night, but I have to say it was worth it. It suddenly occurred to me that Gordon, too, is anxious about being hurt, something I thought guys rarely experience. I'm glad we spent the night together and were able to resolve our differences and air our feelings. We're going to have rough spots, but if we discuss our issues rather than running away from them, I think we may have a better chance of a good future together. Our conversation brought us even closer, and I'll have plenty of sexy memories to take with me this morning as I head out to Hawaii.

Unlike most of my colleagues, I've not been to Maui. In my twenties, Emily and I managed to find a great deal at a hotel in Waikiki Beach. We met a few servicemen on leave from Hickham Air Force Base and had a great time. We stayed at the Waikiki Prince Hotel. It sure sounded great online, but the advertised one-minute walk to Waikiki Beach turned out to be an hour, as it wasn't exactly on the beach, but near the beach. "Near" being about three miles away. Still, we were happy to be there.

Tonight I'll be staying at the luxurious Ritz-Carlton in Kapalua, Maui. I've read all about the hotel, with its seventeen-thousand-square-foot spa, fifteen treatment rooms, private outdoor shower gardens, six restaurants, two golf courses, three-level swimming pool, fitness center with beautiful views of the Pacific Ocean, and tennis and basketball courts. This is a far cry from my last visit to the state.

Sylvia manages to catch a flight to LA so she can leave with us this morning. She and I talk the entire way to Maui. Well, I talk about Gordon. Maybe being thirty-nine thousand miles above show business finally allows me the opportunity to escape into another world. Sylvia simply asks about Gordon and I can't wait to tell her everything. Well, not everything...

"Gordon went to Indonesia with Doctors Without Borders," I say. "I mean, I don't know people who do that. Do you? Just the folks I see on *Nightline*. He truly believes part of his mission in life is to help the less fortunate." I'm eager to share this with Sylvia, who nods now and then as she flips through the *National Enquirer*.

"We're from another planet," Sylvia says. "We don't know people who give so much of themselves. Kinda makes me feel guilty."

"Yeah, me, too," I say as Sylvia asks the flight attendant for more pretzels.

"Did I tell you he lives at the beach in Venice? It's really very cool. We should go roller-skating on the boardwalk some time."

Sylvia puts down her paper and glares at me.

"Are you cracked?" she asks. "Us, roller-skating? Get real."

"OK, you're right. Well, they have some pretty interesting vendors there."

Sylvia doesn't respond but thanks the flight attendant for the pretzels and tears the bag open.

"I went to his place last night," I say. "We had a fight. Long story, but it's OK now. I hope. I just can't screw this up. Gordon doesn't understand my constant drive to succeed. Maybe it comes from not having had much and feeling I need to work constantly just to survive."

"Yeah. Maybe," Sylvia says, munching on her pretzels and completely focused on a story about Kate Middleton, barely listening to me.

"He's far more Zen than I am," I say wistfully, "and enjoys so many other interests and cares deeply about the world at large. I can't get over that. He's an amazing guy."

Sylvia barely looks up from her paper.

"Totally amazing," Sylvia mutters while focused on an article about Prince Harry.

"Are you listening?" I ask.

"Absolutely." Sylvia puts down her paper and smiles.

"I know you like him, Lex," she says. "He seems great. You've told me he loves restoring his car, is a Chiefs fan but will root for the Packers along with you. And the world stops when there's a Lakers game."

"Yeah. Wow, I'm surprised you remembered all that."

"You're very into him." Sylvia smiles. "You talk about him a lot."

"OK, well, give me a break. I haven't had a boyfriend in forever. It's better than talking about the alpha-holes sitting around us."

"No kidding." She smirks.

Sylvia's right. I'm definitely into him. While she reads about Prince Harry I dream about Prince Gordon.

———

The second we step off the plane in Maui we're overwhelmed by the exquisite floral scent of the Hawaiian Islands. Sylvia and I fill our lungs with the fragrant, humid air. As we approach the baggage area a representative from the hotel greets us with the traditional leis. I close my eyes and hold the orange-and-yellow flowers up to my nose and inhale their sweet aroma. Ah, it's great to be here. Soon we're met by a couple of vans. Our luggage is loaded, and we're whisked off to our hotel. I'm in awe of the gorgeous landscape around us. We drive along Highway 380 from Kahului Airport to the hotel as Clyde Bennington, the head of human resources, announces the schedule for the next two days.

We won't have a lot of time to relax, as the purpose of this retreat is to figure out ways to synergize and work together. However, Sylvia and I fully intend to squeeze in workouts and spa treatments.

We pull up to the hotel. It's extraordinary. As we exit the van, Clyde reports his staff has checked us in and has our keys. All is taken care of. I feel like royalty. He adds that cocktails are at five, followed by dinner in a private room inside the Banyan Tree restaurant at seven. Sylvia and I are thrilled.

"Let's meet at the fitness center in an hour, OK?" asks Sylvia as she grabs her envelope from Clyde's assistant. "Let's see if we can get in a massage also."

"I opt for just the massage." I laugh.

"Great. I'll see ya there." Sylvia runs off to her room. I take a moment to look outside at the stunning three-level pool and glistening ocean. I overhear Steve, Jerry, and Chester setting up a golf game. They try to figure out who the fourth might be. Jerry suggests Pete, who's only too eager to be included.

Later, we all have cocktails and then dinner in the beautiful restaurant. Although we don't get to savor the glorious ocean view, as all thirty of us are crammed inside a private room. Of course, that was the purpose of this adventure, to connect with our colleagues—or our enemies. Whatever the case may be.

Chester toasts our great November victory, singling out Jerry's efforts. Not one to miss an opportunity, Jerry leaps out of his seat and takes an enormous bow. He clinks glasses with the others at his table. Chester says he hopes this brief trip will help us work together as a team.

By midnight, we're at the Alaloa Lounge. Sylvia, Molly, Steve, Jerry, Chester, Pete, Noah, and I are beyond wasted. I'm playing my own game of Can I Outlast Jerry tonight. I refuse to leave before he does.

"Great game today, Jer," says Chester as he raises his glass.

"Yeah, man, thanks. Was OK, but not nearly as good as my brother's. Nick was a brilliant golfer. My pop idolized him."

"Was?" Chester asks. "Doesn't he play anymore?"

"Fatal car accident. Twenty years ago." Jerry finishes his beer and orders another. "Hey, shit happens."

But Chester doesn't let it go.

"I lost a sister to leukemia," Chester says, averting his eyes for the moment.

We certainly weren't expecting that admission.

"Four years old. Just two years younger than me. My old man was an oncologist and couldn't save her. They never got over it."

I look at Jerry, who remains stoic. But I think for the first time he actually appreciates the shared experience. However, the moment must be too uncomfortable, because Jerry quickly changes the subject, and the conversation turns back to golf.

After a while, Sylvia, Pete, and Chester decide they've had enough and call it a night, leaving Steve, Jerry, Noah, Molly, and myself to drink ourselves under the table. Soon three attractive young women enter the bar. I'm not sure if they're locals or guests, but they clearly have the guys' attention. Within seconds, our little group has migrated to the Jacuzzi just off the bar and next to the pool outside. Although there are signs saying "Please do not use the pool or Jacuzzi after ten o'clock at night," it seems the rules don't apply to us.

The Victoria's Secret models, or at least they could be, remove their flats and skirts. They're left wearing colorful tank tops and thongs. They lower themselves into the whirlpool and sit on the bench. They even brought their piña coladas and margaritas. They're holding them above the surface and giggling. The guys are watching them and practically coming in their pants. Suddenly all three of them whip off their pants and shirts, leaving just their boxers, then jump alongside the girls in the whirlpool. Molly and I share a lounge chair, sipping our mai tais. I'm glad she's here to witness Steve Hansen's crude behavior.

"C'mon, Alexa, your turn," says Jerry, who's sitting on one of the girls' laps. Noah and Steve are jumping up and down in the center, splashing each other like twelve-year-olds.

"I don't think so."

"C'mon, we're s'posed to bond, remember?" Steve shouts as he kicks water out of the whirlpool at Molly and me. "We're supposed to get to know each other better. I wouldn't mind knowing you a little better. Especially when you wear those sexy duds."

"You mean that red number she wore last week?" Noah shouts. "Man, Alexa, I just wanted to reach in and grab a handful."

The guys are falling all over themselves, knocking themselves out, thinking they're absolutely hilarious. I'm aghast at their behavior. Molly sits quietly.

"You know what? You guys are sick. I'll see ya tomorrow." I get off the chair and start back to the room.

"Oh, c'mon, Lexican, just take off your bra. I'm sure it's no big deal." Jerry laughs. The others find this, too, hilarious. So much for bonding with the boys. Jerry outlasts me once again. I look to Molly, but she doesn't move. Seems she's going to wait it out.

I walk through the lobby toward my room. I look back to see if Molly's decided to join me. But she hasn't. Instead, I see her lower her jeans, pull off her top, and get into the whirlpool in just her thong and bra. I can't believe it.

———

The next morning Sylvia and I enjoy breakfast by ourselves on the veranda outside the dining room while the guys recover from their big night a few tables away.

"I heard what happened last night at the Jacuzzi. Sounds disgusting," says Sylvia.

"It was. I don't know what happened, but thank God I had my wits about me. I could have easily jumped in that hot tub with them. Molly did."

"I heard. Molly's young and vulnerable. Like you and I were at her age. She just has a better job, thanks to you. But it doesn't mean she understands the game. Obviously, you do."

We both stare at the waves as they roar toward the shore.

"Gosh, I really hate that this is such a short trip," I say. "I wish we didn't have to go back tomorrow."

"I hear ya," says Sylvia. "Hey, by the way, that was a great article about you in *Broadcasting & Cable*. Finally getting some good press."

"Yup." I continue to look out at the ocean, trying to plant this lovely picture in my mind so I can call upon it next week when I'm back in the grind. "Nancy's been great. She's certainly turning things around for me."

Sylvia doesn't respond. We sit for a few more moments, taking in the tranquility and serene landscape. We know that within twelve hours we'll be out of the promised land and back into hell.

———

Two weeks later the rain is pounding on my office window. I'm on the phone with Nancy as I stare at the Ritz-Carlton Maui postcard I remembered to pack so I could recall its glorious beauty and tranquil atmosphere. I can't believe it's only been a couple of weeks. It feels as if it's been a year since we were there.

"Things are going pretty well, Nancy. We're starting production on some of the pilots. So far, no major fires. And in between set visits, watching dailies, and recasting roles, I'm doing interviews. You're amazing. You have me everywhere. In fact, someone stopped me in the supermarket yesterday who recognized my photo in *The Wrap*. I definitely like the attention."

"That's nice, but you need to get to Gower Studios today," Nancy shouts. "I don't want to hear you don't have time; you need to start on-air training, and I want you to do some public speaking."

"OK, I'll make it happen," I say, submitting to her urgent tone. "I'll be there." I don't know if I'm intimidated by Nancy or simply enjoying all my publicity. Maybe both. Whatever she says, I do. Whenever she calls, I drop everything. Rosie can't stand her. Nancy screws up the perfect schedule she prepares each day.

"I've got to head over to Gower Studios this afternoon, Rosie," I shout into the intercom. But that's not good enough. Rosie opens the door and enters.

"You have casting and you're two days behind dailies on *Mrs. Sippy*," she says. "Are you going to blow them off for an interview?"

"Yup. Let them know I won't be in the casting session. I'm not worried about the dailies. I can access them on my iPad."

"OK. Sure," Rosie says. "By the way, you're on the cover of the *Hollywood Reporter* tomorrow. I'm sure Nancy told you. They think your drama pilots are the best of all the networks. That's really terrific. Oh, and Gordon called."

"I'll call him later. I wanna do that radio interview in the car. Then, Rosie, get that HR reporter on the phone, I can't remember her name, so I can thank her." I gather my things and head out the door.

As soon as I exit the office suite, I run right smack into Chester.

"Hey, how's my primetime princess?" Chester puts his arm around me and pulls me close as we travel down the hall together. He forgoes the elevator to take the stairs with me. "Your shows have buzz. Proud of you. You're everywhere, in every publication. You're becoming our little star."

"Yup. I'm happy. And of course I'm happy that you're happy." We're on the main floor and out of the stairwell into the lobby.

"I'm a little worried about the comedies, though," says Chester. "Not sure they're looking quite as good."

"Yeah, well, that's Jerry's department, not mine." I smile broadly.

Chester smiles back, knowing exactly what I'm saying. He has pitted Jerry and me against each other and is achieving exactly what he wanted. Two executives are dueling it out for the highest position.

His favorite cockfight. Except only one of us has a prick.

"Well, you've got eight weeks to show us something fantastic. So far, you're looking good, sweetheart."

"Thanks. We'll have some great pilots. I have to go." I leave Chester standing in the lobby and head through the big glass doors to my car. I can feel his eyes on me.

In the car, Rosie tells me she's about to put through Laura Hartung, a radio reporter who covers entertainment news. I put on some makeup as I swing out of the lot and haul ass to meet Nancy at Gower Studios. She wants me on *Access Hollywood* and a number of other syndicated shows, as well as CNBC. It's all about perception. The more I'm out there, the bigger player I become. Kind of crazy how perception trumps reality. I used to hate it. But now that it's my turn, I'm kind of digging it.

"I'm putting Laura through. Are you there?" asks Rosie.

I make sure my Bluetooth is secure and tell Rosie to go ahead.

"Hi, Laura, so happy to talk with you today," I gush when she comes on.

"We're hearing about some of the great shows you're developing," says Laura. "Do you think any will see the light of day?"

"Oh, yes. I expect we'll get quite a few on the schedule. The shows are terrific. I couldn't be happier."

I'm becoming quite adept at this game. The fact that these lies just roll off my tongue is a bit disconcerting. In my former life, I would've been at a loss for words trying to come up with the best way to disguise the truth.

"What about diversity? Are there a fair number of minorities represented in the casts this year? Because HBS, in particular, has been singled out for being somewhat insensitive to this in the past."

"We hire the best actors, Laura. We don't care what color you are. We want great actors."

"But minorities often don't get the opportunities to show how good they are because there just aren't that many roles for them."

"Oh, but the opposite is true. I'm thinking of *Forced to be Family*, a really fun new show that has a great chance of getting on the schedule."

"But that's about one family, isn't it? An Irish one? So clearly there's no diversity there." Laura laughs.

"Oh, but there are quite a few supporting roles," I say. "I believe we have a few minorities in there. Anyway, be on the lookout for *Bound to Score*, about four young men just out of business school who can't find jobs. They support themselves as paparazzi and stalk celebrities. That show is great. We have a dynamite cast and a feature director. It comes from a hot new producer."

I hear a beep, indicating I have another call.

"Oh, Laura, I hope you got enough for your show today. I have another call coming through. You know the busy life of a TV executive." I laugh.

Sometimes I honestly can't believe this is me talking. Where am I getting the gumption? How I've changed. What seemed impossible before comes so naturally now. Do I have more confidence? Is it because I think I'm winning and Jerry's losing? Whatever it is, I'm lovin' it. I can spin the spin with the best of 'em.

"Sure, thank you for talking to me," Laura says. "You're doing so well at HBS. It's nice to see a woman in senior management there. I appreciate your time."

The second I end the call, I hear Rosie's voice on the other line.

"Nancy got you the cover of *Emmy* and wants you to do an interview with them tomorrow," Rosie says. "It's during the time you set to see Marisol. What do you want to do?"

"Oh, Rosie, you had to interrupt the interview with Laura Hartung for that? Was it really necessary? I mean, we could easily have discussed this after that call." I'm exasperated. Why doesn't she think these things through more carefully?

"I'm sorry, I thought the interview was over," she says.

"What was the question again? I can't even remember."

"Do you want to cancel your appointment with Marisol, or do you—"

"Yes, definitely," I interrupt. "Call Gordon and cancel it. Of course I want to do the interview with *Emmy*."

"I'm sure he expects that," says Rosie.

There's a beat.

"What do you mean by that, Rosie?"

"Well, you've canceled several sessions with Marisol. I don't think he'll be surprised."

"Well, fine, then," I say. "Also, can you please call Stan, my landlord, and ask if he'll feed Joe this week? And see if he'll take care of him when I'm in New York. I hope you thought to take care of that already. Also, can you make sure I have lunch delivered in tomorrow? Get yourself some, too. It's gonna be a long day, and I don't want to have to go out. Thanks."

The weeks fly by, and suddenly it's mid-April, an incredibly busy time. It's a nonstop race to get the new shows shot and edited in time for pilot screenings, which begin in a week and last until mid-May. We'll screen the pilots, pick the ones we want, cancel the low-performing shows, and set the new schedule. Pilot screenings are a family affair at HBS. Chester wants everyone's participation. So for two weeks, we'll watch pilots together. We watch new show after new show and then spend hours commenting on them.

I feel pretty confident. My writers and producers delivered great scripts and I gave good notes. My shows are the ones getting the buzz. I've heard the comedies aren't working. I couldn't be happier. I'm not the least bit surprised. Jerry has no idea how to fix a show.

It's the first day of May, and the pilot screenings go well. At lunchtime, after viewing two dramas and one comedy, Sylvia and I take a break and head to the commissary to get some coffee.

"*Forced to be Family* looks pretty good. Lotsa great-looking white people." Sylvia laughs.

"Yeah, so what? They're Irish. How many black Irish families do you know?" I'm annoyed by her comment.

"Well, I don't know about your world," she says, "but in the world I live in, we've kind of crossed the color barrier. There are all kinds of families now. Some are like the United Nations. Yours are like *Father Knows Best*. You're living in the fifties."

"Well, I don't care," I say as we wind ourselves down the hall and enter the stairwell leading to the lobby. "As long as my shows get on the air."

"Are you serious? What's going on with you? Is the publicity going to your head? You're becoming kind of a bitch." She stops before we open the door at the bottom of the stairwell.

"Look, all that matters are the ratings," I say. "Remember? I'm in the business of getting numbers, and you're in the business of getting dollars. I killed myself on these shows. I had to fix the drama shows I inherited. I gave notes. I worked with the directors, many of whom didn't have a clue how to direct a pilot. I revised rough cuts. I made cast changes. It was hell, and I'm short-tempered." I open the door leading out of the stairwell. But Sylvia slams it shut. She won't let me out.

"What is this *I* stuff?" Sylvia asks. "Do you honestly believe your shit doesn't stink? What is with you? You're talking like you and you alone got these shows done. If it wasn't for *your* notes, and *your* casting ideas, and *your* great negotiating, and so on, these shows wouldn't see the light of day. And you're suggesting that the directors can't do their jobs? Have you forgotten this is a collaborative effort? What about the work the writers are doing? Or your colleague, Stacey? Or even people like me, who read every single script and let you know what's appropriate and what isn't? Next thing I'm going to hear is that you actually wrote the scripts." Sylvia's on a rampage.

"In some cases I did," I say defensively.

"What's happened to you, Alexa? Where is the great girl I used to know?"

There's a long pause as I contemplate her question.

"She's gone." I move her hand away and swing the door open. "She wasn't successful. I am."

I hold the door so Sylvia can pass through, and we continue on to the commissary, where I'm greeted with many slaps on the back and high fives for some great pilots this morning. I guess they went over well.

We've been sequestered in pilot screenings for five days. We take intermittent breaks to catch up on the most urgent calls. It's grueling. The last of the pilots trickle in. We've seen more TV shows than we ever dreamed possible. The madness of May.

None of us have eaten anything but pizza. We're bleary-eyed. Chester holds additional senior staff meetings every day, sometimes three. We're discussing and analyzing and poring over details. Barnsworth is in every meeting. It's too much to ask him to wait and see the finished schedule. It's his network, and he wants to be part of the process.

We're now into the second week of screenings and just four days away from setting the schedule. In the meantime, I've forgotten what the sun looks like, if we had rain today, how warm it was, did I have breakfast? What day is it, anyway? I pray Joe has enough to eat. Did I remember to give Rosie the key? Maybe she can feed him. Or is Stan taking care of him? I can't even remember.

Gordon and I haven't spoken much. Most of our communication is via e-mail and text messages. I haven't seen him in almost ten days. He's been training for a bike-a-thon to benefit Save the Children. The ride is from LA to San Diego, although I can't remember when it takes place. I can't get over how he does this. His ride sounds grueling. But Gordon's an outdoorsman. If he's not bike riding on the coast, he's skiing in the Alps. Just thinking about those activities exhausts me. But we agreed to have dinner tonight at Pinot Bistro in the Valley so I can get back to HBS quickly. This will be our last chance to get together before I leave for New York this coming Friday night.

————

It's Thursday. We've screened all the pilots and are ready to put the new schedule together. It will be under wraps until we finally announce it on Monday. I'll present the new dramas, and Jerry, the comedies. Back in September, Barnsworth said he wanted eight comedies next year, but it won't happen because Jerry didn't have good development. He'll be woefully short of that goal.

If Jerry's comedies aren't good, they can't get on the air. There's some justice. He can skate all over the place, but bad shows are pretty obvious, and with many voices chiming in, it will be hard for him to succeed. I'm beginning to feel as if I may have finally won this battle. The proof of the pudding is in the work. Not in the genitals.

A giant grid is secured to the wall in the meeting room behind two big oak doors under lock and key. Noah opens the doors, and the board reveals itself.

The board has all the broadcast networks' current primetime schedules on it. Each network is color-coded. Jerry is first to go to the board to make his case for the comedies.

"I'm looking at eight comedies on this schedule. I'd like to see *Even the Dog is Ashamed* on Monday night at eight o'clock, leading off the evening. I think it's a strong show, and given the research, I think we could do well with women."

Jerry pulls the *Dog* rectangular magnet and slips it into the eight o'clock time slot on Monday night.

"On Tuesday, I think we nix the drama at nine and add two comedies there. I'm recommending *I Wanna Be a Teenager* and

Jiggle." Jerry moves the drama rectangle off and replaces it with his two comedy shows.

I watch Jerry as he goes through the HBS schedule night by night, trying desperately to sound in control and on top. But something's missing. I don't see the bravado. I think on some level, even Jerry knows he failed, that I might have eclipsed him. I might finally get recognized for my contributions and talent and soar above him. He's nervous and sweating. So am I, but for different reasons. I'm excited. I can't wait to get to the board. I have great shows. And everyone knows it. Jerry's shows suck.

But Jerry talks about their ability to slam the competition. He pleads with us to understand that the shows will improve as time goes on. He's the consummate salesman. Whether it's fish boils or bad shows, the man cannot stop selling.

Jerry returns to his seat. I leap out of mine and head to the board and take all of Jerry's comedies off except for two, and replace them with four new dramas. After a moment, I show my schedule.

"Unfortunately, I don't think we'll be able to have eight comedies this year, which is too bad because comedies can be cost-effective," I say, taking a beat to make sure this resonates. I smile at Jerry, who's looking at his BlackBerry. "I believe these four new dramas, *Forced to be Family*, *Steven Gets Even*, *Handsome Dude*, and *Bound to Score* represent a great cross-section. We have one family drama, two cop shows, and one dramedy. I think they're all solid shows and fit well within our schedule."

I return to my seat as Barnsworth gets up and simply moves two shows. Chester adds another comedy, replacing a reality show. The marketing guys talk endlessly about which shows they can promote and which they can't. Business affairs talks about how expensive adding a new show can be and advocates for fewer changes. There's a lot of conversation about the economics and whether we want to take that risk or try to build up some of our existing shows.

Occasionally the door opens and Chester's assistant, Jan, brings Cokes, water, coffee, and tons of junk food, stuff that will help us stay awake. We've been at it since eight this morning. In between meetings, we have calls and e-mails to return. It's a bottomless pit. We can't ever seem to catch up. All of us are reaching the end of our ropes. We're tired. Irritated. Stressed. Exhausted.

––––

It's two in the morning, and we're still working out the schedule. I manage to open a text from Rosie that says she has my boarding pass and Nancy wants to see me tomorrow. There are empty pizza boxes and Coke and Red Bull cans everywhere, as well as half-eaten bags of Doritos, doughnuts, and Sun Chips. There are Oreos smashed on the floor and several old coffee cups on the window-sills. I hear Tony snoring in one corner while Chester is huddled under a blanket in another. Noah's trying to keep his eyes open as he moves more shows around the board.

It's beginning to look like Jerry will have four comedies on the air. A far cry from the eight Barnsworth targeted in the fall. He'll add just one new comedy, *Jiggle*, to the three comedies currently on the schedule. I'll get four new dramas, bringing my total to eight.

Jiggle. A comedy about Hooters' waitresses. The pilot stank. But in Steve's words, it's a home run. We'll see. Last year Steve was coming all over *Bimbos Are People Too*, which the press decimated and was canceled after the second episode. And so much for Jerry's amazing pilot *Hey, Good Lookin'*, which he promoted at press tour as being a great vehicle for diversity. I guess it wasn't so terrific, after all. In fact, the pilot wasn't even screened.

So, I'll get four new shows on the schedule while Jerry gets one.

Jerry lost. I won.

It's four in the morning.

We're back in five hours.

As soon as we arrive the next day, Noah reveals the schedule. There's little discussion. It may be we're all too tired to even think about it anymore. Four new dramas, one new comedy, and two reality shows. Noah locks the schedule. On to New York.

I drag myself out of the conference room and slowly limp across the hall back to my office. I'm drained, whipped, and wasted. Rosie barely recognizes me. I've hardly seen her in two weeks. There've been glimpses and grunts. She follows me into my office as I quite literally collapse on the couch, wanting to fall asleep.

"I feel sick," I say, barely getting the words out. "Or like I'm getting sick. I'm nauseous. Do we have any 7UP, Rosie? I feel like I'm going to puke."

I'm so tired. I have to get on a plane tonight and head to New York, where I have to write a speech about the new shows, attend rehearsals, and present my dramas to a packed room full of cynical advertisers, reporters, and colleagues. It's moving so fast. I just want to sleep. Just for a minute.

"Alexa, you can't crash right now," Rosie says, handing me a 7UP. "You're not going to throw up. You're just exhausted. Nancy's on her way up. She wants to see you before you leave."

"Oh my God, Rosie," I scream. "I just remembered Joe. I haven't fed him. Oh my God!" I want to leap up off the couch, but there's no way. I feel like I have lead in my shoes.

"Don't worry," Rosie says. "Stan has Joe. I brought him dog food and gave him a good walk. He's at his apartment. Do you want some coffee to keep you awake? Also, the car is coming to get you at four, and your friend Emily left a message that she'll call you at the hotel. You have just two hours left if you want to make calls."

My face is crushed into the cushions. I can hardly breathe but don't seem to care. My new Holmes and Yang black pantsuit is worn and wrinkled. I'm sure I smell like the molded cheese in the pizza containers. I can barely lift my head. But when I do, I see Nancy staring down at me.

"What is your problem? You have to get up and put your face on, girl." Nancy shoves seven pages in my face. "Here are some ideas for your speech. You have to fill in the blanks because I don't know what shows got picked up."

I pull myself up. My hair's all over my face. Did I even brush it this morning? I know I didn't take a shower, just rolled out of bed and came here. Or, wait, did I even go home? Maybe I slept in the conference room. I can't remember. I have no makeup on. Whatever I have must be from days ago. My eyelids are so heavy, I can't make out the words on the page. I reach for my glasses, but I haven't a clue where I left them. I squint but it's all blurry.

"I'll look at it on the plane," I say, my eyes closed, slurring my words. "I slept just ten hours in three days. I'm zonked. I'll deal with it later. Thank you." I drop back down on the couch.

"Alexa, you're a good kid," Nancy says, standing over me. "You paid me for a month. I worked for two and a half. I'll knock off the charge for the half month. I think you have a really good shot at being president of this loony bin." She hoists me up again and makes me sit on the couch. Then she leans over and hugs me. "We built you up and changed the perception. You're a star, baby. Good luck."

"Thanks, Nancy. You did a great job." I can barely get the words out. I yawn and try to sit upright. I squint as the bright light of the morning sun envelops my office. I rub my face, yawn again, and try to stand as Nancy exits.

Rosie frantically blasts through the door and storms into my office.

"Alexa, did you forget you had plans to meet Gordon for dinner at Pinot Bistro on Tuesday night?" Rosie shouts, trying to get me out of my stupor. "I thought you were on your way there. You didn't tell me to cancel them."

Oh my God. I haven't spoken to Gordon since Monday. And it's Friday. "Oh, no. I never canceled dinner."

I sit upright, my eyes wide. My heart starts pounding as the door opens and there's Gordon. He doesn't look happy. Rosie senses it's time for her to leave. She rushes to the door and closes it behind her. Now I'm really going to be sick. I pull my feet out of my shoes and hoist them up on the couch, sitting cross-legged. I squint as I look up at Gordon, who's standing a few feet in front of me.

"I'm so sorry," I whisper. "I forgot we scheduled dinner for Tuesday night. I don't know what to say." Gordon looks angry. He's never been in my office. I watch him as he surveys the room. He scans the accolades on the wall, the M&M's in the bowl, the furnishings, and the metal balls on my desk. "You've never been to my office. So, do you like it?" I ask, trying to sound cheerful.

"It's very nice." Gordon comes over to the couch and sits next to me. "You look really tired. And sick. Are you OK?"

"I am," I say softly. "It's been a helluva week. Or weeks. I'm not sure which. I'm actually pretty confused. I feel like a prisoner of war suffering from sleep deprivation."

There's a pause as he just stares at me.

"I'm sorry." I say it again, looking down at the ground. "I should have canceled our dinner. I don't know why I thought I could make it that night. I just wanted to see you. But I wasn't thinking. I never should have agreed to it."

There's a long pause as Gordon's eyes peer around the room. He doesn't say anything for a while. Then he gets up, leaving me doubled over on the couch, and leans against the TV monitor facing me. I'm not quite sure what he's thinking. And even though he's clearly annoyed with me, I can't help but notice how great he looks in his navy-blue V-neck sweater, plaid oxford shirt, and crisp jeans. He looks very professorial and so handsome. Even now, in this very painful moment, I still find myself terribly attracted to him. He puts both hands in his front pockets and stares at me.

"You mean kind of like the dinner at press tour?" he asks. "The one where Barbara and I were your guests but you were too busy to be with us?" Before I even have a chance to defend myself, he comes at me again. "Or maybe like the dinner we were having at Craig's until you found another that seemed more important than the one we were having?"

I just look down. I'm not going to win this.

"I see you're tired," he says. "I'm sorry you don't feel well. I didn't want this moment to come." Gordon doesn't move. He's very serious and doesn't stop staring at me even though I can barely look up at him. "Don't you find it odd that I'm here in your office right now? I have a job, too. I'm not sure, however, that in your world, anyone else's life matters more than yours."

Gordon moves away from the TV and comes over but doesn't sit down. He simply stands in front of me. I'd like to interrupt, but frankly, I'm too tired, and I'm not sure I have a leg to stand on. I'll just have to keep saying I'm sorry till this torture ends.

"Again, Gordon, I'm sorry, I just—"

"You can stop apologizing, Alexa. It means nothing. You're married to your job," he interrupts. "Nothing else matters in your life. Not me, not Marisol, who you discarded like used tissue. Nothing matters except beating Jerry Kellner. It's sick, and it's driving you to the edge. It's pushing away everyone who's ever cared about you. How long has it been since you spoke to your best friend, Emily? And what about Rosie? Did you know her cat died? Do you even care?"

Gordon certainly has my attention. I feel terrible. I did not know Rosie's cat died. He comes around the table and sits right next to me on the sofa. He doesn't touch me. Just stares. I can't look at him. Instead I stare at the carpet below and strangely catch a glimpse of a tiny glittering object stuck in the tufted fabric of the carpet. Within seconds I realize it's a jade bead that must've fallen off my charm bracelet.

"You told me you'd be busy during this time and feared I wouldn't be able to handle it," Gordon says. "The fact is you can't handle it. You're no longer the beautiful, sensitive, fun woman I fell in love with. You've completely sold out. You've become someone I don't want to know."

He gets up and heads for the door. I still can't look at him. I feel totally ashamed and guilty.

"Enjoy your press. I hope it was worth it." He reaches for the handle and opens the door. "You've become what you hate the most, Alexa. You're nothing but the female version of Jerry Kellner." He slams the door and is gone. After a moment I reach down and carefully pick up the dainty jade stone. I hold it tightly against my chest and burst into tears.

Chapter Twelve

I call Gordon the second I leave the network for the airport. No answer. His words shook me to my core. How could I have forgotten to cancel our dinner? How could I have been that neglectful? Didn't I see his e-mails? How could I not respond to him? I was so involved in the schedule that it didn't even occur to me to go back and reread his e-mails. Am I that insensitive? That self-involved? What in the world is happening to me? This is not who I want to be. I'm devastated by his accusation that I've become the female version of Jerry. How could he say that to me?

I'm exhausted, but my heart's racing. I'm so upset and tired that I pop an Ativan the second I get on the plane so I don't stay up and cry all the way to New York. The second we land I call, text, and e-mail him. No answer. I leave a detailed message packed with tears and apologies. I beg him for forgiveness. No response. Not that I expect one. He made it pretty clear that it's over. And frankly, I don't blame him.

I drag myself off the plane. I'm in a complete daze. Exhausted, stressed out, and apoplectic that I lost the best guy I've ever known. How could I let this happen? I beat myself up all the way from the arrival gate to baggage claim.

Harry, a limo driver, holds a sign that says Alex Ross and is astonished that I'm female. He pushes the metal carrier alongside me into the baggage claim area while I call Rosie.

"Why didn't you tell me Mr. Pickles died?" I ask breathlessly. "I'm so sorry, Rosie. I feel awful." I point to my bag, which comes crashing into the metal carousel. Harry expertly retrieves it, and together we start walking outside to his car. "I didn't even get to say good-bye to you. You were gone by the time I left the office."

"It's OK," Rosie says. But she doesn't sound like herself.

"When I get back, let's talk about it, OK?"

"I don't need to talk to you about it," Rosie says flatly. "I have friends and family. They're very supportive. Just do your job." I feel the sting. "You had a zillion calls, all about the schedule, a lot of press. Your apartment manager, Stan, is still taking care of Joe. And no, Gordon didn't call. I'm sorry he broke up with you. That's sad. He was a good guy."

There's a long pause. I don't really want to say anything, but I'm glad she told me he didn't call, because I would have asked. Harry opens the door, and I slide into the backseat of his town car.

"It's about one in the morning there, right?" asks Rosie. "The Regency Hotel has you scheduled for late arrival. You're on the fifth floor. And, by the way, so is Jerry. You can use the stairs. Chester wants you in his office at ten o'clock tomorrow, which is Saturday, by the way, since you seem pretty confused about every-thing. He wants to go over the script for the presentation. There are two rehearsals scheduled for Sunday morning, one at eight in the morning and the next at ten. United Talent's party is at nine o'clock that night at the Stone Rose Lounge. On Monday after the presentation, there's a party in the Tent at Lincoln Center. Then a VIP party at Lincoln Ristorante, next to the reflecting pool. Then there's the Gersh Agency cocktail reception at Juliette Supper Club at five and the William Morris Endeavor dinner party at Peter Luger's in Brooklyn at seven. Tony DeMeo's private party is at The Spotted Pig. I e-mailed it all to you. Text me if you need anything." Rosie doesn't even wait for me to ask a question or say thank you.

I wanted to say I'm sorry (again) before hanging up. She clearly wasn't interested.

I call Gordon again. No answer. Not even voice mail is picking up. I'm sure he knows it's me. Stalking him. I call the school and leave a message. I text and e-mail him again. Nothing.

The cab drops me off at the Regency. I get to my room around two in the morning and collapse on the bed. I don't even take off my clothes or unpack my bag. I just lie flat on my back, and I'm instantly asleep.

I'm jolted out of my bed by a six thirty wake-up call on Saturday morning. I've slept four hours and haven't moved from this position. Thank God I had the presence of mind to schedule a wake-up call or I might've slept the entire day. I better get up, shower, and start moving.

I take a brisk walk to the HBS offices on Forty-Ninth and Park Avenue. On the way I stop at my favorite coffee shop, grab a latte, and continue on. It's the second week in May, and though there's still a chill in the air there's not a cloud in the sky. Normally I'd cherish this moment, as I love New York on a beautiful day. But I'm upset and shaken by Gordon's words. I can't get them out of my head.

As I travel down Park Avenue I take a moment to admire my bracelet, which has never left my wrist. It brings back the memory of our first night together and how euphoric I was the morning after. I smile when I think about Gordon singing to me in the car so I wouldn't think about the cold. And then I recall our romantic trip to Carmel and how he surprised me with this beautiful and thoughtful bracelet. The memory brings tears to my eyes. How I long for that moment. Something I took for granted at the time. And now I would simply die to have again.

I truly may have lost the best man I've ever met. I start to weep but have to stop because I'm not in the privacy of my car but on the streets of Manhattan. I've got to pull myself together. I'm going to be with the guys soon. I certainly can't break the *Never let them see you cry* rule even though male athletes and coaches do it all the time. I'm going to take a page from Bill Clinton's book and try to compartmentalize. It seemed to work for him...for a while. I'll see if it might work for me. I take out a tissue and wipe my eyes and blow my nose and continue walking toward midtown.

When I enter the cavernous steel-and-white lobby reminiscent of so many others in Manhattan, all I see are crowds of people with briefcases and suits. Everyone is moving purposefully and fast. It's infectious and invigorating. I love New York and its great energy, and I hate New York and its abundance of elevators.

As I approach the elevator bank and see the glut of people rush into each car and cram in like sardines, I start to panic. There's no way I can do this. I can't believe this building is crowded on a Saturday morning.

Don't these people ever stop working?

I walk over to the guard and ask if there are accessible stairs. Of course there aren't. There never are in big buildings like this. Something I know all too well. The guard takes me around to a door in the back. He unlocks it and walks up the stairs with me to the fourth floor. He explains I can exit this way, as well, but it will lead out into the alley instead of the lobby. Fine. I don't care. I thank him for escorting me up and hand him five bucks for his time. He's deeply grateful, as well as amused by my peculiar behavior, despite telling me this happens all the time.

Sure it does.

Out of breath, I reach the glass doors bearing the name HBS. I pass the guard and flash my pass and am led down another long hall to a meeting room where I see Chester, Steve, Tony, Jerry, and Noah already seated and working on tomorrow's presentation. Tony's staff dominates the room. They're at computers and on the phone, making arrangements to get the actors and producers to New York by tomorrow and also preparing the presentation. Chester's New York assistant is hovering over him. Although it's full of energy, it's a far more civilized scene than last week's. And it's delightful to see fresh coffee and donuts.

I greet the guys and take my place at the long oval table in the middle of the utilitarian conference room. Noah's brought a miniature scheduling board, which lies flat at the center. Jerry brushes past me and gets coffee.

"Heard the schoolteacher broke up with you," Jerry shouts. "Couldn't take the pressure, huh?"

"Thanks for your concern." You piece of crap. That's really what I want to say, but I hold my tongue.

I won't reveal any feelings to this monster. I just hope I'm not wearing them on my face. Nice to know news travels fast. Fortunately, no one else seems to be the least bit interested. Everybody's mired in the script, throwing out quips and offering ideas and solutions to problems.

"Chester, let's head over to the theater," Tony says, pointing toward the door. "I want you to see how we're setting up the stage. Our staffs will continue on here."

Great. I just arrived and we're already on the move.

While the guys wait for the elevator, I whisk around the side and find the stairwell. I frantically race down the stairs, out the door, and into the alley, and then go back to the lobby to meet them.

But they're not waiting for me. In fact, they're already on the street getting into the limo and are totally wrapped up in some sports-related conversation. I fly over to them and get in the car just before it takes off. They are nonplussed. No one even wondered where I was. I'm like a lost penny.

We arrive at Carnegie Hall. This place is nothing short of spectacular. Every year we present our new schedule in this glorious theater, and every year I'm humbled by it. The auditorium seats two thousand on five levels. It's enormously high, and its curvilinear design allows the stage to become the focal point. This will be my first time speaking at the most prestigious venue in the United States.

The six of us walk through the grand foyer and down the red carpet and peer at the enormous stage before us. Tony points to where the lecterns will be placed, where the clips will be shown, and where the teleprompter will be. My eyes sweep around the theater, and I try to picture what this will be like on Monday. I shiver just thinking about it. I don't think I'm the only one daunted by this great concert hall.

After a while Chester suggests we go to his favorite place, the Carnegie Deli, across the street, to grab some lunch. All of us follow. Even though it's Saturday, work never ends. Everyone has his or her phone, iPad, or BlackBerry on the table for easy retrieval. The guys are chowing down gigantic corned beef sandwiches, while I have an omelet. Tony, Noah, and Steve can't stand to be away too long and head out of the deli before we've even finished eating. Their phones are ringing, and fires are raging. They've hardly had a moment to breathe.

Chester's phone rings, and from the look on his face, it seems personal. He steps outside, leaving Jerry and me alone, sitting across from each other at the table. At first we say nothing. We continue eating like an old married couple. But Jerry can't help himself.

"You know, you're the same stupid bitch you were years ago," Jerry says as he pigs out on his sandwich. "Always flaunting your sexuality in guys' faces, teasing them, trying to get them to come on to you. Not sure it's gonna work this time."

"Are you sick?" I say, astonished by his outburst. "What're you talking about? All you think about is sex, Jerry. You're a perverted misogynist who lives to trash women." I feel those old angry feelings rise up again.

"The truth is, you want me," Jerry says, leaning into my face, practically spitting his food. "You've always wanted me.

We both know it. But I'm not for sale. And frankly, I'm just not into you. Isn't that the movie or book, whatever it is? Well, babe, let me tell you right now, you don't do it for me. I'd fuck Bin Laden's sister before I'd ever do you." Jerry grins, his eyes on fire.

"You're gross." I say, leaping out of my seat.

"You're gonna be working for me again, babe, just wait," he shouts as I quickly race through the restaurant to the exit.

"Over my dead body," I shout back.

"You caaaan't always get what you wa-ant," Jerry sings as I barrel out the door of the deli.

Chester's still on the phone outside the restaurant. He gives me a thumbs-up, which is supposed to indicate something, but I haven't a clue what. He puts his hand over the receiver and shouts that he'll see me at rehearsal tomorrow morning. I guess our day is done. OK, fine with me. I can take the day off and shop. Anything to get away from Jerry.

I'm still fuming and disgusted by him. Every time we have an encounter like this I get nauseous. I decide to call Sylvia. No answer, so I leave a message. I'm on her home turf. I'm sure she has plans. I call her again and leave another message. As I walk through midtown Manhattan and take in the wonderful smells and excitement of the city, my phone rings.

"Syl?" I ask. "I'm walking into Rockefeller Center. I'm gonna get some magazines. What're you doing?"

"Meeting with some Home Depot guys about buying time in one of Pete's shows," Sylvia whispers.

"Oh, sounds like it's a bad time. OK, well, I had the day off, so I wondered—"

"That's nice," Sylvia interrupts. "Why aren't you doing some press interviews? I picked up the new *People* and noticed you weren't on the cover. Is something wrong?"

"Well, that's a nice dig. What's going on? Are you mad at me or something?"

"Are you that pigheaded? For a change I've got some stuff going on, and I can't really talk or play with you right now simply because it meets your needs. I've got to go." And with that, Sylvia ends the call.

OK, I've had enough pain. I hail a cab and take off for SoHo for some shopping and chocolate at Dean & DeLuca. Anything to alleviate the tension and anxiety I feel after these last two conversations.

When I arrive at Prince and Spring and see my beloved Dean & DeLuca, I finally feel a little better. I grab a package of DeLuca's assorted chocolate bars, tear one out, and start eating it. I travel along Spring Street, passing the Mercer Kitchen, which makes me think about the time Sylvia fixed me up with Rich Cates, a banker at Goldman Sachs. The guy did not stop checking his BlackBerry the entire date. Such a turnoff. It only makes me think about Gordon again and how I had a great guy and managed to really screw things up. I promised myself I'd try to compartmentalize my feelings, but I'm really not great at this.

I turn at the corner of Spring and Broadway and stop in a small café to get some coffee. I hear Celine Dion singing "When I Fall in Love" faintly in the background. My mind drifts to the night Gordon and I were having dinner at Craig's. That song was playing in there, too. I remember listening to those words wondering if our relationship would last forever. I remember feeling slightly annoyed with myself for falling so hard for Gordon. I knew that if it didn't work out, the pain of losing him would be overwhelming. And it is.

I go through the motions of ordering my coffee, but my thoughts are back in the restaurant that night. I think about how rude and selfish I was leaving Gordon at the table. How our dinner started out so lovely and ended so badly. I think about the conversation we had on the phone, how I begged him to forgive me and then bullied my way into seeing him that night. I realize that I took advantage of his good nature. And he continued to hang in with me even when I mistreated him. He really was invested in our relationship. Apparently I wasn't. I was more invested in getting even with Jerry. And in doing so, I took on some of Jerry's behaviors. How could I possibly let that happen? To be like him? The person I detest.

"Here's your coffee, ma'am," I hear the waitress say as she shoves a coffee cup in my hand. I've been lost in the memory of that night. I totally forgot I had ordered the coffee and quickly find some cash. I pull out a bill and hand it to her and notice she's wearing a sterling silver Save the Children pin on her lapel. It's similar to the one I saw on Gordon's nightstand. I can't bear to stay in this café any longer. Hearing that song is heart wrenching. Why is it that everything I see, hear, or touch reminds me of Gordon and what I've lost?

It's Sunday morning, and both rehearsals at Carnegie Hall go off without a hitch. Sylvia drops by. I try to engage her, but she's still angry. I'm not sure how to resolve this. But I have to stay focused on tomorrow. I've come this far. I can't give it up. Or can I? Strange how I'm starting to have conflicting thoughts. I know the presentation will be the deciding factor as to who gets the job. Me or Jerry. I definitely have the better development. Now it'll be about the presentation and who will do the best job selling the shows to the advertisers.

It's been a long day, and I'm tired. I want to get to bed early tonight, so I blow off the United Talent Agency party, especially since Sylvia's not around. I can't imagine having a good time at any one of these events without being with her. I'm only excited by the prospect of eating another chocolate bar, which is waiting for me on the end table next to the bed.

I approach the hotel's stairwell and start my climb to the fifth floor. Strangely, as I ascend the staircase I hear someone crying softly. It's late and I know I shouldn't be in hotel stairwells. Gordon and Emily tell me this all the time. But I'm almost at my floor.

As I move closer, I think I see someone sprawled out on the landing. It's a man who is sobbing uncontrollably. I start to turn back but catch a glimpse of his shoes and instantly realize they're Jerry's familiar Gucci loafers. I'm dumbstruck. Jerry sees me and calls out my name. He uses his jacket sleeve to wipe away the tears. I just stand there shocked and unable to move. Something is terribly wrong. This is not the Jerry I know.

"Are you OK?" I ask.

Jerry glares at me. There's a long pause.

"No." I notice he's clutching his cell phone.

He pulls his feet back, signaling that I should continue up the staircase. I approach the landing and stop for a moment. Jerry leans against the wall and looks up at me.

"That was my brother, Craig. Pop died this morning."

I stop cold in my tracks.

"I'm so sorry, Jerry."

Strangely, even though Jerry is the most wretched person I've ever known, I actually feel badly for him. I know how difficult it is to say those words. But Jerry shrugs.

"The old man went quietly. Died in his sleep."

There's a long pause. I decide to stay on the landing a moment longer. We're just inches apart.

"I know how devastating it is to lose a father. Are you going to Wisconsin?"

"Nope. The man's dead. He'll be cremated tomorrow."

Jerry wants me to believe he doesn't feel anything, yet he's sitting on the landing in a hotel stairwell crying his eyes out. I decide to take off my heels and plant myself beside him on the floor. I can smell beer and see an almost-empty bottle in his other hand. He's clearly bombed. After a moment I break the silence.

"It's been eighteen years and I still miss my dad," I say.

"My dad was different. He didn't care much for me. I could never live up to his expectations. His dreams died with Nick. Nick was the prince."

"Well, you've done pretty well for yourself. I can't imagine he didn't take some pride in your achievements."

Jerry shrugs and changes positions. He takes a swig of beer.

"I shoulda been with Nick that night. I never would've let him drive home drunk. I've been plagued with guilt for years."

"That wasn't your fault, Jerry." There's a pause as I lean back against the wall.

"Sometimes I feel that if I had gotten to my dad faster, maybe he wouldn't have died. But I know it's not true. We just can't control everything."

Jerry looks up at the ceiling. I can tell he's starting to tear up again.

"I was never the son Pop wanted," Jerry says softly. "His whole life was wrapped up in Nick. And I could never be Nick."

Jerry pauses as he takes another swig of beer.

"Nick was smart, handsome, and athletic. Everyone in Sturgeon Bay adored him. Pop was devastated when he was killed in that car accident. So I decided I'd become the success Pop had hoped for with Nick. I'd make the old man proud."

There's a long pause as Jerry fidgets with his belt buckle and then takes another gulp.

"You know how I've told you that you don't aim high enough? That you need more confidence in yourself?"

Unfortunately, I do remember. Jerry said it all the time and most recently at the press party earlier this year. Not something I really want to recall.

"My dad would say that to me all the time. Aim higher, Jerry. You need to be more like Nick."

He starts to sob. I reach in my purse and hand him a tissue. I move a little closer and drape my arm around his shoulder. Stunningly, he almost collapses into my body. I feel like I'm having an out of body experience, because I'm not acquainted with this Jerry. Yet I understand how death changes a person and wonder if his father's death is giving birth to a new Jerry.

"I'm sure he loved you, Jer. In his own way. Some people just have different ways of expressing it. You were a good son. I remember the big box full of Styrofoam cheese-heads we sent. Remember that? I'm sure he loved that stuff."

And yet I recall Jerry being very angry that his father never even thanked him. Granted, I'm the one who did all the work putting that box together, trying not to smash the cheese-heads so they wouldn't lose their spongy form when he received them, and buying the birthday card. But Jerry gave me his credit card, so I guess to him, it was the thought that counted.

Jerry's head is on my shoulder, my arm across his back. He seems very comfortable. It's extremely quiet. It's actually rather peaceful in this carpeted stairwell. Whose ever heard of that? In New York of all places. But I guess the Regency makes sure to pamper its guests, even the ones who prefer stairwells to elevators.

"Your dad died eighteen years ago, so you were like, seventeen, huh?" Jerry asks.

I nod. Jerry smiles. "Nick died when I was seventeen. Seventeen, not such a great year for either of us, huh?" Jerry asks.

I realize the irony. I'm surprised Jerry has the ability to even think about something like this. The fact that in some strange way we are in the same club and yet chose to handle the circumstances surrounding those deaths differently. I chose to grieve the loss and

Jerry chose to blame himself. How these horrific tragedies shaped our lives is not lost on me.

"Ya know the teacher you were seeing? He kinda reminds me of Nick. Nick was a really good dude. Everyone loved Nick. Pop was so proud of Nick. Nick was his prized possession. Everything was Nick, Nick, Nick." Jerry reaches a crescendo.

Then suddenly he slams his fist on the floor so hard his phone pops out and falls all the way down the stairwell. I'm struck by his rage and start to pull away. Jerry doesn't move. Instead he leans against the wall and starts sobbing again.

"Jer," I say, "maybe you should get to your room, lie down, get a good night's sleep. I don't think you want to stay on this landing all night. We've got a big day tomorrow. Lemme help you. Rosie told me you're on the fifth floor, so we just have one more flight."

I stand up and extend my hand. He takes it and we walk up the staircase together. Jerry opens the door and we walk hand in hand to his room.

"I took the stairs 'cause I didn't want anyone to see me, and then there you are—the person who wants me dead. Who hates me." Jerry holds my hand tightly.

"I don't hate you." I think I'm lying. But I'm not sure, 'cause right now I'm completely confused.

Jerry slips the key in the door and we enter. He tosses his now-empty beer bottle in the wastebasket, empties his pockets, and crashes headfirst onto the bed. I can barely make out what he's saying, as he's speaking into the bedspread.

"I need my phone," Jerry says. "Can you get it? I can't believe I'm on the fucking fifth floor. The worst room in the place. I'm never gonna be able to sleep 'cause I'm gonna hear the street traffic. I never stay on a low floor. I'm on your floor. 'Cause you can't take elevators. What's that about, Lex, have you ever figured that out?"

I roll my eyes. The old Jerry is back. In some ways it's a relief to know he didn't travel too far. At least I know who this Jerry is and how to deal with him. The other one, though much nicer, is a complete alien.

"Jer, I'll call the front desk and have them bring up your phone. Don't worry. Go to sleep. I'll see ya tomorrow."

How interesting that I slip right back into my old role of secretary-slash-caretaker. I bite my lip and start to exit.

But suddenly Jerry leaps off the bed, grabs me from behind, and swings me around so we're face-to-face. I'm completely startled and pray he's not going to kiss me. He looks directly into my eyes. He's instantly sober.

"Lex. Nothing happened tonight. I don't want anyone to know about this." Jerry is very intense, and even though I can smell the beer on his breath, he seems very aware.

"Sure, Jer. I understand. Don't worry," I say. "But, you're not going to tell anyone your dad just died?"

"No. It's no one's business. It's just a blip on the screen. What happened tonight is our secret. I don't want to discuss his death. Got it? Please?"

I just stare at him and nod. He extends his hand to me.

"It's a promise, right? Can we shake on it?"

We shake hands. I turn toward the door to exit. As the door closes behind me I hear Jerry softly in the distance.

"Thanks, Lexican."

I walk down the hall to my room and take out my key. I think about how sad it is that Jerry can't really express himself. He's so blocked. So unable to move past his brother's death. That incident forever changed him. And for the first time I wonder about Nick and who he was and what a dramatic effect he had on Jerry. And I find it interesting that he thinks Gordon is similar to Nick. He trashed Gordon to me and yet Nick is the one person he most admired in his life. I never realized how complex Jerry really is and how the tragic death of his brother so greatly impacted his relationship with his father. I'm glad I was there for Jerry. I wonder why I ever doubted him. Maybe he's a good soul after all. Maybe he even has a heart and is human. The thought of it makes me laugh.

Finally a breakthrough.

When I get to my room, I see there's a message. I hope it's Gordon. But it's not. It's my great pal, Emily, wishing me luck and telling me to call back anytime. It makes me smile.

I take another Ativan. My third today. I feel like a zombie. Or a drug addict. I get into bed, watch some TV, and fall asleep.

It's Monday. The day of reckoning. All eyes will be on Jerry and me. How well our shows are received will probably determine our fates. Will he work for me? Or will I work for him? Will I shatter the glass ceiling at HBS? Or will HBS dig in its heels and promote yet another guy to the top job?

After a restless night, I pop out of bed at six thirty. I'm excited and anxious and ready to roll. The presentation begins at eleven o'clock. I'm eager to get going. I check my e-mails, get in the shower, and grab my garment bag with the dress and accessories Gabriella Mannucci so carefully assembled for this momentous occasion. I race downstairs and hail a cab.

I approach the stage door on Fifty-Sixth and Seventh. My name is checked off, and I'm escorted inside. The place is buzzing. Technicians, security, production personnel, and Tony and Steve's entire staff swarm the premises. There is tremendous energy and anticipation.

"Alexa Ross?" A young woman on Tony's staff approaches me. "Hi, I'm Sami. I'm going to take you to your dressing room, then you'll need to go to hair and makeup, and you have some press interviews, so we need to get moving."

It's frantic backstage. I follow Sami into a dressing room that looks like Marilyn Monroe's. Something out of the fifties that's been restored with every kind of modern amenity. There's a lighted mirror, a gray love seat, and a tiny restroom. Chester's and Jerry's rooms are next to mine. They all open onto a large green room dominated by a sprawling buffet. It's an elaborate spread with flowers, fruits, and vegetables. There's also a table of cheese, as well as one with salads and grilled vegetables. A carving station serves tender slices of a variety of meats, and a seafood station serves piles of crab legs and shrimp. Two big TV screens hang on opposite sides of the room.

The morning goes by fast. I hardly have a moment to see the time. I'm escorted from hair to makeup to interviews, back to makeup, then to another interview, then to my dressing room, where I put on my Prabal Gurung blue-and-black silk dress. Gabriella suggested fuchsia, but I'm not that crazy. I'm even wearing my sensible Kate Spade midheel pumps, as I don't feel like tripping onstage. Then it's back to the green room to schmooze the agents and talent who have arrived. The stage manager shows me where I'll stand.

Suddenly it's ten o'clock. Chester, who's dying without a cigarette, is watching SportsCenter on one of the TVs above. I hear the sound of the audience assembling. I peek out from the wings and see a swath of suits climb into their seats. Just like a real television production, I hear the band start to play as more and more and more folks file into the theater.

Chester moves over to a monitor that sits on a small table in the wings. It features the empty stage with a large neon sign that says Hawkeye Broadcasting System in orange, green, and blue. I can see three lecterns. One in the middle, one to the left, and another to the right side of the expansive stage. Speaking to no one and sucking on an unlit cigarette, Chester paces back and forth between the monitor and the TV screens in the green room.

Jerry's the opposite. He's glad-handing every person. He's the welcoming committee and hospitality chairman all in one. He'll be on stage in fewer than ten minutes. His hair and tie are askew, but he doesn't seem the least bit concerned. Instead, he's hitting on the new lead actress in one of my shows. She's gaga over him.

I cannot believe this. The man who sobbed in my arms just over ten hours ago in a hotel stairwell over the loss of his beloved father whom he could never please shows no signs of wear. His ability to compartmentalize this tragic loss is not lost on me. Last night I wondered how he would get onstage today. On the other hand, he referred to his father's death as a "blip on the screen..."

No matter how old you are, the death of a parent is hardly a blip on the screen. I've spent years trying to reconcile my father's death, thinking about and talking through the pain. Jerry bears no visible scars. Just a few revealed for the first time last night, buried deep beneath the surface. Jerry and I are completely different. I take everything to heart. Jerry has no heart.

Jerry's defense mechanisms and he are one. He's become his version of Nick. But tragically, it's a fantasized one. Because it was clear from Jerry's conversation last night that Nick was the opposite of Jerry. Who knows whom Jerry might've become had Nick survived. He still may never have lived up to his dad's expectations, but he might also never have had to try so hard.

I'm decidedly nervous. This is scary stuff. Although I've had my share of speaking engagements, this is the grandmother of them all. The music is blasting. The seats are full. The green room is buzzing with excitement as all the stars on the new shows wait for the program to begin. Sami is at my side with her headset and clipboard. She hasn't left me for one minute. The stage manager, a fortyish guy with a long gray ponytail, dressed in jeans, a black T-shirt, headset, and safari vest with bulging pockets, enters the green room.

"May I have your attention, please?" he shouts above the din, trying to get everyone's attention. It takes a moment for things to quiet down.

"The show will start in three minutes. Please pay attention to the TV monitors above. This is a two-hour presentation. Those of you on shows, please stay in the green room at all times. We'll be calling out shows five minutes before you go onstage. Good luck, everyone." And with that, the music escalates and a disembodied Don Pardo–like announcer begins speaking.

"Ladies and gentlemen, Hawkeye Broadcasting System welcomes you to their primetime television presentation. Please welcome chief executive officer and president of Hawkeye Broadcasting System, Mr. Chester King." The music blasts, the drums roar, and the audience cheers.

Chester walks to the lectern in the middle of the stage. Jerry and I stand in the wings and prepare to make our entrances. My heart is thumping so loud I'm afraid I'll pass out before I get to the lectern. My mouth is so dry I can hardly swallow. Sami waits for the signal from the stage manager, who I see kneeling by the stairs, listening to the director on his headset. I watch Chester as he stands before the crowd and reads from the teleprompter. His salt-and-pepper hair has become more salt than pepper. The lines in his face are deeper. He looks focused and intense. And anxious. The glib, fun, relaxed fella I'm so familiar with seems far away. Today, he's the corporate salesman talking about the November sweeps and the success we've had and how we've managed to stop the bleeding. We're on our way back. We expect to score many more touchdowns. The house applauds.

"Traditionally I've had the pleasure, if you want to call it that"—Chester strays from the script and rolls his eyes, and the audience laughs in response—"of being up here alone every year. However, today I'd like to share the stage with my two lieutenants, who work in the trenches and are the blood, sweat, and tears of this company. They're the ones who deserve the lion's share of the credit for our recent success. Ladies and gentlemen, please give a warm welcome to our fabulous new head of drama development, and the person who is on the cover of every magazine, the very beautiful and talented Alexa Ross."

I walk onstage; the word *beautiful* makes me cringe. I know every woman in this room is rolling her eyes. When are guys going to realize we aren't running for Miss America? I knew this would be difficult, but as I cross the stage, stopping to shake Chester's hand in the middle and then continuing to walk to the lectern on Chester's left, my body's trembling and my heart's thumping. I reach the podium as the music and applause wane. I look out into the audience, and all I see is black. I can't make out one face. I haven't a clue who's out there.

Now it's Jerry's turn. Will he crack? Or is he so good at sequestering that he'll make it through with flying colors?

"And now I'd like to introduce the newest member of our team at HBS, that incomparable, unsinkable showman of all time, and truly the king of comedy, Misterrrrrrr Jerry Kellner." Again, the music rises with the applause.

Jerry races across the stage, smacks Chester on the back, shakes his hand, then goes to the middle of the stage, smiles broadly, takes a deep bow, winks, and waves to the crowd before returning to the lectern on Chester's right.

I forgot the stage is Jerry's comfort zone. He once told me it's his womb, where he feels safe. It's interesting because he said his father never once came to see him perform at the Third Avenue Theatre, next to their restaurant. And yet this is truly where Jerry thrives, where he can be his true self.

"Ladies and gentlemen, the vice presidents of comedy and drama development at HBS are going to help me present next season's primetime TV schedule," roars Chester. And with that, the very large screen behind Chester comes down from the ceiling and the new HBS primetime schedule is projected. I'd like to say there are oohs and aahs, but by now, the schedule's out. Nikki Finke posted it Friday afternoon. It's been tweeted and retweeted a zillion times and even has its own hashtag: #hbsschedule. Comments, both good and bad, have poured in, and it's not even officially announced. Chester's determined to find the source, but it happens every year. There are no secrets in Hollywood.

Chester reads from the teleprompter like a used car salesman. He wants the executives from the ad agencies in the audience to get their clients to advertise on our shows. That's what this whole show is about.

Every slide is about a win we've had this past year. Because we can't say we're the number one network across the board, we suggest it in different ways. For example, men between the ages of eighteen and thirty-four who make between sixty and one hundred grand per year and live in the Midwest love *Let's Get the Girls*. It's their number one show. Spin, spin, and more spin. Are they buying our bullshit? Chester continues on, raving about our current schedule and the new one being announced today.

He starts with Monday night and goes through each and every show, underscoring every possible positive thing about it. He gets to Tuesday night and talks about *The Candy Stripers*, which is a disaster. The show's ratings are declining significantly. CBS put a new comedy against it, and it's dying. But Chester and his merry research team managed to find a silver lining somehow and offer a few demographics that prove that the show is still successful, despite the ribbing the *New York Times* gave it last week. They figure it's a sure bet for a midseason cancellation. They're not wrong.

Each time Chester comes upon a new show, whether it's a comedy or drama, he defers to either Jerry or me. We read from the teleprompter how over the moon we are about every one of our shows. As each is introduced, the new cast leaps onstage. They're all smiles and giddy out of their minds.

I'm definitely more nervous than Jerry. He reads with bravado and excitement.

Suddenly, without any warning, Jerry grabs the microphone off the lectern, moves across the stage, and begins to rant on about why his comedies are going to kill the competition, going way off script. All of us are stunned. No one goes off script at this event.

"Let me just say that we will kill. HBS is no longer the little network that can't. We're the powerhouse network that cannot stop. We are focused on a huge win this season. We are on a roll, and we are unstoppable."

Oh God, I pray this isn't embarrassing. Is this going to be like Clint Eastwood's ad-libbed performance at the 2012 Republican convention?

"As the Chinese philosopher Lao-tzu said, *A journey of a thousand miles must begin with a single step.*" Jerry pauses, sweeping his eyes over the crowd. "And that is how we're going to attack the competition and make our way back on top. We're going to take single steps in pursuit of a big sweeps and season win. We aren't there yet. We haven't reached the top. But we're on our way. We're a motivated group. An excited team. We're going to bust through that ceiling and deliver the biggest numbers you've ever seen."

Jerry is gesticulating wildly. He's pacing back and forth across the stage. He uses every single bit of the platform for his dramatic performance. Perspiration drips down the side of his face onto his collar. He is so worked up, so animated, that I wonder if he's on crack.

"Count on us," he shrieks. "We will take nooooo prisoners. We're on a winning streak. Bring those ad dollars here. We are bettin' on you to bet on us. We won't fail. I promise you that. Win with us. Say it with me, folks. Win with us! Say it louder, I can't heaaaaar you. Win with us! Win with us! Louder. With me folks. Win with us! Stand up and shout it! On your feet. Together now. Win with us! Win with us! Win with us!"

Jerry's voice is high-pitched and shrieking as he reaches his crescendo. The audience loves it. They're on their feet, laughing and applauding wildly. Chester seems dumbstruck but happy. Jerry certainly woke up this crowd. They're finally paying attention.

How in the world am I ever going to top this?

I can't.

It's all downhill from here. There's nothing in our presentation that comes close to Jerry's Howard Beale outburst.

The presentation draws to a close. All the actors assemble on stage one last time. There's wild applause. The reaction seems good. Doesn't seem to be any booing, something we've heard in the past. So maybe we dodged a bullet. The music stops. The audience departs. We leave the stage and reunite with the rest of the team in the green room, where Jerry receives a standing ovation. Tony, Steve, and Noah fawn all over him. The actors think Jerry is the second coming and many seem to think he's the president of entertainment. Of course, Jerry does nothing to correct that impression. Instead, he praises their performances in the pilots he may or may not have seen.

Agents are all over the green room. More gushing over Jerry. He's the star of the day. Chester makes his way over and pats him on the back. "Good show, man. I gotta tell you, I was nervous as hell. But you pulled it off. You're quite the showman." Chester has a cigarette dangling from his mouth. It's not lit, but he doesn't care. As long as it's there. He'll be out of here shortly because he won't be able to resist lighting it much longer. He turns toward me. "Jerry was great, wasn't he?"

"Was great," I say, faking a smile.

Jerry envelops me in his arms, squeezing me so tightly I want to scream. He whispers in my ear so no one else can hear him.

"Don't fuck with me. I'm always going to win."

I rip myself out of his embrace. And then, so everyone can hear, Jerry says, "Hey, baby, hearing that from you is great. Finally a compliment. What I have to do to get her to say just a few nice things about me." He laughs.

I look at Jerry in stunned silence. Did I just dream what happened last night? Wasn't I present and aware? Am I being gaslit? I can't believe this is the same person who rested his head on my shoulder and divulged his darkest secrets to me.

I stare at Jerry, while he smiles back at me.

I'm about ready to reveal all. But then suddenly Jerry extends his hand to shake mine, just as he did last night when we made *the deal*. I don't take it. But I know what he's trying to say to me. If I were not my father's daughter, I would ignore that deal and tell all. But I'm Alexa Ross. I am a good egg. An honorable person. I will hold up my end of the bargain. And Jerry knows it. He simply walks away, and it appears that that chapter is now closed.

Soon the talk turns to the after party. Like a herd of cattle the entire audience, along with the producers and casts of the new shows, begins the trek from Carnegie Hall to the after party at the Tent at Lincoln Center. Some hail cabs, some jump in their limos, and others, like me, simply walk.

It's another beautiful day in Manhattan. I see several colleagues. Many agents, managers, studio executives, and producers congratulate me on a successful drama season. The agents also pitch writers to staff some of the shows. I see the producers who got shows on the air, and we embrace. Everyone's excited.

Sylvia is a few steps ahead. I hurry to catch up to her.

"Syl?" I move up alongside. She acknowledges me, but that's about it. "What did I do? Can't we just talk about it?"

Sylvia starts to slow down. "You've changed. I don't know who you are anymore. You totally sold out."

"I'm sorry you feel that way." I can't help but notice that line again. "You're a great friend and colleague, and I miss you."

Sylvia stops, lights a cigarette, and then continues walking.

"Are you OK?" I say.

She nods. But I sense things are not OK.

I grab her arm and maneuver us away from the crowd, which is storming out of the theater. We end up standing in the doorway of a Chinese restaurant, the only semiprivate area around. Sylvia doesn't look at me. She takes a long puff on her cigarette.

"I crossed the line," she says immediately. "I sold some time on *Texas Cheerleaders* to a pole-dancing website."

"Why?"

"Because they offered to pay double what we were getting for a thirty. Why not? I hated myself for it. But hey, I don't care anymore."

"Yes, you do. That's the problem. Or you wouldn't even mention it."

"My boss isn't happy. Even he didn't like it."

"I'm sorry, Syl. I'm sorry you felt you had to do that."

"I sold out." Sylvia flicks her ashes to the side. "But you did, too. I guess somehow that made it all right for me. Your stupid press and crazy transformation."

"I'm doing my job. I'm just better at it now. I'm learning the game and—"

"You're full of shit," Sylvia interrupts. "You'd give your right arm for that promotion. You want it so badly you don't care who you step on or what it takes to get there. Or who you hurt along the way. As long as you get what you want. And that's why I'm angry at you. You abandoned your principles. And because you did it, I felt I could do it, too. But it's wrong. It's not who we are."

There's a long pause. Sylvia takes another drag of her cigarette. Neither of us looks at each other. I watch the crowd as they march toward Lincoln Center. Sylvia peers off in the other direction. I think about her words, which are hurtful.

"I can't possibly report to Jerry," I stammer.

"You may not have to. Your shows were great. You deserve the job."

"I do."

"But you know it's not about that," says Sylvia, softening. "It's about who Chester wants in that job, irrespective of talent and success. Who he's most comfortable having at his side. Managers hire mirror images of themselves. It's why men keep hiring men. It's why there are more of them and fewer of us at the top. We don't get those opportunities."

"It's true," I say. "There's room for maybe one female at the top, which is why women tend to be competitive with one another."

"It's easier just having a pal around," Sylvia says as she takes another hit on her cigarette. "Men hire women to work for them. But not necessarily with them."

"Well, you're right," I say. "We do the work while they're focused on the big picture."

"Ya know, my old colleague," Sylvia takes a long puff on her cigarette, "Spencer Petry once told me that when he accepts a new position he's completely engaged in it for the first six months. He does everything he can to impress management. Then he focuses on finding his next job. He doesn't wait to be laid off or fired. He's looking for his next job six months after he begins. I thought that was very interesting."

"Wow," I say. "Women just don't think like that. We kill ourselves to do the best we can. We believe that if we do a great job we'll be rewarded."

"Exactly."

"You know," I say, taking a deep breath, "sometimes I don't even know if I really want the promotion. I've invested so much time and energy trying to get it. But I'm not sure if what I really want is the job or just not reporting to Jerry again."

"Well, how about if we not think about it for a while," says Sylvia as she tosses her cigarette on the ground, crushing it with her heel. "I'm so sick of this place. Maybe we just go out, have a good time, and party our asses off."

"Sounds good!" I'm relieved to have my friend back.

Sylvia grabs me, and we walk arm in arm toward the party.

"By the way," she says, "will you please tell me what the fuck Jerry was saying onstage? Is he trying to be Charlie Sheen? He sounded like an imbecile."

"And the guys ate it up." I laugh.

"And how, dear God, am I ever gonna sell *Jiggle* to advertisers?"

"Eh, I wouldn't worry, it'll get panned by the press and off the air after two episodes."

"What are these guys thinking?"

"Oh, c'mon, Syl, do you really have to ask that?"

We both laugh as we walk down Amsterdam, talking about the presentation and Jerry's antics. We finally arrive at the Tent at Lincoln Center, which has floor-to-ceiling glass panels. We mingle with all our colleagues, press, and advertisers. Then we walk over to the Lincoln Ristorante for the VIP party. This is just for the producers and casts of the new shows. We hang around for a while and congratulate the winners of the marathon.

Later, Sylvia orders a car, which takes us to the Gersh Agency party at the Juliet Supper Club. From there we head to the William Morris Endeavor dinner at Peter Luger's in Brooklyn. As we continue our tour through the evening, we run into all the guys. All of us are exhausted and eager to let loose. We can finally enjoy ourselves after the past few intense and anxious weeks. It's time to unwind. Each time Sylvia and I get in the car, we rip off our shoes and hike up our skirts so we can sit comfortably. Finally, we approach our last stop of the evening. It's one in the morning, and I can hardly stand up. I've been on the run without a moment to relax since six thirty this morning. This is Tony DeMeo's private party at The Spotted Pig in the West Village.

The place is smoke filled and mobbed. We can barely get in the door. There are people everywhere. It's so loud I can barely hear myself think. I see Steve sitting in a chair being hoisted up high by a bunch of rowdy partygoers. To my left are a couple of girls in bras and bikini panties dancing on the bar. As Sylvia and I inch our way through the extremely crowded room, barely able to move, we reach the back, where I see Chester sitting in the corner, smoking a cigarette, deeply entwined with Adrienne, his temp secretary. In the other corner, on the floor and under a table, are two girls and Jerry. They're smoking a joint. Molly and Stacey are seated with five male agents I recognize from another agency, who are pawing at them.

"Hey, congrats, kid," screams Chris Joseph, my favorite agent. "Great schedule. Your shows look good. You getting the top job?"

I smile and try to scream above the din, but Chris is shoved from view and can't hear me.

"Great show today, Alexa, congrats!" shouts Jenna Devlin, a manager at The Connection whom I've known for years. "So great to see you up there."

As we make our way through the crowd, I receive more and more kudos from agents and producers congratulating me on the drama pilots and the presentation. Everyone seems exuberant, excited, energized, and loaded.

The room is spinning. I'm extremely tired, frazzled, and spent. Sylvia sees her boss, Larry, sitting at the bar with his arm wrapped around his assistant. She turns toward me and mouths something, but I can't hear her above the ear-splitting noise.

"I can't take this," Sylvia screams. "Are you ready to leave yet?"

I'm more than ready. The place is a zoo. I feel as if I'm back in college at some sick fraternity party. We're extremely happy to be outside breathing fresh, cool air, our ears still ringing from the clamor inside. Sylvia calls the driver, and we head back to my hotel.

"I'm glad we're friends again. I need you in my life, Syl. You make working here tolerable."

The car finally pulls in front of the Regency Hotel to drop me off.

"I feel the same way," Sylvia says as we embrace. It feels so good to have my friend back. I missed her.

"Think about what you want, Lex. Is it really worth all this?"

"I hear you," I say. "I don't know. I need to think about it."

The driver opens my door, and I retreat into the hotel, climb up the stairs, and into my very quiet and peaceful hotel room.

Boy, am I ever glad to be back in my room. I'm whipped. I kick off my shoes and tear off my suit. I'm so happy to lie down and thrilled to get out of my Spanx, which I swear cut off my circulation. Gosh, what women will tolerate in order to conceal the slightest bulge. I inhale deeply, happy to breathe again.

I'm done. I did the best I could. I just want to go home. And I miss Gordon. More than anything, I'd like to call and tell him about today. But that was part of the problem. It was always about me. I took advantage of his good heart. Now I have to get used to not having him around.

It's almost three in the morning, and I can't sleep. I watch the ceiling fan rotate above me. I think about what I've lost and what I've gained. And then I think about what Sylvia said. Is it really worth it? I've come a long way over the course of this TV development season. I've watched Jerry Kellner come in to work for me. Then work with me. And now he wants me to work for him.

Again. I feel sad. Not euphoric. Not relieved that it's over and I did well. Maybe the excitement of the moment is meaningless if there's no one to share it with.

I look at the clock. I'd really like to call my pal Emily. It's midnight on the West Coast. Do I dare try her? Her message said to call anytime. I'll take her at her word.

"Hello." Emily is groggy when she answers the phone.

"It's Alexa. I'm sorry to call you so late. I'm still in New York. Can you talk?"

"Oh my gosh. Yes. Are you OK? I've missed talking to you, but I know you've been crazy busy the past few weeks."

I assure her that I am but that this is really the first time I've had a chance to relax and I just wanted to hear her voice.

"I'm feeling lonely and sad, Em," I say softly. "I delivered a great presentation and killed myself developing outstanding programs, many of which got on the schedule. But Jerry managed to steal the show with a spontaneous rant."

"Oh, lovely." Emily sighs.

"And worse, Gordon broke up with me."

"I heard," she whispers. "When I called your office Rosie told me. I'm sorry. Let me get out of bed and go downstairs so I don't disturb anyone."

"I'm sorry to call so late, I just wanted to talk to you. I've been busy and—"

"It's OK," Emily interrupts, speaking softly. "You don't have to apologize. We're friends."

"Thank you," I say, relieved to hear her say that. "I just had what should have been one of the most successful experiences of my life, and I feel empty and hollow. Gordon told me competing with Jerry has turned me into a female version of Jerry, probably the worst thing anyone could say to me. Sylvia wouldn't talk to me, and Rosie hates me. I think Gordon may be right. I can't believe I didn't see it." I go on and on, letting it all come out as Emily listens. I tell her what Jerry said in the deli, his abusive and nasty accusations. The sexual nature of his every breath.

"He's a horrible pig. But, ya know, I have a theory," Emily interrupts.

"About what?"

"Well, first, you can never really escape the fact that there's sexual tension in the workplace. When men and women are together like that, there's always some kind of sexual dance going on."

"What do you mean?"

"I've always thought Jerry might be into you," Emily says. "He knows he could never get you. So in order to protect himself, he masks it by being mean and angry."

"Ugh, that's disgusting. The mere thought of him wanting me is revolting."

"Well, I know," Emily laughs. "But what happened at the deli shows how he probably feels about you. Even the Stones' song, 'You Can't Always Get What You Want,' may be him talking about himself. Not you."

"Yick. I can't even think about this," I say.

"You've done well, in spite of that macho environment," Emily says.

"But I'm confused," I say. "Because here I am in a luxurious hotel in New York, at the peak of my career, about to possibly be crowned president, and I feel empty. Like, this is it? This is what I've killed myself for? Why aren't I ecstatic? Why do I feel like listening to Peggy Lee singing, 'Is That All There Is'?"

"Because now that you possibly have what you've worked so hard for, what you thought you wanted, you may not want it at all. That's something you should think about. Do you still want it?" Emily asks.

"I dunno."

I'm stunned how that reply just rolled off my tongue.

"You're certainly qualified for the job, Lex. But HBS may not be ready for you. They may be too dysfunctional to appreciate your talents. Their culture resides in the past. You are the future."

There's a pause as I try to take in what Emily said.

"Meanwhile," Emily says, "I know you must be very sad about Gordon. I know you really loved him. That's a terrible loss."

"He won't talk to me." I can barely get the words out. "I do really love him, Em. I really do. Of course I realize that now more than ever, but it's too late."

"Well, nothing's over until one of you is dead," she says sweetly. "When you get back to LA, why don't you try calling him again?"

"He won't return my calls. I've called numerous times."

"When are you coming home?"

"I was supposed to stay a few more days, but I want to come home tomorrow. I'm gonna change my flight and get out of here."

I want to tell Emily what happened with Jerry. But I can't. Not even to Emily, my closest confidante. I made a promise. We shook on it. Somehow I came through my dad's death with integrity and a greater understanding and appreciation for humanity. I need to become that person again. That was such a truly vulnerable moment for Jerry. As much as I positively hate him, for the first time I actually kind of understand him. Yet I might have grown more from that experience and his reaction this afternoon than he will in a lifetime.

"Good," Emily adds. "Let's get together and toast your amazing success. I'm proud of you. And I love you."

I tell Emily I love her, too, and thank her for being such an unselfish friend. Now I can get some sleep.

"Oh, one more thing," Emily says.

"Yeah?"

"The thong is working."

"Told ya." I laugh. "Which kind did you get?"

"I went hog wild and got the low riders."

"Ewww. You're so brave. Soon you'll be telling me about your Brazilian wax."

"Ha. No way. I'm not a masochist." Emily laughs. "God, where were thongs when I was single?"

"On our feet. They call them flip-flops now!"

We both laugh. Something I needed. We wish each other a good night and hang up.

The next morning, I check out of the hotel, grab a cab, and head to the airport. In the car, I change my flight to eleven o'clock, which gets me into LA at one. I couldn't be happier. I call Stan and thank him for taking care of Joe, who I miss and can't wait to see. I call Rosie and tell her I changed my flight and am on my way home.

"You changed your flight? Yourself?" Rosie asks.

"I did," I say. "And I want to take you to lunch soon. We need some time to just get to know one another again."

There's silence. Then Rosie starts going through the calls I've missed. She tells me what I need to do when I get in today, but I interrupt her.

"Rosie, let's take a break. I want you to take the day off. Have a little fun. Enjoy yourself."

"Are you OK?" Rosie asks.

"I am. I know you don't believe this is me talking, but I mean it. Nothing's going on. You work so hard. And you're so good to me. Please do something for yourself. Something you truly enjoy. We'll talk later."

I turn off my phone and don't even turn it on when I arrive in LA. Enrique, the driver, meets me at baggage claim and carries my bags to his town car. I'm thrilled to be home.

The palm trees never looked so great. Soon we're in traffic, but I'm relaxed and calm. We drive along Sepulveda Boulevard because the freeway's a mess. As we head north, we come into Culver City and stop at a light. I look at the scenery in a neighborhood I hardly ever frequent, as it's far from where I live and work. I see folks going to Target and the car wash, and wonder what it's like to have a simple, nonstressful day. Do I really need this life? Is becoming president of HBS the be-all and end-all for me?

Finally we get to my apartment, and as Enrique unloads my bags and brings them up the stairs to my door, I stop at the mailbox and see someone's *Variety* sitting in the magazine rack. The headline catches my attention. It reads, "NBC wins May Sweeps; HBS a close second. But Who will Win the Top Job?" I start to reach for it, and then decide to let it go. Instead, I get my mail and return to my apartment.

Chapter Thirteen

It's early Wednesday morning. A week's passed since I arrived home last Tuesday. I've not heard anything about who got the job.

Chester was in Nantucket, while the rest of the guys stayed in New York in case there was more partying to do. Sylvia heard Jerry stayed on a few days longer, as he was invited to play golf with Barnsworth at his fancy country club. We have a brief respite before the shows start production in July, then summer press tour, and then the new season opens and the whole cycle starts again.

In the meantime, I have to renew my driver's license at the DMV in Culver City, which happens to be right by Crestview Elementary. Just the thought of being in that area makes my stomach churn. It's been almost two weeks since Gordon appeared in my office.

As I slowly coast along Olympic Boulevard approaching the school, I can't help but think about Gordon and Marisol and how empty my life is without them. As I pull up alongside the entrance I see a parking space across the street. I feel like Lucille Ball hiding in the shadows, and yet that's exactly what I want to do. I turn off the engine and peer at the school that in some ways has changed my life and certainly has changed me. I long to have it back. I guess that's why I'm staring at a world I once had but may never experience again. And I'm not sure I can do a darn thing about it.

Then suddenly I see kids gather on the playground for recess. I notice Olga Hernandez, and shortly thereafter I see Marisol skipping alongside. I'm riddled with guilt thinking about the commitment I made, and how I let her down. My body collapses into my seat. As I watch Marisol, my mind drifts to the last time we were together when I held her hand and told her I'd return. I made her a promise, which I failed to keep. I feel ashamed and disgusted, as I haven't seen her in weeks. I have to find a way to make up for this. I just hope she forgives me.

As I sit in my car staring at the schoolyard, I'm startled by a driver screaming at another car to either park or move. I realize it's time for me to move on, too. Figuratively and physically. I start my engine, but out of the corner of my eye I catch of glimpse of Gordon. I turn off the ignition and slump down in my seat, hoping he won't see me, but I'm desperate to see every inch of him. He lifts the trunk of his car, retrieves what looks like a jacket, lingers for a moment, then shuts it and returns to his office. I sit up and stare above the steering wheel, taking in all that I can. Part of me wants to leap out of the car, yell out his name, and fly over to him. But I know I can't do that. This is the wrong place, and I'm not sure if there will ever be the right time.

Just before he arrives at his office he stops to chat with another teacher. I catch a glimpse of his face and broad smile. What I would give to just hear his calm, soothing voice, just to be held by him again. Just one more time.

Maybe I should get out of the car. Maybe I shouldn't let this moment pass. Maybe the time is now. My heart flutters and my body tenses. Instantly, I grab the door handle and start to make my move, but at that precise moment, the bell rings and Gordon races off and out of view. Just like that he's gone. I look out my window, searching high and low, but he's vanished. The time has come and gone.

All I can do is bury my face in my hands, thinking about the mess I made. The next thing I know a car has pulled alongside and the driver is asking if I'm planning on pulling out, as he'd like the space. Sure, why not. What else can I possibly do here? I need to leave this part of my life behind and move on.

I continue on my journey to the DMV, making a quick stop at Whole Foods to get fruit, yogurt, and even some flowers. I rarely get them for myself, but they're so beautiful and fragrant and I could really use a pick-me-up right now. As soon as I return to my car, the phone rings.

"Alexa?" Rosie asks. "I have Chester on the line. Can you speak to him?"

"Sure," I say as I set the bag of groceries on the passenger seat next to me.

"Hey, great stuff in New York," Chester says. I hear him puffing away.

"Thanks, Chester. How was Nantucket?" I ask, settling into my seat and closing the door.

"Oh, good," he says, but his tone doesn't reflect that. I wonder what mess is going on now. Something tells me the relaxation is about to end. I hope I don't have to rush back for a meeting, because this DMV appointment was hard to get.

"Listen, where are you?" Chester asks.

"Well, I'm at Whole Foods in Culver City," I laugh. "Actually, on my way to the DMV to renew my driver's license. I haven't been able to do a darn thing for the past few weeks, as I'm sure you know."

"Yeah, I know." Chester sounds serious. "Well, listen, I hate to have this conversation on the phone. I was hoping to have it in person. Except I want you to hear it from me rather than the trades."

Suddenly, my heart rate skyrockets, and it is hard to breathe. I don't say a word. I let Chester continue.

"You know, Lex," Chester continues. "You're a very valuable executive. You've risen to the occasion in a big way. Your shows were tremendous. You managed to take some mediocre development and turn it into gold. Your efforts were spectacular. I'm darn proud of you, and you should be rewarded for that hard work." I hear Chester inhale and then exhale with a loud cough. I think, oh my God, I'm going to be rewarded with the top job now? In the car? This is the big moment? Right here in the parking lot of Whole Foods? Where's the drumroll? The applause? *Is that all there is?*

"Well, thank you, Chester. I'm glad you appreciated how hard I worked this season."

"So I'm going to promote you to a new position I'm creating just for you. It's executive vice president of programming. You'll be in charge of comedy, drama, and reality."

I take a beat. I don't even want to ask, but I have to. "And who's going to be president of entertainment?"

There's a long pause. As if Chester knows this isn't going to be easy.

"Jerry," he says flatly. "Jerry will be president. But I made it very clear to him that you'll be in charge of programming. I want him to focus on marketing, scheduling, business affairs, those other areas. I think you guys will make a great team."

I don't respond. I look straight ahead. The world has stopped as I try to take this in.

"Who will I report to?" I fear the answer, but I have to know.

"You'll be reporting to Jerry."

As I look out the window I see women pushing shopping carts, some with children in tow, some not. I am present and aware, listening to Chester as he drones on, and yet I feel as if I'm having an out of body experience. I try to absorb the words I never wanted to hear.

"You'll be reporting to Jerry."

"Alexa, are you there?" Chester asks. "I don't know if we got cut off or not. I've been talking and talking and haven't heard anything from you. Are you there?"

I decide I'm not. Thank God for cell phone disruption. I disconnect. Within seconds, it lights up and I see it's Rosie, no doubt trying to reconnect us. But my cell phone just isn't working right now. Nor am I. I let it ring, and watch as it finally stops.

After about ten minutes, I turn on the ignition and decide to go home. I don't want to deal with the DMV today. My world has collapsed. I killed myself for a job everyone told me I'd never get, alienated friends and colleagues, and lost the boyfriend I always wanted.

My car is driving itself. Instead of heading toward West Hollywood I find myself driving farther into Culver City, down Sepulveda Boulevard toward Jefferson. I'm traveling to a favorite place. My womb. The place where I can be alone with my thoughts. Where there's no judgment. Where it's just Dad and me.

I enter Hillman Cemetery on this now-overcast Wednesday afternoon and head up the familiar path, passing two funerals that are just getting underway. I see a long black limo, the mass of black suits, and a few chairs perched near a freshly dug grave with a green tarp over it. As I drive slowly up the incline, I can't help but remember my own dad's funeral eighteen years ago. I remember standing just like those folks, watching as my dad's casket was lowered into the ground.

I continue my journey around the bend toward a spot on the hill overlooking the freeway. I park my car next to the curb, which says "Eternal Rest." I decide the flowers will be for my dad. I wander over the grassy knoll toward his grave. I take the flowers out of their cellophane wrapper and pull out the heavy metal vase that sits in a hole in the earth. It's cold and filled with worms and insects. I walk to the fountain, fill it with water, and toss in the new cream and lavender roses. I saunter back to the gravesite and carefully lower the vase back into the ground.

Other than the two funerals in progress down the hill and far away, I'm alone. There's no one in sight. A few groundskeepers rattle by in their carts. But other than that, I just hear the sounds of the freeway. I sit cross-legged on the newly shorn grass, gazing at my dad's headstone lying flat in the ground. "Samuel Ross, Beloved Husband and Father." I lean over and sweep my index finger over the letters of my dad's name engraved in the polished black granite marker.

I start to tell my dad what's going on in my life as if he were sitting across from me. But I can't seem to get the words out. Instead, I start sobbing. The tears pour down my face onto the blades of grass. I can't seem to stop. It's deep, gut-wrenching pain. I'm doubled over, bawling my eyes out. The sleeves of my sweater try to keep up with the onslaught of tears.

When the tears finally start to recede, I try talking again. But I realize my father has been gone for so long that I honestly don't know what kind of advice he'd offer me. I would hope he'd tell me to follow my gut. Do what I feel. Stay true to myself. And pick myself up and find the strength to carry on.

As I run my fingers over the grass I notice a single blade is caught between the links of my bracelet. Interesting how it managed to land right near the shimmering gold football bearing the words my dad taught me so early on in my life. Is this a sign? A message from beyond? The truth is I don't need one. Those words are etched in my memory and have shaped me into the person I am today. I am resilient, and I will live to see another day and many more. That is what my dad would want. And it's what I want, too.

I begin to feel the prickly tingling sensation in my toes suggesting that I've been in this position a long time. The sun begins to set behind the oppressive clouds. It's probably time for me to move on. I remove one bright-lavender rose from the vase and take it with me. I lift myself up and walk to the car. I place the single rose on the dashboard as if I'm taking part of my dad with me. I drive the ten miles back to my apartment slowly and carefully. I think about my life, what it's been and what I want it to be.

———

Two days have passed since I spoke with Chester. It's Friday, and I haven't been to the office in days. Nor have I returned Rosie's calls or others. I haven't even looked at my cell phone. And I'm sure there are hundreds of e-mails. I've begun to accept that Gordon is out of my life and no longer hope for an e-mail from him. That part of my life is over. Instead, I'm hunkered down in my apartment, lying on the sofa with Joe, listening to music, reading a book, and enjoying the fine spring breeze as it blows softly through the window.

After some time and much reflection, I decide to return to HBS.

I'm wearing casual black Levi's and a beige cotton blouse. I've gone back to my Victoria's Secret bra and am thrilled to be wearing my Nine West flats instead of those insane high heels. It's the beginning of the three-day Memorial weekend. I expect everyone will get a head start on their holiday and be gone by three o'clock today.

I drive over Laurel Canyon to Moorpark and into Burbank. I swing into the HBS lot and pull into my parking space. I pull out my badge and flash it in front of the guard, who buzzes me through the security door. I go into the stairwell and climb the three flights of stairs. I turn into the hall and head toward Chester's office suite, where I see his assistant, Jan, talking to Dawn.

"Hi, is he in?" I ask.

Jan looks at me and shrugs. "Sure, go in."

I'm always a bit nervous approaching Chester; however, today I'm not. As I enter his office, I see him sitting comfortably in his black leather chair smoking a cigarette, deeply immersed in his five TVs, each of which is tuned to a different sporting event. Chester smiles when he sees me and waves me over to my usual seat next to him. But I'm not doing that today. Instead I stand by his chair.

"Hey, so good to see you," he says, looking up at me. "How've you been? Did you see we came in second in the sweeps? Amazing work. Thanks to you, Lex. C'mon over, why don't you sit down? Let's talk. I wanna bring you up to speed on what we want to do in reality, now that you're going to oversee that, too." Chester pats my chair, waiting for me to come over, and turns off all his TVs, an indication he wants to give me his full attention. But I don't move.

He's doing everything and anything to compensate for his bad decision.

I would call that too little, too late.

"I'm glad HBS came in second," I say. "I'm happy for you. Thank you for saying all those wonderful things about me and the work I've done at HBS. I appreciate that, too."

I take a deep breath as I glance across the room at the various pieces of art around Chester's imperial office. I suddenly see details I never noticed before. Like the frayed wallpaper in the upper corner of the room and a small hole in the wall next to the doors leading out to the balcony. There was never any time to stop and smell the roses while working here. And never any time to notice the defects. I rest my hands in my back pockets and turn my attention toward Chester.

"I'm not sure I understand why you chose Jerry to be president of entertainment," I say. "I want to know why you made that decision."

Chester hastily reaches for his lighter and lights a cigarette. He hates confrontations and would like to be anywhere but here right now. He chooses to look at his lighter instead of me. "Well, Alexa, you did a great job, and it was a very tough decision and—"

"Chester, that's bullshit," I interrupt. "I want to know why."

There's a long pause. Chester stares at the five blank TVs in front of him. I'm sure he regrets turning them off because now there are no distractions. He'd rather die than have to deal with me right now.

"Jerry's a showman," Chester says, continuing to stare at the TVs instead of me. He takes a giant puff and coughs as he exhales. "He's a great seller with a big personality. But, despite what you might think, it was a hard call. Barnsworth and I went back and forth because you both have great abilities. But we felt Jerry fits in well here. He's also very connected to the community. But his willingness to do anything on behalf of HBS is what really gave him the winning edge."

I let this sink in. But just for a moment.

"And what about his ability to develop TV shows? What about the eight comedies Barnsworth wanted? Jerry got just one new comedy on the schedule. What about that?"

Chester takes another long hit from his cigarette, his eyes glued to the five dark TVs, not able to look up at me.

"Well, that wasn't a realistic goal," Chester says as he coughs again. "Comedies are hard to develop these days. You know things change. Sometimes you want one thing, but you end up with another. It's the natural ebb and flow of business."

"Is that so?" I ask, crossing my arms. I stare angrily at Chester, whose eyes remain fixed on the blank TVs. "Do you remember telling me what you were looking for in a president? We sat right here a few months ago. You said it was about challenging the troops, embracing change, and getting others to follow you. Developing great shows. Being able to manage crises and lead the team to a Super Bowl win. Can you give me examples of what Jerry did that led you to believe he possessed those particular skills you told me were imperative and essential to lead HBS?"

There's a pause. Chester hasn't moved except to flick his ash in the tray.

"Jerry began here eleven months ago," I say as I uncross my arms and place them in my back pockets again. "He was invited to play golf and enjoyed lavish lunches with Mr. Barnsworth. More than a few times. I don't recall you telling me that was a prerequisite to the position. Nor do I recall ever receiving such invitations."

Chester continues to stare at the TVs. After a moment he finally turns and looks up at me.

"I'm sorry, Alexa, I know you wanted this position."

"What you got is someone who's willing to sacrifice their principles for HBS," I say, looking squarely into Chester's eyes. "Someone who can't do the work but who will hire others to do it and then take the credit. Someone who can spin bad numbers. Someone who can talk about what it takes to win, but hasn't a clue how to actually do it. Someone who is well liked by the community because he stands for nothing."

I'm surprisingly calm but focused, and stunned that Chester is looking directly at me.

"HBS was my life, my passion, and my future," I continue without missing a beat. "I made many sacrifices in my personal life to help this network succeed. But I've been marginalized and minimized every step of the way. This was never about the work. Never about the skills. I've been working in a boys' locker room. This is no place for women to thrive and succeed. I did whatever I could to try and change the culture. I tried to break the glass ceiling here. But I can't do it. I thought it was about talent, hard work, and great shows. But it's not."

I take my hands out of my back pockets and put them on my hips.

"I'm done here, Chester. I quit."

I don't wait for a response. I don't want one. I turn on my heels and head out of his office. I can't help but notice Jan and Dawn, whose eyes are fixed on mine. I walk quietly out of Chester's office and back down the long hallway.

As I return to my office suite I see Rosie sitting at her desk. She smiles when I appear. She's happy to see me. "Gosh, I've been calling you for days. Why aren't you returning my calls? What's going on?" Rosie asks, looking worried. I walk past her and into my office.

"Please ask Sylvia, Molly, and Stacey to come in here right away," I call out to her. "I'd also like you in this meeting as well." I hear Rosie getting them all on the phone.

I sit down at my computer and open e-mails for the first time in two days. As expected, there are about three hundred. I highlight all of them and press delete. I pull a box out from under my desk and place some frames, plaques, photos, and other accessories in there. When it's almost filled, I carefully place the box with the stainless steel balls on top.

"Everyone's here," Rosie shouts into the intercom. I place the box beneath my desk and tell them to come in.

Sylvia, Molly, Stacy, and Rosie file into my office. They look concerned.

Rosie closes the door. This is unusual. They see me casually dressed while they're all in their pretty, professional suits. I point to the couch, where they all take a seat. I pull up a chair next to them. No one says a word.

"I quit my job today," I say matter-of-factly. "I choose to leave because there's nothing more for me to do here. I've done all I could. HBS needs to change its culture. I tried. But I couldn't do it."

They don't appear surprised, but clearly disappointed.

"I want you to keep fighting," I say. "Hopefully, someday everyone will be treated respectfully and fairly at HBS. You're the ones that have to make sure that happens. Don't give up." I try to sound perfunctory, but reality is starting to hit me. I'm leaving HBS. And no longer working with these terrific women. And that's something I will truly miss.

Rosie's starting to sniffle. Molly and Stacey put their arms around her.

"I'm going to leave now. I'll send for my things."

My throat tightens as I see the three of them holding on to each other. I'm trying to keep it together. I adore these women, who are more than just colleagues. They're my friends.

"I can't say too much more," I say, my voice cracking, the lump in my throat growing bigger by the second. "'Cause, well, 'cause I love you guys. And I don't want to burst out crying. Just know...just know I'm grateful for your dedication. Your support. Your loyalty."

I'm doing everything I can to remain stoic, but I'm upset and my eyes are welling up with tears. It hurts to see them huddled together. I return to my desk. Sylvia gets up, comes over, and hugs me warmly. And then I collect my purse and the box from under my desk and bolt out of the office.

I run down what will be my final flight of stairs to my car. As I hurry through the lobby, I stop as I hear loud voices coming from a conference room.

"It's my pleasure to congratulate Jerry Kellner, the new president of entertainment at HBS. I know he'll do a great job, and I want to thank you all for coming to celebrate with us."

It's Chester's voice. There's a lot of applause. This must be a company meeting, the notification for which was probably sent via an e-mail I deleted. And I'm glad I did. I continue on through the glass doors to my car. I lift the trunk and put my box inside. I get in my car and leave HBS for the last and final time.

My route home is quiet and peaceful. No calls. No texts. Just classical music, the slow tempo of which is soothing. It's the middle of the day, and I have nothing to do. Nowhere to be.

I arrive at my apartment, pour myself a glass of merlot, and let some light in the room. I lie on the window seat and gaze at the mountains as Joe rests comfortably on my leg. The phone rings. I decide not to answer it. It rings again. I wait for the machine to pick up.

"Hey, it's Emily. I called your office and Rosie told me what happened. I want to see you. Can I come over this evening? Around seven or so? Actually, I'm not even going to ask. I'm telling you. I'll be over at seven. Be there. Love you."

Joe and I haven't moved. I'm sure he's wondering what the heck I'm doing home in the middle of the afternoon. He may have to get used to having me around. I feel like I'm in an altered state. Still in shock. I keep going over and over the conversation I had with Chester, trying to understand what really happened. How could he have chosen Jerry over me? What does "fitting in" mean? And what about the work? Why wasn't there any reference to the work?

At precisely seven o'clock, the doorbell rings. I hear Emily's voice and let her in. When she walks through the door, I can barely contain my emotions and start to tear up.

"I want you to pull yourself together," Emily says instantly. "You have company."

Suddenly about twenty women come marching up the staircase behind her.

Leading the way is Sylvia, followed by Rosie, Molly, Stacey, Jan, Dawn, even Merisa, the lone female writer on *The Candy Stripers*, along with Sophie, the writers' assistant, and some others. Each of them walks into my apartment. No one says anything but "hi" as they swarm my living room. I'm dumbstruck. I don't know what this is about. Some take seats, others stand. Most are familiar faces, but some are not. Sylvia walks to the center of my living room.

"Alexa, these are the women of HBS," Sylvia says, glancing around the room.

"Some work there and others work on HBS shows. We came together because we're outraged and furious that Jerry Kellner has risen to the top position at HBS when it was clear you earned that promotion. Given your accomplishments and expert management skills, we think HBS's decision to promote Jerry to president over you is both offensive and despicable. In its forty years, HBS, a major broadcast network, has never had a female president of any division. At one time or another, every other broadcast network has had a female president. No woman has ever risen above a vice president at HBS. It's clear that HBS fosters an environment that encourages sexism."

I sit on the floor, watching Sylvia and the rest of the group. Everyone is very serious and focused. I look over at Jan and Dawn. I'm astonished to see them here.

"And let me just tell you something." Sylvia pauses for effect. "We aren't going to take it anymore!"

For the first time, the room erupts in cheers.

"We've decided to file a class action sex discrimination lawsuit against HBS. We need your participation because we need every bit of evidence we can get to take this on." Sylvia turns toward me. "You left HBS today telling us not to give up. To continue our quest for equality. This is the first stop on our way. Will you join us?"

They know I will. I'm shocked that within four hours this group came together and forged this effort. I've never been a part of any women's group. I was never the one to cry foul. I never reported any incident for fear of reprisal. I never wanted to be *I Am Woman*, as Steve disparagingly referred to one of my shows.

But I feel different today.

"Thank you," I say. The lump in my throat has returned. I can barely get the words out. "Thank you for standing up. I'm speechless. I thought I was alone. But clearly I wasn't." I look around the room and see strength and determination. I'm overcome by the outpouring of warmth and solidarity. "Of course I'll join you." There's a burst of applause. I look at my watch. "But I have something I need to do. So I'm going to leave this room and encourage you to share your stories and write them down. I need to make two calls, and then I'll rejoin you."

I burst out of the room and into my bedroom, where I see Emily. Neither of us says a thing. We both embrace. I've never hugged anyone so hard in my life.

Chapter Fourteen

Four days have passed since the women of HBS declared war on their employer. The headline in today's *New York Times* hasn't escaped anyone's attention. There it is in bold print: *Women Intend to File Sex Discrimination Suit Against HBS*. Beneath the headline it reads, *HBS strongly denies the allegations made this morning by twenty-five female employees. The company says it will strongly defend against these claims in court.* Sylvia tells me the network was totally caught by surprise, or with their pants down, so to speak.

Patricia Wielding had long left *Elle*. Her new position at the *New York Times* couldn't have been more fortuitous. Her card has sat on my nightstand for months. I guess there was a reason for that. When she picked up the phone and heard it was me, she knew immediately I was ready to talk. And talk I did. We spoke all through Memorial weekend until her deadline on Monday afternoon. I knew the article with my quotes would be in today's paper and online the night before.

Aside from Patricia's article, there are numerous items relating to the impending lawsuit. Some of the more resourceful journalists delved further into Jerry's past. Most wanted to know about the inappropriate behavior that led to Jerry's termination at Tiger Films a mere eleven months ago. They discovered an unreported skirmish involving a subordinate whom Jerry accidentally strangled in San Francisco at their annual retreat. Jerry pleaded no contest to misdemeanor battery, paid a one-thousand-dollar fine, and went to domestic violence counseling. It was all handled very quietly.

My second call on Friday was to Michael Weaver, the instructor at the sexual harassment seminar in January. He wasn't surprised to hear from me. He didn't ask too many questions but said it sounded as if there were some legal violations and therefore suggested I consult an attorney. He gave me the name of one.

Fortunately, I had learned many things at the network over the years. One was to cover my bases. I kept e-mails about various situations in a file. I always wondered if this was just a diary or if it would be useful one day. I didn't feel I could safely turn any of it over to human resources without reprisals, so it just sat in a file.

However, when I contacted the attorney Mr. Weaver suggested and advised him of the *New York Times* article and the file I had along with numerous other documented accusations from colleagues, I was told we might have a case. And I guess he would know. This attorney's law firm was co-counsel for the plaintiffs in a national sex discrimination class action suit filed in early 2000, representing a class of over one million women in one of the largest sex discrimination cases in the history of the United States.

I believe we're in good hands.

That sex discrimination case rocked the entire country. Within my own industry, a sexual harassment case was brought by a former *Friends* assistant who claimed she was improperly subjected to vulgar and coarse language by the comedy show's writing staff. The California Supreme Court shot it down, saying the comments were part of the atmosphere of the show's writers' room.

It's Wednesday, one day after the *New York Times* article appeared. The dust has started to settle. My attorney advises me and the other women not to speak to the press. My phone rings off the hook. I'm surprised by the rabid desire to know something, anything. I answer my phone a few times. After a seemingly innocuous conversation with Nancy, my former public relations flak, I realize she wants information for professional gain. Knowledge is power. That's Hollywood's motto. And being one of the first to know something is even better. It would certainly help Nancy. However, her unsubtle questioning only prompts me to tell her I have nothing to say. I thank her for working on my behalf, wish her a nice day, and hang up.

I even get a call from Gabriella Mannucci, my professional shopper, who is far more blunt, coming straight out and asking me what happened. I decide not to answer the phone or the door anymore.

Two more days pass. It's now Friday. I'm getting cabin fever. I'm used to a twenty-four seven nonstop life, and this is hardly it. I start to wonder what I'm going to do, how I'm going to pay rent. The reality of my situation sets in.

Joe and I get in the car and drive a few blocks to Trader Joe's for some much-needed food. The calls have subsided. The press is gone. Suddenly my life is Joe and me and a lawsuit that may or may not ever see the light of day.

My phone is deep inside my purse rather than in the cup holder, where it always was during my HBS days. When I hear it ringing, I almost don't answer, especially since Joe is dancing on my purse, barking his ass off at a dog that happens to be in the next car. I dig into my purse and pull out the phone. I answer without even looking at the caller ID.

"Alexa, I know you're engaged in a lawsuit against HBS," I hear Chester say, "but I wondered if you'd consider meeting with Mr. Barnsworth and myself. We'll meet anytime at your convenience."

Huh? You'll meet anytime at my convenience? I pull the car over and pray Joe stops barking so I can respond to this invitation. I find a space in front of a Starbucks in West Hollywood.

"OK. I'll meet you later today," I say. I look at Starbucks. "At Starbucks on Santa Monica Boulevard in West Hollywood. How about three o'clock?"

Chester says, "Fine," and hangs up. I sit for a moment, wondering what this could possibly be about. Is he offering me a settlement? Does he want me to get the other women under control? Do they want to berate me and say how cruel I am to do this to them? It occurs to me I probably shouldn't attend this meeting, given that we'll be in litigation. But thanks to the many seminars I was forced to attend at HBS on legal issues, I'm expert in knowing what to say and what not to say under the circumstances. HBS trained me well. And, frankly, I'm curious. This is Chester's meeting. Not mine. My job is to listen. Though I'm sure I won't be able to do just that.

As long as I'm in a parking space, I take Joe and we go for a walk in the middle of the afternoon along Santa Monica Boulevard. Something I've never done in my entire life. A walk on a lovely weekday morning.

As we saunter along my phone rings again. It's Emily.

"Hey, Em," I say breezily. "Can you believe I'm in West Hollywood with Joe, just taking a walk in the middle of the day? I've had two calls and that's it. I didn't realize what life was like outside that insane building."

"Well, maybe you're finally discovering your feminine side." Emily laughs. "I just want to know how you're doing, but I guess the answer is OK."

We talk about a few other things. She tells me what's going on with her sons, and then she changes the subject. "Did you ever hear from Gordon?" she asks.

"No, I never did," I say, changing my tone. Every time I think of Gordon now, it's with sadness. "It's over. It's been a few weeks, and he hasn't tried to get in touch with me."

"Why don't you call him?"

"Call him? Why?" I ask, shocked that Emily would suggest such a thing when she knows he won't return my calls. "He's not responded in any way to me. I think that says something, don't you? I don't think he wants to hear from me. Ever."

"Have you checked out what he's doing on Facebook?" she asks.

"Gordon? On Facebook?" I ask incredulously. "No, he doesn't do Facebook. He barely uses his phone."

"Maybe he needs to see you."

I think about this.

"I don't know," I say. "I miss Marisol and feel horrible and very guilty about abandoning her. I'd like to see her again."

"Well, think about it. I have to go. Just wanted to make sure you're OK." She hangs up.

As Joe and I continue walking by the numerous trendy cafes that dot Santa Monica Boulevard in West Hollywood, I think about Gordon. I kept him at arm's length, too afraid that if I gave myself over to him, I'd risk suffering the unbearable pain of losing him if things didn't work out. And it happened, just as I thought it might. Maybe I needed him to break it off with me in order for me to see that I could survive. And I did. I'm still standing. Yet I miss him terribly.

It's almost time to meet Chester and Mr. Barnsworth at Starbucks, but just as we're about to end our walk I see a jewelry store. I've been meaning to reattach the jade stone that fell off my bracelet, so since I have a few minutes I take it out of my wallet, where it's been since the day I discovered it on the carpet in my office, and approach the clerk.

"Ah, this is a beautiful gem," the clerk says as he gazes at the stone and carefully reattaches it to my bracelet. "You know what they say about jade?"

"I do. It provides harmony, balance, and peace," I say, smiling, remembering those exact words. The words Gordon recited the day he put it on my wrist.

"Yes, that's true, but do you know what else?" I shake my head. "The message of jade is to love and accept yourself." He smiles.

"I didn't know that." I offer him a few bucks, but he waves it away and winks. I thank him and mull over those words as Joe and I slowly step out of the shop and onto the busy boulevard.

We return to my car and drive back to my apartment. I realize that despite the fact that Gordon and I are broken up, I've never removed the bracelet. Maybe wearing it makes me feel he's still with me. Still loving me. I guess it will always hold a special place in my heart. And then I wonder what Gordon's thinking. What he's doing. Is he having as difficult a time getting over me as I am over him? Or is he already on to someone else? Was I simply a blip on his screen?

When I get home, I take off my sweats, put on nice jeans and a top, and get back in the car and head to Starbucks. I'm the first to arrive. I grab a latte and sit in the corner. Soon Chester and Barnsworth join me at the small table in the back. It's a large room and not very crowded. Chester and Barnsworth don't seem terribly at ease. This is not their kind of place.

"Alexa, I'm going to get right to it," Chester says, tapping his lighter on the table as his eyes dart back and forth across the room. "Mr. Barnsworth generously offered to turn Rhapsody, the music cable network in HBS Industries' portfolio, into a women's network. We're offering it to you to run. You would be president. You can hire whomever you want. You wouldn't even interface with me. You'd report directly to Mr. Barnsworth. We can't think of anyone better to do this, and knowing you, it would be enormously successful."

I look at Barnsworth, who smiles broadly. I wait a beat before I respond.

"So," I say slowly, "if I were an African-American man would you turn Rhapsody into a black network and ask me to run it because I had just filed a racial discrimination suit against you?"

The smile on Barnsworth's face disappears.

"That's ridiculous. Of course not," says Chester. "We really do see the need for a women's network. It didn't occur to us that we had the perfect person at HBS." Chester, the master of spin, is trying to spin me right now.

"Really? You mean it didn't occur to you until you saw the headline in the *New York Times* on Tuesday." I don't know where I'm getting the chutzpah, but these days I'm fearless.

"Look, we didn't come here to start an argument—"

"Mr. Barnsworth," I interrupt, "you have one hundred and twenty-five divisions at Hawkeye Industries, and not one of them is run by a woman. And now suddenly you want to turn one of your precious cable operations into a network run by and for women? Really? The timing is rather curious, don't you think?"

"Alexa, we believe you're the right person to run this network," Barnsworth, who's remained mute the whole time, suddenly responds.

"What should occur to you is that fifty-one percent of the viewing audience is women," I say, staring at both of them. "Continuing to rely on men to make choices and decisions about what women want to watch on HBS is a mistake. Just as it's a mistake to suggest that white men understand the plight of African American men or Latinos. The network can't sustain itself without true diversity. The world has changed, Mr. Barnsworth. It's not just a world of white men. The sooner you understand that, the better your business will be. I know you think offering me the opportunity to run a women's network is a fine solution to your now huge problem. But I find it positively insulting."

My Academy Award performance is about over. I grab my purse and start to get up, but realize I have one more thing to say. "You have no idea what awaits you, Mr. Barnsworth. You won't just suffer the loss of millions of dollars. You're going to watch the demise of HBS. Because you now have the perfect person to lead that effort in Jerry Kellner."

I swing my bag across my shoulder, take a final sip of my latte, and exit.

I walk out of Starbucks and never look back.

It's close to five o'clock, and I have nowhere to go, nowhere to be. I just turned down the opportunity to run a women's network, something many of my colleagues would kill for. But not me. Apparently, I've become Susan B. Anthony and Gloria Steinem rolled into one.

Puhleeze. What am I doing? It might've felt good to unload on those guys, but the fact is I'm without a job. And I need to make a living. I'm suddenly starting to feel very anxious. I get in the car and start to drive. But I don't know where. I have no place to go. What *am* I going to do?

I think about what Emily said earlier today. About Gordon. Maybe I do need to see him. If nothing else I want him to know the profound effect he had on me. I was able to finally let someone love me, and I allowed myself to love back. I'm not sure I'm ready to throw in the towel.

I laugh as I recall the words, *It's not whether you get knocked down, it's whether you get up.* Funny how Lombardi's message still inspires me. Just like he used to inspire my dad. And how those words have guided me through my life. I guess my dad was right after all. He said the key to success was the ability to bounce back. Well, Dad, I've had my fair share of rejections, and believe it or not, I'm still bouncing!

I gaze at my bracelet and hold the football charm between my index finger and my thumb. I move my thumb back and forth over the inscription and then take a deep breath. Should I really do this? Am I ready?

I drive for twenty minutes to Crestview Elementary, but I'm traveling very slowly, as I'm not sure I can carry this off. I'm starting to cough, a clear sign that I'm anxious. Very anxious. Maybe I'll just drive by. But as I approach the school I see Gordon's car and a parking space right in front, which I take as a sign and pull in. It's peaceful and quiet. I turn off the engine and sit in the car. I stare at the school and begin coughing again. I know he's there. Oh God. Can I do this? Do I *want* to do this? What if he hates me? What if he doesn't want to see me? After a moment I decide yes, I'm going to try.

I carefully open my car door and walk toward the entrance. As I get closer I take a few deep breaths. I want to see Gordon, but I'm trembling. My mouth is dry, my stomach's in knots. I can barely put one foot in front of the other. Boy, am I a wreck. I just don't want to be hurt again.

I approach the main office. I see the door to the tiny room next to it is closed. I know Gordon often uses that office to grade papers after school. But he may not even be in there. Someone else could be. I start having second thoughts. Maybe I shouldn't be here. It's his place of work, after all. Maybe I shouldn't do this. Maybe I should leave. But I decide I've come this far. I need to at least try to see him. I tell myself that even if I suffer the worst possible scenario, if he throws me out of his office, if he tells me he's already seeing someone else, whatever it is, at least I gave it one last shot. As I stand at the entrance to the little office I've been in so many times, I stop and take another deep breath. My body trembles as I knock very lightly on the door. I wait, but there's no answer. Whew. He's not there. I start to relax. OK, it wasn't meant to be. I had a feeling he might not be here. I'm relieved. I don't knock a second time. Instead, I turn to leave. But then suddenly the door opens and Gordon appears.

I'm speechless.

Gordon stands in the doorway looking at me, and me at him. My heart is pumping faster and faster, my muscles are so tense I can barely move or catch my breath. And then without warning he slowly reaches for my hand, brings me inside the office, closes the door, and embraces me.

The floodgates open, and I'm sobbing all over his shirt. He holds me in his arms. I'm overcome with emotion. I think this journey has wiped me out and everything is culminating right here. I was such a wreck, never dreaming I'd find myself in Gordon's arms again.

"Gordon, I'm so terribly sorry," I say, releasing myself from his grip while wiping the tears from my eyes. "I really thought I had to change and become someone else—just for a stupid promotion. I couldn't see the forest for the trees. I lost my way. And...and I lost you. I don't know why you should forgive me, but..."

I find it hard to breathe. I find it hard to finish the sentence, and so the end of it comes out weak, almost inaudible.

"I'd give anything if you would."

He embraces me again. As he holds me in his arms I'm filled with worry, wondering what he might be thinking. He hasn't said one word. Is he just being nice? Maybe it is too late. But I need to tell him how I feel. I may never have another opportunity. I let go of his embrace and look in his eyes.

"Maybe you don't want me back, Gordon. I understand if you don't. I just wanted you to know how much I love you and how grateful I am that you let me be your girlfriend."

I start to tear up again, but I want to get it all out. If he still doesn't want me then fine. At least I'll have given it my all. Something I haven't done till now.

"After my father died, I never let myself love anyone...until I met you. In a way, before, maybe I was afraid of really opening up to you. But I'm ready now. I know what I've lost."

Gordon rests his hands in his front pockets. I know mascara must be running down the side of my face. My cheeks are flushed; I must look awful. I wish he'd say something. Anything. I feel like my heart's going to explode out of my chest. I'm starting to feel cold and shaky. Then finally, after what seems like an eternity, Gordon takes my left hand. He reaches for my bracelet and turns the gold football charm around so he can see the inscription. Then he looks into my eyes.

"Sometimes it takes these kinds of experiences to really grow and change," he says. "I had time to think about us as well. And I missed you terribly. Everywhere I went, everything I did was over-shadowed by thoughts of you. As much as I wanted to call you, I couldn't because you had to get to this place yourself. I just hoped you'd get there someday."

"Will you give me another chance?"

Gordon smiles, brushing the tears off my cheek.

"I guess we're just gonna have to keep trying till we get this right." Gordon laughs, and I smile for the first time. I can finally breathe again.

"By the way," Gordon says as he kisses my forehead, "I read in the paper that Jerry got the job."

"Yes, he did."

"I'm sorry. I know that must've been a huge disappointment," he says. "But your efforts will pave the way for other women. And for that you should feel great. More glass ceilings will be shattered because of what you did."

"I also quit my job and am part of a class action lawsuit against HBS," I say, dropping my head. "I'm not sure what I'm going to do next."

There's a pause.

"I know. I read about it," he says. And then he places his fingertips under my chin and gently lifts it up. He looks right into my eyes.

"You're going to follow your passion, Alexa. You're a highly creative young woman. Let your instincts guide you. You're going to be fine."

Gordon's eyes never leave mine. There's a long pause. This time I don't want to avert them. I'm enjoying the intensity of his gaze. All I can think about is how I've missed him and how happy I am to be near him again.

"I've learned a great deal from all this," I say. "I don't know where to begin."

"We'll have a lifetime for that." Gordon says, offering a slight grin. "But first I want to show you something."

Gordon takes my hand and opens the door. We start walking across the playground. I'm instantly at peace. My muscles begin to relax, the tension in my neck is gone, and my breathing is back to normal. I'm where I want to be. I love the sound of his voice. I love holding his hand. I just love being with him.

We walk slowly, like we have all the time in the world, across the vast playground, which is empty and peaceful. I feel the warmth of his hand. It feels exactly how I remember it, soft and secure. I hear crickets and the sound of a lone car coming to a stop. I glance up at the sky, which is clear and just starting to darken. I see the sun beginning to set in the distance and feel a dry and gentle Santa Ana breeze.

As we continue our journey Gordon tells me about the improvements he's made to the tutoring program and Marisol's progress. I tell him I want to see her on a regular basis. That no matter what I do next, I'll always keep one hour during the week open for tutoring. I tell him how badly I feel because I haven't seen Marisol and that I promised I'd be back, but I am fully committed to be there now and help in any way I can.

We arrive at the school library. The door opens and the place is abuzz. There are several men and women helping students. Some are painting. Some are reading. Some are working on math problems.

"Wow." I'm bowled over. I sure wasn't expecting this.

"The program's thriving," Gordon says happily. "We have a lot of volunteers who help students after school now."

"This is really wonderful."

"I think there's someone else you might want to see," Gordon says.

In the corner, I see Marisol, who is sitting on the floor, wearing glasses and reading a book. The second she sees me, she jumps up and flies over. She hugs me at my waist.

"I missed you so much, Marisol," I say, running my hand over her hair. "I'm so glad to see you. I'm sorry I haven't been here and—"

"I knew you'd be back," Marisol interrupts, looking up at me. "You promised you would. I'm happy you're here."

And then, without missing a beat, Marisol, who was always quiet and reserved, takes my hand and introduces me, her tutor, to the other students. She shows me the work they're all doing. She's especially proud that she finished *A Wrinkle in Time* and wants to tell me about it. The shy and reticent young girl I saw a month ago is turning into a vibrant, confident student. I'm beaming with pride.

———

It isn't until the *Los Angeles Times* quotes four unnamed sources who say Jerry Kellner not only sexually harassed them but sexually assaulted them that HBS starts to realize it has a problem. Nikki Finke reports she's heard about the other incidents involving Kellner and women at HBS, and that it has all been quietly "handled" by the network. She rails against HBS, a public company that has chosen to support Jerry's employment despite the numerous claims against him.

HBS realizes it's in deep shit.

Today, Thursday, June 13, the Hollywood trade papers announce that Jerry Kellner has been fired.

The headline is all over the place. It was the lead story in Nikki Finke's blog with her trademark *Toldja So* headline, putting HBS in the crosshairs. The entire town is buzzing about Jerry Kellner and how he's single-handedly taken down HBS.

Jerry Kellner has gone from president to pariah.

The press is calling me again. My voice mail is loaded with messages begging for a comment.

Rosie sent boxes filled with my files and mementos. I see them stacked up in the entryway to my apartment. Before I tackle them, I look at the stainless steel balls with the note that says *Now you have four* on my coffee table. They make me smile. We will continue together on our next journey.

The phone just keeps ringing. I accidentally answer, thinking it's Rosie, but it's Laura Hartung, who interviewed me on the radio a while back. She said she's heard I've had several offers, including one to run a TV studio and another to head a cable network. But I tell her I'm not sure what I'll be doing next.

"I'd like to take some time to explore other areas," I say. "I want to open myself up to what the world has to offer. I've worked in television a long time. Maybe there are other challenges for me. Maybe it's time to try my hand at something else."

Laura wishes me luck as my phone continues to ring with more calls from reporters who want comments about Jerry's demise. The one call I answer immediately is Gordon's.

"It's a great day, sweetheart," he says. "Let's celebrate."

"OK. Where are we going?"

"Wear your red dress. Be outside at seven. We're gonna have a good time." "OK." I'm thrilled. There's no one I want to celebrate this wonderful day with more than Gordon.

He arrives right on time. He looks so handsome in his blue jacket and khaki pants. He even has on a tie, something I've never seen him wear. His beautiful smile and blue eyes are sparkling with excitement. This is not a relationship I ever want to screw up again. I'm finally going to take Gordon's advice and try for a little balance in my life. The Alfa's top is finally fixed. We drive along Sunset Boulevard. I'm happier than I've been in a long time. When we approach the stoplight, Gordon hands me his wallet. But I don't take it. Instead I open mine, pull out five bucks, and hand it to the elderly vet holding a sign asking for money. We continue down Sunset almost into Beverly Hills. But right before we get there, Gordon turns left into the parking lot for Soho House, a private club and restaurant on the top floor of an office building.

"Uh, are we going to Soho House?"

Gordon nods.

"But we can't go here," I say as my jaw tenses. "We'd have to take an elevator to the restaurant on the roof. And besides, you have to be a member to dine here."

Gordon gets out of the car and takes the ticket from the valet. He comes around to my side and opens the door. He offers his hand to help me out of the car.

"I know. You're going to be fine. A friend got us in tonight," he says.

Gordon takes my hand as we walk toward the elevator bank. There's just one elevator that goes straight up the fourteen stories to the restaurant. I start to feel a lump forming in my throat. I stand a few feet away and watch as the elevator door opens. But I can't move. I just look at Gordon, begging him with my eyes.

"I'm scared," I say, as I feel myself tremble in anticipation. "I don't take elevators. You know that."

"I know. It's OK." Gordon is calm and relaxed. "I'm going to be with you."

"I can't do this," I say, my voice quivering. "I don't want to go. I feel terrible, Gordon. I'm so sorry to ruin this evening for you."

But Gordon won't give up. He stands in front of me, cupping my face in his hands, staring deeply into my eyes.

"You're not weak, Alexa," Gordon whispers. "You're just frightened. There's nothing wrong with being frightened. It's going to be all right."

Gordon walks to the elevator. The door has now closed. I can't move. My mouth is dry, and I feel as if there's an elephant on my chest. I can hardly breathe. We're standing a few feet away from each other as Gordon perches himself right next to the elevator, facing me with an outstretched arm.

"Take your time," he says. "There's no hurry. If you want to, take my hand."

I'm shaking. I've not been in an elevator since my father died. I honestly don't know if I can do this. I'm terrified of being in such an enclosed space for so long. But there's no one I trust more than Gordon. If I'm going to do this, he's the person I want with me. I take a deep breath. One step. Then another. And another. But very small steps. Baby steps. My heart feels as if it will explode. It's thumping so loud inside my chest that I can hear it in my ears. I stop and take a few more deep breaths. But my palms are sweaty. I'm desperate for some water. I look at Gordon, who waits patiently watching my every move. His arm is still outstretched. I reach for my bracelet, find a jade stone, and hold it between my index finger and thumb, praying that it might offer the comfort and safety I need so badly right now.

I inch my way over to Gordon and am finally within a few inches of his hand. I very carefully slip mine in his.

"Are you OK?" Gordon asks.

I nod. I don't want to say anything. I can hardly breathe.

Gordon presses the call button, and after a few minutes, the door gradually opens. Gordon holds it with one hand and watches as I cautiously enter the elevator. As we turn around to face the front, I take another deep breath. Gordon puts his arm behind my shoulder and pulls me very close to him. He kisses the top of my head as the door begins to shut.

"Going up?" he asks.

I nod. "Yes, I am."

Then he presses the button, and as the elevator starts to ascend, he sings "Dream a Little Dream" very softly in my ear.

Gordon's singing is comforting and sweet. I'm as rigid as a rock, but eventually my body starts to give way, and I am actually feeling happy. I did it. I'm in an elevator, smiling on my way to the top.

Acknowledgments

After practicing it in the mirror for years, it appears I'm finally able to give that Emmy speech. I'd like to thank two important people. Without them I wouldn't be standing here in this very fancy tight dress, high heels, and Spanx, because they made it all happen.

Thank you to my agent, Jane Gelfman, who rolled the dice. I'm forever grateful. And to my editor, Kelli Martin, for her enthusiasm, passion, and patience. My heartfelt thanks to both of you for simply believing.

And to the fabulous team at Amazon Publishing, who got on board and never looked back. Special thanks to Susan Stockman, Jessica Poore, Nikki Sprinkle, and Laura Klynstra. And to Jeff Bezos, for creating this brave new world.

Thank you to my first readers, Jennie Fields, Elizabeth Higgins Clark, Debbie Simon, Megan Crane, Rhonica Petty, Carla Janus, and Karen Graci. And a big round of applause to Andrea Hurst and Bev Rosenbaum for their skillful editing. To Carrie Simons and Ashley Sandberg for their publicity efforts, and Jared Levine and Alex Kohner for their counsel.

Thank you to my galpals who promised they'd buy a bunch of books if they got a mention. Bonnie Raskin, Kay Hoffman, Sandy Gleysteen, Kathy Kloves, Lori Openden, Karen Winnick, Linda Michaels, Pam Morton, Dana Davis, Lori Shaw, Gwen Potiker,

Liza Wachter, Wanda McDaniel-Ruddy, Heather Roth, LaTanya Richardson-Jackson, Mary Jane Clark, Geena Davis, Jill Baffert, Stacey Ray, Maria Shriver, Nichelle Robinson, Jackie Herzig, Marci Gold, Alessandra Rizzotti, Sela Ward, Jackie Singer, Liz Goldberg, Anna Rawson, Barbara Yaroslavsky, Barbara Fisher, and Judy Ranan.

Special shout-out to my fabulous brother, Rob DeKoven. Thanks to Jeannette Davis, Marilyn Adams-Gogul, Andrew Leynse, Cindy Bryan, Merisa Levine, Ali Nuger, Cindy and Ron Levine. And to Hy and Edith Israel, Jordan and John Davis, Mike Growe, and Marty Stern. And to Flo and Eddie for picking up the crumbs under my desk.

This is beginning to feel like a miniseries. But if you're still watching to see how it ends…Thank you to my great bosses who taught me how to survive and thrive in their man's world: Alan Landsburg, Leslie Moonves, Don Ohlmeyer, Bob Wright, and Jack Welch.

Thank you to my husband, David Israel, the smartest person on the planet. If you don't believe me, just ask him. And, who despite the humorectomy he contends I had at birth, provides a daily dose of nonstop laughter.

Last, I'd like to thank my parents, Marcia and Sidney DeKoven, who I miss dearly and think about every day. "Believe. You've done it before. You can do it again." Words ingrained in my memory.

About the Author

After stints as an executive at Walt Disney and Warner Bros., Lindy DeKoven was executive vice president of NBC Entertainment. She has served as chair of the California Commission on the Status of Women and is a former member of the California Film Commission. She lives in Los Angeles with her husband, David Israel. This is her first novel.

Made in the USA
Charleston, SC
22 August 2013